RESISTING THE GRUMP

MOUNT MACON
BOOK 1

ASHLEY MUÑOZ

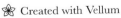 Created with Vellum

To my younger self

There are still stories never told.
Still pieces of our broken heart that we've never examined.
Still an empty echo from that moment when our first love chose not to love us
back.
And we learned for the very first time that unrequited love has claws, teeth,
and an above all…an appetite for hope.

For it devoured mine.

RESISTING *the* Grump

PROLOGUE

Raelyn
Age 18

THE DAY HAD BEEN EATEN UP BY THE ENDLESS CEREMONIAL TASKS OF graduation, leaving me with crumbs of twilight and little time to prepare for what might actually be the most pivotal moment of my life.

Did people really have to practice how to walk across a stage and where to sit? It was still alphabetical, like always, and these had been the same people we'd been with since grade school. But all the meetings, rehearsals, picnics, and breakfasts for graduating seniors were worth it, because it all led me to this moment.

I put the finishing touches on my lashes and shoved the mascara into my small makeup bag.

"Nora!"

My best friend popped her head into my doorway, frizzy curls framing her heart-shaped face. "You rang?"

"I need an outfit assessment."

Scrunching her dark brows together, she stood tall, filling my doorway.

"Your makeup is perfect. Hair…" She put both thumbs up. "I love that you straightened it."

Frowning at her, I slid my hands down my chocolate tresses. "Does it normally look bad, when it's curly?"

"No, of course not," she said easily, her eyes still moving along my low-cut mustard tank and dark leggings. "I think you're ready."

I felt ready. Deep down in my bones, I knew I was.

Nora crowded my bed as I sat down to pull on my sandals. "Let's see the letter again."

Excitement thrummed in me from head to toe as I pulled open my bedside drawer and handed her the carefully folded piece of white paper.

"Rae, meet me at the library Friday, nine p.m. I have something I need to tell you. Davis."

Hearing Nora read it out loud made me flash back to the moment two days ago when Carl, my father's best friend, handed it to me at my graduation party. It was better than any gift I could have received.

"I still can't believe he knows who you are—like *actually* knows who you are—after all these years of you crushing on him and secretly—"

I put my hand up to stop her. "We don't need to go into what all I did; I think we're both on the line for what was done in the name of getting his attention."

Her eyes sparkled as she gripped the letter. "Yeah, but it actually worked! The love of your life knows you exist and now he wants to meet you!"

We squealed in tandem, and my heart soared.

"I just knew it was the fact that I was in high school that had held him back all these years. I just knew it." I sighed, shaking my head while staring at the small spot on my carpet from a permanent marker that leaked through a poster board. I was fairly certain it was from that time I tried to reserve Davis a parking spot in front of the diner. That particular incident hadn't gone over well.

"Okay, so it's almost time... Are you driving there?" Nora adjusted her legs until she was facing me.

I mimicked her pose, nodding.

"I'm not sure what to expect, but I'm ready."

My best friend smiled at me, gripping my hand. "I know you are —you've been waiting for this for so long. I'm so excited for you."

We hugged and then she helped me finish getting ready. Little flyaways were sprayed, perfume was spritzed, and necklaces were traded in and out until I found the right one. Then it was time.

It was inventory night, so my parents were at the diner working, as was Carl, who was their shift manager. I assumed he'd read the note, seeing as it was from the crush he told me I shouldn't have. So he likely knew where I was headed tonight, but just like all the other Davis-related conversations he'd had with me over the past three years, I knew he'd keep it a secret.

"Call me as soon as you're on your way back home." Nora walked with me to my car.

"I will," I vowed, pulling open my door.

"If he goes too fast, remember that move I showed you." She thrust her wrist out, indicating the one we'd practiced.

Assuring her I would, I secured my seatbelt and started toward the library, hoping my heart would relax before it burst through my tight chest.

I couldn't exactly tell you when I started loving Davis Brenton. In my head, all the moments were made up of little fragments of time, smiles, and laughter. Things that wouldn't have mattered to a regular person. To me, they were everything.

He was everything.

The town thought he was a grumpy recluse—a nobody who lived up on Mount Macon, only coming down a few times a month to gather supplies or get gas—but in my eyes he was a forgotten king, hiding away in his fortress. Deep down, there was rusted armor that just needed someone to help him unearth, so he could be brave again. I recognized the sadness, the heaviness that he carried, which he likely assumed no one saw.

But I did.

I heard his silent words, and they were loud enough to drown out everything else.

Through the years, I'd watch him, and I'd fall a little further. A little harder.

I had always hoped he'd see me and fall, too, and while I had made several attempts, I was beginning to give up hope. And then Carl handed me that letter.

The drive to the library went by in a blink, and before I knew it, I was pulling into the empty lot.

No lights were on, but Davis had planned for us to meet here, so I assumed the front door would be unlocked.

Swallowing the thick lump of panic and anticipation rising in my throat, I exited my car and walked toward the entrance.

My palms were sweaty as I tugged on the brass handle, but it eased open on silent hinges, just like always, which proved that the note was real. Davis really *had* asked to meet me here tonight. A new wave of excitement hit me in the chest, making my breath hitch in my lungs.

I couldn't see much, given most of the lights were off, but making my way near the center of the building, I could see back by the illuminated study tables.

The silence in the space was nearly overwhelming, but it added to the gravitas of the moment. I walked up the small ramp leading to the young adult section and bypassed the lounge chairs and computer stations. My pace quickened as I moved along, my heart hammering with every step.

I had tried to interact with Davis multiple times over the years, but he'd never really looked at me. He looked through me, over me, or past me, but never directly at me. He never once said my name, and honestly, I didn't even think he knew who I was until that letter appeared, so that note felt like winning the lottery.

Would he hold my hand? Touch my hair, maybe kiss me tonight? I smiled, watching the familiar, worn carpet at my feet.

That's when I heard it.

The giggle.

I paused, frozen for a second, because the lilt of laughter sounded feminine…but that couldn't be right.

I powered on, cautiously.

Peering through the stacks, trying to catch a visual of Davis, I tiptoed around a study carrel, and *that giggle* erupted again.

I held my breath as I curved the last row of books and edged close to the open study area, staying in the shadows as much as possible. There in the back was Davis, hovered over a woman lying flat on her back on one of the battered wooden study tables, her hair splayed out behind her.

I couldn't really process what I was seeing, my brain whirling into overdrive to make sense of it all.

That was until his lips landed against hers in a hungry way, a way that I had dreamed about a thousand times. His navy blue eyes were closed as he devoured her mouth, making a groaning sound deep in his chest that nearly sent me to my knees.

I watched, hand pressed over my mouth to hold back a sob, as he pushed up her shirt and peeled down her bra. My eyes filled with tears when he sucked on her breast, slowly moving down her frame until she was naked underneath him.

My cheeks were flaming, but my hands were cold as ice, in disbelief that he would tell me to meet him here, knowing he'd be with someone else. I was still firmly in denial that this was real until his hands moved to his own pants, lowering them enough to show a flash of skin, and then the woman on the table was crying out as he plunged forward.

I was still a virgin, but my brain was putting the pieces into place, and it all coalesced as Davis and this woman started moving in unison, his head dipped against hers while her hips rocked forward, her sultry cries hitting me in the chest like a sledgehammer.

He was fucking her in front of me.

He'd asked me here, to witness this—to see him give another woman the one thing I had so desperately wanted.

There was something shifting inside of me, slowly breaking and shriveling.

Shock.

Hurt.

I had loved him for so long, and I had believed in him…his existence made mine make sense.

It wasn't until Davis looked up and locked eyes with me that my instincts kicked in. It was fight or flight.

I heard a low curse, and the woman asking something, as though confused.

What he did after that, I had no idea. Because I ran from the bonfire of my hopes and dreams like a rabbit flushed out by a predator.

Once safely inside my car, I pulled out of the lot at a reckless speed, careening around the corner and heading for the edge of town. I had to get out; I had to get away.

I had been in love with Davis for as long as I could remember, and the fact that he'd invited me there, only to destroy me… It left me shattered beyond repair.

For the first time in my life, I had no idea what the future held for me, but I knew with chilling certainty that Davis Brenton would never be a part of it.

1

RAE

FOUR YEARS LATER

My calves burned as I climbed the stairs to the fifth floor, my lungs screaming at me to move out of this stupid building, but I couldn't afford anywhere else. Hell, I couldn't even afford *this* place.

The humidity in the sweltering stairwell was an invisible wall of resistance, barreling into me with each step I took, until I finally crested the last one and hit the landing near my apartment door.

"Made it!" I huffed in victory, wiping the sweat from my temple.

My neighbor Darrow exited his door and quirked a brow at me. "You say that every time you get to the top."

Still catching my breath, I waved him off and headed toward my door. "Gotta live for the little things, D."

He snorted, reflecting his opinion of my totally pathetic life. Darrow was cool; he had way more friends than I did, and he dated a million different girls—and a few guys—and I'd be lying if I said I hadn't been drawn to him the first time we met, but it was impossible not to be. He was tall, past six feet, with a jawline so sharp it could cut glass, and eyes as blue as the ocean.

Not that I had spent any amount of time cataloging his looks or anything.

That was old me; new me didn't give a shit. Darrow was just objectively hot.

"You around tonight?" he asked, three steps down the stairs.

I paused, head turned toward him, exhilarated that he was finally inviting me to something.

"Because, I'm going out, and I was wondering if you could feed Dunk?"

False alarm. I hadn't made it into the friend circle. I was just the neighbor he asked to watch his cat every now and then. Feeling my face heat, I nodded.

"Sure, no problem."

He beamed at me. "Really? Thanks…here's the key, I'll grab it from you tomorrow." His long legs carried him toward me as he tugged the silver key from its little spot on the ring in his hand and dropped it into my open palm.

"Have fun."

He smirked, "Yeah…you too."

Then he was turning away and walking down the flight of stairs, likely laughing at the awkward girl next door who just admitted to not having any plans on a Friday night and was now feeding his cat. I would definitely be eating that fancy Gouda cheese I knew he hoarded. This called for retribution.

Pushing my house key into the deadbolt and ignoring the chipped wood near my face, I shoved my shoulder and pushed. Good thing about my apartment? I'd know in an instant if someone were breaking in, because between the rusted hinges and a sagging frame, my front door was like a boulder to move.

The box I called home looked exactly as I left it earlier that morning: Two piles of clothes waited for me on my twin bed. A small, thin paned window that hung over my small dresser let in a slice of light, and of course my kitchen, where I could spin in a single circle and reach anything I needed.

A familiar, discouraging feeling bubbled inside as I looked around. There was no air conditioning, and the humidity on the fifth floor was at rainforest levels. My freezer had broken two days ago, so there wasn't even any ice that I could put in front of a fan for a makeshift swamp cooler.

It was moments like these that made me think of home. How August would be warm, but completely bearable at the high altitude, and how the shops in town bustled with people. How the flower baskets exploded with color, hanging from dark, antique lamp posts, lining the pristine, white sidewalks.

A heaviness settled in my heart, forcing my hand to bring up my cell and dial my mother. I'd been calling her more and more frequently over the past few months. I'd finally graduated from college, and I was struggling against a persistent wave of homesickness. I told myself I was just lonely. Still, I put the phone on speaker and waited for it to connect.

"Rae, honey, so nice that you called! Your dad and I were just talking about how we were going to call you tonight because we have something to discuss," my mom said happily.

I walked over to my ancient, rattling refrigerator and tugged it open. "Really, what?"

I had nothing in the fridge but ketchup and some questionable carrots, and I wouldn't until my next paycheck came in, which was a week away. Thankfully, I had bread, peanut butter, and honey.

"Well..." Mom hesitated, and it caused me to pause with my hand over the handle of my two-shelf pantry.

"Is everything okay?"

"It's just"—she started again, still slightly hesitant—"well, we know you're not doing so wonderful in New York..."

I let out a sigh. "Mom, I'm fine, I promise."

I wasn't though, truly. I hadn't been fine a single time since moving here, but I'd always kept that truth to myself.

"Nora called us." She paused, and my eyes narrowed at the phone.

My best friend knew how dire my situation was, but she was under strict order not to ever tell my parents, so I only had one choice.

"She's a liar, Mom. Whatever she told you, she's lying. She's on drugs now. It's really sad."

My mom snorted. "Hogwash. She moved back here about two weeks ago, and we've enjoyed catching up with her, but that's not what we wanted to discuss."

I didn't know Nora had moved back, but it made sense that she hadn't told me. Macon was a bit of a taboo subject for us.

"The reason we wanted to call you is because we're starting a delivery service for the diner."

I tugged the jar of generic peanut butter out and reached for the honey, but just as I did, something scuttled across the kitchen floor out of the corner of my eye.

"Shit," I hissed, jumping up on the counter, as my mom continued talking.

"We thought it would be a good idea to drum up some extra business—you okay, honey?"

"Yeah, just...uh..."—I peered over the counter, my knees pulled to my chest—"I stubbed my toe." If my mother knew that this building had rats and roaches, she'd send in the National Guard.

"Well, anyway... We're having a difficult time getting the service up and running."

Concentrating on the floor, while still slightly curious, I asked, "Why do you guys need to drum up extra business? I thought you were doing really well."

A beat passed, which had my eyes focusing back on the screen as worry slithered through me. I cradled the phone and took it off speaker. "Mom?"

"Things are..." There was another pause and my heart thumped harder as my brows caved in.

"Things are what, Mom?"

She let out a sigh, one that seemed heavy, and if I were there, I imagined her chest expanding and caving with the levity of it.

"Well, to be frank, they're not so great. The town is struggling, sweetie, and Nora mentioned that you were also struggling over there in New York, and well...I just wondered if you'd consider coming back to help us out, that's all."

I was already shaking my head, because regardless of how much my life sucked, and how much I hated New York, going back wasn't an option. Unless *he* had moved.

"Mom, I—"

"Just think about it, honey, please. No pressure, okay?"

I paused, biting my lip because the pain lacing her voice was too much.

"I don't want to be a burden on you guys. I wouldn't be able to get my own place for a while." Or ever, if the housing market was as horrific back home as it was here—although nothing was as bad as inner city New York. Macon was likely extremely reasonable; maybe Nora would want to get a place together. Ideas began taking flight in my head as I imagined getting on a flight back home.

That's when my heart squeezed tight. I didn't have enough money for groceries, much less a plane ticket to Oregon.

"Honey, your room is still exactly how you left it. There's plenty of space here, you know that."

I wouldn't bring up the plane ticket, especially if she already had admitted that things were difficult.

"Well, what about Nora, did you ask her if she could help with the deliveries?"

Another heavy sigh left my mother's lungs, like this was a taxing conversation for her, which made me feel like shit.

"Nora is stepping in to help *her* parents, while trying to start her interior decorating business."

My best friend was a kick-ass designer, so that made me feel proud and happy she was pursuing her dreams. Meanwhile, I'd be here, dodging rats and ignoring roaches because acknowledging them would send me spiraling into paranoia and I'd never sleep again.

A tiny tendril of curiosity wound its way through my mind, wrapping around my heart. An image of working on my laptop from my parent's back porch, staring at the outline of Mount Macon while maple leaves fell across the green lawn. If the small businesses in town were hurting the way my mom mentioned, this could be an amazing opportunity to test out my marketing degree and help the owners revamp their businesses.

"Well, anyway, think it over, honey. We have airline miles to get you here, and we'd love to see you. But we support you staying there too, whatever is best for you."

"Love you, Mom," I said, unable to get that image of me on their back porch out of my head.

Once we hung up, I slowly left my perch on the counter and briskly checked the floor. Usually when the lights were on, I was fine, which was why I left on several lamps at night, but every now and then one of the suckers would run across the floor.

I could withstand the roaches—they were fairly small—but the rats or mice, whatever the fuck they were? Yeah, I couldn't deal with them.

Eyeing the wall that separated my apartment and Darrow's, I suddenly had the best idea ever.

2

RAE

A KNOCK ON MY FRONT DOOR BROUGHT MY HEAD UP FROM WHERE I'd been staring at my laptop. I'd been researching plane tickets, connecting flights, and whether or not a certain someone from Mount Macon was on social media.

Peeling myself away from the screen and out of the nest of blankets, I walked over and pulled open my door.

Darrow stood there, all muscles and smoldering jawline perfection.

"Hey."

I dipped my head. "Hey."

"So…how did it go last night?"

It went fantastic. I brought the cat over and let him hunt for three hours while I binge watched Vampire Diaries.

"Really good. Fed him, cleaned his litter box, and then peeked in on him this morning."

Darrow shoved his hands in his pockets, "Cool, thanks."

Sure, maybe pay me this time. "No problem."

"So, uh…"

Was he finally about to ask me out, or to have random next-door neighbor sex with him?

Because I'd turn him down. Definitely.

Probably.

"Can I get my key back?"

He'd asked me a total of fifteen times to watch his cat over the past two months. You'd think at this rate he'd just give me a key. Instead, I turned my back on him and dug into the drawer I kept my junk in.

"Here you go." I handed it to him, and he just stood there, staring.

I had entertained the idea that he might ask me for a random hookup a million times since moving in, but he never had. Not once.

But now, he was glancing at me in a way that made me think it might finally happen, and he'd—

"So, um, I'm taking a trip next month, and I'll be gone for like a week. You think you can feed him for me?"

Well, that went an entirely different direction. I didn't know why I cared. I mean, in some strange way, I thought Darrow and I were friends. I had built up the image so much in my head that I had believed I wasn't alone in the city, but he wasn't my friend.

He wasn't my anything. Well, he was my neighbor, but it wasn't like I was asking him to kill roaches or lend me his cat to kill the rats in this fucking place.

Suddenly, with an overwhelming clarity, I realized I didn't want to be here anymore.

I'd graduated three months ago, and since then I've worked as a bike messenger, in the mailroom of a law firm, and as a dishwasher. I could put practically nothing against my student loans, and I had no friends. None.

They had all left the city the second we graduated. Now I was here, and I had no idea why.

"Actually, I'm leaving," I said numbly as my resolve firmed up.

Darrow's head snapped up in surprise, his eyebrows arching. "Really? Where are you going?"

I never went anywhere, unless it was work, so his shock was warranted.

I turned away from him, thinking I might actually kind of miss his cat.

"Uh, home, actually." I started for my bed, grabbing for the suitcase underneath it.

"Like right now?" He sounded like he was watching someone unravel, both pity and caution lacing his tone.

"Yeah… Well, no." Not right now; I had to contact my landlord and quit my jobs. "In the next few days."

"Oh." He continued to stare at me. "Well, okay then. I guess I'll see you around."

I rolled my eyes. He wouldn't see me around if I was moving, but whatever.

He walked away without so much as a goodbye. I strode over to my door, which he'd left open, slammed it shut, and continued to pack.

Two Weeks Later

A STREAK of lavender lit up the sky, ridding the world of darkness, and more importantly the stealth required to enter Macon undetected. Hurrying down the street, I pulled my suitcase, willing it to roll faster.

"Come on you piece of discount trash," I grumbled as streaks of orange began to fill in the graying spots above my head. Soon, all the early busybodies in town would be out, getting their paper and starting their walking routines.

Macon was one of those tiny mountain towns, full of charm and quiet whispers. Everyone stuck their noses into everyone's business because we didn't have efficient Wi-Fi or cell towers up here, so we relied on the newspaper to efficiently deliver the news every morning, and of course a part of the news was always a heaping dose of local gossip.

Thus, my rush to get to my parents' front door.

Down the street a loud slamming sound echoed, indicating someone had left their home, but I refused to look. I was almost to my house and nearly clear of the street.

"Rae?" I heard my name called from a block down, but I didn't turn.

"Almost there," I murmured to myself in an encouraging tone.

"Rae!"

No, no. I would not yield.

"Raelyn Vernon Jackson!"

Oh shit. I stopped midstep, turned on my heel, and was nearly bulldozed by two long arms that came around me in a tight grip.

"Why were you ignoring me?" Nora asked, pulling away and inspecting me. She wore a white fluffy towel on her head and a pair of fleece pajamas with little clouds printed all over them.

"I didn't know it was you," I laughed, while a few tears strained to be set free.

I hadn't seen my best friend in over two years. I still came home to visit when I could afford it, but I hadn't been able to for the last couple of years, and she wasn't always here when I was.

"You're home?" I asked, even though I already knew from my mom telling me.

Nora rolled her eyes. "My parents guilt-tripped me, but the better and more curious question is…why are *you* home?"

Panic bunched up inside my chest, along with relief that my mother hadn't told her yet.

"Here, let's go inside." I hurried to the front door.

Nora looked around and seemed to realize her error, especially as a few morning walkers had started down the street.

Once inside the safety of my home, I let the luggage go, which toppled over from the weight of the three bags I had hanging from the handle.

"You put way too much stress on that poor suitcase," Nora observed, walking past me to the kitchen.

Ignoring my bags, I followed her, padding across the living room floor.

"It must be so weird being back… I mean, knowing you're here to stay."

It *was* weird, and embarrassing, although I wasn't exactly sure why.

I was grown up. I had graduated from college. I had moved past the lame indiscretions of my youth…and yet, there was still a strange stinging sensation in my chest when I considered being back permanently.

"It is…" I trailed off, unable to comment fully on all that I was feeling.

Looking around the house, I realized my parents had kept it mostly the same, save for a few newer appliances and updated photos on the fridge. Most were from me, but there were a few from my dad's family, and one of Mount Macon during winter. It was serene and beautiful. Someone in the photo had their back to the camera, hiking up a steep incline.

"So, she convinced you?" Nora sunk into one of the chairs surrounding my parents' small table.

I shrugged, as if that would explain it.

My best friend leaned closer. "I'm glad she did."

I narrowed my eyes on her. "Is that why you spilled the beans about my living situation?"

Laughing, she arranged the salt and pepper shakers in front of her. "At least I didn't say anything about the roaches."

"Thank you for that." I slumped into the chair across from her. "So, what now?"

Toying with the edge of the placemat, I continued taking inventory of the house. Mom had grown her house plant collection, from the looks of it. There were several draped along the side of the sink. Nora would likely walk over any second and start inspecting them. She loved house plants.

Nora clicked her tongue and reached forward to grab my hand. "Now we become grownups, I guess."

I wanted to comment that I had been a grown up, working three jobs just to make rent, but I didn't want to make her feel bad. My thoughts drifted toward what had driven me away, making my stomach churn.

"But what if he—"

She shook her head, cutting me off. "He doesn't matter. I hate that you left because of him."

"I left for college." My voice dimmed, betraying the lie.

Nora's scoff told me she had picked up on it. "You had no plans to go to college, Rae. Before that night, when you found that asswipe Davis, you hadn't applied anywhere, and the two grueling years at that community college in New York proves it."

Hearing her say his name was like a quick slap of reality. The hurt, the humiliation—the entire reason I had moved so far away. The fact that what he did still outweighed all the things I had overcome these past four years. Living in a tiny box while working three jobs, attending community college, breaking my neck to get across campus because I chose not to add on-campus housing to my growing debt. The endless night shifts, the early morning classes, the smell of living in New York with no money. It wasn't glamorous. It was shit.

Pure shit.

Yet, this gaping wound from Davis still apparently bled, while all the other battle scars were stitched up.

I didn't respond to my friend's comment, because she was right. I hadn't planned on going anywhere back then, because I couldn't bear the thought of leaving Davis. I honestly had thought he'd fall in love with me after I had graduated from high school.

So pathetic.

"You think he's still up there?"

"Rae, are you hearing me?" Nora stopped inspecting her nails, and leaned closer. "It doesn't matter. *He* doesn't matter. You matter, and this town matters, and believe it or not, Macon really needs you."

I sobered at her tone and the serious glint in her eye. She was right, but my thoughts still churned like lumpy butter.

"Besides," she suddenly piped up. "If he were to still live around here, would he even recognize you?" Nora eyed me while digging into the basket of fruit my mother had on the table. Peeling back a banana, she ignored my confused expression.

"Of course, he would." I laughed at my friend, because the object of my obsession and the man who broke my heart would recognize me in a heartbeat. I had stood mere inches—well, feet—from his face. I mean, he didn't really *look* at me, but he saw me. *I was right there.* Of course he would know me. I hadn't changed that much.

She raised a dark eyebrow. "You had short, curly hair with chunky highlights, braces, a flat chest, and acne—on a much rounder face."

"Hey!" I slapped her arm.

She reared back, holding her hands up. "I'm just saying, Rae… you looked totally different back then, and you're definitely not flat-chested now."

I rolled my eyes. "It's the bra."

"Okay, but what about your long hair, with all those flattering layers and highlights, and your skin? Bitch, you're hot." Nora suddenly leaned over to deliver a slap to my arm, but the banana was half in her mouth, causing the other half to fall.

"Nora, eww! Keep your banana in your mouth." I playfully slapped her back.

She was laughing so hard now that she had to spit the remaining mouthful out. On a labored breath, she wheezed out, "That's what she said!"

I rolled my eyes. "I'm not cleaning that up, and you realize that made no sense, right?"

She rubbed a napkin over the mess she'd made, giggling to herself. "I'm just jealous because we're both single and going to have to pull from the very shallow dating pool of Mount Macon."

Groaning, I laid my head on the table. "Don't remind me."

Maybe she had a point about not being recognized, and it wasn't like *he* ever really saw me anyway. All my antics, and he never, *ever* acknowledged me.

Nora toyed with the placemat, softly offering, "You know I can ask my parents if he's still around, if you want, just to be sure."

I waved her off. "No, it's fine… I would rather not know."

"Great, then let's not dwell on it, and even if he does still live here, it's not like you'll have to see him."

"Yeah, you're right." We both stood.

"You're going to ruin your curls if you don't go home and take that off." I pointed to the towel wrapped around her head.

"Oh my God, I totally forgot to put any product in." She ran past me, and I laughed as she flew out my door, slamming it shut.

I walked over and opened it, calling after her. "I missed you, Nora-Bora!"

Holding her towel, she half turned and yelled back, "Missed you, too, Rae Bae!"

Securing the bolt, I sagged against the frame, allowing my forehead to kiss the wood. So much had changed in the span of the past two weeks. Once I gave notice at my jobs, I gave notice to my landlord and then packed all my stuff. I didn't have any need for any of the furniture I'd scavenged, so I asked Darrow if he wanted it. Turns out, he had a sister who did, so he had moved all the large stuff out. I packed my belongings in my suitcase, and then boarded a flight and left New York.

Slowly padding down the hall, I embraced the silence of the house and allowed it to cradle my tender heart. This place held so many memories. It all looked the same, but different. The living room had a new area rug, and the appliances in the kitchen had been updated, but everything else was the same. I looked over each photo frame and ensured my parents had not snuck in any photos of teenage me. They were still completely oblivious to the fact that I had taken all those pictures before I left and stashed them away. I smirked as I took in the two steps toward the cramped staircase that led to the top floor, where my parents' bedroom and the master bathroom were. The narrow hall in front of me led to a guest bathroom, my mother's office, and then—the last door on the left—my old bedroom.

Opening the door, I inhaled the faint smell of dust and a burst of something floral. Eyeing my small desk, I saw a small air freshener propped up, which explained the fresh scent. I stepped inside, the carpet still soft under my toes, the walls still filled with posters, awards, drawings, and pictures from different people and periods of my life. My queen-sized bed was made up with freshly washed blankets, with a small pillow in the middle that said *Welcome Home* across it. Suddenly, tears clogged my throat as the heavy burden of living alone began to slip away.

I knew why I had left, but my parents hadn't. Not once had I uttered a word about that night, or the years that had led up to it. I had a feeling Carl had never let it slip, either, otherwise my mother would have called me, or at least gotten on a flight and demanded I return home. In retrospect, leaving was a rash decision.

One that I had suffered for the past four years of my life.

Blinking away fresh tears, I tipped my head back and fell against the bed.

Peace was like concrete, filling in all the fissures and cracks that now outlined my life. Calm swept over me as I acknowledged I'd done the right thing by coming back, even if the humiliation burned like a soldering iron along my chest.

3

DAVIS

Heavy clouds, rimmed in navy and gray, hung over my workshop, making me eye the few pieces of work I had out drying. Weather forecasts weren't very accurate for us mountain dwellers; it could forecast sunshine all day, but within the blink of an eye it could be snowing again. Made it difficult to really plan efficiently.

Heaving a sigh, I began dragging in the pieces I had just finished, hating that my space was so cramped. Half my warehouse was full of sold work I had yet to deliver.

My customers didn't know any different, mostly because I put an extra two weeks on the bids just to give myself time to deliver. I never needed it, but there was always that fear in the back of my mind that I would disappoint someone.

I'd done enough of that to last a fucking lifetime, so if I could prevent it in my line of work, I would.

I stared over at the finished iron work and felt a pinching in my chest. Selling meant socializing, and if I hired someone to do it for me, the appeal of my small business model that so many of these people wanted would be forfeited. They wanted to support local; they wanted a personalized experience and were willing to pay extra for the perk of saying they had a "guy" for their new housing renovations or hotel remodels.

It worked in my favor, and yet it also actively functioned against me. It wasn't that I couldn't socialize. I just wasn't precisely charming, as the people of Macon would say. Finesse wasn't in my skill set, even when trying to make money.

Hearing the crunch of gravel creep up my driveway, I swiveled my head to track a large black Dodge making its way up the hill.

Gavin.

He was my best friend and biggest ball buster. Dude kept me in check, and while I appreciated it, I was in a piss poor mood. Didn't even know why, couldn't exactly pinpoint it… Every now and then, I just felt like a shadow hung over me. And while I could really dig into why that shadow existed, I'd been denying the existence of that shit for years and didn't see a point in changing my ways now.

Parking his truck, my friend hopped out and walked over to me, tugging his hands through his straw-colored hair. Knowing him, he'd worn a hat all day.

"The fuck are these?" He gestured toward the artwork I was about to take inside.

I met him near the outlier piece and swung my head toward the bay door. "Help me move' em in."

He didn't hesitate to grip the edge of the larger piece of iron.

"Seriously, since when do you do shit like this?"

We gently settled the massive globe structure in the open space of the warehouse. He was referring to the fact that I generally had contracts for light fixtures, mostly sold to massive chain hotels or resorts. But these pieces were massive.

"Is it yard art?" Gavin lifted his brow at me.

I laughed at him, grabbing the end of another section. "Fuck you."

"I'm not judging," he said with a smirk as he walked backward through the opening.

"A few of these places want shit set up for their outdoor fire pit areas. They're also asking about creating a wet bar to match."

"Made of iron?" Gavin settled the bottom hull to the sphere gently.

"Yeah, they want the rustic aesthetic throughout their entire hotel, or in this case, their resort."

He slid his palm across the smooth surface of soldered iron. "Which one is this going to?"

"Bravada." It was a five-star resort that boasted of its expensive rooms and sprawling mountain views.

"Fuck, that's swanky."

I laughed, shutting the doors and leading my friend out of the workshop. Gavin came out once in a while, but he lived in town, so he usually came up on the weekends.

"What brings you up the mountain?" I asked, pushing through my front door. My two huskies perked up but immediately rested their jaws on their paws once they realized it was just Gavin.

My best friend walked to my fridge and ripped it open, grabbing for a beer.

"Can't I just come visit my friend?"

He reached back in and handed me one, then twisted the top off his and took a long swig.

"It's Wednesday," I countered, sipping mine.

I hated when he got secretive. It usually meant he was sticking his nose into something that wasn't his business.

"What would you say if I asked you to go on a double date with me?" He held his beer but settled against the wall, watching me with a curious expression.

I shook my head, withholding the ire I wanted to deliver. Instead, I tried to sound nonchalant, and like it didn't really bother me, but fuck, he already knew this.

"I'd say no."

Plain and fucking simple.

I turned toward the back door and pushed through the screen, hearing him groan behind me.

"You haven't been any fun in forever, man. I can't figure you out. What the fuck happened to you?"

We settled into opposite sides of the patio loungers. The sky had turned an angry cobalt color, with a nasty wind picking up.

"You know I hate town; I never go in."

He shook his head. "Yes you do. You go for food, gas, books… You just like to talk yourself out of staying and sitting down at the diner for once or going into one of the coffee shops to get your coffee instead of having it here."

"I don't see the point." Which he was well aware of. Why were we talking about this?

He studied the table in front of us then looked up with renewed energy. "Okay, but a few years ago you actually dated. You went out with me—or at least agreed to meet up if we kept it private."

I shook my head, bringing the lip of the bottle to my mouth.

Gavin's eyes narrowed as he studied me. "I can pinpoint it."

"What?" I scoffed, but I was curious where this was headed.

Pointing a finger at me, he stared at me, incredulous. "I remember…it was right around that time you had a stalker, and that girl—"

"Stop." I snapped.

I didn't want to remember that night. Just thinking about it nearly made my breath hitch.

His eyes narrowed. "Why? What happened?"

I had never told him. I had never told *anyone*, and for years the guilt of that night had eaten away at my sanity.

"That girl…she was young." I swallowed the lump in my throat.

Gavin must have mistaken my hesitation as something else, because he powered through it.

"No shit, that's what made it so funny." He laughed, but I didn't follow, so he sobered, waiting for me to finish.

"I knew she liked me, and I knew she was borderline following me…but one night she actually followed me into the library."

Gavin's brows dipped. "So?"

I rubbed my face. "I was with Lydia…"

Understanding bloomed on my friend's face, his eyebrows arching and his mouth going slack.

"She saw you."

I nodded, even as shame threatened to bury me.

"I have no idea how she knew. I mean, it was freaky because I realized the extent of her following me was actually pretty serious, but the look on her face when she saw me with Lydia…" Shaking my head, I tried to get the memory out of my head. But it wouldn't budge; it was branded on my conscience. "She was destroyed, and after that, I never saw her again. I think…"

This was the part I could never say out loud, one of my deepest fears.

"You think what?" Gavin asked.

Sighing, I sipped my beer once more before explaining. "It's just…sometimes I wonder if she hurt herself because of me. I mean, she just disappeared. I even started hanging around town more often, just to see if I'd catch sight of her, but I never have. I just couldn't live with myself if she did—you know what I mean?"

Gavin's face shuttered, his head ducking. He knew what I was talking about.

He knew why my fears were controlling me.

He understood, because it wasn't the first time someone would have gotten hurt because of my actions.

"Davis, man… You can't live your life like this. You need closure."

I knew I did. I had considered it, but I had no idea what her name was, or where she lived.

I knew she had worked at the diner in some capacity, but they always had kids in and out of there during different seasons, and it wasn't long enough to really grasp what she'd done there. Otherwise, there was nothing. I had no idea who she was.

"It's weird that she knew you'd be there. I mean, even if she had followed you, hadn't you been at the library for a while that day?"

"Yeah, I had. Lydia met me after I had installed a few light fixtures. I'd been there since closing. She came around eight thirty, we had dinner, then the girl showed up somewhere after Lydia and I started—" I hesitated again, unable to form the words.

"Fucking?"

I nodded.

My best friend shook his head, draining the rest of his beer.

"So weird."

"Yeah…" I trailed off, but my mind was still on that night. How I still had trouble being intimate with women all these years later, because it was her face I'd see. Big blue eyes, short black hair, red pimples on her face and metal stretching across her teeth. It was the first time I had ever really looked at her, and that image was stuck with me forever.

Penance.

"What if you ask around at the diner? I mean, there's bound to be someone who knows."

I looked up at my friend's suggestion, and there was a rumbling in the sky above us. I hadn't really thought to do that because it required socializing, but given I now knew the owners, it wouldn't be so bad.

"That's not a bad idea. Not sure why I hadn't considered it before," I muttered, although I did know. That girl's crush was a shameful thing in my head. I felt like I had done something wrong, even though I had never encouraged her. I wasn't eager to ever tell anyone about it.

But…

It would put to rest this nagging feeling in the back of my mind that I had ruined yet another person's life.

"While you're asking around, maybe you could accompany Tiffany and me on a date?" he asked hopefully.

I laughed and shook my head. "We'll see. I can't make any promises, but if it's not in a crowded place, I might be able to make it happen."

"Yesssss!" He jammed his elbow back in an excited gesture. "I knew I could talk you into it."

"Uh-huh," I drawled. My friend was an idiot, but he was helping me, and after the past four years, I was ready to put this burden behind me once and for all.

4

RAE

"WHY DIDN'T YOU TELL US YOUR FLIGHT CHANGED?" MY MOTHER
scolded as she walked in the door.

I had showered, napped, and then called to tell them I was
home, at which point they'd rushed right over.

Waving her off, I sighed. "Because it was no big deal. I caught a
ride, and this way you two didn't have to drive me."

That, and I was way too prideful to be picked up two hours
from home and driven back by my parents. All of Macon would
start talking about how I'd failed college or was bailed out of jail.
Either way, my parents would be the poor victims, and I would be
painted as the villain, so I caught the bus, which dropped me near
the small bookstore, and then I walked the rest of the way home.

"Hey, kid, how are you?" My dad pulled me into his arms next,
kissing the top of my head, the sensation of his strong arms taking
me back to feeling small and protected.

Pulling away, I surveyed them both and tried to ignore the tug in
my stomach that I'd missed so much of their lives. My father was
still just as tall as always, but his hair was definitely receding, and the
sides had turned an ashy gray color. My mom's hair was still a dark
chestnut, but her temples were also starting to turn silver.

"So, how was the diner this morning?" I asked, hoping to ease the awkwardness I felt being back in their presence after so long.

My mom moved around the kitchen in a hurry. "Slow, but that's okay. It'll pick up, especially with you back."

I brushed off the nerves rattling my insides at her hopeful tone and watched my father start a pot of coffee.

"Tell me more about this delivery service that you have in mind?"

My mom grabbed the butter dish and the box of bread, blushing just the slightest bit.

"Your mom is really proud of it; there's several people who can't get around easily, so having a hot meal delivered has been a real help to them," my dad said, yanking the glass pot out of the way and shoving his mug under in a practiced fashion. I held back a laugh when Mom gave him the side eye. She hates it when he does that because it always splatters.

"Well, we added in grocery delivery, too, and it just becomes a big help to the community. I mean, aside from the financial assistance to us." I could hear how proud my mom was in spite of her efforts to sound casual. This truly meant something to her.

"Well, when can I help?"

My mom grabbed my dad's cup and sipped from it, her eyes big and round. "If you're sure that you're ready, I could actually use your help this weekend. We usually have at least ten orders that come in, and getting anyone to drive up the mountain has been difficult."

"Is old man Ford still living up there?" I asked, deciding coffee didn't sound too bad and grabbed for a mug.

"He, Mrs. Kuami, and the others are all still scattered up there. Some like coming down, but we realized how many of them just prefer to have their food delivered. It's real nice though; Mr. Ford has a whole station set up by his mailbox for the delivery, so you just push a button when you drop it, and then he zips down on his four-wheeler and picks it up."

Mr. Ford had a driveway over a mile long, up a steep embankment, so it was kind that the delivery person wouldn't have to drive it.

"That's nice," I mused, checking the fridge for creamer, coming up empty. "You don't have any hazelnut creamer?"

My dad moved to the cupboard. "Your mom finally quit it. Only does half and half with a little bit of sugar."

"Wow, Mom, that's"—*new, different, I hated that I had missed it*—"awesome that you finally were able to finally quit." It squeezed my heart a bit that she'd never mentioned it in any of our many phone conversations, but that was just how my mom was…never thinking to talk about the tiny changes in her life, just the major things.

Mom smiled, crinkling her nose. "It took a while, but now I can't stand the taste of it."

"Well, if it's okay with you, I'm going to go catch up with Nora and look around the town." I shut the fridge and gave up on the idea of coffee.

"Of course, honey. If you get hungry, come see us down at the diner." My mom walked over, kissed my cheek, and then headed toward the door.

"Save some time in your schedule tomorrow so I can check the oil on that car that's still sitting beside the garage," my dad said, trailing Mom.

"You guys kept my car?" I asked, feeling hopeful.

They both looked at me like I had lost my mind. "Of course we did."

Because they loved me. I should have come back months ago.

I was going to make this work.

RED BRICK BUILDINGS lined the street as we walked along the main strip of Macon. Hanging flower baskets that should have been exploding with color were instead still filled with last year's dead vegetation. The street was still attractive, with the massive mountain as a backdrop to the small town, but no expense used to be spared in maintaining the beauty of Macon, especially during tourist season.

"It's so weird being back," I mused to my best friend as we walked shoulder to shoulder.

Nora let out a sigh, taking a long sip from her iced coffee. "It feels good, though, like a piece to my puzzle has clicked into place."

Looking over at her, I smiled. "Your puzzle?"

"Yeah...like my life puzzle. You know"—she moved her free hand in the air—"life is like a puzzle."

Sipping from my own coffee, I added, "Yeah, one without the box, so you have zero indication what the picture is supposed to look like." I looked ahead, recognizing a few faces here and there, but was relieved when they didn't seem to notice or recognize me.

"What if my puzzle doesn't have a corner piece, and the whole integrity of my life is screwed?"

I laughed, nearly spitting my coffee. "I don't think that's how it works."

"With my luck that's exactly how this whole thing would work."

We ventured closer to the edge of Main Street, bypassing the bookstore and the hair salon. A few shops had "for sale" signs in their windows, and others just had a slew of thin boards covering the storefront. It made my heart sink, because four years ago these businesses were thriving.

"Maybe the pieces we need belong to the people we're going to end up with?"

Finally, we stopped in front of a shop window boasting all things Mount Macon, including homemade jam and locally sourced honey.

"Your parents still saying that berry jam is made here?" I quipped, slurping my coffee until it rattled with an annoying empty sound.

Nora let out a heavy sigh, turning with me to face the storefront. "First of all, I think you might be on to something about our puzzle-piece keepers."

"Is that what we're calling them?" I turned my head, raising a brow.

Nora kept her face forward, toward the store. "Yes. Also, if you tell a soul that the jam is from the valley, and not up on that mountain"—she pointed toward the snow-capped peak with her finger—"my mom will totally end you."

"I've kept the secret this long!" I protested, and we laughed and continued walking.

Crossing the street, we stood in front of my parent's diner. Similar to all the shops, it was all glass windows with cursive signage, welcoming patrons to "Millie & Mac's Restaurant." Most people around here knew the Mac portion of the name was all for show—it just happened to sound decent next to my mother's name—but my father liked the gossip it would stir every so often when transplants would arrive in town. Peering inside the broad glass panes, you could make out the faded blue leather booths inside, and the long counter stretching along the back wall. Two swinging doors off to the right led back to the kitchen, where my mom and dad were. Watching people drink coffee and eat pie, I huffed out the same sigh Nora had earlier.

"I'm starting the delivery thing this weekend."

"Shut up!" Nora laughed, pushing my shoulder.

"I'm serious!"

"I didn't think you'd actually do it." She laughed into her hand, clutching her stomach.

I hip-checked her. "It's your fault…"

She wheezed, straightening. "You're welcome. You wouldn't have lasted much longer in that tiny apartment. You needed a reason to come."

She wasn't wrong, but I was still nervous about delivering up the mountain—not that *he* was up there…nor would he likely use something like a delivery service, but still. My nerves frayed like the ends of a rope.

We stood in silence, watching the people bustle inside the diner.

"Maybe I should start doing Uber driving until my design business picks up," Nora droned, clearly still pondering her future.

I elbowed her. "You won't have time in between selling that infamous 'local jam.'"

She elbowed me way harder than I did her.

"Ow!"

"Well, you did it first."

We eyed one another for a second before the diner doors opened, letting out a glorious aroma.

"When do you start the delivery service again?" Nora asked, lifting her nose like a puppy smelling a steak.

"This weekend, but I think I should do a test run, like right now."

Nora kept watching the store front, so I elbowed her again.

"Hey!"

"Call in an order and I'll deliver it to us, and we can eat our weight in blueberry pie."

She rubbed the sore spot on her arm. "Can't you just get it for free?"

"Can you get me some *local jam* for free?"

She deflated, pulling her cell free. "Touché."

Holding the phone to her ear, she waited for the phone to connect before looking back at me. "I'm glad we're back. This whole living in the same town thing is going to be awesome."

I sipped the melted coffee water in my cup and smiled at her, but then the sound of a motorcycle echoed somewhere a few streets over, and it was like a dark thunder cloud rolling over me.

Chills swept up along my arms as the sound reverberated down the corridor, and I stood there, looking over my shoulder, terrified that the one reason I stayed away from this town was about to speed past me.

Within seconds, and in a gleam of chrome, I realized it didn't matter that it wasn't him. The memory of him would continue to haunt me as long as I lived in this town, which meant I couldn't stay here.

This had to be temporary.

5

RAE

There was a low hum coming from the small speaker in the corner of the kitchen. When I was growing up, it used to be a massive boom box that my father would drop a million large batteries in, so he could take it outside with him. He'd play the classic rock station, and it would always be a low hum in our house, smothering any silence that dared creep into our quieter home. Now he had these speakers all over the place, and it was odd getting used to it.

"Honey, did you bake the cherry rhubarb?" My mom craned her neck, directing her question at my father.

Dad was the baker in the family. My mother was a decent cook, a kick-ass host, and a killer business manager, but the baking was all my dad.

He cleared his throat and nodded. "Yep, it's ready for delivery."

Wiping the crumbs from my hands, I cleared my throat and asked, "A delivery order?"

It was Thursday night, and while I had planned to help by the weekend, I figured it wouldn't hurt to get started sooner, especially considering I had literally nothing going on. I'd completed a puzzle with my mom and sat in the garage, hearing my dad talk about the boat he was still restoring. He'd been working on that boat for years, but he was confident this was the year he would finish. I'd tried sitting on the back porch with my laptop to fulfill the fantasy I'd had while in New York, but I just sat there staring at the screen. I had to get out in the community and talk to the struggling businesses. I had to figure out who needed the marketing help, and where the greatest weaknesses existed.

"Yeah, this one is a part of the few orders that had been scheduled for this weekend, but I was actually thinking of having this one picked up..." My mom's eyes narrowed on the chicken in front of her.

My dad furrowed his brows as if he was considering a problem of some kind.

"Hey"—I waved my hands at them—"I'm right here, no need to have him pick up. Remember, this was sort of the entire reason I came home?"

"Oh honey, that's okay, this particular order is delicate, and it might just be better to have him pick it up from the diner."

Delicate? What the hell did that mean?

"Who is it for?" I stood, moving around the kitchen and tugging open the fridge.

No one answered.

Abandoning my quest for food, I turned around. My parents were silently communicating with one another, using their eyes.

"Seriously, what's going on?"

"Nothing, honey. Thomas is just cautious about who knows about him, and we try to be respectful about his wishes."

I perked up at the name. "Thomas, as in the guy you're always talking about?"

I pictured the strange old recluse they must be referring to, remembering all the stories my parents had shared about this man who had become close to them over the past few years.

"I can meet him; I mean, I don't mind or anything."

Suddenly my dad's eyebrows hit his receding hairline. "That's actually a wonderful idea."

My mom gave him a long look before returning her gaze to the chicken in front of her.

"He'll come…I know he will." My dad softened his tone and reclaimed his seat.

My mom shook her head, staying reserved.

I felt uncomfortable, like maybe I was intruding on a private moment, and then my gut shuddered the slightest bit at the idea that maybe they weren't comfortable with me being here.

"Mom, if you're unsure of him meeting me then I don't have to—"

"No, honey," she interrupted, shaking her head, "it's not you. I think it would be wonderful for you to finally meet him. I know you've heard us talk about him quite a bit over the years."

"If you're sure?" I snagged a can of Sprite before slinking back into a chair.

"Of course I am. We'll plan to have him over for dinner tomorrow evening."

"That's sort of short notice, isn't it?" I asked, gauging the reactions from my parents. Most people wouldn't be able to just drop everything and attend an impromptu dinner.

My mother only waved me off. "Oh, no, he's not usually busy."

I let it go, still a little weirded out by how guarded my parents were regarding their friend.

Over the years, there had been an endless stream of casual references to the man, but I still had no idea what he looked like, if he was older than my parents, or what his story was. But if he was this important to my family, it would be a good idea to meet him.

I decided to drop it and head to bed. Tomorrow would at least bring me one day closer to being useful with deliveries—I started Saturday morning and had eight clients, which meant I would be busy all day.

Smiling, I sauntered down the hall and considered the last time I felt this happy.

It had been too long to even remember.

"DO you think your parents will mind if I crash the dinner? Your mom makes the best pot roast." Nora walked next to me as we lazily shopped for my mother's dinner.

Thomas had said no, apparently, but then my father called him and had a private conversation in the garage, after which, the recluse had agreed to show up by seven. Truthfully, the man sounded a little grumpy, and I was apprehensive to meet him.

"Sadly, no, because this Thomas guy is so skittish when it comes to people that he barely agreed to come, but I'll save you some."

My best friend let out a sigh. "Better than nothing, but make sure your mother doesn't open her windows. I swear if I smell that pot roast, I'm going to die."

Letting out a little laugh, I continued walking down the aisle. My mother had given me a list, most of which I had already grabbed, save for a few things.

"You want to come with me to deliver orders tomorrow?" I asked, grabbing for a can of green beans.

"You know your mom wants fresh green beans, not the canned kind," Nora warned me, pointing her finger at me as I crouched down to grab the can.

"Pshh, this is for me."

"Oh my gosh, you don't still eat green beans with melted cheese, right from the pan, do you?"

Slightly blushing, I aptly ignored her.

"Ewwww, you're such a weirdo."

"I am not," I defended earnestly. "But when you have to live off nickels and dimes for food, you learn to lower your standards. Don't let me near the ramen aisle."

She giggled and let out a sigh as we continued to move. "I can't go with you tomorrow. I have to help my parents, but let's meet up tomorrow night. I want to get a feeling for the nightlife of this place."

We both waited a beat before bursting into laughter, because this was Macon; there was no night life, especially not now that a ton of businesses had shut down.

"I did hear there was a bonfire of some kind and alcohol was involved," Nora offered, sobering.

"Oooh, kinky." I waggled my brows, reaching for a cold bottle of Diet Coke.

Nora grabbed one too. "Better than nothing."

Unfortunately, my best friend wasn't wrong.

THE HOUSE SMELLED DIVINE, and I opened the window closest to the street just to piss Nora off, knowing she'd be outside at some point. She'd punch me for it later, but it would be worth it.

"Rae, honey, is the table all set?" my mother asked, wiping her hands on her apron.

I nodded, grabbing a carrot that hadn't been cooked.

"Good, he should be here soon. Listen…you should know that Thomas is different. He's not very social and can seem rude, but really, he's just nervous."

Patting my mother's hand, I smiled. "Yeah, I sort of got that when you guys nearly had an aneurysm at the mere idea of having him over for dinner."

My mother blushed and ducked her head.

"Well, just don't be put off by him. We've actually wanted you two to meet for a while now."

That threw me. From her reaction, she didn't seem like she had wanted me to meet him. And why on earth would they want me to? Unless he was my age…and not some old man…

Panic gripped my chest, and I felt a little faint.

"Mom…he isn't—"

"Oh, he's here." My mother moved past me, looking outside. There was a silver truck that had pulled up against the curb. It looked tall, probably too tall for an older gentleman to drive. She wouldn't try and set me up with someone, right?

Suddenly, I hated that I didn't push to have Nora invited.

Breathing a little harder than necessary, I looked down at what I was wearing. A Star Wars T-shirt, with a few bleach spots, and leggings that had melted chocolate on them from when I fell asleep out on the patio. She wouldn't…not without telling me to clean up, right?

I heard voices, and it all coalesced.

The one that should have been old instead sounded young and gravely.

My mother was totally trying to set me up with Thomas, and I was totally giving her shit for this later. Because at least warn a girl. I had no makeup on. My hair was at least smooth, and neatly tucked into a ponytail, but the rest…

The rest!

"Come on in, the table is set," my mother said encouragingly.

Gripping the counter behind me, I tried to wait out the impending train wreck. My father came in first, followed by my mother, and then a head, hovering much higher than either of theirs, full of dark hair, popped into view. And then he looked up, a familiar pair of navy eyes landing on me, sending me back four years to a night that had changed my life. I waited for his expression to break, showing recognition, but his eyes quickly darted away.

This wasn't Thomas. Unless…did I just hallucinate?

My father said something, but I couldn't process it.

I realized too late that I hadn't been breathing.

My mother touched my elbow, but all I could see were those navy eyes.

I don't want to be here.

Everything in me screamed to run. My heart hammered in my chest so hard that I thought I might throw up.

"Rae?" my dad asked.

All at once his words hit me, and I sucked in a breath. "Sorry, it's just hot in here."

"Oh goodness, let me open a window," Mom fussed, heading to the window while my dad stood close to the man I had hoped to avoid for the rest of my life.

Waiting for my mother to face me again, I whispered, "Sorry, maybe I should just go—"

My mom moved me toward the table. "Oh, you're fine, just need a little food."

After being physically forced into my seat, I was suddenly face to face with Davis, who looked as though he might be as uncomfortable as me.

"Now, let's eat." My mom sat down with a heavy sigh, my father trailing her, after grabbing the glass pitcher of juice that I'd made.

"Sorry, in the chaos, we missed introductions," my mom said, smiling, forcing the conversation to circle back to the two twenty-somethings at the table.

"Thomas, right?" I asked with a bit of a bite, because for all I knew he'd catfished my parents into loving him.

He was a liar.

His dark brows caved as a flare of red tipped his ears. "Uh...no, that's reserved for Millie and Roger. It's Davis to everyone else."

Fuck.

He just said it—threw his name out there like it was nothing. Did he remember me? Did he realize who it was that sat across from him? I stayed quiet, having a difficult time wrapping my brain and heart around the magnitude of what was happening here.

For years I had desperately wanted Davis here, in my house, meeting my parents. But now, I just wanted him out of my sight. I didn't want to be in the same hemisphere as him, let alone the same room.

"Honey—" My mother cleared her throat, bringing my gaze up to meet hers. "Aren't you going to introduce yourself?"

What were we, five?

"Raelyn. People call me Rae."

It was rude, I knew it. They knew it. Davis probably knew it.

My tone explained exactly how I currently felt about introducing myself to him.

Silence expanded in the room, hovering over us like a wet cloud, so I decided to ask the one question that kept popping into my head.

"Why do they call you Thomas if that's not your name?"

Davis didn't say anything, and the moment stretched awkwardly until he finally set his fork down and cleared his throat.

"It's my legal name. Your parents heard about…" He hesitated, staring down at his plate for a second too long for it to be casual. "Uh…my upbringing, and well, it's a long story, but they decided to call me by that instead of what everyone else called me. They know I go by Davis, but it's special for them to call me by the name I was given, so they call me Thomas."

Feeling my face heat from his direct attention, I let my chin fall to my chest.

Why did it seem like hurt laced each word when he talked about his name and his parents? Why did I care?

"Thomas, I finished that book." My mother took over the conversation, cheerily.

The low chuckle I heard from across the table had my reluctant gaze traveling up. The sound was deep and throaty, like sunshine found in between a sliver of rock, somewhere in the darkest cavern.

But his laughter was nothing compared to the smile that stretched along his face, and the dimple that popped out on the side of his cheek. My stomach flipped, immediately followed by a gripping fear.

Through all the years of tracking him, of following him as often as I could, he had never once smiled. A frown had always tugged along his devastating jaw line, a dark cloud hanging over his head. Happiness wasn't an emotion he seemed familiar with, and yet, seeing it on him…

It could ruin me.

Again.

"You're lying." Davis called my mother out good naturedly, still with that smile intact.

Laughter echoed from both my parents as they all joined in on an inside joke.

"I goaded her into finishing it," my father added around a bite of his food. "Every night that she would work on a puzzle instead of reading, I'd say something."

All three of them were laughing now, and I was left feeling like an outsider.

Keeping my eyes on my plate, I felt the murmur of conversation shift and suddenly Davis was clearing his throat.

"So, Rae—you just moved back from New York?"

I lifted my head as my thoughts strangled any response I could deliver. Instead, I just ended up staring.

His face flushed the smallest bit, his mouth working—surely to finish the bite of food—and then his throat cleared.

"You grew up around here, right?" Navy eyes implored an answer from me, but I remained frozen, unsure of what to say and unwilling to play whatever game this was. He had to remember me —how could he not?

"She did," my dad replied on my behalf, filling in the silence.

Davis's gaze swung from me to my father, and that's when I realized I was embarrassing my parents. Shame fluttered alongside my pulse as I tried to recover.

"Yeah, sorry. I did."

There. Short, honest, and to the point.

His gaze was back on me as he dug into his mashed potatoes.

"Well, I was just curious…because there was this—"

My knee jumped under the table. It was completely subconscious, but the table jerked, and Mom jumped up.

"Rae," she whined accusingly as she swiped red juice from her shirt.

"Mom, oh crap, I'm so sorry." I turned toward her, jumping up to help, and my hasty movement toppled my glass too.

Davis dove forward to catch it, while I turned and tried for the same thing. Our heads cracked together, and suddenly I wanted to cry—and not because of the pain radiating through my temple. I'd take roaches any day over this crater in my chest that kept expanding each and every time I seemed to do something that embarrassed my family.

"Ouch!" I rubbed at my forehead while using a potholder to mop up the excess liquid.

"Shit, sorry about that," Davis grunted, rubbing at his own forehead.

Normal me would have reassured him it wasn't his fault—that

this was all mine because it was, but hurt and angry me just turned away and let him sit there in pain.

"Here, Mom...I'll grab some towels." I darted toward the sink, reached for a few from the drawer and walked back to the table, wiping and cleaning while my dad said something that made Davis laugh. I didn't miss the way Davis continued to cut a look in my direction every few seconds or so.

Cradling the wet potholder and towels, I stood and addressed the table. "I'm going to go throw these in the wash."

Darting toward the living room, I cut down the hall and practically dove into the laundry room. Dumping the soaked mess in my arms on the top of the dryer, I braced myself on the ledge of the washer.

If only I had included my parents in what had happened all those years ago, they'd never have agreed to befriend this man. Now it was too late, and they loved him more than me.

"So stupid," I muttered out loud, pushing open the top of the machine lid and swiping my load inside.

"What was that?"

Davis had walked up behind me, holding the center of his soaked shirt away from his chest. I hadn't even realized he'd gotten juice on it.

"Nothing, sorry..." I looked down at my feet, hating this feeling notching in my gut. It was a swelling of my pride, a shrinking of myself and a whole lot of pain that hadn't been addressed. I had taken advantage of the school counselors three years ago to try to work through these feelings, and I realized now how foolish I was to have assumed I was all fixed.

Davis stepped around me, pulling my thoughts from the past, and that's when I realized I had missed a rather large development. His shirt was gone. I sucked in a silent breath and quickly averted my gaze. I had never seen him shirtless; even that night he was with that woman in the library, he had been fully clothed. I allowed one look, darting my eyes to the side, so he wouldn't know I was peeking. But holy shit! He was cut like stone and molded into a magazine-worthy masterpiece.

"Your dad said I could just borrow one of his white shirts, said they were folded on the counter in here?"

Trying not to gulp awkwardly, or shake—I pointed toward the pile I had finished earlier that day. "Right there."

My eyes returned to my feet, which needed to begin moving out of the room and away from him.

"You don't like me very much," he said, matter of fact.

Shrugging, I turned and grabbed the soap, filled the washer and started it without offering to add his sullied shirt.

"I have no reason not to like you." The first lie of the evening. "I just wasn't prepared to meet you. My parents have talked about you quite a bit over the years, and I had no idea you were even remotely close to my age." Or named Davis Brenton.

He shook his head, smiling before turning away and slipping into a shirt. The fact that I would be thinking about him shirtless in my house later tonight made me hate him just a little bit more, if that were even possible.

"So, the fact that I was close to your age made you nervous—is what you're saying?"

I could tell without even looking at his face that he'd have a dark brow raised in an attempt to be funny, or flirty…either was unacceptable.

"I'm saying…" I inhaled a deep breath and looked up. "That I just moved back, and I'm tired…and the last thing I wanted to do was meet some recluse that can only seem to make friends with people old enough to be his parents. It's obvious you don't have much of a life, but now that I'm home, you won't have them all to yourself anymore. Sorry, but the meal ticket is up."

My heart raced as I bit out each venomous word, hating that I was forced to watch his playful expression turn hard and resentful.

Steadying myself, I went to leave when I felt a tug on my elbow and suddenly his palm was against the door, shutting us in with my back flat against the surface.

"Let's cut the shit. I was nice for the sake of your parents, but that obviously was a waste. I don't know what your problem is, but you don't know me," he seethed, one palm above my head, his face close to mine.

But I did know him—he just had a shit memory, which was not my fault.

Smiling, I lifted my chin, daring him to move closer. "I don't need to know you to know that you're a leech. You're sucking the life out of my parents, and now that I'm back, I'm going to put a stop to it."

There was a storm in those eyes that I once adored, a violent, turbulent tempest.

"You got back from being away for over four years, with what... a handful of visits throughout the entire time you were gone?" Shaking his head, he snapped, "Say whatever the fuck you want, but your parents deserve better than having their spoiled brat finally grace them with her presence and immediately start throwing her weight around."

Guilt tugged hard at my chest, a rusty chain around my heart, aching with all the words I still owed to my parents about why I had stayed away. I had no idea why I wanted to taunt him into becoming this vile thing in front of me, but his words hit harder than a cement block to the face. I was too stunned to respond, so he continued.

"You think you know anything about me at all? You don't know anything. I, on the other hand, know everything about you, Rae, and I know that they got the short end of the stick when they got you. I've been good to them, and I will continue to be good to them because we both know you being here is only temporary. You're too selfish of a person to stick around."

With that he tugged on the doorknob, forcing me forward. He moved so we didn't touch, and then he slipped out into the hall, taking the last word with him.

6

RAE

SIX YEARS AGO

The bell rang, echoing through the restaurant, causing me to drop my ball of dough, and for what had to be the millionth time that day, I ran to the front to see if he'd come in.

"Raelyn Vernon Jackson, if you drop that dough one more time!" My mother scolded me from the back of the kitchen as I moved out front, searching for the newcomers, and other patrons sitting around tables, but the counter, where he usually sat, was empty. The spots were filling up fast.

"Excuse me." I moved a sign that I had printed and laminated and taped it in front of the space he liked to sit. "This spot is reserved."

"Reserved?" Jonas Stellate whined, sipping his coffee. "For who?"

I stood up straighter. "A VIP."

He shook his head, muttered a few things under his breath, and moved down a few spaces. I pulled the name I'd also printed and laminated from my apron and set it down on top of the tag.

Davis Brenton.

The first draft I had made had little hearts circling his name, but Nora talked me out of keeping them on there.

"Rae, get your rear end back here right now!" my mother yelled from the kitchen.

Taking one last glance around the space, I ran back and hoped I wouldn't miss him this time. Nora said he'd come in last Friday, while I was at school. The only reason she knew about it was because she'd been sick with strep, and her mother's store sat across from my parents' diner.

I worked the dough without thinking, without feeling. All I could think about were his eyes, and whether or not he'd be smiling when he saw the sign.

Thirty minutes later, I wandered back out on my break, not hearing the bell ring or any fuss, and there he was talking sternly to Carl, the shift manager. His navy eyes were murderous as he pointed a finger at the counter where I'd put his name sign. I crinkled my brows. I'd reserved him a spot; why wouldn't he be happy about it?

I couldn't hear what they were saying, but it ended with Davis picking up the sign I had made and throwing it in the garbage on his way out.

It felt as if he'd tossed my heart in there with it.

Later, Carl had gently taken me by the arm and walked me out back, sitting on a milk crate.

"You can't make those signs anymore, kiddo."

My face flushed.

"Davis is an oddball, and he doesn't like to be noticed. So things like that, they make him uncomfortable."

Nodding, I kept my eyes down, still too embarrassed to look my father's friend in the eye.

I asked, "Can you keep this between us?"

He stood, let out a sigh, and placed his hand on my shoulder. "Honey, he's five years older than you...a crush is harmless, but I need to know you understand that he's too old for you. But yes, I'll keep it between us."

I smiled, my face turning a horrible shade of pink. I was going to die of embarrassment.

"I know he—"

"That means he's twenty-one, Rae. He can drink, and you can't even drive yet, baby girl. Let the crush go."

I had just turned sixteen…I didn't have my license yet, but it wasn't too far-fetched to imagine myself with Davis. Carl was acting like I was in middle school or something.

Placating the man whom I knew more as an uncle than a boss, I gave him a firm nod and stayed outside for a while longer after he went back inside.

I understood the age difference, I did. I just also knew that soul mates wouldn't care about a thing like age. Davis was my soul mate. There was no one on this planet that could tell me any different, and I'd wait as long as I had to for him to see that.

7

DAVIS

THE PRESSURE UNDER MY AX FELT GOOD AS I SPLIT ANOTHER massive log. The crack in the air was my only soundtrack as I worked out my aggression from the previous night's dinner. I was angry, but mostly at myself, because over the past few years, as Roger and Millie had talked up their daughter, I had actually looked forward to meeting her. I wouldn't call it a crush, so to speak, but I wanted to meet the daughter of my two favorite people.

Shit, maybe it *was* a crush.

Regardless, the notion of wanting to meet her was stupid.

I had known back then that this amazing woman, living in New York, following her passions and dreams, would likely never settle down again in Macon, and if she did, she'd never be interested meeting the likes of me. Not a broken, antisocial recluse that would rather be alone and miserable than surrounded by people.

Humiliation spurred me on, lining up log after log. Each hit landed harder and harder until my hairline was soaked, my shirt too. I thought over the words I said to Rae, and how I had envisioned our first meeting going so many times that it was pathetic.

When the Jacksons had first requested that I come to dinner, I was so nervous that I had turned Roger down. I wasn't ready to

49

meet Rae, not after I had pictured what it would be like so many goddamn times.

But then he had mentioned that she was having a hard time adjusting—that her time in New York hadn't been easy on her. He hadn't really expanded too much, but I knew by his tone that he was worried about his daughter. I also knew that it was only a matter of time before our worlds connected due to how close I had become to her parents. So, I agreed.

I had even bought flowers but left them in my truck at the last second because I didn't want to seem like a complete idiot. Thank fuck for that.

Still, I hadn't been prepared for her ire toward me. She detested me, and wasn't that just sobering as hell?

The girl I had been secretly somewhat crushing on for years hated me and wanted her parents to have nothing to do with me. Not only that, but she also thought I was pathetic.

I turned to grab another log, swiping at my forehead when my dogs started barking. Turning, I watched as Roger Jackson made his way toward me in his truck, stopping just short of the woodpile.

Tossing the ax, and calming Duke and Dove, I waited for him to exit the car.

Roger Jackson was like a human pillar: strong, stoic, and always thoroughly thought through his questions before he asked them. He wore pleated pants, loafers, and sweater vests, but he didn't have a judgmental bone in his body. He gave more than he had of his time, money, and resources, to everyone he knew. I constantly felt honored that he'd drive all the way up here to see me; that he laughed at my jokes and he took interest in my life.

Best of all, my past didn't scare him.

So Little Miss Sunshine had another thing coming if she thought she could scare me off.

"Roger." I held my hand out for him to shake.

"Thomas, how are we today?" He gripped my hand and then went to pet my dogs. "Hello, you two, you keeping him in check?"

I walked over to the wood pile and started stacking the fresh pieces that I had cut.

"So…" Roger started, and this was why I appreciated him so much. He didn't waste time with bullshit; he wouldn't skirt the issue for half an hour, working his way up to telling me something—he'd always just come right out with it. I knew why he'd come up, though, so it was nice that we could just get to it. Cut it off, and then hopefully we could move on.

"I wanted to check on you after yesterday…you left rather abruptly." He paused, looking up toward the top of the trees surrounding us. "And wearing my shirt…."

"Had to get back."

He clicked his tongue, which made my dogs lift their heads. "We don't lie to one another. You've always been free to speak, no matter how blunt. Don't start keeping things from me now."

Fuck. How did I talk about Rae with him?

Letting out a sigh, I gestured toward the house. "Want some coffee?"

"Always." Roger followed, until we crested the porch steps and pushed through the screen door.

Roger knew the way to the coffee mugs and began filling his. I took a seat at the table, needing to rest after cutting almost an entire cord of wood.

Once his coffee was done, he joined me, and waited.

I toyed with the edge of a stray napkin, letting the silence stretch, until too much time had passed and half of Roger's cup had been emptied.

With an annoyed clip, I finally conceded. "She hates me. I just wasn't expecting that."

Roger sipped his coffee, patient as always.

"Rae has always struggled with expressing her feelings."

I scoffed, shaking my head. "She expressed them perfectly fine."

Leaning forward, Roger set his cup aside. "Her *real* feelings. Whatever she said to you last night was just fear, maybe a little insecurity…but don't give up on her. You of all people know better than to give up on someone so easily."

Because of my brother.

51

Fuck, the reminder still twisted inside my chest like a butterfly knife.

I didn't want to give up on Rae, but Roger might have a different opinion if he knew about the developing crush I had on his daughter. Then again, maybe those feelings were just superficial after fantasizing about this idea for so long. Maybe if I got to know her, I'd lose interest, and then her anger toward me wouldn't matter.

"So, it's settled. You'll place another order…and I'll have Rae deliver it."

"Here?" My voice was pitched too high, but in my defense, I didn't have people in my space, ever.

Roger laughed, "Yes, here. You two need to try again, and she feels useful helping with the deliveries. Let her pick up your order that you forgot to grab and bring it to you."

Shaking my head, I looked outside at the yard and animal pens that needed repair. Just a few tweaks here and there, tightening of the wired fences and cleaning out the straw and muck.

"She won't want to deliver if she knows it's going to me," I muttered rather pathetically, looking down at the floor.

I wondered if the real reason Roger was here pushing the two of us together was because he had an inkling that I had secretly harbored a flimsy crush. Anyone else and I'd tell them to get their nose out of my business, but Roger had earned the right to pry, even to play matchmaker if he wanted to. I trusted him and Millie implicitly, and if I played along, then they couldn't blame me when it inevitably fell apart.

My friend's smile was broad as he leaned closer. "Then we don't tell her. Let it take place naturally. I know she felt something toward you, because she wouldn't have been so uncomfortable last night or so snarky. She's likely threatened by your connection to us, but I think there might be more to it than that."

He shifted in his seat as a small grimace broke his features apart like one of Millie's puzzles. He had a thousand stories in that sad expression, a thousand unspoken truths, and maybe a decent number of regrets.

"Truth be told, although she's home, I don't really feel like I have her back. Something in her is broken, and I don't know how to fix it. She won't open up to us. She's always been independent, but after hearing how she was living in New York, it really hit hard that we don't know her at all. But, typical Rae...she's our little burst of sunlight, never dulling anyone's moment with her own problems or issues. We don't want to press too firmly, but we want to be there for her as she works through being home again."

He paused, slowly spinning the coffee cup toward him and then back, while his mournful gaze fixated on the movement. There were things he wasn't saying, and it tugged at me in a way that I wanted to fix. I wanted to physically get Rae here and make her look her father in the face and put all his fears to rest.

"I don't want her to leave again," Roger whispered, raising his gaze to meet mine.

Clenching my fist under the table, where he couldn't see, I nodded my agreement.

If I had my choice, I'd just wash my hands of his daughter, because I knew deep down that I wouldn't be the guy to fight for someone that didn't want me. Someone who thought so little of me. I would rather just live up here and forget about her...but for Roger?

I'd place that order, and I'd try to get his daughter to at least see me as a friend, so maybe she'd stay in Macon.

Maybe she'd find purpose here again, and maybe my friend list would grow by one.

8

RAE

My mother wasn't a fan of the attitude I had developed overnight, specifically minutes after Davis had left. She aggressively washed the dinner dishes, and ignored my offer of help, all while muttering about manners and how I had been ruined by New York.

Eventually I left, wandering outside, and finding my way to Nora's front door.

My best friend had grabbed a box of wine and sat on the front porch with me, while I poured out the story of Davis coming to dinner.

She'd stared ahead, unblinking, while sipping. We both had, long enough that the light had waned and the streetlights blinked on. There really wasn't much to say. The strangest and weirdest twist of fate had landed right in the center of my back with a metaphorical blade.

Now it was Saturday, and my distraction had arrived in the form of delivering meals and groceries up the mountain.

I carefully read over the list in my hand, tracking the items on the shelf as though the two could line up. "Mouthwash, hair gel, deodorant…" I placed each brand specified in the cart and headed toward the food section, but at the last aisle, my phone started vibrating, and I paused to pull my cell free.

Nora: I have a dare for you.

Smiling at the screen, I stood in the middle of the aisle and punched out a reply.

Me: What did you have in mind?

Nora: Throw something random in one of the orders, something that will make whoever gets it laugh.

Peering around the items on the shelf, my face heated.

Me: I'm staring at a rack of condoms.

Nora: Perfect!

Me: You're an idiot.

I pushed away from the spot and continued down the lane, when my phone buzzed again.

Nora: Think of the kick they'll get out of it! Obviously pay for it yourself, but this should be your thing...add one surprise item to each order.

Biting my lip, I thought it over and considered that maybe she was right. Maybe while I was home, I could carve out a fun little existence for myself. Maybe one day I'd start stealing lemons and collecting teddy bear figurines, too. I turned my cart around and veered back toward the condoms, smiling at the glossy box as I tossed it into the cart.

I STOPPED at the restaurant before I plugged the addresses into my phone. Right as I was about to tug the back door open, I inhaled a sharp breath. I hadn't walked through this door for years. When I had visited over the past few holidays, I never once came to the diner—not when there was a chance Davis might visit it.

I walked through the large kitchen that was bustling with people, nervous that no one would recognize me here. People in town seemed not to, and I wasn't sure the same would be true for most of the people I'd been around since I was a little girl. A few familiar faces appeared, a few polite smiles and waves were given, until they were followed by gasps.

"Oh my goodness!" I heard someone mutter, and a clanging sound that would indicate a dish had been dropped.

"That can't be Millie and Roger's little girl!"

"My heavens, she's all grown up!" I smiled as the polite smiles turned into watering eyes and wobbling lips. It made my chest warm with familiarity and comfort. It was peace in the midst of the chaos that had been the last four years of my life.

"Rae, my goodness, my girl!" Claudia, an older woman that I had known since I was ten, corralled me into a tight hug. I patted her back, embracing her with a smile. Her greeting caused a few more to chorus through the kitchen, until my eyes locked with a pair of warm gray ones, and my heart faltered. Carl was standing there, like an oak tree—just ready to protect me from the world. I thought over how happy he was for me when I had moved to New York— we'd talked about how good it would be for me to spread my wings. He'd even come to visit me a time or two over the years, and of course he was always present when I was home visiting, but he'd been gone the last time I came.

Once Claudia released me, I took careful steps toward the man I knew as a second father, feeling tears well up, and suddenly his arms were around me.

"String bean."

"Hey Car-Car." It was a nickname I had used ever since I was a little girl. Feeling a burn behind my eyes, I realized I was going to cry if I didn't pull away soon.

"I can't believe you're back." He let me go and stared down at me.

Giving him a light punch to the arm, I accused, "I can't believe you were already hunting when I came home! Dad said you wouldn't be back until tomorrow."

Shaking his head, he let out a small laugh and then messed up my hair by rubbing my scalp, like I was seven again.

"Sorry, kiddo. Bad timing. Let me make it up to you—your dad just baked this delicious pie. You came to eat, right?"

I took in the graying hair that filled in all the dark brown he used to have. It hadn't completely consumed his hair, but it was starting to. Shaking my head, I looked over my shoulder. "I'm here to help with mountain deliveries."

His bushy brows bunched in confusion right as my dad came up and interrupted us.

"Here, honey…it's all packed up. I'll have Carl walk it out and load it into the back."

Carl grunted, and I tried to decipher the odd look on his face, but I was distracted by the delicious smells all around me.

I eyed the pies, the scones, and the cinnamon rolls, and my stomach let out an audible grumble.

My dad chuckled. "Hungry?"

I watched as my father gently rolled the dough out on the counter and sprinkled flour like it was gold.

I had missed this. All my life, I had sat on a stool and watched him roll out dough and sprinkle flour, magically turning raw ingredients into the most delicious treats.

"No, I ate earlier."

Lifting his eyes, he smiled. "Well, I packed a sandwich for you just in case, plus water and a bag of chips."

"You're the best." I pulled him into a hug, inhaling the smell of sugar and butter.

He kissed my forehead and led me out of the kitchen. "Best get on the road if you're going to make it back before dinner."

The rear hatch to my parent's SUV was open, so I walked around the car, watching as Carl's bulking height maneuvered under the hatch that was oddly low.

I tried to push the hatch up a little further, but it wouldn't budge. "Wow, that doesn't raise up much at all, does it?"

Carl let out a huff. "It actually has a nickname. We call this car the "goose egg" because so many people who've helped load it have hit their head on this piece of junk door."

I laughed, even though I probably shouldn't, but the image of person after person falling prey to this car was too much. "Have you told Mom and Dad to take it in to get it checked?"

Slamming it shut, he clicked his tongue. "You know I have, but your dad says it's fine."

"Of course he does," I sighed.

Carl set his large hands on his hips, watching me closely, like he was hesitant to address something he'd been thinking about for a while.

"You sure you're ready for this?"

I met him with a wide smile. "Yeah, of course I am."

Why wouldn't I be?

He ducked his head, stepping closer. "I just want you to be okay, String Bean...I still remember what you went through, and..." He looked over my shoulder, speaking quietly. "I know the real reason you left home."

His eyes searched mine, as though I would spill the beans about Davis. Carl had known about my crush all those years ago, but he didn't know what had happened in that library, so he couldn't know the real reason I had left. Only Nora did.

Smiling up at him, I shook my head. "I just left for college, no big mystery. Mom and Dad need my help—that's why I'm back."

He watched my eyes, as though he was sensing that I wasn't being entirely truthful, then let it drop.

"Just be careful up there and don't give him more than just a polite hello. He hasn't earned more than that—and call if there's any issues whatsoever."

Giving him a firm nod, I veered toward the front and tugged on the door. As I settled into the seat, I tried to let go of the strange sensation taking root in my gut.

Who was he talking about?

I took a few clarifying breaths and tried my best to shake off Carl's words. But even as I pressed my foot to the gas, his words echoed in my ears.

9

RAE

THE DRIVE WAS BEAUTIFUL.

Tall evergreens lined the black asphalt, seemingly growing taller with each mile I put behind me. The sky was a bleak, grayish color, worsening as I climbed in altitude. Memories of when I'd driven this dangerous road haunted me, rankling as the cringe factor surfaced. I had no idea where Davis had lived, so I would drive it for hours, thinking fate would lead me to him. Except it never did, and I just ended up wasting my time and gas.

It was mortifying remembering that period of my life...and thinking over the dinner with Davis the other night only reinforced the sentiment. It wasn't just the humiliation from being obsessed with him; it was the fact that he'd gotten to witness my shame first-hand in that library, while confirming how pathetic he'd known I was all along.

It was still a fire in my veins and smoke in my lungs, leaving me burning and choking on my past, because Davis had a front row seat to my downfall. It was even worse that he didn't seem to remember me now—that or he was just lying—but why act nice, almost flirty even, if he did remember?

The man who had secretly invited me to meet with him and

then hooked up with someone in front of me wouldn't casually ask where I had been the last four years with that easy smile. He just wouldn't.

It was a few more miles before I realized I was gripping the wheel with so much force that my knuckles were white. Deep down, I knew I had to start getting past this anger and hurt. It wasn't healthy.

A clearing in the tree line caught my eye, distracting me from my negative thoughts. It was so breathtaking that I pulled the car over along a spacious viewpoint and parked. Pushing the door open and slowly walking to the edge of the overhang, I looked down, seeing a serpentine river. White rocks littered each side of the water and sprawled in every direction. The quiet that cradled the world was so magnificent it made my eyes water.

I had lived in the shadow of Mount Macon my entire life, and I had never once hiked its trails, or stopped to take in its unending beauty. I had never stood on the edge of the wilderness, looked down and felt so hopeful. It was as though every gust of wind was blowing fresh air into my lungs for a future I could actually be excited about. This sacred place had no past, and the only future would consist of the yellowing of leaves or white tips of the trees.

Rubbing my arms, I closed my eyes and breathed.

I stood there on the edge of what seemed to make up my whole world and inhaled. With every breath, I released pieces of my past. Not all of it, but something was left there, and for the first time in four long years, I felt lighter.

MRS. KUAMI WORE soiled overalls and a straw hat. She had a small cottage, with free range goats and chickens which sprawled over nearly every inch of her small driveway and yard. She offered me tea, which I accepted, knowing part of this delivery service would be a way to socialize with the forgotten men and women on Mount Macon. Surely they had to be lonely up here.

Which only proved right as Mrs. Kuami droned on and on

about her late husband and her son, who was thinking of moving to Alaska. After about forty minutes, I apologized and told her I had to get going. I still had other deliveries to get out of the way.

The day went on as I continued further up the mountain.

Ford and Mr. Carlson both had wooden boxes set up for the case of groceries, with a walkie left near the front of the gate. All I had to do was inform them their order had arrived. Mr. Carlson had even left a tip tied to a river rock for me, which I had put inside the cup holder of my parent's car. I'd use the twenty to help buy a few groceries for the house or maybe just grab dinner for them sometime.

My last stop was at the very top of the mountain, my logic slightly failing as I continued up the grade. I definitely should have started with the furthest house first then worked my way down.

It was nearly four in the afternoon when I started internally kicking myself for saving the furthest for last. I was trying to gauge whether or not the customer would want to engage in small talk merely based on their last name, but the packing slip for the last delivery was blank.

Something I hadn't realized before.

Keeping my eyes on the road, while quickly flicking to the packing slip, I realized they'd filled out everything else on the sheet, making it seem complete, which is why I had missed it, but sure enough there wasn't a name listed. First or last.

"Shit."

I'd have to just let my parents work it out, I had the address at least, so I knew they would be expecting me.

The client lived about twenty miles up the mountain, so it wasn't a crazy venture to get there, especially without snow on the roads, but it was still a drive. After about thirty minutes, I began to slow down and watch for the big tree and iron gate my mom had told me would act as a marker.

Pulling to a stop in front of the gate, I parked and slowly opened my door to get out. There was a latch that had to be pulled open to go up the driveway. The feel of steel pranced along my fingertips as I lifted and pushed the gate until there was enough of an opening for my car to go through, then I got back inside and drove up the path. It was mostly gravel, with tall spires of trees that lined the narrow drive all the way up to a curve, where it evened out into a large opening.

Leaning forward, I gaped at the massive, two-story house sitting in front of me. It was white, with attractive black shutters. The paint seemed fresh, and the windows on the top floor looked clean and clear, complete with gauzy white curtains. A porch swing hung to the left, and two chairs dotted the right. Off to the side of the house was a double garage, and on the other side was what looked like a large shop.

All of the siding and shutters matched, making it look like a mountain aesthetic dream. That, paired with the trees and mountain peak as a backdrop, made me want to groan in pity for myself. I wanted this: a secluded mini mansion with matching outlier buildings and a deep inset porch where I could watch the snow fall while bundled under a blanket. I wanted to wake up every morning to that view.

"Some people are so fucking lucky," I sighed, parking somewhat far from the porch, so I didn't seem intrusive.

The back hatch slowly opened and I exited, walking around the car. The plan I had set up in my head was that I would set the boxes on the wide porch, and then knock two seconds before making a run for it back toward the car. Maybe I'd throw a rock at the door once I was in the car and then just speed off, that way I didn't have to interact with whoever lived here, since I had no idea who it was.

My mind was busy as my hands grappled for the first box; I completely missed the sound of a screen door snapping shut.

"Hey, thanks for driving this all the way up here, I really appreciate it," a deep voice called out, laden with a roughness that belonged up here, as if his voice was birthed in one of the deep caverns, locked away in a mountain. He didn't sound old, he sounded... hot. Alarm ripped through me. I moved so I could convince my eyes that that voice didn't belong to who I thought it did.

My heart sputtered as panic seized it in a vise-like grip, the box slipping from my hands as I stared at Davis Brenton, the man I had so rudely told off just days before.

With his box of groceries sprawled all over the gravel, I stared at his proximity, and how his boots kept increasing in steps, bringing him closer. Suddenly, I had to get away from him any way possible, so I went to my knees and started repacking his groceries.

"Shit," I murmured, gently tugging at the carton of berries that had busted open.

Large hands were suddenly reaching for the items from me, setting them into the box that had been turned upright. My face was blotchy—I could feel it as the heat in my chest invaded the upper part of my body.

Why had he placed an order, knowing I would be the one to deliver it?

God, this was embarrassing. I didn't know what to say, and I didn't want to look up.

"Rae, it's fine." His soothing voice cooled the fire in my veins, but tears still clogged my eyes just from sheer humiliation. It wasn't about the berries, or the groceries...it was still just *him.*

"Sorry, here. I'll just get out of here." I stood briskly, slamming the top of my head right into the metal frame of the hatch door. *Damn it, stupid goose egg car.*

"Shit, are you okay?" Davis asked.

Rubbing my head and closing my eyes, I made some sound that it was okay, but damn, it hurt. A dull throb was pulsing in the crown of my head, radiating down to my ears and neck.

"Let me see." His body was nearly flush against mine, and my eyes flew open. That navy gaze was narrowed in concern, his dark green shirt complementing the tan skin stretched along the prominent veins in his forearms. A lump formed in my throat as I stood there, feeling the heat from his body in the air around me. I had to get some space from him, but at the moment I couldn't move, so I dropped my eyes to the gravel at our feet.

His large hands went up to my hair, gently prodding where I hit the hatch.

"It's fine," I muttered, but the pain was a searing stinging sensation along my scalp, and I couldn't stop myself from jerking away when his fingers tested the injury.

Davis let out a hiss. "There's blood, Rae...you need to come inside so we can get this cleaned up."

That would be an automatic no from me. I instantly began shaking my head when Davis's fingers caught my chin in a gentle grip.

"I'm not asking."

Before I could say anything more, my feet were swept out from under me, and the graying sky was stretched overhead as Davis walked with me, tucked snug against his chest, into his house. This was my high school fantasy made real, but now it felt like a nightmare...a long, humiliating nightmare.

10

DAVIS

Fucking hell.

This was exactly the reason I had told Roger that I didn't want Rae coming up here. This right fucking here.

My dogs barked at the woman hanging from my arms, as though a princess had just dropped out of the heavens, and I was the villain keeping her captive. That's the story the town will spin when they get wind of this, so might as well embrace it.

"Dove, Duke! Fucking sit before I kennel you both."

That shut them up, and they gave one last little collective whine before padding off toward their places in front of the fire.

Slamming the front door shut with my foot, I walked over to the couch and gently laid Rae down. She let out a small hiss, bringing her hand to her head, trying to gauge where the wound was.

Once letting her go, I stood and turned away from her—stretching my fingers to get the feel of her out of them. The last thing I wanted to do was get used to how soft her skin was, or admit that I liked how she felt pressed close to my chest.

"I'm going to call your dad." I said matter of fact, but she seemed to panic at the suggestion.

"No! Please…I don't" —she paused, wincing as she adjusted her hand—"I don't want him to worry."

Fuck, she was bleeding and hurt, and I was standing there staring at her like a prick.

"I'll grab you some ice and pain meds." I didn't wait for her to respond. I grabbed ice, a wet rag, and some peroxide—along with a water bottle and a container of aspirin. Padding back toward Rae, I noticed she'd shifted her body so that she was more reclined, relaxing into the couch. The sight of her closed eyes and supple body made my breath hitch. I had never had this, a woman in my space. It felt strange, but not in a bad way.

Blinking away the image, and clearing my head, I stepped closer and took a seat on the coffee table across from her.

"Here…" I hesitated, trying to sound a little less like the Davis Brenton in all the rumors she likely heard growing up. "Be careful as you sit up."

My hand was out, careful not to touch her as she moved. I wouldn't make her uncomfortable, and I sure as shit wouldn't touch her again if I could help it, but that didn't mean I didn't notice how good she looked. She had smooth, creamy skin, with a few independent freckles—one above her left brow, one on her nose and one near her jaw. Her dark lashes fanned the top of her cheeks, and her lips were plump and pink. She looked like a fucking princess: hair too perfect, and shiny, skin too clear and creamy, lips too kissable.

Her lashes fluttered, and two bright blue eyes stared back at me. For one small moment, she seemed completely at ease just staring at me, but then her gaze narrowed, and her face went from pale to slightly red. I was sitting so close to her that my knees practically touched her hips.

"You okay?" I asked, hoping to ward off her panic.

She thrust her palms back, trying to adjust her back into a sitting position.

"Careful," I reiterated, finally applying pressure to her back to stabilize her.

She muttered something under her breath and kept her gaze low, as though she didn't want to look at me.

"Can you say something coherent, so I know that you're okay?"

Wincing, she finally settled her gaze on mine. "Why did you place an order and not add your name?"

Her confusion made my composure break, forcing a smile.

"I did add my name."

Her confused stare stayed in place as she waited for me to elaborate, but I needed to be sure she was physically okay first.

"Now that you're sitting up, I need you to take this." I nodded toward her injury and reached for the bottle of aspirin.

"Here." I handed her a bottle of water, and medicine.

She gave me a long look, her left eyebrow arching, as if she was weighing how likely I was to poison her.

I glared back. "It's not drugged or anything. Look, the seal is still on the bottle."

That eyebrow stayed arched, challenging me.

"What?" I asked, trying to shake off the feeling she stirred in me. She looked at me like she knew that deep down I was just a piece of shit, trying to hide from my sins.

"Why are you being nice to me? We didn't end our last conversation on good terms..."

I smiled. "No, we didn't, did we?"

Those eyes flicked to mine as though she were searching something out. If she was starting to pick up on the fact that I was attracted to her, well, good. It would save me from having to explain that I had liked her long before she ever showed up. That I used to think about her after those long summer nights when her parents would get done talking to her, or share a new story about her escapades in New York.

"I'm not being nice. I'm just trying to make sure you don't die." Shaking my head, I popped the lid off the aspirin bottle.

Seemingly at ease, she carefully took the offered water and pills. I stayed where I was but leaned over her to see the cut on the top of her head. With her dark hair and the graying sky outside, I didn't have a clear view.

"Hang tight, I need to grab a flashlight."

Rae's eyes moved upward, while shaking her head, which made her flinch. "It's not a big deal."

I walked toward the laundry room, ignoring her calls from the couch about it being fine, and tugged open the junk drawer.

Grabbing the slim flashlight, I headed back and settled into the same spot I had before.

"Come here," I ordered gently, placing my hand around the side of her head.

She leaned into me, allowing me to inspect the top of her scalp. She smelled like some sort of floral blend that made me want to sink my nose into each and every silky strand on her head. Pushing past my odd, yet growing obsession, I focused on her injury.

With the flashlight, I could see the gash, which was still bloodied but had already clotted.

"This is going to hurt," I whispered, letting her go and reaching for the antiseptic and the rag. Gently pouring a small amount over the cut, I wiped at the blood with the rag, pressing it into the wound to ensure it was done bleeding out.

Rae let out a small hiss, moving her hand up to grab my wrist. The jolt of heat from her touch ran up my arm, instantly making me think of having her in my bed, her gripping my wrists while I fucked her slowly.

Working to get that image out of my head, I cleared the lust from my voice. "Sorry."

"It's okay, thank you…" Rae said softly.

Things were silent for a few seconds as I continued cleaning her wound, and she continued holding my wrist, maybe she didn't realize she was doing it. Maybe it was because it was too painful not to…but I liked that her hands were on me. So, I may have taken a little longer than necessary.

"All done," I rasped out, still trying to clear the attraction to her out of my voice.

She let me go and leaned away from me, the tops of her cheeks flushed as she tipped her head back to let the remaining water drops trickle away.

Sitting back and setting the rag down, I let the quiet fill up the space between us, hoping she'd be the first one to talk.

"I'm going to get going before it gets too dark."

Fuck, that wasn't what I wanted her to say.

She swung her legs, attempting to swing them off the couch, but I wouldn't move from my spot on the coffee table, blocking her path.

I stared at her for a beat, trying to wrangle the emotions clogging my chest.

There was this dam inside me, bursting at the seams with her nearness. Thinking how throughout the years, Raelyn Jackson had become like a celebrity to me. I had begun salivating for stories about her, and before I knew it, a small crush had developed over this girl I had never met, nor seen. The Jackson's had never once shown me a photo of her, never once introduced me while they facetimed her. Yet, this girl never left my head. She was there, lurking the back of my mind like a shadow.

Now she was here, and she was about to leave. Something about it ripped at my insides, screaming at me to make her stay. It wasn't that I was just lonely, it was...*her.*

"Do you drink coffee?" I stood, looking down at her.

She just sat there, staring up at me.

Blinking, and closing those sapphire eyes off to me, she exhaled through her nose. She stayed like that for a few seconds then looked up at me from under her lashes and said, "I need to use the restroom."

I held out a hand to help her up, but she ignored it.

"First door of your left, down the—"

She stood, took one step and nearly fell over. My hands were at her waist in the blink of an eye, which made her inhale sharply.

"Can you wait for one goddamned second or let me help you? I don't need you falling and getting hurt any worse than you already have."

She half turned toward me, a glare firmly in place as her lips turned down and she jerked away from my hold.

"I'm fine."

I ran a nervous hand through my hair, realizing I'd snapped too harshly at her.

Once she was tucked into the bathroom, I ran outside to grab the box of groceries and food she'd delivered, right as it started to sprinkle. Bounding back up the steps and back inside, I set everything down on the counter and settled a few perishables in the fridge before letting out a small sigh. I shouldn't have been such a dick; it wasn't like she'd want anything to do with me even without my gruff nature…but now.

Sneaking a quick glance toward the hall, where the bathroom was, and hearing the sink turn on, I checked the mirror hanging in the living room. Without thinking, I smoothed a hand through my hair, so it didn't look so lame. I was out of hair gel, so mine was flat today. She probably dated guys that wore suits and had three-hundred-dollar haircuts; there wasn't a chance she'd be interested in me.

"You have a nice bathroom." Rae said kindly, coming out of the restroom looking refreshed and still a little nervous.

I took a second to appreciate how her dark hair framed her face, the long locks trailing past her breasts, which were high and perfectly round. In fact, the way they pushed against her shirt, and the way her hips flared, the denim clinging to her toned thighs, I could feel myself getting worked up over how beautiful she was, which was insanely virginal of me.

Clearing my throat, I grated out, "Thanks, I renovated it last year."

I moved to the Keurig and refilled the water tank. "I have a few flavors of coffee over here, if you want to pick one."

I could hear her move behind me, slowly. *Nervous.*

I hated that I made her feel that way, but it wasn't like Millie and Roger were talking me up to her while she was in New York, like they had been with me.

"I really should be going. I splashed water on my face and feel much better… I think the aspirin is kicking in."

Fuck, she wanted to leave again.

I lifted my cup, gesturing toward the ceiling. "It's pouring outside. Just stay for a few minutes…have some coffee."

Her blushing face told me she was more nervous than anything else—maybe uncomfortable because she didn't like me—but we were both adults… We could get past what happened the other day. I sipped my hot drink, trying to keep my eyes anywhere but on her so she'd relax, but it wasn't easy. She was the prettiest fucking thing I'd seen in a long time, and truth be told, it made *me* nervous.

Finally, she seemed to let out a sigh, and tucked the hair behind her ears. "What sort of flavors do you have?"

She was elbow to elbow with me, and I could smell her subtle floral scent, which had my thoughts returning to her hair and burying my face in it.

"I have about every flavor, decaf too if you want it."

She nodded while tracing the different tops of the flavored pods. Just then, the rain started hitting harder against the skylight, making her look up.

"I like that." She smiled, and it caused my breath to hitch.

I wanted to kiss her. *Really fucking badly.*

Her eyes lit up as she picked up a hazelnut pecan pod and pushed it into the top of the coffee maker.

"So you recently graduated, right?" I asked, taking a sip of my coffee but keeping my back against the counter so we still stood close.

"You trying to pick up where we left off at dinner?" She raised a dark brow in my direction.

I tried not to react, but it was obvious she didn't like me, and that just fucking grated against my pride.

I simply replied with, "Yep."

Then there was just silence between us, which again, normally I wouldn't care about, but I wanted her voice. I wanted to hear her, but maybe talking about what we did the other night wasn't a good place to start.

"What made you want to move back?"

The rain clashed against the roof and glass like rocks, which meant there might be some hail coming down. That, with the wind howling through the cracks and crevices of the house, made the silence between us echo.

She watched her cup fill, ignoring me, until finally she let out a sigh.

"I'm surprised you don't already know that too."

Again with that fucking attitude.

"Your parents *are* protective of your privacy, more than you probably realize." I sipped my coffee, ignoring the frustration that was beginning to build in my chest.

She made a sound of agreement, finally pulling her cup free and slowly sipping it with a wince, like she didn't like the taste. This wasn't going the way I wanted it to at all. Roger was wrong; there was no getting through to his daughter, and truthfully, she might be beyond help. She seemed to have a stick up her ass, and there was not enough lubricant in the world to get it loose.

"How about I just drive you back? My truck is down, but I could drive Millie's car. I know these roads a lot better than you do." I didn't trust that she'd be able to handle the curves of the mountain with that head wound. What if her vision went blurry and she didn't realize it, or she passed out?

That icy glare cut through me as she set her cup down.

"No thank you. I know these roads like the back of my hand."

I narrowed my gaze, inspecting her for the lie. "Bullshit, no one knows these roads unless they drive them every day."

"Well, you don't know me, *at all*," she bit out angrily, before shaking her head and turning on her heel. I knew she had emphasized the tail end of her comment in response to when I had said I knew her better than anyone the other night in the laundry room. I probably needed to apologize for what I had said because while she had started it, by the way she'd flushed and almost cried—I had definitely ended it.

"Fuck. Okay. I'm sorry about that comment, and the one I made the other night."

She paused in the doorway of my kitchen, a pensive expression on her face that crumpled after a moment. "I've taken up enough of your time. I honestly just want to go home."

"I get that, but..." Dammit, I didn't want to say what was about to come out of my mouth next, didn't want to show how desperate I was, but I also didn't want her to leave. "I wouldn't mind the company; it gets quiet up here."

Blue eyes flashed, searching mine briefly before she gave me a single nod.

I backed away from the counter and walked over to the back window. I didn't want to spook her, so I watched the rain instead of inspecting her every move.

"So..." Rae drawled, "How did you meet my parents and get to know them well enough to where you're all they talk about?"

Adjusting my stance near the window, I looked up, thinking back on when I first met Roger and Millie.

"They have been delivering up here for the last couple of years, trying to make us mountain dwellers feel less disconnected from the town. They started with Thanksgiving dinner, and then Christmas pies. They were so nice, I couldn't even be mad when they kept showing up. We struck up a friendship, and then all the sudden both your parents were up here once a week, delivering food and whatever groceries I needed from town."

Such a shitty way to summarize my only relationship of substance.

"Wait." She wrapped her soft coral nails around the ceramic mug, while her brows crowded her delicate forehead. "So they were delivering up here before they even started the delivery business?"

I nodded, sipping from my cup. "We joked about me giving them the idea, actually."

She made a surprising sound from the back of her throat. It caught me off guard, so much so that I gently set my cup down and glared at her.

"Did you just scoff?"

Mimicking my movement with her mug, she stood away from the counter. "Yeah, I did."

Was she serious? "Why?"

She shrugged, her face reddening. "Just sounds like my aging parents were endangering their lives a ton just to appease someone who's too lazy to leave the house."

Gritting my teeth, I tried to focus on what Roger had said about his concern with Rae, and how badly he wanted her to stay. I could be nice. *I would be fucking nice if it killed me.*

"That's quite an assumption."

"Well, how often did you visit them at their house?" she asked, flicking her wrist out as if to encourage me to answer.

I was silent because the dinner the other night had been the first time. Not that I hadn't been invited, I just...

I liked my space, my privacy...and I hated town and all the people in it, except for Roger and Millie, but even the idea of being in their home made me anxious.

Rae shook her head. "That's what I thought. Well, thanks for the coffee, and for..."—her tone took on a sarcastic ring—"helping me."

"Did I do something to make you hate me?" I asked, not able to hold in my own scoff, because this was bullshit. "Because the way you treated me at dinner, and now this...I have to wonder what the fuck I did to make you so angry."

Walking toward the front door, her dark hair swaying with the movement, my eyes managed to betray me and drop to her ass.

"No, you did nothing... I'm just glad I'm home now, so I can talk some sense into my parents regarding the hermit up in the mountains."

What the fuck?

Now I was practically chasing her to keep in step with her.

"Hey." I placed my hand on the screen frame right as she tugged on it, my posture blocking her exit. This was just a repeat of what we'd done the other night, her saying shit and running away and me not able to let her.

"You don't know anything about our relationship, or me—and while we're on the subject, let's talk about how you're stressing your parents out." My voice shuddered from the anger fraying my nerves.

She turned her red face my way, her blue eyes sharp, her lips thin. "What are you talking about?"

"You lied about how bad things were in New York, and now you're being a snobby bitch to the important people in their life, stressing them out."

I didn't actually know if she'd lied about New York, but Roger had implied as much.

Tears gleamed in her eyes as her lip curled in disgust.

"Fuck you."

"Fuck you back," I snapped, although my voice came out raspier than I intended. My eyes were unable to stop tracking the movement of her lips, or how close we were standing to one another.

Her gaze fixated on my mouth, like mine had with hers.

Her chest rose and fell in heavy rhythm, and if she placed her hand over my heart, she'd realize mine was doing the same.

The silence expanded, stretched, and nearly exploded as we stared at one another, and through her stare I felt something so familiar. Instead of wanting to kick her out on her ass, like I would every other person, I wanted to shut and lock the door with her inside.

"Great, glad we got that out of the way. How about you stay away from me, and I'll stay away from you," she whispered in return and turned her face toward the screen door.

Her hand jerked on the metal handle, but mine was still above her, boxing her in, and I wasn't going to move.

Not until I had a few more seconds of this charged electricity with her. It was the most alive I had felt in…well, ever.

"Stay. Have another cup of coffee," I whispered, brushing my lips against the shell of her ear.

Her head turned, her lips parted, and those eyes were wide.

"You can't be serious, you just—"

I did something stupid then.

Something I knew I'd regret.

But she was burning under my skin. So, I leaned down with my hand above her head and slammed my mouth to hers.

The rain poured as I held the door in place with one hand and grabbed her waist and pulled her against me with the other.

She let out a small sound, but it wasn't a protest because her head slanted to the side, and she moved her lips against mine in a quick, erotic cadence that seemed to match the pounding of the rain.

I'd never kissed someone like this before. I'd never wanted to touch someone as badly as I wanted to touch her, and I had no real reason why. She was like a burn that needed to be soothed. An itch that needed to be scratched. Whatever it was, I needed her mouth, her body...*more.*

She was flat against the screen door now, both my hands at her hips, and her hands were gathered at my neck, tugging the hair there, her mouth moving with mine, easing enough that my tongue had access to slide inside and move against hers.

Another groan escaped her lips, and when a crack of thunder split the air, resulting in her eyes popping open, and then her hands were moving down my chest and she was shoving me away.

Her surprise mirrored my own.

So much so that I faltered back a few steps, giving her enough time to open the screen and slip through. My chest heaved as I watched her stomp toward the white Rover, and while I wanted her to be okay, I also knew that I had crossed too big of a line to keep her here any longer.

She'd never want to talk to me again.

Running a hand through my hair, I decided I could at least trail her to ensure she made it down the mountain alive—even if that meant doing it from the back of a bike in the pouring rain.

11

RAE

My hands shook as I gripped the steering wheel, my eyes flicking to the rearview mirror over and over, ensuring I was really seeing what I thought I was. Davis Brenton was following me, on a motorcycle, in this crazy thunderstorm that had streams of water running along the road and my windshield wiper blades moving back and forth at a breakneck speed.

Why on earth was he on that bike, and in this freaking weather?

I eyed him once more in the mirror. "He's going to kill himself."

I had begun talking to myself out loud, but it wasn't like it was safe to call Nora. Although, that idea did have merit. She might know what to do. Maybe she could run interference for me if his plan was to kidnap me before I got to my front door.

What *was* his plan?

This entire situation was insane and couldn't really be happening.

He kissed me.

His lips had molded to mine, his arm braced above my head, making me feel protected and safe. *Wanted.*

"Wake the fuck up, Rae," I scolded myself, feeling my face heat. I forced myself to put my focus back on the road.

The steady grade led into several sharp turns until it evened out, then there was an entirely new set of curves that had me crawling at a snail's pace out of sheer terror. A steep cliff dropped off to one side, and a single wrong move would have me flying down it. Suddenly I wasn't worried at all for the man enduring a little rain— I was panicked for myself. I had no clue how to handle these roads. I had lied to Davis earlier, trying to be the more experienced one in the room and gain the upper hand. He obviously saw through it, which was why his dark helmet was currently a black spot in my peripheral.

Finally, after nearly an hour, I saw signs for town, and my grip slackened on the steering wheel. I expected the man behind me to turn around, maybe veer off back toward the mountain now that I was safely in town. That was assuming he was following me to keep me safe, but his headlight stayed fixed on my bumper.

More determined than ever, I sped past the signs to slow down and ventured toward my parents' house. He continued to follow.

Oh my gosh. Was he going to tell my parents about the kiss? I mean, I wasn't a kid anymore, but he couldn't just come right out and say anything to them about it. How awkward.

Before I had a chance to come up with an alternate plan on what to do, I'd turned on to my street and then into the driveway. I watched in horror as the motorcycle behind me eased next to the curb and his boots landed on the street, steadying his bike.

Fumbling with the buckle, I released it and hurried out of the car, bypassing his stride up the walk. If I could just get in first... But as my hand wrapped around the door knob, it wouldn't turn. *Locked.*

Fuck.

I had left my purse in the car in my rush to get out, which meant I was going to have to stand outside with him.

Just as I crossed my arms, his presence seemed to envelop me from behind. He kept enough distance that we weren't touching, but I still felt how warm he was, and how close.

"Don't tell them anything," I said in a rushed whisper.

Right as I heard the deadbolt unlatch, he leaned down to whisper in my ear.

"I wouldn't dream of it, especially because we aren't even close to being finished with *that* conversation."

The door jerked, with the same urgency as my heart seemed to thump.

His voice still trailed up my arms, leaving little bumps behind. I felt completely out of control around him.

"Rae, my goodness...and Thomas?" My mom gasped, shock evident in her focus toward the man behind me.

I walked past her but faltered two steps ahead, curious what she must see to have made her face twist like that.

"Did you ride here, on your bike, in this storm?"

Each word was punctuated with rising alarm.

Now being able to see what she did, my gut twisted uncomfortably. I wanted to hate the man, but he'd just spent an hour in the pouring rain on the back of a bike to ensure I made it here safely. His hair was drenched, the strands sticking to the side of his face, and his skin was ashen, his lips blue, along with the beds of his nails. He hadn't grabbed his leather jacket; instead, he had on a black hoodie, which was laden with water, same with his boots and jeans.

"Come in, my goodness." Mom seemed to snap out of it, while Dad rushed around him to grab a blanket.

"It's no big deal," Davis murmured quietly, his eyes catching mine every few seconds.

I felt frozen, unsure if I should just leave and take off to my room or help him.

"What on earth made you drive that bike down the mountain in this storm?" Dad asked, incredulously.

"Just making sure Rae made it safe. The mountain is dangerous in this kind of weather." Davis sounded more exhausted than he did before, but there was still an undercurrent to his tone that kept those chills in place along my skin.

I walked forward, trying to escape the conversation—and more importantly the feelings attached to being so close to him—when my mother stopped me.

"Rae, go start the shower. He needs to get out of these wet clothes. Get him a fresh towel too."

79

Inwardly, I made some sort of immature gesture, but in front of my parents, I nodded and did as they said. It wasn't that I didn't want him to be warm and get dry. I just didn't want to care either way. I wanted to be as apathetic toward him as I was a week ago.

Starting the shower and grabbing the biggest towel I could find for him, I checked to make sure there were toiletries.

Then I turned, ready to leave, but stopped short.

Davis stood there, his dark hair hanging in dripping silky strands that nearly cut into his eyes. He was so tall that he filled the entire door frame, still wearing the black hoodie. I sucked in a sharp breath as his eyes trailed down my body, and with his eyes locked on mine, his arms raised and reached behind his neck, tugging the thick material over his head.

"Rae, is everything all set up?" my mother asked from down the hall.

I shook out of my reverie, blinking away the sight of Davis smirking at me, and called back.

"Yes!"

He smiled, slow and sensual, as I continued to stand in front of him, and he continued to block my path.

"Then tell him thank you for ensuring your safety, and let the poor boy take a shower!"

Summoning all my will power, I stared at the object of my high school obsession.

"Thank you for making sure I got here safely."

His eyes went to my lips, and it made me want to scream. He wasn't supposed to kiss me at his house, or look at me the way he was now.

"You're welcome."

I waited for him to say something else, but he didn't.

He did, however, finally walk past me with a low chuckle.

My face heated the entire way to my bedroom.

LATER THAT NIGHT, I cracked my bedroom door, peering out to ensure that after hours of being stuck inside my room, Davis wasn't still in the bathroom. Seeing the door ajar, I bolted toward it and locked myself inside.

Once I had finally relieved my poor bladder, I grew a bit bolder and padded down the hall to see if anyone was still up. I was starving, and just wanted to throw some bread in my mouth, preferably slathered in peanut butter and some honey. Seeing that no one was in the kitchen, I began acting on my desires, pulling free the ingredients. I was mid-swipe with the butter knife when I heard laughing coming from the garage.

Keeping my eyes on the sliver of light coming from the door, I grabbed my sandwich and began shoving it in my mouth in a very unladylike way, tiptoeing to the entryway to see who was up talking with my dad.

Through the crack, I could make out Davis, in his now-dry hoodie, standing with his back to the door I was peering through. My father was next to his boat, drinking from a coffee mug.

"You don't have to do that," I heard my father mutter with a heavy sigh.

Davis looked down at the floor. His legs were spread wide, looking relaxed in a way that I hadn't seen before. "Roger, you and Millie—you're my family. It's something that makes me happy."

There was a long pause, and then my dad spoke up.

"And Rae...do you think she could ever fit inside that small circle you've created?"

Davis waited a second before he responded, and I don't know why it mattered so much to me, but I needed to hear his response more than I needed my next breath.

"I don't know, Roger. I did what you said to do. I didn't put my name on the slip, but she still seemed annoyed with me. We ended up getting into another fight. I know you're worried about her, but I don't think I'm the right guy for the job."

Uhhh, what the actual?

I felt lightheaded.

My dad...

He'd set me up?

Asked Davis to ask me up there, and to be nice to me?

Did that mean the kiss was fake? Suddenly, I was reliving feelings from that night where he'd embarrassed me. I was triggered. I knew enough about my pain to know that there were still frayed edges that would come apart if anyone tugged on them.

Someone said something, but I didn't hear it. There was a rushing in my ears, a whooshing, like I was sitting next to a waterfall. Tears creased my eyelids as I slowly slipped back toward the kitchen and finally turned toward my room.

I was more determined than ever to never open myself up to the grumpy recluse on Mount Macon.

Not my heart. Not my mouth.

Fucking nothing.

12

RAE

I sat at the small coffee bistro, waiting for Nora. I had initially texted her that I had major news, and that it involved Davis. She wanted to see me last night, but her parents had her attend a business function for her father. Now, she was ready for all the gossip, and all I wanted to do was forget anything had ever happened.

While I waited for her, my fingernail trailed the small plastic menu, noticing the worn edges and how a few of the drink options had a dark permanent marker sliced through them.

Furrowing my brows, I walked over to the counter and thumbed through a few more menus, noticing the disrepair repeated with the others as well. Distressed edges, wrinkles, permanent marker, and sticky spots. Looking over my shoulder, I eyed the empty tables and frowned.

This would be an easy fix to give the impression that they cared about their image to the public, and with the location of the shop, they should be getting the majority of the tourists who wanted a latte before heading up the mountain, and yet there didn't seem to be anyone in, and I had been there for well over twenty minutes.

This was a big reason I wanted to meet Nora here, because I

wanted to start inspecting a few of the businesses to gauge where they needed help and how I could offer my services. Unfortunately, my rebranding help would have to be done for free, as I already knew these businesses didn't have the money for it. If it helped keep my home afloat and my parents employed, then I wouldn't mind.

"Hey, Rachel?" I called out, standing at the counter.

The girl in question had introduced herself, made my Americano, and then promptly ducked into the back.

A flash of red hair caught my attention as Rachel jogged back out, holding a sudsy dish.

"Yeah?"

Dear Jesus, why would she drip soapy water along the floor? Gah.

"Sorry, didn't mean to bother you, I was hoping to chat with you about something for a second."

"Oh, okay." She looked around, as if she wasn't sure where to put the dish. Settling on the counter, she set the plate down and walked over to me.

"What's up?"

"I was just curious if you reprint and laminate menus on a quarterly basis or what the rotation usually is?"

Her dark brows hit her hairline as surprise swept over her features. "Oh those? No, we've had them forever. I don't think they've been swapped out for at least two years or something."

Just as I suspected.

"Okay, thank you. Um, do you have the number for the manager, by chance?"

Panic flooded the poor girl's features. "Is something wrong?"

Shaking my head, I set the menu back down. "Not at all! I promise, I'm just hoping to talk with the manager about a business opportunity. You have been amazing, don't worry."

"Okay, good, just making sure." She exhaled and walked back toward the back, forgetting her soapy dish.

Right as she exited, I heard the small bell over the door jingle. I turned, seeing my best friend enter, hugging a cross-body purse to her chest. Her eyes widened as she took me in and hustled toward the table I had snagged for us.

"I literally don't even need caffeine; I just need details," she gushed, barely balancing her ass in the small seat she'd half untucked from the table.

Feeling my face flush red, I settled in across from her and decided to just spill everything, like ripping a Band Aid.

"Well, I may have oversold it. I mean, it wasn't that big of a—"

"You will not skimp on this, Raelyn Vernon. Tell. Me. Everything," she demanded, leaning over my cup of coffee.

Exhaling a heavy breath, bristling at the flicker of embarrassment that came with the feeling of what happened, I just blurted it out.

"He kissed me."

"What?" she shrieked loudly, making Rachel drop something in the back. The barista came rushing back out, eyes wide and chest flushed.

"Everything okay?"

"Sorry," Nora and I apologized in unison.

Rachel shook her head, probably in irritation, and trudged into the back.

"He kissed you? Okay, back up." Nora sat back, shaking her head.

"Okay, so when I got up there, I had no idea it was his house, until he walked out."

"How is that possible?" Her brows came together, piecing little bits together, and it made me want to just let her try and draw her own conclusions. Confessing felt like swallowing glass.

"Well…funny thing about that, I found out last night that my dad had actually set me up and asked Davis to place the order without putting his name on the ticket."

"What?"

Something crashed again in the back. We winced and yelled together toward the kitchen, "Sorry!!"

"Yeah, we'll circle back to that. So, I was surprised, and because of how stunned I was, I ended up standing too fast by the rear hatch and hit my head."

"Oh my God. He totally took care of you," Nora presumed, slack-jawed and wide-eyed.

"He took me inside and offered me water and helped me." I carefully left out about a gazillion details, like the fact that he carried me, and how he cradled my head to his chest like I was the most fragile thing he'd ever held. Or how I'd grabbed his wrists because they seemed strong and, in the moment, I had felt weak.

Gathering my thoughts, I pushed on. "Anyway, we started talking and I got annoyed because he's been forcing my parents to drive up the mountain for like two years, just to take him stuff, because he's too lazy to come down, so I told him to fuck off, he told me to fuck off back, and when I tried to leave, he pulled me in and kissed me."

Nora's eyes searched my face, "like in a sweet way?"

Slowly, I shook my head, as a defiant smile twisted my lips, betraying my truth.

"Oh my God, you liked it!"

Pushing my cup forward, then tucking my fingers into the handle, I tried to ignore the rush of heat hitting my chest at the memory of his lips. "No, I didn't."

"You did," she argued, as though it were as plain as the sky being blue.

I sipped from my coffee, shrugging my shoulder. "So, the man can kiss…doesn't change the fact that I hate him. Like hate, hate, totally despise, so it doesn't matter."

Nora sat back and finally let her gaze drift up toward the ceiling, like she was considering everything I had said, trying to find a way to fix it.

"It definitely matters, Rae…this is your lifetime crush. The man you—"

"It wasn't real," I said more forcefully than necessary. Softening my tone, I added, "It was a crush, and it died. My feelings are no longer active, so it doesn't matter."

It *was* just a kiss. And a lie.

Nora's eyes sparkled with amusement as she sat back and smirked, drawing her gaze from the patron who opened the door, face down, eyes glued to their phone. We both watched as the man looked up, saw there was no one behind the counter then turned on his heel to walk out.

"So the kiss meant nothing at all?" She raised a thin eyebrow at me in challenge.

Shaking my head vehemently, I smiled. "Nothing at all. It was just physical, like two magnets that clunked together because of proximity." I couldn't bring myself to talk about what I had over-heard him say to my father.

"Huh…interesting."

I narrowed my gaze on my best friend. "Why is that interesting?"

She shrugged, sagging in her chair. "No reason… It's just that… a kiss from Davis isn't *just* a kiss. It will always mean more because of what he meant to you for so many years."

"It's not like that at all." I swallowed the thick lump in my throat, hearing his voice as he spoke last night. "I think it was all just for show, for my dad. I think Dad is worried or something about me. Either way, it wasn't a real kiss, Nora. So this entire conversation is just a waste of our time."

Her expression crumpled and then her left brow arched, which meant she was ready to throw a few more reasons on top of why she likely thought the kiss meant something. But I couldn't talk about this anymore.

I stood and smiled down at my friend.

"I need honey—Mom and Dad are fresh out. Let's go."

THE NEXT MORNING I found myself yawning as I exited my bedroom and padded down the hallway.

"There she is!" my dad exclaimed loudly.

Wincing, I blinked against the brightness of the room. "Why are the shades open?"

"It's almost ten, sleepyhead."

Oh.

"Sorry, I was up late…" I scrambled to think of something clever to say. "Doing a puzzle."

My mom's eyes lit up. "You should have come and grabbed me, I was up late doing one too." Of course she was.

Giving her a warm smile, I moved into the kitchen and grabbed a mug, pouring myself a cup of coffee. It was when I went for the creamer that I heard a gasp behind me.

I jumped, startled at how close my mom had come up behind me.

"Mom!" I huffed. "What are you doing?"

"Is that the hazelnut blend?" She eyed the creamer bottle in my hand.

She looked crazed, like she was ready to snatch it from me any second. Slowly returning the bottle to the fridge, I shut the door and put my back against it.

"I think I'll try that milk and sugar thing you've been doing."

Her eyes narrowed on the closed door. "No, don't be silly…just let me smell it."

I watched her, trying not to crack a smile. She was a total addict, about to break, and my dad was going to kill me if she did.

"Dad!" I called, and he was there a second later, eyeing my mother's posture and gaze toward the fridge.

"Mil, you worked so hard," he said reproachfully.

"I just want to smell it, Roger, that's all."

I burst out laughing, unable to hold it in any longer. "Why on earth are you so determined not to drink it anymore?"

Finally, my mother clicked her tongue and turned away. "It was just something Thomas encouraged me to give up. We all gave something up as a summer thing." She waved me off as though I wouldn't understand, and the pinching in my chest echoed her sentiment. I had grossly underestimated how close they'd gotten over the years.

"So, you guys know him pretty well then?" I toyed with one of the magnets on the fridge, my eyes going toward the photo of a man hiking up Mount Macon.

"Yeah, we've gotten pretty close…" my dad said, biting into a piece of toast.

I eyed the photo once more, already knowing that person wasn't either one of my parents. I pointed at the picture, "This is him, isn't it?"

"That was two winters ago. We went Christmas tree hunting up there, but that image right there, I just loved how he looked at the mountain—like it was a friend instead of a foe, or something to be afraid of. He taught us how to listen to the mountain, how to safely be on it, and how to respect it."

More pinching sensations took root along my lungs. Anger surged like an ugly storm head, battering all my logical sense away, turning me into a petty teenager again.

"Yet, he's never come here, until the other night for dinner?" I raised a brow. "Sounds like a one-sided relationship to me."

"You just don't know him, sweetie," my dad chided, and the pull in my center threatened to detonate. They'd never known of my obsession with Davis; they never knew how madly in love with him I was, or what a fool I had made of myself.

I'd grown accustomed to not telling my mother and father things, and Davis had fallen under that umbrella. They were always missing big cues where I was concerned, and it hurt like hell that they'd gone and adopted the one man on the planet that had hurt me so badly.

"Well, I find this entire relationship ridiculous…and I didn't have a very good interaction with him yesterday." I wanted to set my father up for failure with the way I worded my statement. I wanted him to admit that he'd set me up. Maybe I was looking for a reason for them not to want me, to send me back to roach-infested New York with a new chip on my shoulder.

Fuck, I needed to go back to therapy.

My dad's eyes narrowed. "Well it must not have been that terrible if he drove all the way here on his motorcycle, in the rain."

His implication was clear—Davis had risked his life just to follow me home. My anger split me in half like a log, forcing my voice to break.

"He wouldn't have had to drive me home if I hadn't gone up there in the first place! You played me, Dad."

My father's shuttered expression made me feel as though I had gone too far, but I was hurt over their lack of involvement with my life, only to stick their nose in it at the worst possible time.

"Sweetheart," Dad said softly, right as my mother's expression caved.

"What are you talking about?"

At least she wasn't in on it.

I shook my head and walked through the kitchen, my molars clenched tight as I worked to wrangle my frustration.

"Dad told Davis to place the order, but leave his name off the ticket, so I didn't know who I was delivering to. Then, I don't know…told him to flirt with me, or whatever else. Essentially, get me comfortable enough to want to stay here in Macon."

I glared at my father and added, "I heard you last night, talking in the garage."

My mother's eyes flicked to my dad's for a brief second before they landed back on me.

"Are you not wanting to stay?"

Fuck, that's not what I wanted to slip, or for them to hear. It didn't sound right.

I backpedaled. "No, of course I want to stay, but Dad seems to be worried that I don't and roped Davis into helping."

"Rae, honey…" My mom moved to come after me, but tears clogged my eyes as embarrassment flushed my face. I was so angry about the interaction with Davis, about not knowing that he was the client I was delivering to. It all hurt too much, and I couldn't tell them about any of it because then they'd want to know why.

And why was she coming for *me*, and not yelling at my dad?

"I'm fine…but I can't believe he did that and—"

Strong arms wrapped around me, crushing me in a warm hug. My words cut off abruptly, and as another set of large arms wrapped around my back, I realized I didn't need to say anything more.

My dad's voice rasped into my hair. "I never meant to hurt you. I only wanted you to be friends. I thought you could use an extra one. I'm so sorry, honey."

A burning sensation blazed behind my eyes as I worked to hold back tears, but it was useless.

"Don't give up on us, sweetheart. Just understand that we're trying, and we love you so much."

Who were these people? I hadn't ever felt so loved and protected in my entire life. Where was all this support when I wanted them to come and visit me, or when I had graduated? The hurt I had used to guard my walls where they were concerned started to crack. Ever so slowly.

And for once, I welcomed the break.

THAT AFTERNOON, as I was helping at the diner, trying to nurse my wounded ego, Carl popped into view, which reminded me that it wasn't just my father who seemed to be in on the delivery scam with Davis.

Seeing Carl haul a box of fresh blueberries from the back, I waited for him to set them down and then inclined my head for him to follow.

Following me out, his big, burly presence was like a wall of solid brick as we hedged near the trunk of my car.

"How come you didn't warn me about that delivery?" I asked evenly, wanting to hear what he had to say before volunteering that my dad had set me up.

His eyes narrowed. "I thought you knew!"

I shook my head vigorously. "No, I had no clue!"

"Sorry, String Bean...I never would have sent you up there without a little warning."

I had to remind myself that my father wouldn't have either, if he'd known what sort of past I had with the grump up on the mountain. A few seconds of silence stretched as stray leaves clustered around my car tire, and Carl's eyes searched the pile of debris.

"Did you see that another order came in from him?"

"Seriously?" The nerve of that man, after he'd told my father that he didn't want to deal with me, that I was too far gone. A lost cause. He was spoiled enough to assume that I'd just rush back up there and play delivery service? Fat fucking chance.

"Here." Carl handed me a phone. "This is the employee phone where orders come through; you can respond to his order with a red X and leave a note why you're not able to fulfill it." I loved that this man already knew I wasn't planning on taking his order, and that I didn't have to explain.

Taking the sleek cell phone in my hand, I smiled as I stared down at the screen. This would do perfectly—anything to send a message to Davis that he didn't call the shots anymore, and no one would be catering to him, least of all, my parents. *Or me.*

13

DAVIS

SIX YEARS AGO

I watched from my truck window as people walked through the hospital's automatic sliding glass doors. A family huddled together, wiping their faces as they hurried toward the parking lot. Macon's hospital was only two stories tall, and could only withstand a marginal amount of activity, but the emergency department had efficient nurses, and the surgeons here were respectable.

Still, part of me wished they'd just move him out of this fucking place and away from me. It was the same mental battle I had every week, when I'd make a trip into town. I'd make my rounds, grab my grocery order, food from the diner, reserved books from the library, and the order from the hardware store. Then I'd drive here…and I'd watch.

I'd yet to go in, and I had no idea what he thought of that, if he was even conscious, or knew that I was out here, struggling with my fucking guilt. I'd gotten as far as the walkway, and that was only once. Every other time, I was here, just watching.

I'd done this for two months, and with each week, a part of me withered away a bit more.

Ironic, considering my brother actually was withering away.

The accident was my fault, and now he was in there, alone, and

I couldn't make my body work right so I could go to him. My parents were sick of my excuses, my extended family disgusted by what they saw as indifference.

The town...well, most of them knew about my past, at least what they thought they knew... and most still talked. The rumors I heard circulating about the mountain recluse were getting more intense each time I ventured into town, but I didn't care.

I just wanted to see him, but every time I tried, I shut down.

I deserved to be in that bed, not him, and that regret would drown me.

14

RAE

I was rolling out dough for a cherry pie when my father made some sort of sound next to me. Looking over, I watched as his face contorted.

"What was that?" My hands stopped mid-roll as worry cut into my movements, making them jerky.

He laughed, rubbing his chest. "Nothing, don't worry, I've already seen a doctor about it."

I was worried.

"How long ag—"

"Did you see who's out there?" Rudy, one of the servers asked, interrupting my trail of questioning. I watched as he walked to the sink to wash his hands, then flicked my worried gaze back to the man at my shoulder. My father gave me a look that told me to drop it, but I would definitely be bringing it up again.

"Is it Susan Bowker again? Because I told her she can't come in here unless she's fully dressed."

I laughed along with Christy, the woman who frosted cupcakes next to me.

Rudy barked out a laugh. "No, it's that recluse guy."

"Thomas?" my dad asked with a hopeful tone, but hearing that name did the opposite for me, and the lack of recognition bounced off everyone's faces.

Dad corrected himself. "Davis, I meant Davis."

"Yeah, he's outside, across the street, leaning against his motorcycle."

It had been over a week since our kiss, and the betrayal. And just as long since I had begun turning down his order requests. Every day, a new one came in, confusing me on too many levels. He knew that I would be the one who would be delivering to him, and yet he told my father I was too much work…but he had also said that the conversation around that kiss wasn't finished. But maybe that was only in regard to coming clean—explaining that my father had asked him to take pity on me. Maybe he hadn't wanted to kiss me at all.

"I better go out and talk to him." My dad started untying his apron and washing his hands.

"Why do you have to go out there? Why can't he come in here to talk to you?"

Not that I *wanted* him to come in here, but I would have preferred that to my dad having to go out. Especially after his weird behavior just a moment ago.

"It's just how things are with him, honey."

This again. We hadn't broached the Davis subject again, since that day where I had an emotional breakdown. We all just moved on from it, like it was taboo, which I suppose for them, maybe it was. Regardless, I wasn't okay with my dad giving in to that spoiled mountain brat's whims.

Letting my dough go, I copied my father's movements. "Fine, I'll go with you."

"There's no need, honey. It would help if you stayed here."

"Oh no, I insist." I followed.

Anything to remind Davis that he needed to stop treating my mother and father like stand-in parents. Their daughter was back in town, and she would be stepping up to stop this abuse.

Shaking his head, my father bypassed customers and headed outside. Davis sat with one leg kicked back and the other long leg extended while his ass rested lightly against the black leather seat of his bike. He had his head dipped looking at his cell, and he was wearing that leather jacket, despite the warmer temperatures.

As his eyes tipped up and he saw me accompanying my dad, my arms crossed, an angry scowl on my face, he straightened his spine, pushing off the bike and running a hand through his hair.

"Thomas, my boy, how are you?" My dad asked as we approached.

I narrowed my eyes at his 'my boy' comment.

Davis opened his arms, and my father stepped into a hug.

A hug.

My scowl deepened.

"Such a nice way to greet someone you forced to come outside in the middle of baking a pie and running a business." I scowled.

Davis matched my expression, stepping back. "Well for anyone who's been here for any amount of time at all, they know this is how people communicate with me when I come into town."

"Cater."

He scrunched his dark brows together. "What?"

I clarified. "How people *cater* to you…"

My dad waved his hand like it was funny. "Just ignore Rae, she's still getting used to being back. You remember she hit her head, and well, things seem to still be a little unsettled."

What in the—?

Davis moved his eyes from my hair down my body and then to my shoes in a suggestive way. A way that made me blush, considering my father was standing right there.

"Yes, I remember."

The way he said that gave me goosebumps, as if he could actually remember teenage me. I'd die if he ever did—pack right up and move to literally anywhere but here. His lingering gaze made my brain short circuit in a way that had me completely forgetting about my father's comment, and instead I began reliving the way Davis's lips felt pressed against mine. The way he smelled, and how safe I felt when he had caged me in.

"Well, I wanted to swing by and ask if everything was okay. My last few delivery orders have been denied, saying you no longer service my area." He stuffed his hand into his pocket and pulled out a white envelope. "And Rae left without this last week, so I wanted to bring it by."

Smiling, he handed it to my dad, whose face had slackened. He must have forgotten that he had followed me home and easily could have brought it with him.

I should have stayed inside, because the way my father turned toward me and glared told me he didn't find my refusal of service very cute.

"I'm so sorry, Thomas. There must have been an issue with the app." My dad kept his gaze on me as he talked, and I felt two feet tall, "I'll be sure to have Carl look at it and see what the problem is."

Davis smiled, flicked his gaze to me briefly before looking away. "No problem, Roger...that's what I figured." His gaze hardened on me as he finished his sentence. "You and Millie mean so much to me; I just wanted to be sure there weren't any problems."

"None whatsoever, you know you're like a son to us." My dad walked forward and embraced Davis in another tight hug.

I flipped the recluse off, while my dad's back was still to me.

Davis smirked.

"Well, I better get back in. Millie will want to see you, have some tea. Will you come over again, maybe for dessert?" My dad's gaze bounced to me as if I were the reason they couldn't go up to his house. Good. I hoped I'd always be the reason they didn't make that dangerous drive.

Davis seemed to understand and lowered his head. "Sure, of course."

Slapping Davis on the back, dad crooned. "I'll have Millie call you."

Davis nodded, and we both watched as my dad turned back toward the diner. I was turning, about to leave as well, when I felt a firm grip on my elbow, holding me in place.

"Not so fast," Davis muttered close to my ear.

The closeness did deliciously wrong things to my stomach. I blinked to remain impassive.

"I wanted to bring back an extra purchase that seemed to make its way into my delivery. I checked the receipt and noticed it wasn't on mine, so it must have been yours."

Oh shit.

I didn't want to look, but he pressed the glossy cardboard box into my chest, his fingers wrapped around it, so his knuckles grazed my breasts.

"You might need these if you're planning to fuck any time soon."

Heat slammed into my face as I took the box of condoms from him. The way he'd said fuck, the tone of his voice…it grated along my skin, like a rough stone.

"You might want to return those ones, though." He smirked, and I turned enough to register for the first time that his face was clean shaven, making his firm jaw stand out even more than it did before. His hair seemed shorter, too, and it was styled.

"Why should I return it?" I asked a little breathlessly.

Clicking his tongue, he stepped closer until our bodies were almost aligned, then he whispered, "Because those won't fit me. You're going to need the magnum size."

My gaze hardened, and my jaw locked tight.

"You son of a—"

His hand came up, gripping my jaw, and within seconds we were turning, so my back was against the building and we were out of sight of the diner.

His nose was at my neck, and his hands on my hips.

"Can I kiss you, Rae?" he whispered, moving along my skin.

Shaking my head, my throat bobbed. "No."

"You don't seem like the kind of girl who likes to be asked, so I'm just going to do it."

"Try it and see what happens," I smiled wickedly.

He stared at me, a tiny smile lifting in the corner of his mouth. "You can't resist me forever."

"Watch me." I glared defiantly, hating that he'd called out something that simmered so close to my core.

His body pressed against mine for a second longer then it

vanished. "I think I'll kiss you when you're least expecting it. Maybe in church or something."

"Why bother with this ruse? I overheard you talking that night in the garage. I know my dad asked you to place the order, and I know you think I'm too much work to befriend." My palms went flat against the brick, so I could somehow find balance.

His stormy glare cut through me, as if I were a cold stick of butter and he was the searing knife, just pulled from the fire.

"You misheard…or at least misunderstood."

Tilting my head, I asked, "Did he tell you to place the order and lie to me?"

Without a single hitch in his voice, or flicker in his gaze, he answered. "Yes."

"Then I don't know what's left to——"

His grip returned to my waist as his body pressed into mine, pushing me tighter against the brick at my back.

"You misunderstood…I don't want to be your friend, Rae, and you are a lot of work, but if you haven't noticed, work doesn't scare me off. I like work. I like trouble. You're a fucking delicious mixture of both, and please understand me when I say this"—he lowered his head, his lips just barely a breath away from mine—"I like kissing you."

I felt like I was spinning in place, like my entire universe had turned upside down. I had run from this town because of him. Picked the furthest college from this place, just to heal from him.

Now here he was *wanting* me? This was madness.

He clicked his tongue. "I look forward to my next delivery, Rae."

With one last skim of his nose against my neck, he pulled away and stalked back toward his bike, leaving me standing there with a box of condoms.

I TUGGED the cardboard monstrosity free from the top shelf and cradled it as I sank to the carpet in my closet. This entire situation with Davis was pulling at the armor I'd built over the past four years. With every encounter, I could feel a piece chipping away, revealing how pathetic my attempts had been at putting it all together. Pulling out my leather-bound journal, I gently thumbed open the first page and swallowed the lump in my throat.

October 27th, 2016

Dear Diary,

It's October, and there's a festival in town. I think Davis might go, and I think this might be my chance to finally tell him who I am. If he doesn't show, I told Nora that I have a plan B...I just hope it goes the way I think it will.

Shutting the journal, tears lined my eyes as humiliation clogged my throat. I was so naive. So in love, and with a man I had never even talked to, but there had been no way to convince me that he didn't love me back. I remembered what happened after that festival, and it jogged my memory about "plan B."

"Oh God," I gasped, remembering that I had left him letters.

Did he ever get them?

A stark memory of him briskly leaving the library one sunny day, gripping a wad of papers in his hand and shoving them into the garbage can, rattled against my heart. Of course he got them, because I took advantage of the fact that he reserved so many books on such a regular basis. I would stuff the letters in between the pages of his books.

I couldn't pair the two, the man I loved from the time I was sixteen to eighteen. I couldn't compare him with the man who had touched me today and made me feel the way he did. The way he spoke, his velvet voice rolling over my skin like thunder, zipping along my arms like lightning.

"This is insane." I pushed hair off my forehead and dug through the rest of my box. High school yearbooks, my journalism notebooks, and photographs. I dug out a pink, spiral bound notebook, creasing my brows.

What had I used this one for?

June 16th, 2017- Davis seen at Post Office wearing blue jeans and white T-shirt.

June 30th, 2017- Davis seen interacting with another woman at the grocery store. Nora saw it first, text to get more information from her. Get specifics on the woman, and whether she's someone we need to keep tabs on.

I slammed the notebook closed and threw it against the closet door as angry tears streamed down my face.

A crater existed inside my chest where shame, resentment, and humiliation lived. I had been so utterly pathetic. I had *stalked* him.

I actually had physical proof of stalking him. Could I go to jail for this?

Groaning, I picked up the box, hauled it out of my bedroom, and out into the hall.

"Rae?" my mom called, likely curious about my determined gait.

I moved without speaking, not wanting to let a single word slip past my lips, but I knew if I didn't give her something, she'd harass me.

"I'm going to Nora's. I'll be back soon," I muttered, slipping on my fuzzy slippers.

My mother's puzzled expression only worsened as I exited the house without a jacket or any other form of clothing beyond my pajama shorts and tank top.

Her voice echoed down the drive as she called after me. "What on earth are you doing, Raelyn Jackson?"

"Nothing, I'll be back soon." I hurried down the street, ignoring the bite of cold that dug into my skin.

I had no idea if my mother was on my heels or not, but she had to know that I was old enough to leave the house half dressed, carrying a box of memorabilia, without having to explain myself.

One block down, with my breath clouding in front of me, I finally made my way to Nora's front door. It was only eight at night, so there shouldn't be any reason she wasn't home. Pounding my knuckles against the wood, I began shifting from foot to foot, pushing down the ache growing in my fingers and along my arms.

Finally, the door swung open, revealing my best friend.

"What are you doi—"

I cut her off, pushing inside, the promise of warmth too tempting. "Hello Mr. and Mrs. Petrov." I smiled at Nora's parents in greeting, walking back to her bedroom. They smiled, looking a little confused at my sudden appearance, but honestly, they shouldn't be that surprised. Nora and I were once inseparable and were constantly at each other's houses over the years.

"Okay, what is going on?" Nora shut and locked her bedroom door.

Setting the box down on Nora's desk, I stood there and stared at it.

"We need to burn this."

My best friend stepped closer, about to peer inside.

Embarrassment rose like bile, forcing me to guard the box. "No need to look inside. I just need help with burning it, and a witness to attest that any and all criminal activity regarding Davis Brenton has forthwith been burned."

Nora's eyes widened, her dark eyebrows arching with surprise. "Wait a second."

My face burned red hot. "Nora...I just—"

"Oh my gosh, is this the box of—" Her eyes met mine, her body leaning closer.

She knew.

Stupidly, I had included her when I had started the journals and *surveillance*.

I gave her a swift nod, unable to even speak the words.

"So, in here is everything?" She inched closer to the box.

Mashing my lips together, I gave her another swift nod.

"I have to see it."

"No way," I argued, moving to block her, but she was faster.

Grabbing it, she carried it above her head and moved around me, toward the door.

"Please, Rae, pretty please? Let's have an old-fashioned slumber party, where we dish about Davis, and we go through your notes."

I reached for her. "No way! I have to burn all the evidence."

"Why are you so hell bent on suddenly burning all the evidence, when you could have destroyed it at any time over the last four years?"

"One" —I swiped at her, but she dodged me—"I honestly

thought I could look back through them and laugh, seeing as I'd never see Davis again."

"Two" —I stood up straight, eyeing her position and trying to gauge where to attack—"I haven't really thought about it, and I've been in New York."

"You could have asked me."

I put my hands out. "I'm asking you now!"

Rolling her eyes, she finally lowered the box. "Fine, but you're no fun at all. We should go out back and drink while we burn everything."

That actually sounded amazing. "Do you have anything?"

"Psshhh, I'm half Russian, half Moldavian. Of course I do."

ONCE I PULLED on a pair of Nora's sweats, I bundled under several blankets while she started the small fire pit in her back yard. Cuddling on her cushioned patio furniture, I reached for the bottle of vodka and took a swig.

"Your parents don't care that we're doing this?"

Sure, we were both twenty-two, but I still felt like her mom was about to come out and lecture us about drinking.

Nora tipped the bottle back and then poured a little on the fire. "They're already in bed. They said goodnight to me when you were changing. They just told me to be sure the fire was out before we passed out or went back inside."

Laughing, and feeling a bit warmer, I started digging items out of the box. "Okay, first…the location journal."

"Nooooo, we worked so hard to track his every move."

Snort laughing, I shook my head, thumbing through the journal again. "I can't believe I kept this. I can't believe we did this to begin with! What were we thinking?"

"Well, you were thinking you were in love, and I was just your supportive best friend."

Sipping from the bottle once more, I pointed it at her. "You should have stopped me."

Nora leaned forward and grabbed the bottle. "It was endearing to see your love. It was vibrant and alive, Rae. I looked up to you for it. Hell, I still do."

Thinking back on how I had loved Davis only made me feel stupid and ashamed. I was completely unhinged when it came to him.

"This stuff is illegal, Nora. I legitimately stalked him."

It was her turn to snort. "You were completely harmless. You just loved him. You didn't even say anything when you saw him with that hussy in the library."

That hussy being the reason I ended up cracking mentally and leaving Macon as soon as I had a chance. Yeah, no harm done.

"I just want to burn it all and forget." I tipped my head back and drank.

Nora studied me for a second then leaned closer. "But he's back in your life, and he kissed you. That has to mean something, like the universe is finally giving you your chance."

"I don't want it," I snapped. "I don't want him, I want nothing to do with him. I just want to carve out a tiny piece of life for myself and leave him in the past."

Nora's concerned expression left me feeling raw. I didn't want her pity, and whether she meant to or not, that's what her face was delivering.

I had to put a stop to all of this, so I ripped out several pages of the book and tossed them into the fire.

15

DAVIS

Gary rolled the toothpick inside his mouth, giving me the side eye. His denim hat was more grease than oil stained, and his face was pockmarked. He wasn't the most attractive man to ever grace the earth, but more so, his attitude seemed to match his looks.

"Weren't you just here for gas a few days back?" he mumbled, grabbing the pump handle and shoving it back into place while my receipt printed.

It wasn't any of his business how often I got gas, but just like everyone else in this town, he was nosy as fuck.

"How about you mind your own business, Gary."

He huffed, while pressing a few buttons on the pump, the loud beeps echoed through the stale, humid heat. "There's rumors 'bout you and the Jackson girl bein' friendly, and I'll tell you right now…" He pinched my receipt between his filthy fingers, while angling toward my truck, but I wouldn't be sticking around to hear what he had to say.

Starting the engine, and pulling the drive gear down, I drove off before Gary could finish his sentence. I hated this shitty town, and how on earth were there rumors already? I thought back over the past few weeks. I had gone to the Jackson's for dinner. I had stood close enough to whisper in Rae's ear that night I followed her home. I might have been seen pinning her up against the side of the clothing store. I suppose his warning might have some merit, considering the town would want to protect poor Rae against the likes of me, regardless that she was in her own right as mean as a snake.

I didn't care. The fact that I was in fact getting gas again meant I had been coming to town more often than I normally did, but aside from Rae taking up every inch of space in my head, Gavin had texted, asking if I found anything out about that girl. So, I decided it would be a good idea to venture in today to see if I could find anything.

If I happened to see Rae somewhere, then oh well.

Didn't mean anything.

The first place I wanted to check was the library. I had no idea if it was merely because that's where the scene of the crime took place, or if it was because I knew she had frequented the space often. Regardless, I'd have to take care with what I asked, because I didn't want people to get the wrong idea, and shit spread faster than wildfire in this town.

Entering the library gave me a familiar sensation of shame, tearing at my insides and reminding me that while I had no idea that girl would be there that night, from the look on her face, I had destroyed her. I was an asshole in most situations, but I'd never be cruel to anyone, not on purpose. Why had I waited so long to check in on her, though? Fuck, what if something *had* happened, and I waited four long years to even check?

I'd never forgive myself.

"Mr. Brenton!" Mabel, the librarian, called out to me, adjusting her reading glasses. Mabel called everyone in town by their first name, so her calling me by my last was her way of snubbing me. I knew people didn't like me, and I didn't like them either, so it didn't bug me.

"Mabel, uh...hello there." Fuck, how did one start small talk?

Her overgrown eyebrows folded together in the center of her forehead, "Well, I..."

"I just have a quick question, actually," I said, quickly cutting her off.

Mabel's eyebrows relaxed as her face twisted into something more akin to a resting bitch face. I didn't wait for her to respond.

"I'm trying to find someone. She would have been..." I searched my brain for how old she had to have been that day in the library. The summer prior, she'd said she was seventeen... "Eighteen or so. This was four years ago." Even as I said it, I began to connect a few dots, slowly but surely. Maybe Rae would have known her?

"A girl who came around here, or?" One of Mabel's eyebrows lifted in question.

"Yeah, she would have been in a lot, she seemed like a bit of a bookworm, always seemed to carry a book bag, had dark, short hair, and braces..." I didn't want to comment on the acne; it seemed rude to point out.

Mabel seemed to consider it while shuffling a few folders. "Let's see...now, I transferred to the Clark County library for about a year around that time. You probably don't remember, but I was working in three different locations for a while there."

Why would I remember that? I assumed Mabel had worked here forever.

"So you have any ideas on who it could be?"

She clicked her tongue. "You probably don't remember that time Miss Frenza's dog got loose and ran past you in the parking lot, and we all begged you to stop it, but you ignored us and let it go, do you?"

Nope, didn't remember that at all.

"Or that time Shelly Harding asked if a few homeschool groups could come to your farm and warehouse for a field trip for their kids, and you rudely turned her down?"

What the fuck was she on about? Oh yeah...

I put my finger up, like a light bulb had just flared to life in my head. "I remember that one,"

She stared at me, expressionless. Her watery blue eyes were lined with dark blue eyeliner, not a great look against her pasty skin tone.

"You know...honestly, even if I did know who this girl was, I wouldn't tell you, and really, I shouldn't help you at all."

"But, what about that time I installed those wall sconces for free? And let's not forget that I donate a shit ton of money to this place." Sure, I was a dick, but a generous one.

Her face flushed, but with a huff she said, "I honestly don't know, but the high school yearbook would be a good place to start. If she was eighteen four years ago, she was likely in the senior graduating class. Start there."

The school yearbook! Genius. I hated when people were smarter than me.

"Aren't you going to say thank you?" Mabel called after me.

I pushed my shoulder into the glass door and yelled back, "For what? You didn't have anything for me." Not true, but technically, she didn't give me a name, so I wouldn't be giving her any credit.

Where would I get a copy of a high school yearbook? Surely the school would have that, right?

Apparently, it didn't matter if they did. It was August, and the school offices didn't open to the public for a few more weeks. Which meant I was out of luck...unless...

Did Rae have a copy?

How strange would it be if I asked to see it? It would be weird, and we weren't even close to being at that point in our friendship, or whatever the fuck it was that we had yet. I wanted to fuck her, not ask to see her high school yearbook.

Shit.

Still, I needed to find someone who might have one, or at least know who I was talking about. Maybe Gavin was right and asking around the diner would be a good idea.

THE BREAKFAST CROWD had mostly dispersed by the time I had arrived, which was good. The fewer people I had to deal with, the better. An older man with graying hair, sharp gray eyes and built like a linebacker pushed through the swinging doors from the back.

I remembered him; he was here when that girl had left me the note
—and I'd talked enough with Roger to know this was his best friend.
Carl.

He seemed to hesitate as I walked over to him, but at the last
second, he tossed a rag down on the counter and crossed his arms. I
ignored the way his eyes seemed to measure my worth, and how his
growing sneer obviously meant he found me lacking.

Most people didn't care for me. This man, in the past, seemed
not to really care one way or the other, but now he appeared to have
taken whatever pill Gary and Mabel had swallowed.

"Hello, sir, I'm Davis Brenton, and I—"

"I know who you are," he interrupted. The increasing hunch in
his shoulders and intense glare would probably deter most people,
but not me.

"Well, I was wondering if you could help me with something?"

The door opened, making the bell over the top jingle. A few
older women entered and huddled toward a booth. I redirected my
attention to the statue in front of me.

"Not likely, kid."

Resisting the urge to tell this guy to fuck off, I took a small
breath and continued.

"You're Carl, right? I remember you…you used to help me
when I'd come in to get my orders."

His grunt was acknowledgment enough.

"Well, a few years back there was a young girl who used to leave
me notes, and reserve spots for me at the counter, do you remember
her?"

Carl's face fell, his silver brows puckered, while his sneer
completely fell into a flat line. It was as though I'd spoken of
someone who died. Unease slithered into my stomach as I considered the worst-case scenario had happened.

"What do you want with her?" Carl's tone was like an ice pick,
slamming down between us. Regardless of his attitude, at least it
meant he knew who I was referring to.

"Nothing…I merely was curious if she was okay. Some years
ago, I had worried that something bad had happened to her and I

—" How was I supposed to explain this? Did I tell him that I was still beating myself up about it? I didn't want to sound like a fucking creep, yet I needed answers.

Carl's eyes bounced around, searching the counter for something. It was as though he was thinking over what answer to give me; maybe he was just battling on keeping her privacy, which I understood. If he couldn't tell me anything, then fine, but that had to mean she was alive, right?

"She's fine. Moved on, away in fact…so don't think twice about her and leave her alone."

"I wouldn't—"

Suddenly he shifted, giving me his back and cutting me off. Slipping back into the kitchen, he shot one last menacing glare from over his shoulder and then he was gone.

That was fine. I didn't need anything more from him, but why had he mentioned leaving her alone? Did that mean she was still around? I hadn't seen her.

Maybe I'd ask Gavin for some ideas, or break down and finally ask Rae, but at least I now knew she was alive. She hadn't hurt herself over me; she had merely gotten over me—over her crush. And while that was good, she had also been the only person on this planet that seemed to give a flying fuck about me.

Shaking my head free of the thoughts surrounding the girl, I pushed outside and climbed into the safety and seclusion of my truck.

16

RAE

My best friend was sprawled out on a flannel blanket under our maple tree. Her brown curls fanned out behind her like a river of chocolate spirals, and her hand was dramatically thrown over her face, shielding her from the sun. A speaker softly played our favorite playlist from the porch, and between the two of us, we had a few notebooks scattered.

"Did you keep any journals or physical evidence of any of your crushes?"

Nora let out a small grunt, then slightly sat up. "No." Her dark brows caved as she considered something, and then she slapped her forehead. "Wait…that's not true."

Smiling, I cut into the notebook, seeing the confessions of love and obsession begin to fall to the blanket in tiny pieces. "I knew I wasn't the only messed up person on the planet who documented her obsession."

"No"—Nora pointed a finger at me— "you're definitely on your own with all this, but I did create a Pinterest board."

My notebook dropped into my lap and plopped to the blanket. "What?"

Nora stared off to the side, while nodding. "A wedding board."

"I have to see it!" I dove for her phone.

"Noooooo." She batted my hand away, but I was already gripping it.

"Rae, let it go! Oh my gosh, you can't!"

"You saw my humiliation, it's only fair!" I stood, holding the phone up in the air like I couldn't get service.

Nora settled in, folding her legs together, criss cross applesauce style, while tucking her arms in tight. She looked like a toddler throwing a tantrum. "You don't even know my password."

"You've had the same one since middle school," I muttered in response, navigating to her Pinterest app.

I heard Nora mutter a curse word from her pursed lips.

"Oh my God." I froze in place, my mouth dropping at the images before me.

Nora jumped to her feet. "You have to understand that I put most of it together when I was drunk!"

"Nora-Bora, you were stone cold sober when you did this, don't lie." I slid my finger along her screen, staring at the lavender colored gowns she had selected for her bridesmaids, and relishing the dog carrying the ring down the aisle.

"You don't even have a dog!" I continued swiping and flipping while Nora let out heavy sighs from the blanket.

"In my alternate reality, where my crush adores me and wants to marry me, we have a cute little dog who's like a son to us and would be our ring bearer."

It was cute, her wedding idea. Stringed lights, outdoor, small, lots of green ivy and potted plants. I could envision all of it, and the more photos I looked at, the more wistful I felt, until...

"Is this...wait a second, is this what he looks like?"

Nora squealed, jumping to her feet and throwing herself on my back. "You weren't supposed to scroll down that far!" She reached for the phone, but my arms were longer.

"Rae, give it back!"

I was laughing so hard, half crouched with her on my back, that I couldn't breathe.

"Two things: first...I have to know who this crush is, and

second, where did you find that photo?" I sputtered, my eyes watering while I stared at the man in question. He had blond hair, long enough to be pushed under his backward hat. He had striking blue eyes and a drool-worthy jawline that was firm and pronounced. He reminded me of a surfer.

"It's on his website. I found it when I was working with my dad. So yeah, I sort of saved the image, and then created the pin, but the board is private. He'll never see it."

"Okay, so there's a real actual person who—"

"What are you two doing?" my mom suddenly called from the kitchen window, interrupting us.

We both spun, chiming in unison, "Nothing."

It was difficult to see my mother through the screen, but she waited a beat before saying, "Come on in, Carl is here for dinner."

Giggling, we huddled together to grab our things and then headed inside.

Carl was already seated at the table, his hulking form folded into one of our small kitchen chairs.

"Hey, Car-Car, how are you?" I sat down next to him and expected him to lean over and hug me, but he just sat still as stone, staring off toward the living room.

"I'm headed home. See you later, Rae!" Nora called before exiting the house, her face still crimson from my discovery of her secret wedding board. I smiled, thinking of what I'd seen.

"What's that smile for?" Carl suddenly asked, brisk and cold.

Put off by his tone, I almost didn't answer, but his eyes were warm and his body language relaxed.

"Just an inside joke."

He nodded, while his brows crowded his forehead. Mom and Dad were still talking by the sink about the diner, unaware of our conversation.

Carl hesitated, eyeing them like I had, then he leaned closer. "I just thought maybe it was from that Davis kid…he was in today asking questions." Carl shook his head, like he was banishing the memory, but now my blood was heated.

"What was he asking?" My voice was raspier than I intended,

but all things Davis related still felt like a cord pulled taut in my belly. It felt familiar, like I owned a piece of him.

Carl glanced over toward the sink briefly then back at the empty plate in front of him.

"Just about some girl…" His gray eyes bounced up and landed on me hard. "Just stay away from him, kiddo. He's bad news."

I nodded absently, mentally grappling with the words he'd said.

Some girl.

He was asking about a girl?

That cut deeper than I wanted to admit. I was purely anti Davis, especially after going through my boxes, but there was still a poisoned well inside my heart where Davis existed, and hearing that he was asking about another girl seemed to be as painful as taking a pull from those waters.

My stomach tilted.

Images of that night in the library played over and over in my head, forcing me to remember how frivolous Davis was with women. I was nothing to him—always had been, always would be.

When chicken pot pie hit my plate, I nearly doubled over. I ended up pushing the food around my plate for twenty minutes before excusing myself. Which did nothing but remind me that I was a fool, and there would never be anything attached to Davis Brenton but pain.

17

DAVIS

Watching Raelyn Jackson was like looking at the most beautiful piece of art, and yeah, that was cheesy as fuck, but it was also true. She was stunning, with the way the sun hit her dark hair, and the way her head flew back when she laughed…that laugh…it was like a song created just for me. Something that could rival the serene sounds of nature, of my mountain. I had yet to find anyone who had the ability to sway me from the mountain.

Yet, here I was, watching Rae while she was at lunch with some girl who had chocolate brown corkscrew curls, and the two guys sitting next to them. I was probably overreacting, but it almost looked like they were on a double date or some shit.

Sitting in my truck with my window down, sunglasses perched on my nose, allowed me to watch her from the street without being noticed. However, this feeling coming alive inside my chest was like a fire, burning hotter than anything I had ever felt. It burned for me to walk over to their table and pluck her away from everyone at it. She'd scream and shriek, and then I'd have to throw her over my shoulder and explain that she was mine, and no one else would ever be able to hear that laugh or see those plump, pink lips wrap around a straw, or get near that silky soft skin.

What the fuck was wrong with me?

I had never felt this way for anyone. Ever.

My mountain had been enough for me, all these years. Yet, now, I craved more. I wanted more. *But only with her.*

I watched as the guy nearest to Rae leaned over, whispering something in her ear. He had to be a stranger—someone she'd just met tonight—because she kept leaning closer to her friend after the fuckface crowded her. He had nicely styled hair, swept to one side, and he wore tailored peach-colored pants with a white collared shirt. He looked exactly like the kind of guy I assumed she'd be with. The rage that simmered in my veins was deadly, especially as this idiot draped his arm across the back of her chair.

It would be so easy to open my door and be up and out of my truck within seconds, crossing the space without a thought of what I was about to do. But, it wasn't like Rae would choose to go with me. In any given scenario, she would side with the stranger and tell people I was harassing her. I'd go to jail because I'd not only punch the asshole who touched her, but I'd end up kidnapping Rae, or kissing her until she listened.

She was mine.

Blinking, I focused on my steering wheel and the hand gripping it. Obviously, she didn't belong to me in any capacity if she was on a date with someone. The realization sunk into place, like a brick in mud. She'd made her choice, made it clear to the world—and that choice wasn't me.

DELIVERING pieces to the smaller town of Hope, Oregon, was always a mixture of happiness and heartbreak. I had been delivering pieces to this little shop for the past five years, and while I had actually turned down about three other stores around Oregon, this was one place I'd keep delivering to no matter what, and it was all because of who lived here.

"These pieces are beautiful!" Matt, the owner of the shop,

beamed as he helped me unload the new fire pit and chandelier fixtures.

"Yeah, they came together nicely."

Matt didn't talk too much, which made working with him easy enough. With practically no time passing at all, everything was unloaded and a hefty chunk of money was delivered to my bank account.

Getting back into my truck, I headed toward the small grocery store and loaded up on clam chowder, saltine crackers, pepper, and a fresh bouquet of daisies. I tried as usual to keep my expectations lowered as I drove to the senior citizen home.

I only came this way about once a month, but I'd been enough for the staff to know who I was, especially seeing that I had donated thousands of dollars' worth of accent lighting to this place. Gwen, the head nurse, greeted me with a smile that turned watery within seconds.

"Davis, so nice to see you, honey."

I nodded at the older woman; her chocolate eyes always went soft when she saw me. I noticed her hair had started turning gray at her temples, but her ebony skin was still wrinkle free and youthful.

Handing her the flowers, I gave her a genuine smile.

"Nice to see you, Gwen. How's he doing today?"

HER DAINTY FINGERS wrapped around the plastic covering the stems as she considered my question.

"He's doing pretty good today, actually."

"Good." I knocked on her desk in farewell and walked around the corner.

Down the hall and through another set of doors was my grandfather's suite.

A nurse was exiting, right as I was about to knock.

"Go ahead and head on in; he's expecting a game of cards with Theo."

Theo would be grateful I stepped in; poor guy hated playing against my pop.

"Theo, you're here!" my grandfather crowed, holding a brand-new deck of cards in his left hand. His lack of recognition didn't hurt; in fact, it did the opposite. I only came to see him because he didn't remember me. If he did... Well, I'd be fucked.

"Hey, old man, ready for a game of cards?"

His toothless smile was wide as he shuffled the deck, and I took a seat across from him.

"Get ready to lose."

This was how it always went. My grandfather's shit talking was on point. We'd joke for a few rounds and then he'd start to remember my brother. It made me wonder if Mom and them ever came back to visit him.

"Did you know I had a grandson?" he asked, eyeing his hand closely. I tried to let the comment slide, because he in fact had *two* grandsons. I just wasn't considered one anymore.

Even still, I acted surprised. "You don't say? Well, tell me about him."

"He's real smart, book smart. Always reading. But inside, I think he's sad."

My chest pinched tight as I laid down a pair of twos.

"Why's he sad?"

My grandfather's bushy, unkempt eyebrows crowded his forehead as he tried to remember. This was where things usually got hazy for him.

"Maybe it's because his older brother is like the sun, and he's like a rain cloud. The two don't mix well."

My breath nearly caught because he never mentioned me. Not ever.

"Thought you said you had just the one grandson?"

Gramps shook his head like he was confused. "I do...but after the accident, I only have one."

I was walking too close to the fire; I knew this. I knew I was about to get burned, and yet I couldn't stop myself.

"Did something happen to one of them?"

A small sigh escaped his mouth as he focused on his hand, laying down a set of cards that didn't follow suit. I let it slide, like all his other hands.

"Well, the bright one…he wanted to shine so bright, the cloud was driven away. But, we decided to keep the cloud and asked the sun to shine somewhere else."

The talking in metaphors was new. Usually, he just came right out and said what happened. I'd sit and listen, as a form of penance. I'd hear what I'd done through my grandfather's memory, and then I'd want to go back in time and change it all.

Like I usually did.

"You have any brothers?" Watery blue eyes met mine, and for the smallest second, I worried he'd remembered me. But his eyes searched mine, no expression on his face. No memory whatsoever.

I cleared my throat and answered how I always did.

"Not anymore."

18

RAE

AFTER A WEEK OF PURGING DAVIS OUT OF MY LIFE WITH MY BEST friend, I was starting to feel better. We'd burned, cut, and laughed about almost everything inside my box, and the two others I found deep in the back of my closet. I hadn't mentioned what Carl had said about Davis, because it didn't need to be mentioned. Davis was nothing to me and always would be. However, Nora had caught on to my demeanor the next day, and while I couldn't bring myself to tell her about it, I knew her sudden interest in finding us dates had something to do with it.

My date, Blake, was a loan officer down at the bank. He'd just returned from college, and based off the number of bad pickup lines he delivered, I had to assume he had been popular enough with the ladies. They didn't work on me, and by the end of the night, I bid him goodbye without setting up a second date or giving him a goodnight kiss. My heart felt wooden, like it was heavy and old, cumbersome to carry within my chest.

Not to mention, Carl's voice was stuck in my head, lodged deep down in my stomach, making it ache and hurt all week. I didn't want to think about Davis and Lydia, or him with whoever it was he was asking about in the diner, but it was as if a loop was playing in my head and I couldn't get it to stop.

Thankfully, it was the start of a new work week, which meant I would have something to keep me distracted from the fact that Davis hadn't reached out since seeing him outside the diner. Even after discussing the misunderstanding, he'd yet to place another order, and while I had been making a few deliveries here and there, most of the mountain orders had stopped over the past week. Maybe it meant I could focus on helping businesses with marketing or look for a place of my own.

"Rae! Oh good, you're here." My dad called out to me as his eyes met mine for only a second or two before returning to the berries in front of him.

I set my purse and jacket down on the small cabinet reserved for the employees.

"Morning, how can I help?"

My mother chose that moment to breeze out of the office, her face was flushed as though she'd been crying, and she had circles under her eyes. She was normally bright and happy, never worried unless something had actually happened.

"What's wrong?" I asked, slowly crowding her. I waited to ensure we weren't being listened to and then turned her around by her shoulders. Her eyes were watering, which made my gut sink.

"Mom, tell me what's going on."

Flicking her eyes to the side and then down to her feet, she sniffed. "We're sinking, sweetie...and the regular delivery orders we used to get kept us afloat," she murmured, keeping her gaze down. "I'm not sure what to do."

Her brows furrowed, and I knew I'd fucked up. I was the reason he hadn't been placing orders.

"Thomas hasn't placed an order in over two weeks, and for whatever reason, the other mountain orders haven't been coming through either. I know everyone is hurting right now, but we haven't had a month this rough for as long as I can remember."

I shook my head, trying to piece together a way to fix this that didn't include me begging Davis. "But you have customers in here all the time; it feels like business is booming."

Her slow shake of her head confirmed a tiny flicker of fear in my chest. "It started a few years ago. The cost of living increased, and more swanky people started moving here. There's a fancy diner just twelve miles up the road, at a ski resort. More and more people have started going there, along with the bigger chain restaurants popping up now."

My throat was tight with emotion as I pulled her into my arms. "It's going to be okay, Mom. I promise."

I'd make sure of that. I'd do whatever I could to help them, including making stupid deliveries up the mountain to the grump.

"What do you need me to do?"

My mom smiled, swiping at her tears. "Well, I don't know how you'd feel about this, but I need to talk to Thomas—er, Davis—and see what the problem is. I need to know if this is going to continue so we can start making contingency plans, but I don't have the time to go up there, and it really needs to be a conversation had in person."

I didn't feel great about it, but for her, I smiled and shook my head. "I don't mind, I'll take care of it."

Because what else could I do?

PULLING up to his house with the sun shining down along the two-story masterpiece nearly had me rolling my eyes. It truly looked like something out of a magazine. The two beautiful huskies were out, lying lazily on the porch, soaking up the sun, just like the wildflowers near the porch and the evergreens standing like tall sentinels along his property.

I parked and lifted the back hatch, not waiting for Davis to come out. I gripped the box of goodies my mother had prepared for him, ducked my head, and started across the gravel drive. The sound of the screen door creaking open had my eyes swinging up.

I froze, mid-step.

Davis walked out, shirtless, dripping wet, wearing a pair of low hanging basketball shorts. His feet were covered by a pair of white running shoes, and the way he ran his fingers through his dark hair was making my brain short circuit.

Nothing marred his skin. Not a single tattoo or scar, from what I could tell. Just bronzed, golden skin, likely from working out in the sun. It was enough to make a reformed Davis addict fall off the wagon and pull out a notebook detailing every minuscule thing about him.

"Rae, hey…" he said, sounding breathless.

"Uh…hey." I swallowed, and tried to regain focus. "Did you just get done with a workout or something?"

He smiled, his navy eyes working their way down my frame. It made my skin prickle with goosebumps.

"Yeah, just got off the treadmill."

I nodded, too transfixed by the delicious V on his lower abdomen. There was no happy trail of hair leading into his shorts; it was all just bare, muscled, tan skin.

He was the grumpy, recluse Mountain Ken doll.

"You're staring awfully hard," he mused, with a smirk. "What are you doing here, anyway?"

Rolling my eyes, I pushed past him. "You're just *awfully* pretty for a mountain man. You should have a beard and be wearing flannel. And my mother sent me."

He followed on my trail. "I thought you liked pretty guys."

I dropped the box on his porch and stood, turning toward him. "Who said I liked pretty guys?"

He shrugged, toying with the tips of his mussed hair.

I smiled, intrigued that he seemed to know about my dating preferences.

"Tell me."

Firming his lips into a thin line, he dipped down to see what I had brought with me, then muttered, "I saw you out the other night with someone who looked the type. So, your mom sent a care package, huh?"

The air nearly burst from my lungs as I tried to catch up to what he'd said. "Wait a second. You—"

He grabbed the box from the porch with an audible sigh.

I was on his heels. "Did you *follow* me?"

His scoff made my heart jolt. "Nope. Just saw you sitting outside. I passed by on my way to a friend."

A friend? Did he mean a female friend, maybe the one he'd been asking about in the diner?

He shouldered through the screen door. "So, you want to explain this random visit? Thought you were done with me."

"My parents noticed you haven't been placing any orders..." My eyes were unfocused, my thoughts spinning—settling in on the conclusion that he'd gone and seen a girl the other night.

Davis tilted his head in my direction, with a small smirk playing across his deliciously evil mouth. "Did they now?"

Asshole.

His teasing tone brought me out of the tailspin, reminding me why I had stopped the orders when I had.

"Yeah, I guess they're used to catering to you so much, they notice when you up and disappear."

He let out a small laugh as he set down the box on the kitchen counter. Memories of when I was last in his house popped into my head, a tiny reminder that I was completely alone with him. In his house.

I awkwardly hung in the doorway, loving how the sun filtered in through the tall windows along his living room wall. The backyard was lush, green grass and a patio set to die for.

"You going to stand there all day?" Davis suddenly asked, walking toward me.

Remembering myself, I blinked and shook my head. "I should get back."

I hadn't exactly talked with him in the way my mother likely hoped, but my actions spoke loud enough, right? It was clear what my showing up had said—*start ordering again, I won't do anything to mess with it.* I could leave now and feel as though I fulfilled my duty.

"You have more deliveries?"

Taking a step back as he crowded me, I tried to find my voice. "No, but I—"

"Then come have lunch with me."

"Uh..." I watched his eyes nearly sparkle as he grabbed my hand and tugged me toward a door that would lead to the beautiful patio.

I pulled, putting up resistance, trying to stop our trajectory, even though all I wanted to do was see the full scope of his backyard. "I should get back. Rain check? Thank you."

Turning on his heel, he gave me a devious smile. "Speaking of check, don't you need to talk to me about more deliveries?"

Fuck.

"That's why you're here, isn't it?" he asked, raising an eyebrow. "Are you finally connecting the dots that I don't order so they'll cater to me?"

He glued me in place with a glare as he let his statement drop between us. He knew I wouldn't respond because I was too proud to admit that I had connected those dots and had realized that I was being unfair to him regarding his relationship with my parents.

In silence, I followed him outside to the back, at which point my breath stalled in my lungs.

A respectable patch of green grass extended past the patio, and a tidy looking chicken coop ran along one side of his yard, which dipped down into a small goat pen. The hen house matched the main house, with the same color siding and shutters, and a few furry goats with tiny horns milled around the enclosure. The porch stretched along the back space with a large hot tub outside a bedroom, and the most beautiful patio set, complete with a gas-lit rock table.

As I looked over the yard, something settled in my chest, some-thing warm and comfortable, like I didn't ever want to leave. "This is beautiful."

"I like it out here, no matter the season," Davis said shyly.

Sitting down on the plush seat across from him, I smiled. "I can see that."

In front of us, on the small table, were two beautifully crafted sandwiches with turkey, avocado and bacon.

"How did you know you'd have company?"

The space under his lashes flushed red. "Uh...I always make two?"

I laughed, tossing my head back. "Liar. My mother called, didn't she?"

His deepening blush told me I was right.

"So, why did you pretend not to know why I was here?"

Moving a glass of tea in front of me, he tucked his chin to his chest. "She didn't tell me *why* you were coming, just that you were on your way, and that I should feed you."

I ignored what it did to the butterfly swarm in my chest that he'd made two sandwiches in preparation of me coming up here.

Davis watched me, not touching his food.

"Do you want to get a shirt on or a coat or something?" I bit into my sandwich, keeping my eyes on his.

He smirked, raking his gaze over me in that seductive way that made my neck feel too hot. Which reminded me of the promised kiss he said he'd give me when I wasn't expecting it.

"Does it bother you to see me without a shirt on?"

It bothered me that he was asking about other girls, and that he hadn't tried to see me again after our last encounter. "Like you mentioned, I'm used to seeing pretty boys and dating them...it's not offensive or anything, just weird for two friends who are just hanging out, I guess."

"We're friends now?" He quirked that dark eyebrow at me.

"You tell me." I took another bite, enjoying way too much how the sun sliced through the trees, cutting into his eyes. I wanted to hear him clearly define our relationship, the boundaries...the lack of anything substantial happening.

He stared at me, waiting, a small smirk playing along his mouth as he pulled his fist under his jaw.

"I don't have friendly thoughts about you, Rae."

Was that relief sagging in my chest like a soaked pillow?

"No? What a shame…here I thought we could be mountain buds."

His eyes sparkled with mischief as he finally leaned forward and took a bite of his sandwich.

We ate in silence for a few peaceful moments, listening to the sound of the forest, the wind whispering through the trees and the light braying of the goats. I resisted the urge to close my eyes, inhale, and try to steal some of the magic for myself.

"Tell me about your work. You obviously make a decent living with how much you order from the diner."

His eyes lit up, making my stomach pull tight, then he stood, pushing away from the table and tossing the remnants of his sandwich toward the goat pen.

"What are you doing?"

He gave me that sexy smirk. "Showing you what I do for work. Come on."

I grinned and did the same with my sandwich, following him around the house to the large workshop. The ground along the side of the house was all jagged rocks and tall grass. With my flip-flops, I was hesitant to walk through the weeds, so I carefully picked out my steps, while still trying to follow him.

But I wasn't successful in the least.

"Ouch!" I bit my lip and lifted my foot away from the rock sticking out.

Davis turned, his eyes narrowing on my feet.

Before I could explain that it would just take me a second to work through the landscape, he was scooping me off my feet, bridal style, walking us the rest of the way.

"It's not that big of a deal," I said in a small voice, although I wasn't sure if I was trying to convince him or me.

The feeling of his smooth, warm skin against mine was too much. His pecs were pushing into my arms, and I was two seconds away from making an undignified sound.

His eyes fluttered, lowering. "You like the feel of me, Rae?"

Fuck, had I been touching him? My face caught fire as I snatched my hands back.

"That's okay…I like the feel of you, too." He squeezed me against him, and that flame licked at my core.

Dammit. The purge week apparently wasn't enough to eradicate Davis from my system.

Gravel crunched under his feet as we cleared the side of the house and ventured to the large bay doors. A regular white entry door was positioned to the side, and Davis led us through it.

The sun shone down from the upper windows, casting a warm glow along the floor as we walked inside. Davis gently set me back on my feet. Flipping a few lights, the space illuminated, revealing an expanse of sealed floors, pallets, worktables, and wall to wall tools. Rolling toolboxes nearly as tall as Davis lined a few of the dividers, but the thing that caught my attention more than anything else were the light fixtures arranged along a few of the tables.

"Oh my gosh!" I darted toward the desk and ran a gentle finger along the designs etched into each piece of iron. "These are amazing."

Davis stood silent next to me, picking up a few of the fixtures. "Yeah, the resorts around here, and a few hotels, have contracts to replace all their current accent fittings with a few of mine."

I lifted my head. "You make them here, like out of nothing, and design them into these?"

I sounded ridiculous, but my brain couldn't quite connect how talented he was. My dumb heart was falling back into obsession territory.

He chuckled, moving around the table. He looked so out of place with his bare skin and those running shorts loose on his hips.

"Yeah, I start with a solid piece of iron or metal, and I weld them into what you see around here. Each different hotel or resort usually has a few variations in their requests, depending on the theme of the room, but here in Oregon and Montana, most go for rustic." He picked up a light fixture that looked like a pair of deer antlers.

My eyes rounded. "You deliver to Montana?"

His soft laugh went straight to my core and warmed it like a hot coal.

"Idaho, Montana, Wyoming, and even Colorado."

Pride swelled inside me so large that I worried it would suffocate me. Tears burned my eyes as I recalled how badly I wanted him to find who he was back when I was an obsessed teenager, planning my future with Davis. I used to hope that he'd find something that would make him feel complete.

Swallowing around all the words that flitted around my head, I blurted, "I want them all"—I stretched my hands over the creations—"in my imaginary home that I will one day have."

I laughed, smiling up at him, but the way his eyes settled on me made me feel like he was seeing something else.

He seemed to shake out of it a moment later. "You think you could afford me?"

I perked up at that, liking this playful side of him.

"How much do you charge?"

He grinned, blushing a little. "Enough, but I'm commission based only. I don't sell to any store fronts or anything yet. Well, except for one."

"That's a good problem to have, if you're making it fine without having to expand."

I walked around a few more tables, loving how organized every-thing was. There was a clear process of parts and assembly that he had set up along one wall, and then packing and distributing along the other.

"Yeah, it keeps me busy enough, and I have more money than I know what to do with from the commissions." He shrugged, like it was no big deal.

His words reminded me that my parents were struggling finan-cially, and I needed to get back and help them.

"Well, speaking of money…" I folded my arms, as though they could create a barrier between us. "I should probably get back and help my parents out. They mentioned that your orders have really been helping them, so uh…" I hesitated, nearly choking on the words. "Thank you. And I'm sorry I was so hard on you about everything."

Davis gave me a slow and genuine smile. "They mean a lot to me. I wish they'd let me buy the building their diner is in; I know that would help them tremendously, because the owner keeps threatening to lease it to someone else."

He moved past me, walking to the door, but this time, as I watched his back, I felt a tug behind my belly button, like he was the only connection I had to my parents. I followed after him, a little sad to be leaving his space so soon. I had a strange urge to dig through his work tools, organize them for him, and see what he needed help with. He was doing everything all alone. Surely there were things he could use an assistant for.

Heading back into the house, I hesitated and hung back on the porch, needing as much space from him as possible.

He noticed, then stuck his head out of the screen door, giving me a confused expression. "I have to find my checkbook. Might take a second, come inside."

Confused, I called after him, "I didn't deliver an actual order today..."

The screen snapped shut once more, but I didn't want to go inside. I didn't, but then again, maybe I could stare at a few of his pictures while he was off looking for his checkbook.

Carefully entering his home, I toed off my flip-flops and pressed my toes into the warmed hardwood. I took in his light walls, and the well-made couch and matching armchairs that faced a large flat-screen TV. His house was charming, warm, and inviting. It felt as if I were seeing it for the first time, which made sense because the first time, I'd practically been concussed.

His steps echoed down the stairs.

"Here, found it."

He took a second to lay the checkbook down on the surface of the kitchen counter, filled in what he needed to, then ripped out the singular check.

"Why are you giving this to me?" I repeated.

"For the care box, and gas..." he said with a small secretive smile, walking my way. He was being sweet, and it was difficult not to feel swayed by his kindness, especially after seeing my mother's tears earlier.

I smiled, gently taking the check from him. "Thank you, this means a lot."

"This time things went a little smoother. That's a good sign, right?" He laughed, standing too close to me.

I laughed, shaking my head. "I guess, if you—"

Suddenly his lips were on mine, his hand cupping the back of my neck while his other went to my hip, nudging me in the direction of the kitchen.

All the emotions from the lunch and having him hold me erupted from my chest, compelling me to kiss him back. I was hungry, desperate for his touch and the feel of his lips against mine. My hands went up his bare chest, feeling the taut muscles under my fingers.

"Rae," he groaned, tugging my ponytail until my head tilted back, his lips slamming against mine once more. The tension from my hair being pulled, and him devouring me, had me practically grinding against him. His free hand moved down my front, hovering over the apex of my thighs. We were against a wall, I think, as the palm of his hand landed against my pussy, still covered by leggings, but he didn't seem to care as his fingers found a way to settle right where my thighs connected. My eyes were shut, the sensations of having him touch me and fuck my mouth with his tongue almost more than I could handle.

He rubbed me through the fabric, kissing me, tugging my hair until suddenly my hips were lifted, my ass slammed on the counter, and Davis stepped in between my legs, spreading them wide.

Gripping the hair at the base of his neck, I brought him closer, kissing deeper, all while hating myself for how weak I'd become. I'd spent the last several days erasing my crush, only to have it all come rushing right back.

He kissed me so hard that I started to tip, and his hand came around my back, bracing me as he laid me on the counter. Within seconds he was hovering above me, his lips detached from mine.

"Tell me you're not seeing that guy from the other night."

My chest rose in heavy thuds as I processed his question. Puckering my brow, I shook my head. "No…that wasn't anything. We never set up a second date or even kissed at the end of the night." With a bit of a rumble, he suddenly disappeared from view, and then there was suddenly a sharp tug on my leggings and the sound of fabric ripping.

"Hey!" I gasped, trying to close my legs, but his hands braced them, keeping them open.

I sat up on my elbows, peering down at him. "What are you—?"

The mischief in his gaze cut me off, and before I could utter another sound, his mouth was descending through the slit he'd just ripped in the center of my leggings.

"I need to taste you."

My hands were back in his hair as his fingers forced my panties to the side and his tongue delved deep into my center. His groan was so fucking hot that it made my hips jut forward into the friction of his ministrations.

"God…yes," I whimpered as he consumed me like a fucking meal.

The panties he had pushed aside were soaked as he flattened his tongue, swiping along my center and teasing the edges.

His eyes tipped up, meeting mine, and I wasn't sure when or how we'd crossed this line, but I was too far gone to care.

Right as I was about to beg him to keep going, he stopped and pulled away, staying kneeled in front of me, his eyes right at the mess he'd made.

"Want me to stop?"

I hated him, and the smirk on his face and that small twinkle in his eye. But I also craved him.

"No."

Under the bright rays of sunshine that his kitchen basked in, I watched as he used his pointer finger to touch my clit then drag it down my slit, making me hiss. "I don't want to see you on any more dates."

If he wanted me to beg, then fuck him. I was so wet and horny that I was going to die if he didn't finish me.

133

"Fine," I agreed irritably.

Another finger joined his first, both massaging. "Say it."

With a huff, I muttered, "I won't go on any more dates. Now please..." I gestured with my head toward my center.

"How do you want to come, Rae?"

I moaned, rocking my hips. "I honestly don't care, just do it."

That wasn't true, though, I wouldn't be ready for his cock to slip inside me.

He must have been done toying with me, because he removed his fingers, sucking them clean.

"Fuck, you're so beautiful. I wish you could see this." His thumb tugged on the left side of my entrance, spreading me open, his eyes half lidded as he stared down at me. "You're glistening. I can see how badly you want me." His other hand came up, that thumb tugging on the opposite side of my pussy, and now I was just spread wide for him.

He made me squirm with how long he stared at me, his eyes devouring every inch of me.

"What are you...?" I swallowed the lump in my throat. "What are you thinking?"

Without removing his eyes or his thumbs, he replied, all husky and hungry. "I'm thinking what it will feel like to be inside of you, and how good it will feel when I'm filling you so completely that you won't be able to speak—"

Those eyes heated, shifting from my center to my face. "Just scream."

His words sent a shudder through me.

"Davis," I whispered in a harsh tone, practically begging him to finish me.

"You need to finish, baby?" He flattened his tongue, slowly separating me with a delicate push. "Do you want to fuck my tongue and come apart?"

I could feel my wetness increase, and he wasn't even touching me. Davis had a filthy mouth, and I was completely caught off guard by it.

"Yes," I whispered.

He clicked his tongue. "I need to hear you say it."

"Fuck you."

"Not exactly. I'm looking for you to beg for me to *fuck you*, baby."

"I am not your baby, or your anything," I snapped, legs still spread, still desperate for him to return.

"No?" he challenged me, his eyes darting to my entrance, his tongue coming out to wet his lips.

"God! Fine!"

"Fine what?" He stroked over my clit, gently.

"Fine, whatever you want. Anything! Just please finish this," I begged.

He practically attacked me, pushing my stomach down and throwing my left leg over his shoulder, delving so far inside me that I cried out.

He filled me with his tongue, pushing it deep inside then slowly bringing it out, swiping up over my clit and down my center, over and over. It was when he added three fingers while sucking on my clit that finally had me coming apart, screaming his name.

"That's right, fuck." He sat back, then he was back at my center, sucking my release into his mouth, watching me as I came down from my high.

Slowly, he pulled his fingers free, then made a show of licking my release with an enthusiastic groan.

"You taste so fucking good."

I watched him as he stood and then smiled at me like the devil he was.

"Well, you can see yourself out, *baby*. I have to go jump in the shower and handle this situation"—he gestured to his erection, bulging through his shorts—"that you left me with."

I had the sudden urge to follow him upstairs and see him undress and take him in my mouth.

"Unless you want to help me with it?" he asked, reading my mind.

Clinging to my pride, I shook my head and jumped off the counter, gripping the edge so I didn't fall.

"I need to go."

"I hope you have a change of clothes in the car." He smirked again and walked toward the stairs. Before he was out of eyesight, he dropped his shorts enough to pull the tip of his erection free and began stroking it. He was fucking huge if that much was in his hand with the band of the shorts barely down.

I turned away, feeling my face heat, and darted for the door.

19

RAE

I OPENED THE EMPTY CUPBOARD AND SCRUNCHED MY NOSE AT THE stale scent.

"Not a fan of these," I mused while Nora tried the kitchen faucet.

She made a sound of frustration. "Not a fan of pretty much anything in here."

We moved onto the garage. We could hear Vanessa Hammond talking loudly on her cell from the front yard, where we had left her. Nora didn't want the realtor to walk through any of the houses with us because she knew she'd succumb to feeling pressured into buying. It was my job to jot down any questions she had, like whether the owner would be willing to fix the roof or upgrade the cupboards.

"Are you sure you're ready to move out on your own? You're only twenty-two, that's still really young. A ton of people still live with their parents."

I ran my finger along the odd storage cabinet in the garage while Nora moved to the access door that would take us around back.

"I need it, Rae. I have to move out. If I hear my parents going at it one more time, I will stick something sharp inside my ears."

I turned her way, just short of the hot tub that was in grievous disrepair. "Are they fighting?"

Her parents had never really fought before, so if they'd started it was news to me. They always acted so in love.

Nora snorted. "The opposite. They act like they're in heat twenty-four seven."

"Oh God, eww—gross."

"Yeah." She rolled her eyes.

"Well, I say we go to the next listing. I don't see you living here."

She let out a heavy sigh. "Yeah, me either."

Once we loaded back into the car, with Vanessa behind us, my phone pinged. Digging through my purse, I tugged my cell free and saw that I had a new text from an unknown number.

Hey, it's Davis…your mom gave me your number. She said I could put my delivery requests in directly through you. She's delegating you to be my personal delivery girl. (winky face)

My face heated as I stared at the screen, completely in shock that I had Davis Brenton's phone number. I had his number *and* he texted me.

Sixteen-year-old me was freaking out right now.

"What is that look? What's going on?" Nora peeked over at me while glancing back at the road.

Tossing the phone back in my purse and purposefully not texting him back—I leaned against the window.

"Boo Radley kissed me again, three days ago, and then he slammed me down on his kitchen counter and tore my leggings open."

"Motherfucking—shit!" The car swerved wildly as Nora's face swung to stare at me. Her hands corrected on the steering wheel, getting us back on course. "Warn a girl before you drop that shit."

Biting my lip to hold in my laughter, I muttered an apology. She was gone for the weekend with her parents and had just gotten back, so this was the first chance we'd had to talk.

"So, did he—?" Nora's eyebrows were jumping up and down as we came to a four-way stop.

"No...I mean, sort of, he kind of...um..." Heat infused my face again as I remembered his tongue on me, swirling over my clit in an expert fashion. "He went down on me."

My best friend stared at me with a jaw that had dropped while a car honked at us from behind. "He went"—her eyes dipped to my lap—"just like that, huh?"

"Yeah...it was a little crazy."

"But no sex? What the heck?" We veered into a nice-looking neighborhood with beautiful aspen trees lining the street.

"He offered, but no, I turned him down."

We slowed to a stop in front of a cute one-story craftsman house, painted an awful brown color. "You turned him down?" Her eyebrows dipped into the center of her face. "Why?"

I thought it would be obvious to her, but maybe not. "Because of the purge, and because I'm not that girl. I have to prove that I'm not. You know how that goes."

"So, was he sexting you just now then?"

We both peered behind us to see if Vanessa had pulled up yet, but she hadn't.

"No. My mother gave him my number and now I'm his own personal delivery girl."

"Omigod." Nora burst out laughing, spitting out some of her iced tea that she'd sipped right after asking.

"Stop."

Her laughing continued, her face reddening. "Yep, that purge week did jack shit for you. I already know you're totally obsessing that he texted your phone. That he actually has your number and used it."

"Stop it, you're such an asshole." I pushed her arm, then went for my door. I hated how well she knew me.

Vanessa finally pulled up, got out, and went to unlock the house for us. "This was built about fifteen years ago, so it's not that old at all, and the backyard is to die for."

Nora rolled her eyes behind Vanessa's back, and I hid a smirk. We knew it was her job, but Nora was the type of person that had to go into a house and get it based on feeling, not any actual information or data, and she always felt like the realtor talked up the house in a way that hid problems. I told her that wasn't necessarily true, but there was no way to convince my best friend otherwise.

She was the same way with buying cars, cell phones…even a big purchase at Costco. She just didn't like talking to people whose job depended on her saying yes. It was too much pressure for her.

"So, I'll stay out here again, or did you want me in th—"

"Stay out here please," Nora quickly said, pushing past her realtor.

I mumbled an apology and followed after my friend.

Right away it was easy to notice how different this house was. Light fell across the wood floors from the windows, creating a cozy vibe. The living room was spacious, with a nicely sized fireplace and mantle.

"Wow," Nora whispered as she tipped her head back, taking in the vaulted ceilings.

"This is really nice." I walked along, bypassing the open dining space, and then ventured into the kitchen, where a modestly sized island sat, with two large skylights overhead.

"There's so much light in here, I love it." I said, tipping my head back.

"It would be good for my plants," Nora mused, running her finger along the counter and the deep farmhouse sink.

Her lack of words spoke volumes. She liked this space.

We saw the three modest bedrooms, and the two-car garage. The backyard was beautiful, but the trees along the property looked old and in questionable health. Nora was in the process of kicking her foot against the base of one of the trees when my phone went off again.

Too curious for my own good, I pulled it free and checked my messages.

Davis: I get the feeling you might want to pretend I didn't taste your cunt a few days ago. That's fine. But I do need a few things delivered, so if you could get back to me somewhat soon, I'd appreciate it. I was hoping for these items by tonight.

He was right; I *did* want to pretend nothing happened between us, and I hated myself for giving him that power. But, if I admitted that something *had* happened then that meant there was something between us, and I wasn't sure I was ready for that yet. Still, it bothered me that my parents' financial situation seemed to depend on these stupid deliveries.

With a sigh of irritation, I texted him back.

Sorry, just house hunting today with my friend. I will be free in about an hour, depending on the order, it might take anywhere from fifteen minutes to an hour to get it ready, then another forty-five to get up the mountain, you should have the order by six.

I reread the text. It seemed professional and non-flirtatious. I wanted to be sure he knew I wouldn't be doing anything else with him, regardless of the deliveries. I wouldn't be falling into any more of his random kissing schemes.

"This thing legit feels like it's about to fall," Nora yelled at me from her spot across the yard.

"Yeah, well, stop kicking it. If it does fall, I don't want it to hit you."

She waved me off, turned, and then froze in place, staring at something over the fence. I slowly moved my eyes to track where she was looking.

Next door was a man hammering away at something that looked like a greenhouse. I could only make out the back of him, so I had no idea who he was, but where Nora was standing, she could see his side profile.

Furrowing my brows as I tried to assess the threat, I was two seconds from yelling, asking who he was, when she suddenly bolted across the yard.

"Time to go!"

I turned with her, perplexed by her parting words, and then picked up the speed behind her.

"What's going on?"

She didn't answer me, just jogged back through the house, exited the front door like the house was on fire, and got into her car.

"Sorry, Vanessa, Nora isn't feeling well. We'll follow up!" I called while darting down the steps, more than a little concerned she might take off without me.

Once inside the car, Nora stared straight ahead, like nothing had happened.

"You ready to go?"

I stared at her, still heaving air. "Want to tell me what the hell just happened?"

She waited a few more seconds before starting the car and pulling away from the curb. "The next-door neighbor is Colson Hanes. He's this guy that worked with my dad on a project two years ago." She blushed a deep red before adding, "Pinterest guy."

"Ohhhhh." The lightbulb went off, and suddenly I was insanely invested. She'd created a fake wedding board for him; this must be a pretty serious crush.

"I met him by accident and thought he was kinda cute. He, however, wouldn't give me the time of day...until I took a page out of your book."

Oh no.

"What exactly does that mean?" I silently prayed that she hadn't stalked him. There couldn't be two of us; that would make us like a cult, right? How many people did it take to start one?

"I sort of started showing up on the work site just to see if he'd talk to me, see if I could get him to organically like me."

She veered toward Main Street, her face reddening with every block.

"And?"

She swallowed. "Well, there was a situation with me spilling something on my sweatshirt and having to change in the bathroom...he sort of walked in."

Confused, I shook my head. "I don't get it."

She parked in front of her house, then gripped the steering wheel until her knuckles turned white.

"My father had apparently insinuated to Colson that I was in the building, waiting for him because I had to give him something. It was just a clusterfuck. Anyway, when he walked in, it sort of seemed like I had stripped and was waiting for him."

My poor, poor friend. I would have died. "What did he do when he saw you?"

Her blue eyes widened as she looked at me. "He blurted that he had a girlfriend and then fled the room like he was on fire."

Bringing her hands to her face, she whined. "I was so embarrassed."

"Have you seen him since?"

"Yes, that's the worst part." She dropped her hands and unclicked her seat belt. "He saw me in the grocery store once and completely changed direction mid-walk."

I cringed. "Oh man, that's pretty bad."

"Yes, and now if I want that beautiful house, I'll have to live right next door to him. I can't do that."

Opening her door, she rushed out.

"Wait, we need to talk about this!" I called after her as she hurried up her steps.

She didn't even wait for me as she unlocked the door. "I need vodka!"

BY THE TIME I left Nora's house, it was close to five. Her parents had gotten home, breaking up our party and ending her fun. I had stayed sober, knowing I had to still do a delivery for Davis, except now there was no way I'd make it by six.

Pulling my cell out, I decided to call him, mostly because I was too mentally exhausted to text.

Davis picked up on the third ring. "Hello?"

I smiled, but it was futile, he couldn't see me.

"Hey, uh…it's—"

"Rae." His deep voice sent shivers down my skin, reminding me what he'd done to me on that counter just a few days prior.

"Yeah. Look, I had an emergency come up, and I'm just now

getting out of it. I know you needed that delivery tonight, and I had said six, but—"

He cut me off. "It's fine."

I hesitated, unsure if he meant it was fine if I came later, or if I didn't come at all.

"So, you want me to arrange it for tomorrow?"

His silence made me feel uneasy as I crested the steps to my house.

"Is that what you want?"

"I…" What did I want? I wanted to see him, but I didn't want him to know that, and more importantly, I was falling for him again, too easily, and deep down, I knew he'd hurt me. "I think tomorrow would be better."

The lie tasted like acid on my tongue, but I couldn't give him a pass. Not when there was still this massive lie and offense that sat between us, whether he knew about it or not. I did, and I owed my younger self the loyalty required to ice him out.

He paused, not answering for a moment.

"Yeah, okay, we'll touch base tomorrow." There was a hitch in his voice, and for some reason when he hung up, my throat burned.

Slowly making my way into the house, I trudged to my room and flopped onto my bed. Why did this hurt so much? Why was there a part of me that now wanted to be nice to him? Was it simply because he'd been secretly keeping my parents afloat all this time? How could someone so mean—who ruined me four years prior— end up being so kind to my family?

It was all so confusing and muddled my head and frustrated my poor heart. Before long, the hole I was staring into my ceiling blurred, and I fell asleep.

"RAE?" My mother's voice echoed from the other side of my bedroom door. I picked up my aching head and peered at the dark space that separated us.

"Honey, are you sleeping? It's dinner time." Her voice was

muffled but clear enough for me to begin connecting dots, my stomach connecting the rest, grumbling as I twisted out of my covers and staggered to the door.

"There you are," my mother said, with a warm smile and an apron tied around her midsection. The smell of her infamous meat-loaf slid into my senses, making my stomach ache.

"You shouldn't have fallen asleep so early in the day. It's going to completely wreck your sleep schedule."

I followed her into the living room, where I froze in place. I hadn't changed earlier, so I still wore a pair of jeans and an off the shoulder sweatshirt, but my makeup and hair were a complete and utter disaster. Yet, my mother didn't seem to want to warn me that she'd invited company over.

A pair of deep navy eyes stared at me from over the brim of a coffee mug that had faded handprints on one side and my face on the other side. I had made them that mug when I was seven, and for some reason it had lasted throughout all these years, no matter how many times I had tried to forget it out on the porch or accidentally let it fall—or slam into the sink. The sucker was indestructible, and now my teenage obsession was drinking from it. My lips twitched as he stared at me, like he was challenging me.

"Raelyn, say hello, it's rude to stare," my mother chided, swatting my arm as she headed back to the laundry room.

I rubbed my arm and moved forward on numb legs. "Hey."

He smirked but tried to hide it behind his mug. "Hey."

Settling next to him on the couch, I was very careful not to touch him in any way as I settled into the cushions. "Thought you were up on the mountain tonight."

Translation: I cowered like a chicken and said I'd see you tomorrow, yet here you are.

That smirk stayed small and tucked along the side of his jaw, like he was in on a secret. Maybe it was a joke, and this whole thing was one big elaborate scheme to break my heart again. The way his eyes warmed as he looked over at me made me think it wasn't. In fact, the way he looked at me made me think this wasn't a joke at all. He looked at me the way I looked at coffee, or the way I looked at my bed after a long night shift at a bar. Like I was the place he wanted to end every night and start every morning.

"Decided I'd swing into town"—he ducked his head, sipping once more—"and ended up here."

My heart pounded in my chest, hammering out a message of long-lost love and lust. He was the storm that had driven me away, and yet he seemed to shine as bright as the sun, ushering me back.

"Well, it's a nice surprise," I managed to say around the lump in my throat.

He'd come to see me.

He turned my way, searching my face for the lie. He must not have found it because the most devastating smile spread across his face a moment later, and right as he opened his lips to say something, my mother announced dinner was ready.

We both stood in quick, silent movements. It was likely obvious that I was nervous. He made me insanely anxious, especially after having his face in between my legs. Was he thinking about that? His gaze stayed focused on the savory meat in the center of the table, but once we took our seats, that gaze bounced up and landed on my lips. My face heated every thirty seconds or so as my mother tried to make small talk.

"Where's Dad?" I finally cut in, burning from head to toe with how close I was to him. Every now and then his foot would brush mine, and for whatever reason, that seemed insanely erotic.

"He's still at the diner, doing inventory. I'm actually going to take him some dinner as soon as I finish here; I was hoping you two could do the dishes and clean up?" She looked in between us and smiled.

"Of course we will." Davis rushed to answer, but all I could think was whether he'd set me on my parent's counter and go down on me again, potentially with one of those damn homemade mugs watching us.

I'd die.

"Rae?" my mom asked, her brows crinkled in confusion as to why her golden child already accepted and her loser child hadn't yet.

"Of course." I waved her off and ducked my head to finish my meal.

I had to mentally prepare to be alone with Davis. This was the entire reason I'd brushed him off tonight, to not see him, and yet, my mother was ditching us. Leaving us alone together. This was very irresponsible of her.

"Okay, you two clean up. There's ice cream in the freezer." She kissed us both on the cheeks and then rushed out of the house in her usual whirlwind manner.

Davis let out a small chuckle before grabbing his plate and the small dish of green beans and walked toward the sink.

"I thought you didn't like coming to town," I mused, needing to hear him say that he'd come for me. I was an idiot, and absolutely fishing for a compliment of some kind, but my poor broken heart couldn't compute why he'd come.

"I *don't* like coming to town," he replied, keeping his back to me.

"Then why did you?"

He turned, soapy suds covering his hands, but that smile was earnest and warm, and it heated me from my toes to the top of my head. "You're here."

His response smacked me in the face as hard as any slap. That was as close to a declaration of love as I had ever gotten, and it overwhelmed me into silence. I worked quietly beside him, cleaning, putting food away, and wiping things down, until he turned off the sink and the kitchen was completely clean.

Slowly turning toward me, he pinned his hip against the counter and watched me.

"So...guess it's late."

I briefly glanced up before ducking my head again. I wanted him to stay. I wanted him to grovel and apologize for what he had cruelly done to me when I was eighteen, but I also realized he didn't know who I was then, and I was unfairly holding him responsible for something he didn't know he'd done.

Blinking, I shoved my nerves aside and bit my lip. "Guess so."

Reaching up, he rubbed along the base of his neck as though he was nervous. I knew I was acting strange—like a high schooler finally alone with her crush and unsure how to make a move.

He huffed a silent laugh—as though it would fit just between the two of us—then he leaned down.

"Rae." His rasp rumbled along my skin as his lips met my hairline. "Show me your room."

Blushing, I lifted my hand, hesitating a moment before pushing past the awkwardness and grabbing his. I reveled at how much bigger it was than mine as I tugged him behind me. The house was quiet as we padded through the kitchen and down the hall, until he was walking into my room and shutting the door behind him.

Seeing him braced against my door, smiling at me with that mischievous grin, lit me on fire from the inside out. I blurted out the only word I could think of.

"Puzzles!"

He quirked a brow.

"Um...do you do them, or did you want to watch something?"

Finally, he peeled himself away from the door and slowly stalked toward me. "This is your bedroom—the one you had when you were a teen?"

He looked around at the walls, scanning the awards and ribbons I had hung up. Internally I thanked myself for not having any photos of my teenage self anywhere, and that the box of him was gone now. Seeing his tall frame next to my dresser was creating a tsunami of emotions. He was a dream—a walking, talking dream—here in *my* room, looking at *my* things.

Nodding, I looked around with him. "Yeah."

His strong fingers picked up one of my stuffed animals and inspected it.

"Did you ever get lucky in that bed?" He smirked at me, still slowly walking through my room, touching small pieces of my past. Each stroke might as well have been made into my skin.

"Uh..." Lucky? As in sex?

My expression crumpled. "No. I was a virgin until college."

That made him freeze. He turned to face me, a dark brow

raised. "Completely, as in you didn't do anything at all until college?"

I swallowed the lump in my throat. How could I explain that I had been saving myself for him? I had honestly thought he'd kiss me that night in the library, maybe do more. I hadn't had any interest in other boys…no one at all was in my world except for him.

To answer him, I merely shook my head. Words wouldn't come. With two slow steps in my direction, I noticed he was moving me backward. The backs of my legs hit the mattress just as he paused in front of me.

"So, you were never touched under the covers?" His question grated against my skin, forcing goosebumps to erupt. He leaned closer, asking rhetorically at this point. He knew I hadn't.

"You haven't been kissed—or licked—under that flowery comforter?" He was whispering now, slowly leaning closer until his lips grazed my throat. I closed my eyes, my breathing coming in and out as jagged as a rusty saw.

He gently pressed a kiss to the side of my neck as he continued murmuring. "Never kissed or licked anyone else, while hoping your parents didn't come home and catch you?"

I shook my head again and his hand came up to my waist, while his lips continued moving against my neck.

"What about you? Have *you* touched yourself under there, Rae?" His tongue flicked out, lapping at the shell of my ear.

"Have you rubbed your fingers through that perfect pussy, closing your eyes tight while you fucked your hand?"

Oh God. I was panting, my eyes slammed shut, picturing every filthy word. If only he knew how often I had done exactly what he'd depicted, while thinking of *him*.

"Yeah, I bet you've done that, haven't you?" His hand lowered, until he was cupping me through my jeans. "You've left a creamy white stain on these sheets, fucking your fingers, haven't you?"

He hummed, adding pressure to my center, making it throb. Then his hands were moving up my stomach until they curved around my breasts, protected by my bra. He seemed personally offended by this, as his thumbs rotated back and forth over my hardening nipples.

Tipping my head back and pushing my chest out, he tugged the padding down, exposing my breasts, while a low hiss left his mouth. Dipping his head, he moved his lips over the outline of my aching nipples.

"I want to see you do it, Rae," he whispered, while his tongue lapped over the material concealing my skin. "Sit back on this floral comforter that you've had since you were a teenager and touch yourself. Let me watch you."

My face was on fire as I processed his words, and how ironic they were in the grand scheme of our relationship. Not that he'd remember, but I had watched him, and now he was here in my room—talking dirty and asking to watch *me*. It made me so hot. I ached to do as he said.

I lifted my chin and stared up at him, wet my lips, and then gripped the edges of my shirt, pulling it over my head. He seemed to grumble his agreement with a few muttered "fucks" and then he was helping me unhook my bra. It slipped down my arms, falling to the carpet as our eyes stayed locked. Without breaking that gaze, his thick fingers moved to the copper button of my jeans and worked them open.

I stood frozen as he smirked up at me, pulling the denim down my legs. Once at the apex of my thighs, he leaned forward and placed a kiss right over my panty-covered center. My fingers dug into his thick hair on instinct.

"Pink is my new favorite fucking color," he said with a chuckle, carefully nipping at my clit. The sensation sent chills sweeping down my spine. I watched as his gaze stayed focused on the tight cotton barrier between us.

Breathing as though I just finished a marathon, I waited as he settled there, moving his lips over my pussy, seemingly unbothered that there was fabric separating him from my wet center. He took his time, groaning as he leisurely licked the tiny section of skin not covered by my bikini-cut underwear. Moving his head to the side, he nipped, this time at the edge of my panties, tugging them to the side.

"I should move this scrap of fabric" —he bit at my center again —"suck on your clit until you're creaming these," he added gruffly while pushing his nose along my slit. His eyes closed and a look of pure devotion bloomed along the planes of his face. "Then I should make you stay in them while you rub against my cock."

I was so on edge that I would literally do anything to get relief. He groaned moments later as he moved from my center, and his fingers finished pushing my pants down, until I was stepping out of them.

"On the bed," he ordered, falling back to his knees. The hungry look in his eyes was a soothing comfort to my anxious thoughts. I felt safe with him. *Wanted.*

So, I did as he said, keeping my eyes fixed on his.

"Fuck," Davis whispered, finally flicking the button on his own jeans, and pulling his erection out. It was as big as it was the last time I saw it. Thick veins ran along the velvet expanse of his impressive length, and the immense, mushroom shaped head was weeping clear liquid while his eyes pierced the spot between my legs. His shirt disappeared next, leaving his smooth, sculpted chest on display. There were so many ridges and grooves I needed to trace, to taste.

I slid my fingers up and down the soaked fabric covering my center, feeling the wetness increase until finally I pushed a single digit inside.

I moaned as I added more fingers and they slid through my soaked folds. I tossed my head back as Davis muttered a few curse words. I knew his hand was moving vigorously over his shaft, because he kept hissing as the bed dipped, and he was inching closer.

"That's it, Rae. You're soaked, look at that."

I opened my eyes and looked down. The wetness along my panties spread, and you could *hear* how aroused I was. My eyes bounced up and saw his engorged cock standing straight up; his left hand gripped the root of it, as he stood on his knees, angling closer to me.

His heavy erection pressed into my soaked underwear, and he pushed as though there wasn't a barrier between us. Fuck, it almost felt like we were having sex. His dick prodded my entrance, and his sculpted chest hovered above mine, while his tongue lapped at my nipples.

"Have you ever dry fucked, Rae? Fucked with your clothes barely on?"

He moved his hips, pushing his cock further into me, but the panties still created a barrier of resistance. It made my hips buck forward, riding the friction and pressure it created.

"No," I breathed, and he groaned.

How long would he last before just tearing the flimsy piece of fabric off? Already, it slid to the side, and I could feel the smooth feel of him against my sensitive lips.

"Oh my God, you're there...you're right there." I looked down, seeing him angled in a way that looked like he was digging from the side to find a way in.

"Feels so good, shit. But we're not fucking tonight...you're going to sit up, straddle me, and dry fuck me with your underwear on. You're going to ride my cock with this barrier between us, Rae. Then I'm going to keep your underwear for the rest of my goddamn life. Do you understand? No one else will ever get to see them."

I was gasping for air but nodded my understanding, and then he shifted us until he was sitting against my headboard, and I did exactly as he instructed. I straddled him, pressing my knees into the bed as I adjusted to being spread open for him. His sculpted jaw paired with that devious smile made my stomach flutter. His eyes settled on mine while his hands landed on my hips.

"I like you here," he breathed. "You fit perfectly."

I smiled, rubbing my aching center against the base of his cock. Looking down, his erection stood like a deliciously dangerous dare —taunting me. When he gripped its girth with his fist, it almost seemed impossible not to give in and beg for him to impale me with it. It was perfect, and still leaking clear liquid that I ached to lap up with my tongue.

Instead, I lifted my hips and rolled them, sloppy and fevered, against him. He grunted and groaned as I found my rhythm, and as I kept pace, the fabric continued to slip, allowing the slide of his silky length against my soaked center.

His smile was devastating as he lapped at my hardened nipple. "You like it, don't you?"

I gasped, clinging to his shoulders, as I moaned my agreement. I picked up speed, rubbing ruthlessly against him, watching his lower abdomen contract as he tilted his head to watch my pussy slide against him. With his hands on my hips, moving me in a cadence that suited him, I was already coming harder than I ever had with anyone else. A scream fell from my lips, a chant with his name and a prayer of some kind. With my limbs complete noodles, he sat up, hands on my back, and shoved me on my back.

Still gripping his cock, pumping up and down with a twisting motion, he gripped the hem of my panties and tugged them down. With a groan, he spilled his orgasm all over my mound and all along the outside of my pussy. Once he finished and I was covered in his release, he put my underwear back in place over the mess he'd made. Bits of white cum splattered my belly button, and now that the fabric was mashing it into place, pieces of him leaked out of the edges and down my thighs.

"Next time, I'm finishing here" —he stroked along my breasts— "then here" — he moved his finger up along my throat and over my lips—"and fuck, I can't wait to finish here." He relocated his hand to my ass, dipping underneath the panty line along my crack.

That's when the front door slammed shut from the front, and we heard my parents' voices.

He smirked, rolling over and pulling me into his arms.

My parents' voices rose and fell from the kitchen then leading into the laundry room.

With his lips right at my ear, Davis said, "Kiss me."

I didn't think twice. Our mouths were already so close; I just tilted my head back and lifted my face and then Davis was there, molding his lips to mine, as if he couldn't wait a second longer for me to place my mouth against his.

This kiss was different, though—it was slow and sweet. Our legs scissored together, my breasts mashed against his chest, his fingers gently running up and down the expanse of my back. But it quickly took a turn, with the thick, hard length pushing into my stomach and Davis letting out a groan.

Breaking our kiss, he rasped, "I want you to touch me." Moving his hips forward and pressing his erection into me, he added, "knowing your parents are on the other side of the door."

I was already getting hot again, and because of that, I gripped his length in my hand, but Davis held my wrist with a click of his tongue.

"Did I say touch? I meant taste. I want to drive home tonight with the image of those fucking lips wrapped around my cock."

"Rae?" my mother called through my door then wiggled the handle. I thanked all the holy saints that Davis had locked it.

"Scared?" he whispered in my ear, tucking a few strands away.

This was insane. My parents were right out there, and he wanted me to suck him off? It was crazy, and yet it somehow made me hotter.

His fingers tangled in my hair, tugging lightly while he started kissing my neck.

Blinking away my thoughts, I moved.

My knees hit the carpet of my floor, right as he sat up and spun around, engorged erection in his fist. With wide eyes, I looked at the massive size of the weeping tip and tried to find a way to begin.

He must have sensed my anxiety, because while I was staring at his massive cock, he seemed to freeze in place.

"You've never…" His voice hitched as he tipped my chin up. "Have you ever done this?"

Heat hit my face, a million different shades of humiliation churning and burning around under my skin. I could lie. I could fake it. But for some reason I didn't want to.

"No…my ex… Well, we just never did. He never seemed to want it, and he didn't even go down on me, so…"

Seconds later my mother knocked again. "Raelyn, I need to talk to you."

154

Davis had a pair of worried brows crowded in concentration as he stared down at me.

"This shouldn't be your first time then. Let's save it."

But it was hot doing things we weren't supposed to while my parents couldn't see and didn't know—so I gripped his thighs.

"No...let me, please."

Without waiting for him to answer, I leaned forward and licked the clear liquid from the tip. Davis let out a low hiss while his hand found the back of my head.

"Shit, that felt good. Just do whatever feels right. You can't do it wrong when you're just navigating and feeling things out. Okay?"

I nodded and went in again, doing as he said.

It was odd at first, unsure how to exactly perform the way I had seen it done in the few videos I'd seen. But remembering that they usually gripped the base of the cock, I decided to start there.

Another hiss left his throat as I stabilized the behemoth penis in front of me, and then I lifted on my knees and marveled at how silky smooth he felt in my hand. The tip of his dick was wet, but so soft and so deliciously sexy. I moaned as my mouth descended and my lips wrapped around the head.

"Rae!" my mother called again, this time sounding out of patience.

Davis increased the grip at the back of my head, encouraging me to take him deeper. I found with alarming clarity that I really liked having him in my mouth. I loved the power it gave me, and how when I went as far as I could seemingly go, he'd groan and then push me deeper. I'd let up when I felt like I couldn't bear the press of him against my throat, and he'd let me. Then we'd do it again. I'd bob my head up and down, sucking as I went, moving down along his shaft as deep as I could take him.

"Fucking shit," he wheezed, now tugging at my hair with more force. His hips were jutting upward too, and I realized I really liked that.

Another knock rattled the door and I sucked harder, gripping his thighs, bobbing up and down as he let out a string of whispered curse words and tore at my scalp. I was completely worked up again, moving my own hips against the air, and damn it, I was two seconds from using my hand.

"Rae, I'm going to come, you need to let me go, or else I'll finish down your throat."

I didn't let up, because I wanted to experience it; I wanted all of it. My false bravado was called seconds later when he indeed finished in my mouth, but the texture was unexpected, as was the sheer volume. Jumping up and covering my mouth, I darted toward the garbage can, but Davis stopped me by gripping my wrist.

"Just relax," he coaxed, gently tipping my head back. "Open your throat and swallow. It's okay."

I did as he said, closing my eyes and ignoring the small amount of jizz that had dribbled down my lip, swallowing what was left in my mouth.

"Good girl," Davis whispered, his eyes focused on my lips. "We're going to do this again sometime, and I'm going to reward you for that."

I let out a small laugh as I took in his serious expression and the way his eyes homed in on my mouth.

"Be right out, Mom," I finally called back.

A firm grip on my jaw forced my focus back on Davis, his thumb pressed directly under the mess that had leaked out of my mouth.

"Lick," he commanded, eyes on mine, heat searing me to my core.

His grip remained as I did as he said, darting my tongue out, lapping up his release.

His groan of approval sent a shudder through my core.

Seconds later, Davis forcefully pushed my underwear down my hips while whispering against my ear, "These are mine."

I stepped out of them, and he lowered to grab them.

"Rae, is Davis still here?" my mother asked, and the man in question smirked at me while he buttoned up.

Still staring at him, I yelled out, "No, he left a while ago."

His truck was likely still out front, but oh well.

He stepped closer to me and whispered in my ear. "Why don't you tell them what we were doing in here?"

I smiled, listening as my mother launched into something about leftovers and Tupperware.

"Tell them that you were just sucking my cock and swallowing every fucking drop of my pleasure, like the good fucking girl that you are." He nipped at my neck, pressing a kiss there. "Tell them how good it felt to have my cock inside your mouth, hitting the back of that throat."

I liked this playful side of him, so much that when he went to kiss my neck again, I moved so he'd catch my lips.

He slowed, bracing my face with his hands, kissing me slowly. My fingers slid up, feeling every ridge and groove of his perfectly sculpted chest. Letting out a low groan, he moved his jaw to the side, deepening the kiss. It was the kind of caress that I'd obsess over later, the type of touch old me would have cataloged and journaled about. A kiss I'd keep tattooed on my soul, lingering long after he left.

Finally, he broke away and whispered in between the slice of space between us, "Come tomorrow, after your deliveries are done. Bring an overnight bag, you're staying for the weekend."

His command was a siren call I couldn't turn down, so I gave him a smile that conveyed what I thought of spending the night with him.

Then before I knew it, he was dipping to grab his shirt and headed to my window. He gave me one last hungry look before popping the screen and crawling through it.

20

RAE

FIVE YEARS AGO

My fingers tangled in my hair as I tried to comb through the tight curls. My eyes were stuck to the black motorcycle parked in spot number five across the street, at the gas station. Earl was slow in getting to each customer, so the man straddling the bike was staring down at his cell phone while he waited.

Internally I chided myself for not applying at the gas station for a job; that was a sure place to see Davis and get to talk to him. It was getting easier to pin down the spots around town he actually went inside or spent any length of time. The library was one, but only once a month or so. Usually, he'd just order his selections online, and then pick them up from the reservation shelf.

The grocery store was another place he went inside, but he was always moving, so it would be too difficult to converse with him in any real capacity, and he always used those self-checkout machines. Even upon exiting, he stuck to himself.

Sadly, the diner was still my best option to see him, or even talk to him. I just had to convince my parents to let me work the front.

Watching Davis sit there, I toyed with the hem of my shirt as I calculated the time it would take Earl to get to him, seeing that he had three other cars to get to first. That was maybe five minutes.

"I could make it," I muttered in encouragement to myself.

Digging my fingers into the small cross-body purse sitting at my hip, I popped a mint into my mouth and reapplied my lipstick then darted across the street.

His eyes were down, so he didn't see me, but deep down, I knew he could feel me. Like if we were both in the same place at the same time, then we'd both just know it, because we were soul mates.

Chills erupted along my arms like little spikes, regardless of the sun bearing down on the world, infusing the asphalt with heat and air with humidity. My low heels clicked along the cement as I progressed along the length of the gas station, but Davis never once looked up from his phone.

Not until I stood close to the chrome handlebars of his motorcycle, linking my arms across my chest.

His eyes flicked up: a dark, navy blue…and I'd never once stood close enough to see the black specks inside them or realize how truly massive his shoulders and biceps looked this close up. He let out a sigh and returned his gaze to the phone in his palm.

Seconds passed where he stared at the phone, and I just stood there, hoping he'd notice my hair, or my makeup…or the fact that I was seventeen now.

"You work here or something?"

His voice rumbled like a thunder cloud, and the way it lingered around me nearly made my knees shake. I could feel my face redden as I unlinked my arms and tucked a stray piece of hair behind my ear.

"No, uh…" I looked over at Earl, and then back to Davis. "I, uh…I wanted to introduce myself." My voice was shaky and uncontrolled, like a train cart off the rails.

His dark eyebrows dipped to the center of his forehead, eyes still on the phone. "Why?"

"Because." I shrugged, smiling. "I—"

"Sorry about that, Davis, you want to fill it with regular?" Earl interrupted, grabbing for the pump.

Davis finally lifted his head, but turned away, dismissing me. "Yeah, thanks Earl."

Then his focus went back to his phone.

I stood there awkwardly, waiting for the focus of a man I shouldn't love. The numbers kept ticking up on the pump, along with the price, indicating my time was running out, but I had no idea what to say to make him see me. I could say my name, but would he think it was dumb? Raelyn sounded so young. Rae sounded older, but it was also masculine.

"You need me to call your parents or something?" Davis asked, peeking up from his phone, but only for a second. He barely looked at me before returning his gaze to that stupid device.

Heat burned through me from the top of my head to the bottom of my feet.

"No...uh...I'm seventeen, old enough to drive, I just..." I needed him to see me; if he just knew who I was and that he could love me, then he'd look at me differently, "I wanted you to know who I am."

I lowered my eyes, hoping my false lashes would pick up the slack and deliver a sultry look.

But he didn't move, the pump clicked, indicating his tank was full. He pulled out the nozzle and leaned over, securing it back in place, not even waiting for Earl. Once his fingers wrapped around the gas cap and began tightening it, I knew my time was up.

The roar of his engine screamed at me to move, to step away... but I couldn't.

"Kid," he gritted through his teeth. His helmet was on now, a mirrored version of myself reflecting from his visor.

"I—" I couldn't let him leave, not without hearing me, "just want you to give me a chance."

I stammered my words, my face on fire, tears stinging the backs of my eyes.

He dipped his head, shaking it. "Seriously, kid, move. You..." He faltered for a moment, giving me the smallest slice of hope, but then his voice spiked, dripping with disgust. "Do you really think I'd be interested in you? You've got braces. You're a fucking kid, and I'm not trying to have any more rumors started about me, so get the fuck out of my way."

Stunned into compliance, I moved to the side as he sped away, taking pieces of me with him. Pieces that he'd always hold, whether he knew it or not.

21

RAE

A ROGUE AUTUMN WIND BLEW THROUGH THE BACK PORCH, RUFFLING my papers. I had three business names typed up, with an equal number of marketable ideas that could be used to help a few spots around the town of Macon. One was Nora's parents' store, which I was saving for last because I knew Nora would have to be the one to express the findings to them. Her mother was too proud to hear any of it from me, but there were some easy tweaks that could be done to fix the signage and window displays.

My parent's diner was also on my list, but for now I didn't want to touch anything, simply because they were so focused on the new delivery service. They would need a little bit of time to test it to see if it was effective at all. Then there was the coffee shop, where Rachel worked. I had managed to get in touch with the owner and had even arranged a meeting in a week's time. Ideas were flowing for the first time since arriving back home. My setup in the backyard was finally paying off, and I was busy enough that I had completely forgotten about the planned sleepover with Davis for a while.

The order he had delivered the night before about sleeping over still thrummed inside me like a chord being plucked repeatedly. I wanted to go; my body was alive and ached to be touched in ways that it seemed only Davis could. I liked that with him it wasn't just sex. It was *sexual*—hot, dangerous, taboo. With my previous partners, we'd kiss, maybe fool around for a few minutes, but then it was just sex: guy on top, me faking an orgasm on bottom. Sex was never as hot or insatiable, which only reminded me how Davis had handled my inexperience yesterday.

My face flushed, remembering how he'd gently tipped my head and didn't allow me to make a fool of myself. Instead he'd talked deviously dark in my ear, leaving scorch marks along my memories. His words still burned in my stomach, making it flutter every few seconds. I never even knew it was possible to play sexually and drag out pleasure in the different ways he did. It was another layer to him that made me crave him. But I was hesitant still and knew I would need to talk through a few things with Nora, especially after our purge session.

Right on cue, my back door slid open, and my best friend popped her head out.

"Hey, I was going to call you!" I called, setting my things to the side.

She sauntered onto the porch and plopped down. "Were you going to tell me about the man who was caught skulking around your house last night?"

Oh crap.

"That's what I thought. I know it was Davis Brenton, and he came from around the back of the house, which is where your bedroom is."

She waited, as the trees swayed above us, singing a silent song.

"Spill it."

Heaving a breath, I launched into what had happened, trying to remain somewhat tactful by leaving out the juicy details of how filthy Davis Brenton turned out to be.

"So, you're going for a sleepover?" Her dark brow raised, critically, making me feel insecure.

Pausing, I tipped my head back and looked at the blue sky. I hadn't answered this question out loud yet, but if I was going to be honest with anyone, it was going to be with her.

"I want to."

She leaned forward and grabbed my attention. "Then I think you need to come clean with him."

"Clean?" I tilted my head, like I didn't know what she was talking about.

"As in the teenage obsession, and the fact that you saw him having sex with someone when you thought he'd invited you there to declare his undying love for you."

Oh, *that*. I hated how tainted the truth made my hormones feel. They had on major Davis blinders, definitely. My vagina didn't give a flying fuck what happened four years ago, just as long as Davis made us feel more of what he did last night.

I balked, sitting back. "Where is this coming from?"

"Rae, just listen. I know you really well, and I know when you're starting to fall for the guy that's been sweet to you, or whatever the case may be. You're falling for him, and you're going to get hurt if you don't just rip the Band Aid off. You need to tell him, and more than that—you need closure with what happened."

My face heated as I tugged at a loose string.

"Why don't you want to?" she asked, as though she truly didn't know—but she had to, especially after running from her new neighbor. She knew.

"Same reason you ran from Colson Hayes."

Nora blanched, rolling her eyes. "I'm not falling for him, though. You are totally falling for Davis."

"The past can just stay where it is." I waved the air aside, as if it were as simple as that.

"Rae…"

"What if he pulls the plug the second he realizes?"

She scoffed. "No, he doesn't get to. He hurt you—remember? He owes you. You were an innocent teenager with a crush, and then he crushed you. You owe it to yourself to put all this out in the open and get healing from it, otherwise it will just be painful down the road."

Shaking my head, I stared down at my lap. "I just want to leave it, all of it. My hurt, the fact that he embarrassed me…"

"That's not just your decision to make. You owe him the truth, but only because you're developing feelings for him. It's not fair to have this creep up in your relationship later."

I stood, suddenly too frustrated to have this conversation with her. Sometimes the past just needed to be left exactly where it was. It would do absolutely no good to tell him that I was his stalker, much less that he had demolished my heart four years ago.

Walking back into the house, I tried to push past the pain, but deep down, I knew she was right.

STILL MULLING over whether I was going to stay at Davis's didn't change the fact that there were still orders to be picked up. So, that afternoon, I walked into the restaurant and started packing the delivery orders. There were only three, not including Davis's order, so it would keep me busy for a little while.

I was looking through a few slips and orders when Carl popped up beside me.

"Is this the mountain order?"

I nodded, still too raw to talk after my meeting with Nora.

Carl examined the tickets and then clicked his tongue when he focused on the last name.

"Is this smart?"

I cringed, hating that he was acting this way. The complete opposite from my dad, except my father had no clue what had driven me from Macon four years ago. Still, Carl's observation and commentary was riding too close to the nerve that Nora's opinion had rattled.

"It's an order, and my parents need the money," I muttered, keeping my eyes on the inventory list.

"But it's late. Maybe you should wait."

"I'll be fine."

"Rae, you're not being smart." He sighed, and I turned to face him.

"What does that even mean? I'm doing exactly what my parents asked me to." My voice held an edge that could cut if people got too close.

Carl watched me with a pitying expression.

"I'm just saying, kiddo—you need to be careful; you're just going to end up getting hurt."

"Then let me get hurt," I snapped, turning away from him.

Between the two of them, my decision to go to Davis's was shaky at best, but maybe I needed to go, just to clear the air.

Perhaps that would be the first step in this relationship—so I knew I had steady ground to stand on and there wouldn't be any secrets between us.

Decision made. I'd go just as soon as I was done with the deliveries, but not to sleep...just to confess.

22

DAVIS

It was close to eight at night. The stars were beginning to wink into view, and I'd started to give up on the idea that Rae was coming. Not that I blamed her, but it didn't change the fact that I wanted to. She was supposed to show up after her last delivery, which would have been much earlier in the evening. I had planned dinner for us; I bought fucking champagne and shit. I wanted to date her, show her that there could be more between us than just fucking, but that would require her attendance and actual consent in this little planned sleepover.

Was she nervous?

There was no way she could be, not after what we did last night. The way I touched her, the filthy things I said to her... There's no fucking way she would be nervous, right?

I felt distracted, and I was never distracted. It was why I enjoyed being in nature, alone, away from all the noise and chaos of the city. It had always been easy to focus, for my mind to tune in on my art and focus on design. Since meeting Rae, my mind has been solely on her.

On the curve of her waist, how her lower back dipped inward, leading to her plump and perfect ass. Her body was what I saw when I closed my eyes, and her taste…

"Fuck," I muttered, heading inside from the patio.

This morning I'd viciously jerked off to the image of her spread open on my counter, my head between her legs, those moans and whimpers she'd made while I devoured her. All I wanted to do was touch her, taste her…fuck, just be in the same room as her, so I could soak her up.

Her resistance wasn't a good sign. In fact, her entire demeanor should have been enough for me to just back off. She might as well have the words "fuck off" printed on her forehead, for as much as she seemed to want to interact with me. Still, I couldn't bring myself to care. She made me selfish, crazed…and insatiable.

Stoking the fire that I'd built earlier in the fireplace, I heard gravel crunching under tires. My heart rate spiked, my pulse hammering as I ran my hands through my hair. I should have taken two seconds to actually shower or shave after the long day of work.

I muttered a curse under my breath while walking to the door. I didn't want her to have to carry in the delivery box by herself.

Dove and Duke barely registered that anyone had arrived and instead stayed glued to their spots by the fire.

Seeing that Rae drove a different vehicle than her parents' Range Rover, I paused on the porch to wait for her to finish parking. Usually when she arrived, she'd park as far away from the house as it seemed she could get. This time, she parked directly in front, so I could see her face as she stopped the small vehicle. The two-door maroon car looked vaguely familiar, but I couldn't place where I'd seen it.

Rae smiled at me, and it made my stomach clench. Then she reached beside her and tugged out a small overnight bag, and it took all my strength not to just throw her over my shoulder and run upstairs.

"Hey," she said, exiting the car.

My brain went dead, and all I could seem to think about was how the other car was so much safer.

"Why did you drive this? It's a shit choice for the mountain."

Those dark brows of hers caved, and her smile slipped.

I rushed forward, down the steps, trying to salvage the damage of my stupid fucking mouth.

"I just want you to be safe when you're driving up here. There's snow coming tonight."

"Seriously?" She tipped her head back, looking up at the sky. "But it's been so warm."

I moved until gravel was crunching under my shoes. "Yeah, it won't hit town, just up here, but it sticks to the roads until the sun comes out."

She seemed to shake herself out of her thoughts and reached back into her car to pop the trunk.

"Shit, I didn't realize it would snow."

She sounded anxious while following me to the back of her car.

"I can always drive you back if you're worried about it," I offered, grabbing for the box.

She paused, watching me for a second before shaking her head. "No, I'm sure it'll be fine."

Closing her trunk and grabbing her large purse, she walked ahead of me and held the door, so I could carry the box inside.

She started rambling while slipping off her tall boots. "Sorry I'm late. I delivered to Mr. Jackson, a few miles down the mountain, but his gate wouldn't open, and I couldn't get service to call him. It was a bit of a mess."

I smiled, watching her. "No worries, but you're probably tired after waiting and having everything pushed back."

Rae's face turned a beautiful pink color as she moved over to the dogs, bending down to pat their heads. "No, I'm good. A little hungry, but that's it."

Relief swelled like one of those fucking congratulatory balloons that people get you on special occasions.

As she made her way into the kitchen and rounded the delivery box, she hesitated.

"Uh...but, about tonight—*if* I were to stay, you know, for more than dinner, then..."

169

"Are you going to pretend you didn't bring an overnight bag?" My shoulders shook, silently laughing at her.

There went that little pink flush that I loved seeing on her face so much. Somehow it brought out the blue in her eyes.

"I just wasn't sure if you changed your mind, and if you did that's okay. I just——"

Walking forward, I gripped her hip and pulled her flush to my chest.

"I didn't change my mind." Needing to convince her, I pressed my lips against hers and let myself relax into her. It wasn't difficult, especially when her fingers came up, winding through my hair and pulling.

We kissed long enough to muss each other's hair and get to second base with a few boob squeezes and ass grabs. Until finally I managed to pull away.

"What did you tell your parents?"

Giving me a small smile, she stepped back and straightened her clothes.

"Uh...they think I'm at Nora's tonight."

I nodded, even though I didn't like that they didn't know where she was. This wasn't high school; she could come clean and tell them where she was. Shit, she would *have* to tell them something, or else they would worry.

I asked, "So they don't know you came here at all?"

"No, I wasn't sure how they'd respond to that." With her hands tucked into her back pockets, and her face flushing pink, it took all my energy not to pull her back in for a kiss.

"Call your parents." I pressed a quick peck to her nose. "So they don't worry, and if there's an emergency, they know how to get in touch with you."

"I doubt anything is going——"

Applying a bit more pressure to her hip, I needed her to hear me. "Please, just...you never know. Okay?"

Searching my face, she gave me the slightest nod before tugging her phone free.

I moved, giving her some space, while she paced near the table, where she ran her thumb along the grain of the wood. "Hey Mom. Just letting you know I had a change in plans. I ended up having a late delivery night and decided to crash here with Davis."

She paused, listening to her mom, and that rosy color deepened, invading her cheeks and neck.

"I know, I'm sorry. I just didn't know how you'd react." Another pause and then, "All right, well, thank you for being so cool about it." She huffed a laugh, and it melted the hard place in my chest.

Her eyes bounced my way, followed by a sultry smile. "Okay, love you, bye." She hung up and set the phone down on the table.

"All good?" I asked, clearing my throat.

"Yep, all good. She appreciated the call and was grateful that I decided to stay since there's supposed to be a storm moving in."

"See, I told you." I winked, moving toward the box of goods she'd brought up.

Rae stepped closer, "I'm starving."

"Great, want to eat it at the table? I, uh—" Shit, I felt like a high schooler again. "I bought champagne."

"You did?" The shock in her voice told me about as much as I needed to know regarding where she thought this night might go. She assumed it was just a booty call. Would it freak her out to know that this was the furthest thing from it?

"Honestly, I'm wiped from the long day. Would it be okay if we kept things a little more relaxed tonight? What if we watch a movie while we eat?"

Picturing Rae lying on my chest, her hair tangled around my fingers while a movie played in the background, did something to me. An odd ache bloomed that I never knew existed before.

"Yeah, let's do that."

"Do you have plates, or?"

I grabbed two forks. "Let's just share it."

She smiled, sauntering to the couch.

Settling in next to her, I started a movie, and she set the chicken pot pie between us, each of us taking turns to dig in. Occasionally, I'd stop and stare at her profile as she laughed or mouthed the words to the film. It was an older movie, debuting in the '90s, but she must have seen it a thousand times for how well she knew the scenes.

I liked watching her. I liked having her in my space. She was like a little ball of light, captured and held here, just for me. She had her phone out, wanting to take a picture of the dogs while they slept, and I decided to do the same, except I captured her—the way she looked at my dogs, the way her hair fell over her shoulder, the way the denim clung to her ass and thighs.

Maybe it made me a creep, but I needed something of Rae's that was just mine. Some part of her light that I got to keep, no matter what.

Once the pie was finished, the tin tray left behind on the coffee table, Rae tucked her legs under her and relaxed into my side.

Wrapping an arm around her, I pulled her close, right as the dark sky outside lit up like a Christmas tree, followed by a crack of thunder.

With a gasp, she sat up. "I thought you said it was snow that was coming."

Stroking her arm, I tried to get her to relax. "Guess it's rain."

With one last glance outside, she deflated into my side once more, until another loud boom sounded above us, followed by a streak of light and the power blinking out. The only light we had was the fire.

"Oh my gosh, the power is out!"

"It'll pop back on in a bit. This is normal. Us mountain dwellers have to deal with pretty bad storms from time to time. You get used to it."

"Is your house all locked up though?" she asked nervously.

I couldn't help but laugh.

"I'm serious! You never know if there's some crazy person out there, just waiting for the power to go out so they can break in and murder you in your sleep."

"Well, to answer your question: yes, all the doors are locked. I have a security system in place, with cameras and motion detectors that run off a generator. I also have two dogs who'd lose their fucking minds if anyone so much as fogged up one of my windows."

She relaxed once more, letting out a long yawn. "Guess you're right about that. Sorry, New York wasn't like this. If the power went out, it was a bad night, and I definitely wouldn't be sleeping, but mostly because of the roaches."

"What?"

Groaning, she brought her hands up to cover her face. "Please don't tell my parents."

"Look, I think you're tired. Why don't we go to bed?"

She seemed to perk up at that.

"Are you sure? I mean, I know you wanted me to come so we could have sex like a billion times. I feel like a loser being so tired."

Standing up, I bent down and scooped her into my arms. "I didn't ask you here for sex, and I definitely don't think I have a billion times in me, at least not this weekend. I asked you here because I wanted you in my bed. Fully clothed, naked, wrapped in ribbon, I don't care how…I just want the chance to hold you."

"Fucking shit, Davis. You can't just say that stuff to a girl."

If only she knew that I had never said that to any girl.

I walked upstairs with her, knowing the dogs would likely stay by the fire. The hall was dark as I walked up until suddenly a light popped on, beaming across the stairs.

"Flashlight app, so you don't drop me." Her smile made me crack one of my own. I liked how silly she was, how happy and bubbly. She was quickly becoming an addiction I knew I'd never be able to break, which meant I should probably slow the fuck down.

"Okay, here we go. Looks great, right?" I joked, setting her down on the wood floors. There was an older than shit rug by the dresser, that she'd hopefully miss, and a bed with mismatched sheets, pillowcases and blankets. Suddenly, I was grateful the lights were out, because I was fairly certain Rae was used to guys having their shit together a bit more than me.

She surveyed the space with her phone light, smirking at me from over her shoulder, "Just have to make sure you don't have any dead bodies in here. Or dolls."

"Dolls?"

"You obviously haven't watched true crime shows or listened to

173

the podcasts. There are some strange fucking people in this world, Davis."

My chest felt too light to laugh her response off. I wanted to absorb it, take all of her in and just keep her there. I was the weirdo. I was the strange fucking person, but I wasn't sure how to fix that about myself. I had never felt this way about anyone.

"Okay, looks good. Can I use your bathroom to clean up, and do you have a candle or anything I can use?"

"Yeah." I sprang into action, remembering I had an emergency kit in the hall closet. "Here you go," I set the stubby candle in front of her, and then lit the wick.

"Thank you. Now please don't laugh at me, but I'm completely afraid of the dark so I am going to pee with the door open, and I know that's a lot for a first date, but just plug your ears. Well, one ear. The other needs to stay available in case someone tries to murder me, and I scream for help."

I laughed, shaking my head as she walked in and cracked the door. She turned the faucet on, so all I could hear was running water instead of her relieving herself. Then a flush, and more water. I chose to use the time to strip out of my clothes, suddenly feeling a little nervous. I hadn't had anyone sleep with me...ever.

I was so caught up in my head, I didn't hear the water turn off, or the door open.

"Whoa! You just went straight for it, huh?"

Spinning around, I saw Rae standing in the doorway, holding her candle. Her hair was tied on top of her head, and she had a fresh, clean face. Her eyes were wide as she took me in from head to toe.

"I was not prepared for the sight of you in just a pair of black boxer briefs. Holy shit. You...you have really muscular thighs. And Jesus, Mary and Judas...that V on your lower abdomen."

My lip lifted on its own as her gaze continued to roam and her mouth seemed to just keep going.

"And did you know that you have really impressive back muscles? I've never noticed that about guys—I mean, at least not the ones I've been with. They just had regular spines, and skin...you know, the usual stuff that makes up a back. But you—you're all muscles, and fuck, how come no one ever told me there was back porn? Because I'd pay a subscription fee to just watch your back as you cut wood or lift tree limbs."

"Rae." I was laughing so hard my stomach was starting to hurt. "Come here."

She stumbled forward, setting the candle on the dresser. I caught her by the hips, staring down at her. She bit her lip, placing her hands on my stomach.

"You need to make things even, so I can gawk at you."

She gave a little snort. "I'm sorry, did you think I was going to strip down to my bra and panties? No, sir. I have a nightgown, a *flannel* one. Goes all the way up to the neck, with a nice collar. Besides, you've seen me naked. This was the first time I've ever seen you like this."

Pulling her closer to the bed, I clicked my tongue. "Well, then, go find your flannel nightgown and put it on, so we can go to bed."

She snorted. "I didn't really bring that. I assumed we'd be having sex at some point this weekend."

Groaning, I pinned my forehead to hers. "Rae, I'd want to fuck you in a flannel nightgown, in a paper bag, in a suit of fucking armor. Just please, I beg of you, get in bed, so I can touch you."

Letting out a nervous laugh, she stepped back and slowly pulled her shirt over her head, her skin illuminated by the firelight. She wore a simple cotton bra that had a thick black band at the bottom and two straps that crossed at her back, but each breast was cupped tightly.

Then went her jeans, which she left in a pile on the floor while she stood in front of me in a matching pair of cotton underwear that was just a tiny band at her hips and barely covered her smooth mound.

Letting out a heavy sigh, I let a few curses free as I realized how fucked I was.

With her dark hair splayed against her creamy skin, and those dark lashes fanning her cheeks, she looked like a dream. A long-lost, soaking wet dream I never knew I wanted.

Bending her leg, she pressed her knee into the side of my bed and slowly crawled on. Leaving her ass on display, she lifted one knee cap and edged along the expanse of my bed. My cock twitched behind my boxers as I watched her, and it honestly felt like I couldn't stop. I couldn't move. I could barely even breathe. She was in my bed, waiting for *me*. How the hell did I get this lucky?

"You going to join me or just stand there?"

Shit.

Jumping into action, I carried the candle to my side table and then pulled the covers back. Assessing her tiny smile, and feeling my heart hurl itself against my ribs, I pressed my knees to the soft mattress just like she had. Rae mirrored my movements as I crawled under the blankets and kicked my legs out, tucking them under the top sheet.

Rae's head landed on her pillow, a relaxed sigh leaving her lungs as her lashes fluttered.

I didn't wait for her approval. I wrapped my arm around her waist and tugged her to my chest, forcing her nose into my neck.

This felt right, her warm body against mine while rain slammed against the window. I caressed her back in soothing strokes, feeling her breathing slow, until eventually it evened out and she was asleep. Smiling into her hair, I let my eyes close and left my heart wide open, willing to accept anything Raelyn Jackson would be willing to give me, secretly hoping it would be everything.

23

RAE

THE SOUND OF CROWING WOKE ME.

Fluttering my eyes open, the room was all murky with strokes of early dawn, making me snuggle further into the cocoon of blankets surrounding me. I wanted to go back to sleep, but I heard fabric shuffling, and then the sound of a zipper. I sat up, letting the blankets fall to my waist.

"What are you doing?"

Davis stopped zipping his jeans, tipped his face up, and smiled at me.

"You sound sexy as hell in the morning."

I returned his smile, leaning back on my palms while I tried to assess where he was headed.

"The sun hasn't come out yet, where are you going?"

He moved around the bed, dipping down to grab his shirt from the floor, "Just have to feed the animals. Go back to sleep. I'll make us breakfast in a little bit."

His lips pressed into my hair on top of my head and then his gaze lingered on my breasts, a fire blazing in them.

"If you're feeding them, I want to help." I swung the blankets off, wincing just the smallest bit as my feet touched the freezing floor.

"Sorry, I should have started a fire in here."

I waved him off, prancing on my toes to the bathroom. "Do you have any socks? I didn't bring any."

"You don't have to help, Rae, just go back to bed."

Now that I could see the details of the bathroom, my jaw nearly became unhinged. Unlike his bedroom, which was a bit outdated, his bathroom looked like someone took one of my Pinterest boards and recreated it.

Porcelain hexagon tile ran under my toes, with a wall to wall glass shower off to the left. Inside was smooth white stone, a stone bench resting on each side of the shower, along with two shower heads. To my right there was a double farmhouse style sink, with dark bronze faucets and a mirror that took up the whole wall.

"I want to," I yelled back, while finishing up. Once done using the restroom, I washed up, splashed water on my face, and dug out my toothbrush. Right as I finished, and I was still standing in just my underwear, he pushed the door open, holding out a rolled-up pair of socks.

Watching him in the mirror, I smirked as his gaze seemed to travel the length of me but stopped at my ass. His heated eyes glued me in place, until finally his gaze traveled up and met mine in the mirror.

With a sly smile, he stepped forward, pulling me into his firm chest. A chest that I snuggled the hell out of the night prior.

"You're so fucking beautiful, did you know that?"

My face warmed and I felt my walled-up heart crack a little.

His hand skimmed my back, lowering down over my ass, where he gripped the cheek and groaned.

His touch continued, moving lower, until he found my wet center, then he demanded with a gruffness that sent shivers down my spine, "Spread your legs."

I complied immediately.

"I like that you have firsts, Rae. I like it a lot." His rasp grated against my skin as I slammed my eyes shut.

. . .

"HAVE YOU EVER BEEN LICKED"—HIS pointer finger circled the tight hole that had never even been touched, much less licked— "here?"

I couldn't answer. Around him, I felt like a virgin, and it was embarrassing.

"Answer me."

I shook my head.

Warm fingers traced my lower back and played with my hair while he hummed.

"Your body is fucking delectable, and I want to touch, taste, and fuck every inch of it. Are you okay with that?"

Nerves rattled my rib cage, but pleasure wound around my core so tight that I squeezed my thighs together.

Letting out a small exhale, I made sure I had his eyes in the mirror. "Yes."

That same pointer finger pressed further into my hole, making my back arch. "Are you sure, because you can say the word and I'll stop."

"I like how you touch me, how you taste me, and..." Watching his heated expression, I added, "I can't wait to see how you fuck me."

That was all it took. He pushed me forward until my chest brushed the counter.

I adjusted my stance, my fingers gripping the basin for support.

"The first thing we need to discover is whether or not you like being licked there." He lowered to his knees behind me.

Warm fingers gently pushed aside the fabric of my underwear as his hot tongue swept along my most intimate space. The feeling of his mouth on that part of my body was overwhelming in a way that I had never experienced before. The sensations swept through me, dragging me under a wave of pure pleasure as his tongue worked me.

I must have let free a moan as I rocked into his mouth, shameless with lust as he worked me.

He groaned then stood, leaving the biting cold to attach to my soaked slit.

I gasped, tracking his movement in the mirror.

"I think you like it," he smirked, catching my gaze. "We're definitely doing more of that later."

Standing behind me, that muscled chest pressed into my back, he gently lifted my knee up on the counter and held it there, pressing his face into my neck. The awkward angle of my leg being bent didn't even phase me as his fingers wound around my hips and pushed into my center.

"I want to watch your face as you come on my fingers," he whispered, tipping his eyes up enough to meet mine in the mirror.

Keeping my gaze on him, I watched the filthy image mirrored back to me: his hand under the fabric of my sheer panties, a soaked spot noticeable. I didn't even feel ashamed. I felt alive, brazen, and sexy.

Rocking into his hand, with the added hardness from the counter, made the pressure feel incredible.

"That's it, Rae."

His fingers increased in speed as his thumb circled my clit.

Before I could even fathom it, I cried out, letting my head fall into the curve of his neck while my leg remained up on the counter and his hand was still shoved under my panties.

"Look at how beautiful you are when you're coming for me," he rasped, increasing the speed of his fingers, milking my orgasm for all it was worth. The sound of my wetness echoed through the bathroom, and I kept my leg lifted unabashedly as he rubbed me.

Davis pressed a kiss to my shoulder and muttered, almost to himself, "That's all for me."

My chest heaved as I watched him stand there, pressing gentle kisses into my skin while he helped me lower my leg to the floor. His hands went to my hips to stabilize me, but he still didn't move. I looked up into the mirror in time to see him smiling down at me, and it lit a blazing fire in my chest, a warning I should have heeded.

"I'll get you a shirt, and some sweats."

Instead, I followed him into the room and pulled on pieces of his clothing, as if each piece was a part of him that I could keep. And maybe I could… Just as soon as I told him the truth about our past.

⌂

I WORE a pair of black rubber boots that were too big for me, but it was perfectly themed with the flannel that swallowed me up, along with the sweats that were so long they had to be stuffed into the boots. I grabbed a bucket of feed and followed after Davis as he walked into the chicken coop. The birds all seemed to hum and cluck lowly as he filled their food bucket.

Wings fluttered as they all crowded the large round dish, and then we moved to fill up their water and replenish a secondary feeding spot for some of the other birds who hadn't joined the others around the first feeding area.

"What's in here?" I asked, as Davis set down his bucket and opened the door to a shed. He smiled at me and held it open, motioning me inside.

"This is where they lay the eggs; we just need to grab what's here real quick while they're distracted with their breakfast."

The floor was covered in straw, the smell of feed and straw heavy in the air, but the space was warm. "This is cozy."

He picked up a bowl and held it to his chest as he smiled at me. "You get to grab the eggs."

Excited, I got to my knees and started looking inside each small cubby for eggs. Some still had hens inside, but they didn't seem bothered by my checking for eggs. Grabbing three, I handed them up to Davis, and then moved to the next, and so on, until I'd grabbed them all. I was about to stand up when I looked up at Davis from my spot on the floor.

He watched me with a starved expression that I'd seen earlier when I was standing in his bathroom, and again last night as I crawled into his bed. I'd never been so insatiable for a man before, but I wanted Davis in ways that I'd never had anyone else.

So, feeling brave, I angled my body toward him and carefully placed my hands on his thighs, slowly moving up until I was at his zipper.

"What are you doing?" He swallowed thickly, setting the bowl of eggs down.

Standing tall on my knees, I unbuttoned his jeans, and slowly slid down the zipper.

"Wasn't it painful for you not to fuck me this morning?" I asked, keeping my eyes on the dark material under his jeans, ignoring how much my face flushed at the dirty language. It would take some getting used to it, but something about Davis made me feel brazen.

He let out a shuddering breath. "Yes."

"Didn't you want to?" I gave him a sultry look, tipping my head back just the slightest bit, then used my fingers to pull the band of his boxers down, freeing his length.

God, he was massive.

Thick veins ran along the length of his heavy, sleek cock. The mushroom shaped head was already slightly weeping, and all I wanted to do was taste him.

"Of course I did," he finally responded, his eyes blazing at the sight in front of him.

I gripped the base of his shaft and ran my hand up and down the full length of him, loving how hard he became under my touch.

"I haven't stopped thinking about the last time I had you, how you filled my mouth, how you taught me to swallow so perfectly. Don't you want to teach me how to take your cock again, like a good girl?"

Keeping my eyes on his, I wrapped my lips around him and moaned loudly.

"Fuck, Rae." His hips jerked. "You want to learn how to take my cock again, learn how to fuck me with your mouth?"

I let him go with a pop. "Mmmmm, yes, please." Keeping hold of him, I wet the tip and then ran my tongue down the length of him.

He hissed and groaned as his hips jutted forward, his fingers tangling in my hair as he pulled me closer.

"Fuck. Fuck. Fuck," Davis chanted as I sucked with fervor, his hips rocking in forceful thrusts. My thighs became slick as lust overcame me. I'd never felt this way before, never this greedy, or needy.

Or this bold.

Needing to feel friction between my legs, I kept one hand wrapped around the base of his cock while I sucked and shoved my free hand into my sweats, cupping myself, riding my hand.

"Shit, that's fucking hot," he breathed, watching me.

I rocked harder into my hand, liking that he was watching, wishing he could see more of me.

Then I was being pulled up to my feet, his length freed from my lips, and Davis's mouth slammed into mine. His fingers twisted into my hair while he walked us to the wall, and my back was shoved into it with force.

I loved it.

"Yes," I breathed, while he viciously kissed me, biting my lip, moving his fevered caresses down my neck. He shoved my sweats down to my ankles, same with my panties, my boot was pulled free and tossed behind us, freeing my leg and then he lifted me.

I wrapped my legs around his waist as his erection throbbed between us.

"I wanted our first time to be in a bed, or romantic somehow, but I need to be inside you."

Gasping, I nodded fervently. "Yes, please."

Eyes glazed with pleasure, my head tipped back against the wall, I felt him grip his length and then the tip of him pressed into me. It was massive and very clearly larger than any other penis that had ever been inside me.

"Wait!" I stared down at where he was pressing into me. "You're going to tear me in half, and that seems incredibly unsexy."

His smile sent a shiver down my spine.

"You're nice and wet, Rae. It'll slide right in, baby. Shit...unless, are you okay without the condom?"

Nodding, I couldn't tear my eyes away from his massive length about to slide inside my seemingly tiny body. "I'm clean, and on the pill. Are you clean?"

His scoff shouldn't have felt like a jack hammer to my heart, but all it did was take me back to that night I walked in on him with someone else.

"I've been on a bit of a dry spell for nearly a year, and yes, I've been tested since then."

Rubbing his shoulders, I swallowed the lump in my throat, my legs wrapped around his waist like an anaconda. "Good, that's good. Okay, then, let's do this."

With amazing gentleness, he held me up with one arm, and used his free hand to tip my chin up, pressing a gentle kiss to my lips.

With a soft whisper, he warned, "Hold on tight."

He slowly advanced, sliding his engorged cock in, inch by inch, and the stretch felt incredible and insanely horrific all at once.

"Shit," he hissed, pulling my hips down against him. "You're so tight, baby. So fucking tight."

"No shit, why did you think I was worried about being torn in half? I've only been with two guys, and they were half your size."

His rumble sent a spasm to my sex as he pulled out and then slammed back into me.

"Oh my God!" My head slammed into the wall as his hips moved, pulling his cock out and then thrusting back in.

"Yes!"

The more he moved, the more I felt like I was going to combust. He was thrusting so hard that my head continually hit the wall behind me. My ankles were locked behind his back, his hands on my ass, pushing me down against his cock.

My mouth gaped as soundless cries fell from my lips as wave after wave of pleasure slammed into me.

"Look at me as you come, Rae." His hips bucked, his cock swelling inside me as he tugged my hair and kissed my neck.

My eyes were open as he came. I saw the flush in his cheeks, the strain in his neck, and with one last hard thrust, I came too, falling apart, screaming his name as I rocked into him, clenching around his shaft as he emptied himself into me.

A small lilt of laughter came from his chest as his forehead pinned mine.

"We're not going to get anything done at this rate."

I gave him a small peck on the lips and smiled. "I'll keep my hands to myself, I swear."

Lowering me to the ground, he pulled out, looking down at his already semi hard cock.

"I probably won't, so keep your fucking panties off."

With that, he gave me a wolfish grin, tucked his semi into his boxers and sauntered out of the hen house.

I did as he said, tucking the panties into my pocket and pulling up the sweats, already aching for him once more.

BY THE TIME we were done feeding the animals, the sun had crested the trees, but the chill of the morning and the rain from the night before hadn't waned. We hustled inside, and Davis started a fire, which I sat cross legged in front of, warming my fingers.

"I told you that you didn't have to feed the animals with me."

He pressed a hot cup of coffee into my palms. I smiled up at him, grateful for the caffeine.

"I wanted to, and besides—we had fun."

He choked on his coffee from his spot near the kitchen then shook his head. I heard him mutter a few things under his breath, but it only made me smile into my mug. I was having more fun than I'd had in a very long time. I also couldn't seem to ignore the fact that being around Davis felt natural, like I'd known him my entire life. Which, I hadn't. Regardless of my early crush, I didn't know anything of substance about the man.

I stared into the fire, thinking over the questions I had about him: how I wanted to know about his past, his childhood, and upbringing...mostly I wanted to know why he didn't like going into town or seeing people. From what Nora had mentioned, over the years—really after I had left—he'd stopped going into town almost entirely. Part of me wondered if I had caused him trauma of some kind because of my obsession with him.

I didn't like settling too long on those thoughts, because guilt and fear mingled like a cocktail, warning me not to get too close to the man.

We ate in silence, while both of us had smiles that stretched along our faces. Rain started to pelt against the roof again, and for some reason I had to watch it. I made a humming sound, grabbed my coffee and sauntered out to his covered patio. Curling up in one of his loungers, I watched the downpour as it washed the tall evergreens beyond his yard, amazed at the thick fog that clouded Mount Macon. That, with the smell of smoke, it was the most perfect autumn aesthetic ever.

Davis was out seconds later, holding a few pieces of birch wood. He loaded the small chiminea with wood then lit it and shut the small hatch. He offered me a blanket and then snuggled in behind me, holding me to him.

It was the safest I'd ever felt in my life.

"Tell me what you're doing with yourself now that you're back? Are you going to do the delivery service permanently? Are you here temporarily?" I could hear the question and worry in his tone; it matched the cadence of concern I had for him leaving or slipping through my fingers, too. He was treasure I didn't deserve; gold I would have to return.

"I'm actually trying to help a few of the businesses around town. I have a marketing degree, so I thought I'd do whatever I could to help a few. It's probably dumb…"

"No." He stroked my arm as the rain poured. "It's not dumb at all. I think the businesses could really use it."

"I wish I had a way of unifying the town look; something aesthetically similar so everyone had a leg up. I know a few towns around the state do it, and it helps add to the overall feel of the city."

He seemed to mull that over for a second. "You mean like different fixtures or physical things to put on the business storefronts, making them match?"

I let out a sigh, my brain still plugging different pieces about it together. "Yeah, something like that."

He didn't say anything else as we sat there and watched the rain.

Eventually we moved back inside, where we both napped on the couch.

Near lunchtime, we woke, and I ate while he ran upstairs and did something with water.

"You done?" he called down to me from the top of the stairs.

I couldn't see him, but I yelled back, "Yeah."

"Come up here."

I set my dish in the sink and did as he said, patting Dove and Duke's heads as I went. Once at the top, Davis held a hand out to me. Placing my small palm inside his massive one, I followed him down the hall, away from his room.

There, in the guest bathroom, was a massive soaking tub, big enough for two, and the water was running, steam rising from the clear water.

"My bathroom has a massive shower, with all the bells and whistles, but this tub..." He blushed, rubbing his neck. "I thought, if you wanted, we could, or you—"

Standing on my tiptoes, I pressed a kiss to his lips and smiled.

"Take a bath with me."

So, he did. Stripping out of his clothes and helping me with mine, we settled into the hot water. Once he was seated behind me, he pulled me to his chest and rested his chin on top of my head.

The rain continued pouring outside, and the peaceful quiet of the room overwhelmed me.

Davis didn't speak. Every now and then I hoped he'd open up, maybe share something about himself, but he never did. He liked to ask me questions: about my childhood, where I grew up, how New York was, if I liked their pizza better than what I had in the Pacific Northwest.

Then, it seemed, he'd had enough talking, as his hands roamed over my body, up and over my breasts, leisurely and slow, until he rested his grip around my neck ever so gently.

In my ear he rasped, "Have you ever been held by your neck while fucking?"

God, some of his questions came out of nowhere, and my whole body would light up like a torch every time. I merely shook my head.

"The kinkiest things I've done have been with you."

He pulled me back against his chest. "So, the other two——" He seemed to hesitate to ask but then forged ahead. "Were they serious?"

"Sort of? I lost my virginity to someone in one of my classes my freshman year of college. We went out for drinks, and made a plan to just make it happen for each other. We watched a few videos to help us get things going."

He rumbled something, but his grip tightened on me, and I hated how much I loved it.

"Second guy was the year after. He was my boyfriend for about a year. We had sex, often—but it was just always the same, in the same positions, in the dark. Nothing very exciting."

"The things I ask of you...are they too much?"

I laughed, and his hold on me loosened. Immediately I reached up and gripped his hand, holding it in place. "Don't you dare stop. I love everything and anything you want. Just do it. I trust you."

"I can think of some dirty things," he grumbled, jutting his hips forward the slightest bit.

I hummed in response.

"But, for now, I just want to hold you."

Feeling my heart pinch tight, I rested against him. I felt his hand drift down to my hand, and he threaded his fingers through mine.

While the rain fell hard, in heavy beats against the earth, I fell for Davis in ways I'd never recover from. I'd tie this feeling to the crushed one I had carried for so many years, and I'd make a solid chain, tie it around my neck, and drown.

24

RAE

"Mom, I'm fine, I promise. Davis is teaching me all about his farm and business," I rattled off in between bites of cobbler.

My mom made a sound similar to when she used to get exasperated with me as a kid. "I just want to be sure you're okay. You can tell me if...if something has happened and he—"

"Mom." I squeezed my eyes shut in mortification. "I like him."

Her silence was louder than the dogs barking outside. Davis had run out when one of his cameras picked up a possible cougar sighting. He told me to stay put, and I had zero qualms about doing exactly that.

"You like him, as in..." My mother trailed off.

I had to just say it, rip it off like a Band Aid. Otherwise it would be a slow, painful death.

"As in, we're spending consensual adult time together and enjoying one another's company." My face burned. She'd never even explained the birds and the bees to me, but I'm assuming she knew I wasn't a virgin anymore.

More silence expanded between us. "Well then, that's..." She trailed off once more. "That's a big piece of news."

For two glorious seconds, I assumed she'd be happy. Her build-a-son was spending time with her daughter. That would be a match made in heaven in my parents' world, right? Besides, she'd practically thrown us together the first night we met; this news should thrill her.

"Sweetie, I really wish you would have talked about this with us first," she reproached quietly.

"Why would I have to talk about it with you first?" I scoffed, licking the spoon.

The little camera in front of me showed Davis still stalking around the same tree that he had been for the past ten minutes, the dogs jumping every few seconds and barking at whatever was up there.

"Well, there's things to consider..." She trailed off.

"Such as?"

"He's just delicate, sweetie."

The image of dirty talking, rough sex Davis flashed in my head, making me laugh audibly. "He's not as delicate as you might think."

"Oh for goodness sakes, Raelyn, that's crass. I didn't need to know that."

Talking with my mouth full, I responded, "Sorry, but you said he was *delicate*."

"He's just had a rough go of it, and with his brother, and the way his parents cut ties with him.... he's just closed himself off to people, and it has taken your father and I a lot of time to get him to open up."

It hurt that she seemed to know all these things about him; that he'd opened enough to them to share about his life.

"And what? You think I'll ruin him?"

Her pause spoke volumes. "That's not what I said. It's just—you just got back, and you're still finding your footing."

"Mom, I'm not sure what to say to that." She was right, I was still finding my footing, and I understood what she wasn't saying. If things went badly, it could ruin things for her and my father. "But I do care for him, more than you probably know."

"I'm sure you do, in your own way, sweetie."

The camera showed Davis moving back to the front door.

"Mom, I have to go. I'll be home tomorrow." I hung up before she could say anything else. Not because I didn't love her, but each word she said had rattled me to my core. And if I let Davis know or show any of that, then he'd lose his only support system in the whole world. So, I'd tuck it away, put on a brave face, and enjoy what time I had left of this weekend.

LATER THAT NIGHT, I found out that Davis still liked to read. He had an obsession with old, leather-bound books. In his study, he had oil paintings—a few modern pieces of art, and hundreds of books, stacked, piled, and tucked into shelves. I begged him to read to me, so that was how we ended our second night, reclined against one another in front of the fire, his dogs curled around each of us and my heart pounding in my chest. It would be too easy to fall in love with all of this...with him.

Too easy to love the rain, or the porch, or the soaking tub and scalp massages.

It was as though my past were taunting me, begging me to stay, but daring me to share my secret and see if he'd still welcome me here. The confession burned on the tip of my tongue, but panic seized my throat so much that when I did speak, it was something else that came out.

"Tell me about your family?"

The fire popped and cracked next to us as my question hung in the air. My chest grew tight as I waited for him to answer, but all I felt was the rise and fall of his chest below my cheek.

Finally, after what felt like forever, he stroked my hair and responded.

"There isn't much to tell. I haven't seen my parents in a few years; they wanted warm beaches and to live as close to the sun as humanly possible."

But my parents had mentioned a brother.

Caressing his chest, I hedged. "How come you don't see them?"

Letting out a heavy sigh, he toyed with the ends of my hair. "I just don't."

That was all he had to say to get me to shut up. Obviously, he didn't want to talk about it. I didn't want to push him. After a few beats, he continued reading. I tried to imagine what his parents looked like, and why they'd actively choose not to see Davis again. Although, I had chosen that too, hadn't I? I moved across the country to get away from him, and I suppose they did too…but why?

Blinking, I pushed past the thoughts plaguing me and focused on his words, but the more he read in that perfect, rough timbre, the more my heart softened and swooped.

I had to stop.

Turning in his arms, I stared down at him while his reading paused.

His lips parted, watching me in fascination as I unbuttoned my shirt.

He closed the book and set it aside.

The silence in the room seemed to scream at all the things I should be saying, and all the things he refused to—it didn't matter. We didn't have to explain ourselves; we'd let our bodies say all that we needed to.

I helped him peel his shirt off and then lowered myself to unfasten his jeans.

"Tell me what to do to you," I whispered, peppering his chest with kisses.

Releasing a sound that could rival a growl, he sat up and gripped me by the neck, like he'd done in the bath.

Planting a firm kiss to my jaw, then a soft one to my lips, he shook his head.

"You tell me what you want."

Flames licked at my insides as I processed his words. I hadn't considered what I wanted, except to be touched and to feel good. But, him asking made me feel cherished, desired, and *powerful*. I could ask for anything.

"I want you to try what you showed me in the bath."

The heated look he gave me told me I was right on track with what he'd been craving.

"Okay, but only if you promise me some slow sex upstairs afterward."

Shit, maybe I was wrong. He wanted slow sex? That seemed incredibly intimate.

Nodding, I swallowed around the lump of emotion clogging my throat. How come every time I tried to categorize this as just sex, he seemed to contradict the sentiment? Every time I expected him to pull away, he'd tug me closer, or be sweeter, more thoughtful...more *into* this than I ever expected.

He moved, pulling off his jeans and boxers, nudging me out of my thoughts. Pressing a kiss to my jaw and down my neck, his voice was rough against me as he commanded, "Come here."

Feeling exhilarated, I followed, until I stood before him, peering down into his dark eyes while his palm stroked his stiff erection.

"Straddle me," he rasped, barely audible over the erratic beat in my ears.

Pressing my knee into the leather, and bracing my hand against his shoulder, I lowered myself onto him, inch by inch, until he was fully sheathed.

"Breathe, baby," he whispered, "because you're going to need every single ounce of air."

Oh *fuck*.

Unable to remain still, I began grinding against him, going slow at first, and as I became more comfortable with his size and feeling stretched, he took the opportunity and gripped me by the neck with one massive palm while the other held my hip.

"Shit, you feel good."

He thrust hard and fast, bouncing me on his cock while holding me by the throat.

"Look at these tits. You're fucking perfect, baby," he muttered, breathlessly, before leaning forward to lap at my nipples. He released my neck and hip long enough to cup my breasts while he ran his tongue roughly across each peaked nub. I continued fucking him while he sucked and licked, and then his hungry gaze traveled back up to mine, and I could see the lust consume him. He used two hands to hold my neck while he thrust as hard as he could into my core.

"Fuck. It shouldn't feel this good. How does it feel this good?" he asked accusingly, with a guttural groan.

I moaned, but as the sound left my lungs, he squeezed his fingers, making me squeak. Right as he did it, his hips rotated up, hitting a different spot inside me, somehow going deeper.

I was soaring as lust consumed me, emptying me out and filling me anew. I moved in ways I didn't think possible, bouncing on his dick at a speed I had never known was actually possible outside of a porno.

Right as I was about to combust into a billion pieces, he groaned and lifted me off his lap. The loss of contact on my neck allowed for a gulp of air, but it didn't last long. His hands went to my ribs as he gripped me then slammed my back into the couch, right before thrusting into me.

Pinning my leg to the side, his hips rotated at a breakneck speed, my orgasm slowly building once more as he slowed his thrusts and gripped my neck again.

"God, you take my cock so well."

Heaving raspy breaths, I turned my head to the side, over-whelmed with sensations as he fucked me raw. At some point, he flipped me until I was half hanging off the armrest, ass up, his fingers spreading me.

"You doing okay, baby?"

It thrilled me when he called me that, and even though he'd only done so during sex, I still cherished the endearment. I moaned in response, a sultry plea that didn't sound like me at all.

"I need more." I had come at least twice, but I still wanted more. He had this way of working me right back up after helping me find release.

"Shit, when you tell me that, it just...fuck."

I gripped the edge of the armrest when he lifted my hips and pushed me forward, causing my head to hang over the edge. I heard him spit and felt moisture being rubbed into my tight hole in my rear. Then he lined himself up and thrust into my pussy once more.

This time, his thumb pressed into that tight bundle of nerves in my ass. Lubricated with his spit, it didn't hurt, but I felt every thrust with a new intensity. My entire body shook with each jolt of his hips, every stroke inside my core making me hiss and beg him to go harder until I had fallen so far over the edge that my hair touched the floor and only my ass was left on the arm. He gripped my hip tight enough that I knew I'd have bruises later, pulling me down onto his hard length as he pushed against me one last time. The moment seemed to hang in suspension and then he roared his release, the sheer intensity of his cock jerking inside me setting off my own climax, leaving me screaming in what felt like another language.

My brain was completely dead, my speech gone. My chest was heaving so hard that I wasn't sure I was breathing. When Davis pulled me up and gathered me to his chest, I finally started to regain composure. I had never had that many orgasms in a single fuck. Hell, I had never had that many with another person, period.

Still out of breath, he smiled. "You ready for bed?"

I hummed in response. Ever so gently, he kissed my shoulder, his lips slowly traveling along my neck and along my hairline. It was so intimate, so perfect, that my eyes began to water. I didn't want him to know how much his tenderness mattered, especially after him being a little rough with me. Not that I didn't completely love being dominated by him, but the soft side of him made me melt.

"Was that okay?" he asked in a whisper, taking my hand and kissing along every knuckle.

I half turned, watching as his lips caught on every single one while his eyes stayed on mine.

Giving him a smile, I took his hand and mimicked what he'd done to me, kissing each knob. "It was more than okay."

"Good, then let's go to bed."

I smiled, knowing deep down I was already adding the way he said *go to bed* to a new mental list. It was ever growing, and if my journals were anything to go by, I was completely screwed. Already I was back to loving Davis Brenton, and it barely took any time at all.

I decided I'd worry about it tomorrow; I'd learn how to unravel this feeling in my chest. Tonight, I'd let him make love to me and then sleep in his arms, imagining he was mine.

25

RAE

THE NEXT MORNING, I WOKE TO THE SOUND OF LAUGHTER ECHOING from downstairs. Someone was visiting Davis, and from the sounds of it, it wasn't my parents. So, who else would it be?

Curiosity gnawed away at me as I lay there, listening to their conversation fade in and out, only to be interrupted by random bouts of laughter. Tossing the covers back, I decided it was best just to make my way down and see what was going on.

I pulled on a pair of sweats that had been tossed to the floor last night. I had no idea where they came from. Honestly, I think they were under the covers, and during one of our rounds, I found them and tossed them over. Davis had more than enough flannel tucked away in his spacious closet, so I pulled one on and buttoned it closed then walked to the bathroom to try to salvage whatever was happening with my hair.

Once I felt marginally presentable, I padded toward the stairs and with one foot in descent, I paused.

"So, what happened with the stalker girl?"

Air constricted in my lungs as my hand gripped the railing with force.

Davis replied moments later. "I found out she's fine. I mean, I started at the library, which led to a clusterfuck. I was half tempted to ask Rae for her yearbook when I decided to check out the diner."

"Why would Rae's yearbook have that chick in it?"

My body slowly sank to the top step, almost as if it were caving in on itself.

Davis sounded like he sipped something, then cleared his throat. "She's around the same age, I think. She just graduated from college, and that girl was barely eighteen at the time, I think. I mean, she walked up to my motorcycle the summer prior and had said she was seventeen then, so she would have to be around that age."

His guest laughed. "Shit, she was probably homeschooled, based off the shit you told me."

My chin wobbled as tears began flowing freely down my face. I didn't even feel the burn that I usually did to warn me that they were coming. Fat, salty drops just fell from my lashes, silently securing my future—and the lack of it here.

"Dude, I was homeschooled, don't be a dick. Besides, she was sweet. A little misguided, but sweet."

"I distinctly remember how fucking pissed you'd get every time you went to the library and found a new note stuffed into one of your reserved books," his friend scoffed, and his voice moved closer. "Shit, I remember when we talked about getting that security system installed because you were worried she'd follow you home."

More tears fell, and my heart clenched tight in my chest. It felt like barbed wire was slowly wrapping around it with each word spoken between the two.

He remembered me.

"So what ended up happening at the diner then?" his guest asked.

I swiped at my face with the sleeve of Davis's flannel, preparing my heart. I already knew my parents wouldn't know anything because in spite of all my stalking of Davis, I had never worked up the nerve to actually give him my name...but Carl would have known.

"The manager, old guy with the gray hair? He seemed to know

who I was talking about because he was the one I dealt with when that girl would leave me those VIP—"

"Reservations!" his friend burst out laughing, finishing the sentiment for him.

My face heated, a hiccup got caught in my throat, and suddenly I just wanted to be anywhere but here.

"Yeah, so he knew who I was talking about. He seemed a little cryptic and protective, like he didn't want me to try and reach out or find her, but he made it seem like she was fine."

The memory of Carl sitting next to me, telling me that Davis had asked about a girl, flashed through my mind. I had assumed it was a one-night stand—someone he'd been with or wanted to find again.

It was me.

He'd been asking about me...and Carl *knew*.

His friend made a loud scoffing sound. "You trying to find her, that's cool. If you're looking to somehow get killed or something."

"Gavin, don't be a prick. You know she wasn't like that."

One of the dogs' collars suddenly jingled close to the stairs, and within seconds, the top of Dove's head popped into view. He trotted up until he reached me, plopping his jaw in my lap, like he knew I needed the support.

Gavin made a placating sound before defending himself. "Man, she showed up at the library, when you were having sex. How the fuck did she know, and who does that?"

What in the actual fuck was he talking about?

Did he lie to his friend? He had given me a note and asked me to show up. He set the whole thing up!

"I don't know man, the whole thing just seemed strange. She seemed shocked when I lifted my head. Not like 'I saw someone having sex in the library' but rather 'I saw Davis having sex in the library.' Like she was expecting something completely different."

"Yeah, you there—alone." Gavin laughed again.

What was he talking about? This didn't make any sense at all.

"I don't know. Anyway, just trying to put it behind me."

There was silence between the friends, and then suddenly Gavin spoke up.

"So, am I going to meet this girl you supposedly have up in your bed? And can we talk about the fact that you have one in there for the first time fucking *ever?*"

"It's not that big of a deal," Davis muttered, almost bashfully.

"Since I've known you, you've always had random hookups in the chick's house, a car, or some other place. Never in your house, let alone your bed. Now, I'm hearing she's been here all weekend and is *sleeping* in your bed?"

Silence stretched, then Gavin spoke again.

"All I'm saying is it seems like a big deal...like maybe she's special."

I couldn't hear anymore. What if Davis said I wasn't special, and he'd just gotten too old to care for uncomfortable hookup places? What if it had nothing whatsoever to do with me?

I stood on shaky legs, about to walk away, when I heard Davis finally respond.

"Yeah...I think this might be it for me."

Never mind, this was worse. Now, I had to break his heart, tell him goodbye, and explain how I was the girl who pathetically stalked him all those years ago. The one his friend laughed and joked about. And because I was her, there was absolutely zero chance for the two of us ever working out.

26

DAVIS

"THERE SHE IS!" GAVIN CALLED, ABRUPTLY STANDING FROM THE couch. I followed his trajectory with my eyes and turned to see Rae walking down the stairs, fully dressed and carrying her overnight bag. I knew she would need to leave today, but still, seeing that she was packed and ready to leave so early made my heart twist uncomfortably.

I liked her in my space. I liked her smell, and that the dumb creamer I knew she liked was now in my fridge. I even liked the way she hummed when she watched me work, or when she saw something that excited her. Being around her, having her here, was like plucking one of the stars from the midnight sky and asking it to be happy with you on earth, in your home, and then being shocked when it said yes.

Clearing my thoughts, I moved to get in front of my idiot friend and greeted Rae with a kiss.

"Hey."

She gave me a tight smile in return. "Hey."

Gripping her hand, I lead her into the kitchen and then let her go to make her a cup of coffee. The longer I was able to keep her here, the better.

"Gavin, this is Rae. Rae, Gavin."

I half turned, not seeing Rae's reaction to having a stranger in the house right when she woke up, but her response was sweet enough. "Nice to meet you."

"Yeah, you too. I've heard a lot about you." Gavin gave me an acerbic look while shaking her hand.

"You're what to Davis?" the asshole asked. Fucker knew we hadn't talked about labels yet.

I sipped my coffee, waiting for hers to brew.

"Fuck buddy, I think."

I spit my coffee out, sputtering the remnants down my shirt.

"What?" I tugged the soaked fabric away from my chest, feeling a small burn.

She shrugged and moved toward the door. "That's what we are, right?"

No, that's not what we were.

I didn't hold my fuck buddies in the bath while the rain poured outside. I didn't read to them in front of the fire, and sure as fuck didn't open up to them about my family.

But had I really opened up to her? She had asked last night about my family, but what I had told her was more than I'd told anyone, save for her parents. It wasn't like I was eager to scare her off—and telling her about my past would do just that. She was pulling on her boots when I realized I hadn't responded to her comment out loud. I gave Gavin a look that told him to fuck off and then responded to her.

"Not exactly. Uh, are you already headed back?" Setting my mug down and abandoning the full cup that was supposed to be hers, I followed her to the door. Why did I have the impression that she was pissed at me?

"It was nice to meet you, Gavin!" Rae called, pushing through the screen.

I was hot on her heels, grabbing for her door as she swung it open.

"Hey, are we okay?"

Her gaze wouldn't meet mine; her dark lashes fanned the tops of her cheeks as she inhaled a sharp breath then let it out. Finally, those blue eyes made their way up my torso. In the early morning light, the hint of pink still in the sky—it made her look like something out of a fairytale. Dark, silky hair, pale complexion and those bold eyes, it was a sight I wanted every day for the rest of my life.

"Why wouldn't we be?" she finally replied, giving out a small laugh.

I may not know her super well, but I knew her well enough to know that she was bullshitting me.

"I'm sorry about Gavin just showing up, sometimes he does that, but I figured maybe it was a good thing. He's the only friend I have besides your parents, and well…I wanted you to meet him."

From how tender and thoughtful Rae had been the past two days, I assumed she'd soften at that confession, but her lips turned down into another firm line.

"I liked meeting him."

"Then what's wrong?" I tugged a rogue piece of hair and tucked it behind her ear. My heart pinched tight, worried that she'd suddenly pull away from me. Leave me.

She shook her head slightly while ducking her chin to her chest. "Nothing, I just—I need to get home."

I paused, letting her finish, but she didn't say anything more. I couldn't find my voice, so I stepped away from her car and let her get in.

"I guess I'll see you when I see you." *Please kiss me. Tell me you'll call me when you get back. Don't break what we just put together.*

"K…" She opened her car door, my throat constricted painfully tight when she slammed it shut. I stood, battling the emotion clogging my chest, and watched as she reversed and drove off. With every stride she put between us, I felt the space pull taut, becoming a lesson and a crude warning.

Hands pinned to my hips, I watched for far longer than I should have then finally turned around and walked inside. I had no idea why she pulled away, but it felt typical. Most people in my life usually did.

DAVIS: Sorry again about the other day. I tried to call you a few times, everything okay?

Rae: I saw that, sorry. I've been crazy busy helping Nora with the details of her new place. I'll call you tonight.

DAVIS: Never heard from you last night…can I see you this weekend?

Rae: Can't. Helping Nora pack. Raincheck

Davis: Am I missing something? I thought we were…

Rae: We were what?

Davis: Never mind. Just call me when you're free.

DAVIS: You're not delivering anymore, or is it just that you don't want to deliver to me?

Rae: I gave the job to a kid who just graduated from high school, he needs the tips.

Davis: Right.

DAVIS: I feel like an idiot even asking, but you wouldn't want to come up this weekend, would you? I miss you.

Rae: I want to…I do. I just…I can't do this right now, Davis. I'm sorry. Please know that I wanted to, desperately, but I have too much going on with my parents and the diner right now. I need to focus on them.

Davis: You just broke up with me via text. Never thought of you as a coward, but I guess people surprise me all the damn time. Have a nice life, Rae.

THE BELL over the entrance clanged cheerily as I sat with my back to the door so I didn't have to see what sorry soul was wandering in. I didn't like being in here. I didn't like being around people, not for any specific reason other than they pissed me off. Always talking, being loud, coughing and sneezing. Just fucking noisy.

But I found myself wandering in here every day for the past two weeks, plopping down and ordering an obscene amount of food, only to have it all boxed up and then dropped off with Saul, one of the homeless guys that held a cardboard sign down on Maple Street. He had the balls to post up in one of the nicest neighborhoods in all of Macon. Unfortunately, he'd likely be better off going over to Salmon and Fir—they're poor, but generous. Pricks with money clogged the whole damn world up, but I was one of those pricks, so I did what I could to give back. Which was why I didn't want Roger or Millie to suffer just because I wasn't putting any more delivery orders in.

I hadn't put one in since Rae explained that some new kid now had the job. It wasn't that I stopped ordering because she'd stopped doing it. I decided to come in person just to piss her off. To rattle her, I guess, even though it was more of a punishment to me on the rare occasion that I did see her. Sometimes, I'd come in, but she wouldn't be here. On those days, I ended up walking around town, down by the coffee shop, and eventually into Rae's neighborhood. I wasn't stalking her…just stretching my legs.

"Oh!" I heard someone gasp to my left. I already knew it was Rae without looking. Sure enough, she had pushed through the kitchen doors, holding a plastic tub between her fingers. I didn't even bother saying anything to her. This was a part of the new dance we did with one another. She'd unexpectedly see me and then scurry away, like her ass was on fire. I must have done a number on her, fucked her in the head or something, because she couldn't even talk to me.

Each time I heard her gasp, or saw the way she blushed when she saw me, made the stone in my chest rattle against my bones. Reminding me that I tried to make it beat, and I fucked it up.

I was a lost cause.

"Can I get you something? We need to clear the table," Carl grumbled from the other side of me, breaking the odd silence between Rae and I. Turning, I surveyed the older man, trying to understand his shitty attitude toward me. What I'd done to him, I had no fucking clue, but just like the rest of Macon—he hated me. I just couldn't figure out why.

Reaching for my wallet, I pulled out a wad of cash, tossed it on the table and barked back, "Get me a few boxes and I'll go."

He grunted but moved to the kitchen. Three agonizing minutes later, Rae came out holding two boxes and headed straight for me, making my chest grow tense.

"Here you go." She gently put the boxes on the table in front of me then stepped back.

"Um..." Tucking a few pieces of hair behind her ear, she hesitated.

I waited.

"Um, I know why you're coming in every day...and I feel bad about that, seeing as you're trying to take care of my parents financially, but I know you hate it. So, I just wanted to remind you that you can place orders online and still have them delivered."

I scoffed, shaking my head. I needed to go, get the fuck away from her before I did something stupid, like drag her to my truck and kiss her. Just to piss her off. Or to get the truth from her lips. I knew she was hiding something; I just couldn't figure out what.

"Whatever you say, Rae."

"You should know..." She paused, her lip wobbling just the smallest bit. "I'm not the one who decided to hire Todd."

I watched her toy with the edge of her apron, chewing on her luscious lip. I thought of how they'd wrapped around my cock when she was in the hen house. I thought of how she kissed the top of my dogs' heads, and how easily those lips were always spread in a smile while she was with me that weekend.

"Right...just like you didn't just decide that we weren't a thing anymore, out of the blue?"

Suddenly she lifted her head and snapped. "Are you saying I did it on purpose?"

"Don't treat me, or this"—I waved my hand between us—"like we're idiots, Rae. It's exhausting." I angled closer, which took us almost to the far wall.

Her blue eyes darkened as they tipped up to meet mine. Her pink lips parted; her throat bobbed as she straightened her spine.

"We were just a weekend fling, nothing serious. Nothing to get upset over...no reason to have an attitude or get offended."

I stepped back. The pull to touch her was too strong.

"If that were true then why are you worried about the deliveries?" Reaching out, I skimmed her cheek with my knuckle. "And why are you barely holding back tears right now?"

She wet her lips, her eyes searching mine frantically. I knew I had her. She couldn't answer without admitting that she had deeper feelings for me.

"For the record, it was never casual to me. It meant something. I wanted to build on that weekend. I—"

"What are you doing?" Carl's gruff voice broke me out of my thoughts.

Keeping my eyes on her, I stepped back, putting distance between us.

"Just on my way out."

"Good. Maybe it would be best if you didn't come back." Angry gray eyes stormed under thick eyebrows, glaring at me. Behind the human wall known as Carl was an entire restaurant full of people who were silently watching our exchange.

"Carl, he's fine. We were just talking." Rae snapped at him, pushing past us both and heading behind the counter. "And you know you can't kick him out, you don't have the right."

She focused on me, her hands on a few plastic menus. "You should go though, Davis. I have to get back."

I gave her one last look before turning and pushing through the glass door.

27

RAE

Gripping the underside of the box, I heaved it up on top of the cluttered counter, letting out a string of curse words. That was only the third box that I had carried in, but they were heavy—full of Nora's design books. The previous one was of all her mother's old dishes and pans. The one before that was all her shoes. She had way too many.

"Oh my gosh, I'm already tired." Nora dramatically swept inside and fell onto her secondhand sofa. It was decent looking once we'd flipped the cushions to hide the stains. Most of the furniture was purchased online at different sales and swap sites, but Nora made it all work with the right accent lamp or pillow. All in all, her new place was cozy and cute, and all hers. I was insanely jealous of the fact that not only did she qualify for a home loan, thanks to a slew of online designs she'd been working on for some time and a portfolio much larger than I initially realized, but she snagged the house and closed within just a few weeks' time.

Once Nora had gotten over her aversion to the next-door neighbor—her resolution involved tall shrubbery and a fence that would go all the way to their shared mailbox—her entire purchase moved along quickly.

I was beyond happy for her, but while she was busy moving and closing on her first home, I was busy burying my feelings and trying to pretend they had never existed in the first place, as well as dodging the man who was like a second father to me. I'd had a heart to heart with Carl regarding his strange comment about Davis asking about some girl, when he could have easily warned me that it had been me he was asking about. He apologized, saying he just wasn't sure what to say, but it still left me feeling raw and a little guarded.

"WHAT ARE YOU DOING?" I asked, popping a carrot into my mouth as I moved around the kitchen. Nora was in the living room, standing on her tiptoes with a sheet, trying to cover the window.

"I don't want him to see inside. Come over here and help me." She grunted as her body stretched along the expanse of the wall.

"Oh my gosh, you're being ridicul—"

"Shut it, Rae, and come over and help. It's almost dusk. What if he goes for a run or something and sees inside?"

"He'll probably just keep running." I wiped my hands on my jeans and took my time getting to her.

"You're so funny. Now hold this up and hand me a tack."

I gripped the edge of the dark purple sheet and did as I was told. "You're using tacks?"

Nora's left foot landed on her side table, while her right balanced on the edge of the sofa.

"I really don't think you understand how desperate of a situation this is."

Was she sweating?

Standing under her, to support her and prepare for the tack, I asked curiously, "Did something happen between you two since you got here? Because you're acting a little unreasonable."

She grunted to herself. "Go into the wall, dammit! And to answer your question—yes, he saw me."

"Got it!" she yelled, jumping down and heading to the other side.

From the outside, this was going to look ridiculous. If I hadn't pushed Davis out of my life, I could probably call him and ask him to come over and help put up the shades, then I could go home with him and snuggle in his bed and wake up to kinky morning sex.

"What happened?" I needed to stop thinking about Davis. What I had done was the only option I had in front of me, but that didn't mean it wasn't ripping me to shreds.

Nora continued busying herself with the sheet, using her teeth to keep the tack arranged, then grabbing it and smashing her thumb into the back to pin the fabric in place. Once she was done, she let out a big sigh and jumped down.

"He saw my ass from over his side of the fence. It was the first night I slept here."

"When you stole my sleeping bag?"

Clicking her tongue, she rolled her eyes. "You can obviously have it back."

I grabbed my water bottle off the floor and sipped it. "Any-way...explain..."

My best friend stomped toward her bedroom, grabbing another sheet, calling over her shoulder, "He yelled over the fence, asking me to please be *courteous* of the other neighbors and cover up."

I choked on my water, wiping at my face while I trailed behind her. "Were you naked?"

She shook the sheet out. "Of course not, I was wearing a robe. It was just a little short, and I didn't realize he was out when I bent over to check my new garden."

"You inherited a garden?" My eyes were huge because Nora loved gardening but was terrible at starting them.

Repeating what she'd done in the living room, I moved to support her as she began pinning the sheet over the window. "I did, and it's so cute. I'm terrified of killing it, so I have been checking it at all intervals of the day."

"So, what did you do—I mean, when he said that?" I softened my tone, hating that this jerk had already seemed to shake my bestie. It was enough that he'd already crushed her; he could be nice. It wouldn't kill the idiot.

With a big sigh, Nora blew a rogue curl out of her face. "I just stood up, turned to look at him and said, 'Maybe you can work on keeping your eyes on your side of the fence, and I'll work on wearing pants,' then I sauntered inside, shaking my ass with every step."

My head tipped back as a cackle erupted from my chest. "You did not say that!"

"I did, and I'd say it again if I were brave enough to go in the backyard again, which I am not."

This wouldn't do. "Nora, you can't give up your beautiful back-yard, especially with your new garden."

"I haven't given it up. I just time it so I go back there when he leaves for work. I don't know if he lives with anyone, but so far no one else has come out and harassed me."

"Are we going to talk about how you know when he leaves for work already?"

Her blue eyes narrowed as her nose flared. "Are we going to talk about what happened between you and Davis?"

I spun on my heel. "Nope, let's figure out dinner."

"Come on, Rae!" She chased after me. "You disappeared all weekend, then came back and wouldn't smile or talk for like two weeks. Now there's no word of him?"

When I dipped down to grab my purse, she placed her hands over mine, stopping my trajectory.

"Come on, Rae, talk to me."

I knew she was right, but it didn't change that I didn't want to talk about it. My feelings after I left Davis's house were locked up inside me, and that's where I wanted them to stay, so I could hold the memories forever and never have to let them go. But Nora was my best friend, and she'd gone through all of it with me. It wouldn't be fair to pull out now.

Deflating, I dropped my purse. "We need vodka, and a comfort-able place to sit."

Nora ran toward the kitchen on bare feet. "On it!"

I EXPLAINED THE WHOLE WEEKEND, leaving out the filthy sex parts. The gas fireplace illuminated the sparse living room as Nora faced me with her feet out, cradling the bottle of vodka in her lap.

"So, he knows," she hiccuped, "but he doesn't know."

I nodded. That was the extent of it. He knew about me...but he had no idea I was *that* girl who used to leave him notes in his library books and walked over to him while he gassed up his bike and tried to tell him my name.

"But I'm confused..." She tilted her head, letting her curls fall off her shoulder. "Why would he go looking for you now?"

That was something I hadn't entirely worked out yet. "From what I can gather, I think it was guilt."

"But guilt over what?"

Leaning forward to grab the bottle from her, I took a large swig. "The note he left me, I'm assuming, telling me to meet him there."

Saying it all out loud felt like tiny pricks from a needle, jabbing at my heart. Reminding me how stupid I was to fall into bed with the man who'd so thoughtlessly hurt me.

"But from what you said, it sounded like he didn't give you the note. He sounded confused as to why you were there."

Concentrating on my lap, I thought over that part of the conversation between Gavin and Davis. It still seemed so confusing. If he hadn't given me the letter, then who would have? And why? What would anyone have to gain from that?

"Well, what did Davis say when you asked him about it?" The vodka must be hitting her, because I had already told her I hadn't talked to Davis in over two weeks, except for at the diner the other day. Which was uncomfortable and painful. He sounded so hurt, but I knew if I had just explained it to him—told him I was his stalker—he'd just sneer and walk out of my life, and what if he cut my parents out too? They loved him so much and would absolutely blame me if he left their life.

There was no future for us as long as we had the past.

"I broke up with him, we can't—"

"You broke up with him?" Nora yelled, staggering to her knees.

212

I leaned back, shielding my face as she began pummeling me with a pillow. "Yes, I had to."

"He"—the pillow landed on my shoulder— "is" —another hit landed to my chest—"the love" —a crash sounded as the pillow hit her lamp—"of your life." She finally sagged back into the couch, drunk and blotchy faced. "He sounds like he really cares about you, Rae."

"He cares about the new me, but once he realizes who the old me is, he'll run away."

I tilted my head, taking a long pull on the vodka.

"So, he loves the new you, but will hate the old you? That doesn't make any sense."

I laughed, feeling lighter than I had in weeks. "Now he *loves* me? He definitely did not say he loved me."

"Rae, you're being an idiot."

Laughing again, I shook my head. "Yeah, and you're a peeping tom."

"Peeping Toms are what *Colson* did. I was a naked victim. I should be able to check my garden while I'm in the nude, Rae. It's biblical."

"You're right, Nora-Bora—you should be able to be naked Eve out in your garden. Colson dumb face can suck it."

The air was getting fuzzy, and suddenly I was so sleepy. "I'm going to sleep here tonight, then I'm going to wake up and kick your neighbor's ass."

"Good," Nora mumbled, settling into the other side of the couch. "Then I'll tell Davis tomorrow that you love him, and you want to have his babies."

"Okay, good." I couldn't remember what else she said. Sleep claimed me, and I dreamed of little babies with navy eyes and dark hair.

AFTER MY DRUNKEN night with Nora, I had an epiphany, and it was all thanks to Nora and her garden.

I sat on my back porch, sketching out the ideas that started coming faster than I could contain. I pulled up my computer and began pulling up tab after tab of research. I would need to start the process immediately if I was going to pull off the idea that had been rolling around in my head.

Finally, after what felt like an eternity of being home, I felt like I had a clear vision for how to help the town before winter hit. Our peak tourist season was about to end, and with it, several business owners would leave for warmer climates until March, and the others just wouldn't entertain changes or ideas until well after the holidays. It had to be now.

"I thought I'd find you out here," my mom said gently. Things between us since I came home that weekend with Davis had been strained and awkward. I refused to talk about it, and it seemed like it was all she could think about. Nearly every day, she'd tried to bring it up in one way or another.

Instead of answering, I smiled up at her.

"Want some coffee or a snack? You look like you're hard at work."

Relief sailed through my lungs. She wasn't going to bring up Davis, for once.

"I'm actually okay right now, but want to see what I'm up to?"

She took the chair next to me, and leaned over to look at my sketches. "Oh, Rae!"

A warm light hit me square in the chest as I realized what her approval meant to me. We might not have addressed the Davis situation, but seeing her smile felt like walking on the sun.

"You think it's a good idea?" Oh fuck, were those tears in her eyes?

"I think it's a wonderful idea, sweetie. This could be so good for the town, and for all the businesses. I know so many people are so scared right now."

I flipped over a page. "I know, and I figured maybe it was time I started digging in my heels, trying to get this started. I have tried getting in touch with the owners, but trying to connect one on one has been a scheduling nightmare."

Swiping at her face, she squeezed my arm. "I'm so glad to have you home, honey. Dad and I will help in any way we can, okay?"

"Okay," I said around the lump in my throat. For the first time since returning home, I actually felt like I had a reason to be here. I had a purpose, more than just fawning over the mountain recluse who broke my heart.

After a few minutes of mom looking over all my ideas, she finally stood and made to go back in the house. She hesitated near the sliding door.

"I just wanted to let you know that Davis is coming over for dinner tonight."

Standing, I began gathering my things.

"No, sweetie, please don't go again." Mom held her hand out, silently begging me to stay.

"Mom, I'm not going over this again." I gathered everything into my arms. "I told you things didn't work out between us, and I just don't care to be in his company."

"This was exactly why I didn't want you two getting involved."

Not the first time I heard her say this, but it didn't matter. I was an adult now; I didn't owe her an explanation.

"I'm sorry, Mom."

"Just tell me what happened. Help me understand." Again, her hands were out in that gesture that said she just wanted to understand me. I hated that gesture.

"Nothing, Mom."

I moved past her, heading inside, but the second I stepped foot inside, I froze.

Davis was there in an untucked gray Henley, opened at his throat. His jaw was covered in a few days' worth of growth, but his eyes were dull, and a sadness seemed to hang around him like a raincloud.

"Rae." He dipped his head in greeting then walked into the kitchen, breaking eye contact with me and ultimately dismissing me.

It stung, but I had expected that. I had done nothing but shut him out for weeks. Of course he walked away like I meant nothing.

"Just sit and have dinner. I'll put you on the opposite end of him, and Dad and I will talk the entire time," Mom said in my ear, sneaking up behind me.

"Mom, no." I couldn't. She had no idea how painful it was to be around him when I had feelings so big—when I hurt so tremendously bad from what I'd overheard in his house.

I heard her let out a heavy sigh as I tucked myself away in my room, starving for more than just dinner.

28

DAVIS

"Mr. Brenton, how nice of you to stop in again...for the third time this week," Mabel said in a tart tone, like she was worried I'd jump and attack her any second.

"Is it a problem that I'm visiting so frequently, Mabel?"

Her face turned a pinkish color. "No, not at all. I just... Well, you've never stopped in so often."

I fucking hated coming into town, but I was still stupidly here, no matter how many times I had talked myself out of coming. Somehow, I still found myself driving down the mountain and spending my days here, with these exasperating people.

I was two steps from passing Mabel's desk when she piped up again.

"Although——" She paused, waiting to garner my attention. "Today, we're closing early, so I don't know if it's a good time to start browsing."

I could feel the sunburn I'd gotten over the weekend pull tight as I frowned. "It's only noon."

Mabel beamed excitedly. "Yes, well, do you know the Jacksons' daughter, Raelyn? She's holding a small gathering in the town square, where she hopes to drum up some extra business for the local shops around town. It's the last warm weekend of tourist season, so she's hosting a big market, with booths and games. There's bouncy houses for the kids and music."

It had only been a week since I had seen Rae. How the fuck did she get all this shit done—and why?

My mind spun back to a few conversations about helping the town, and her being worried about the shops here.

I must have been standing there too long because Mabel cleared her throat. "Anyway, it'll be quite the event."

"Uh…" I grabbed a random brochure about the best place in Macon to get Wi-Fi, something I already knew, but I needed something to do with my hands. "So Rae will be at this event then, since she's spearheading it?"

Mabel beamed brightly, shuffling papers and tucking a few stray pens back into her drawer. "Absolutely. She's going to be stopping at each shop booth to give her marketing tips to the owners. We're all looking forward to it."

"What on earth could the library gain from all that? You're funded by our tax dollars."

Clicking her tongue, she answered tersely. "There's people in charge of how we spend that money, and it wouldn't hurt to hear her ideas on how to make the town look better."

Right. Turning on my heel, I exited the library, wincing as the sun slammed into me. It was nice, but it was also annoying. I should have brought a hat. Climbing back into my truck, I reversed and headed to the town square. There seemed to be a bit of a bounce in everyone's step as I watched families walk down the sidewalks. There were colorful balloons everywhere, and kids with half their faces painted and a shit ton of cotton candy. Somewhere inside me was a flicker of pride for what Rae was doing for this town. I may hate Macon, but it was still where I bought groceries and filled up my tank with gas.

Finding a place to park was nearly impossible, so I parked near the diner and just decided to walk the rest of the way. I was out of the truck and ducking to see if I had a hat stashed somewhere under the seat, when I heard someone clearing their throat behind me.

"Davis, right?"

I spun around, seeing Rae's friend Nora. On instinct, I narrowed my eyes, already defensive. Whatever the fuck this chick was about to dish out, I was ready to—

"I have wanted to catch you alone for some time. Walk with me?" She cut into my thoughts and placed her hand in the crook of my arm.

Slamming my truck door, I walked woodenly next to her. I hated being unsure if I should trust someone or not.

"You know I've lived here my entire life?" Nora tilted her head, then amended her statement. "Well, except for my time in California, when I was in college."

I didn't respond, but we continued to walk. I noticed the flower baskets that had previously been dead weeds were now overflowing with color and fresh flowers.

"Rae has lived here her whole life too, except for New York."

I knew this already.

"She's changed a lot over the years, though. Did you know she had braces?"

Not trying to be a total dick, I shook my head.

"Yeah, and so did I…except I had mine in middle school. Rae didn't get hers until later in high school."

Why did I need to know any of this?

"No offense, but why the fuck are you telling me any of this? The last person I want to talk about is Rae, and I have a feeling you already know that."

She waited a moment before answering, leaving her hand tucked into my arm, until finally she let out a small breath and stopped.

"See, that's exactly why I'm telling you, because I know you *do* want to talk about Rae, and I know she wants you to talk to her."

"She doesn't," I scoffed. "She must be lying to you too, just like her parents, but we—"

"She told me that she had the best weekend of her life with you," she said, and suddenly the air seemed to leave my lungs. "But she felt like the only option she had was to cut things off with you."

What the… "Why?"

"That's what I want you to figure out. I know why, and you have some work ahead of you to get her talking. I can tell you that she cares much more deeply for you than you realize, and based off the talking she did in her sleep the other night, she has some very strong…" Clearing her throat, she laughed and choked out, "sexual feelings for you too."

Searching Rae's friend's face, like it could give me the answer, I waited for her to say more.

When she didn't, I tried to grasp onto what she was expressing.

"So, you're saying I need to push harder for her to explain what happened?"

"I'm saying you need to push, pull, and don't take no for an answer. *Make* her talk to you." With that, she untucked her hand and sauntered away toward a cotton candy stand.

THE FESTIVAL, or whatever they were calling it, was in full swing by the time I maneuvered into the center of the town square. Billy Jameson and a few of his friends were up on a makeshift stage, strumming guitars and singing a happy melody that had people dancing and laughing. The overall vibe of the town was jovial and carefree—it was the happiest I'd ever seen anyone in Macon. That flicker of pride grew into a roaring flame for Rae. I didn't know of anyone else who could have done this for our city. No one else would have cared enough to.

The more I thought over what Nora had said, the more I realized how much of an idiot I had been regarding letting her go. She wanted to end it with a text, and I fucking let her. She wasn't the coward, I was—but I was about to fix that.

Along the outside of the square, rows of partitioned booths were neatly arranged, open and ready to greet customers. From what I could tell, every single shop from Macon had a little tent, showcasing what they offered. Even the coffee shops had a spot, although theirs were set up in small food trucks, serving iced coffees for a dollar and black coffee for just fifty cents. I scanned the different shops represented, seeing Roger and Millie greeting people while they sold pies, and there, two spots down, was Rae.

My stomach flipped, and my chest seemed to expand at seeing her stand there in a pencil skirt and flirty blouse. She was talking to the owners of the Pine Stop—a small market that saw about six customers daily, if that.

Walking slowly, I edged to the side so that she wouldn't see me. Just watching her in her element, pointing to the tablet she was carrying and using her hands to talk, made me smile. I liked seeing her beam as bright as a ray of sunshine. But with that pride came swift possessiveness. I wanted that light all to myself. I wanted her in my life—in my dark, cloudy existence. Currently, it felt as though all of Macon had a piece of her except me. My chest felt empty, my head dizzy as I continued to walk in her orbit without her knowing I was there.

Finally, she smiled and said goodbye, heading in the direction of her parents' tent. There, she set her tablet down, glanced at her phone with a cute furrow to her brows, and said something to them both before slipping through the back of their tent.

Where was she going?

Quickly, I cleared the last tent in the row and veered to the small alleyway that acted as a sort of backstage for the event, cluttered with overflow packing materials, little camping chairs, a portable bathroom, and a few rolling coolers. Just beyond the alley was a glass door leading into city hall. That was where I found Rae, tugging out a key and unlocking the bottom lock then slipping inside.

She had an actual key to the city. The pride growing in my chest swelled.

Within seconds, I was silently slipping in, seeing she was already up a level and seemed to be headed to the public works office. I quickly followed, ensuring I kept pace with her. I cleared the steps right as the glass door to one of the offices swung shut, and a lamp clicked on inside, acting like a beacon.

Twisting the brass knob, I tugged the door open and let it shut silently behind me. The floor was covered in old, worn carpet, but past the receptionist desks were two offices, one of which was a corner office. I would bet money that was where Rae was. Thankfully the door to the office wasn't shut all the way, just cracked. Carefully placing my hand against it, I found Rae inside and tried to make sense of what I was seeing.

29

DAVIS

Rae stood in the middle of the floor with her shoes and skirt on the floor around her. Her ass and white lacy thong was on display and music played from her cell as she began unbuttoning her shirt.

What the fuck? Was someone in there with her?

Anger and jealousy swept through me so fast, I nearly lost my breath. It clouded my vision and made it impossible to think, which was why I pushed on the door and ambled through with a curse on my lips.

I began searching the room frantically, but the room was empty. The shades were slightly open, but not enough that anyone could see her.

"Davis, what the hell?" Rae yelped, grabbing the lapels of her blouse and hugging them close to her body as she stared at me, mouth hanging open.

"What the fuck, Rae?" I argued, my eyes still shifting around the room, searching for her lover.

Clenching her jaw and tapping her foot, she shook her head. "No, you first. What the heck are you doing up here? Did you *follow* me?"

Obviously, I had.

"I was trying to talk to you, but you seemed like you were on a mission. I didn't think I'd find you in here *stripping*."

A little frustrated growl emanated from her chest as she moved to the corner of the room, snatching a bag off the floor. "I wasn't stripping! Well, I was, but only because I can barely breathe or take a full step in that skirt. It's so insanely uncomfortable. It's my lunch break—an entire hour alone, where I get to rest, and eat, and not wear that demon skirt or this fucking bra."

Oh.

Well, shit.

My face warmed a bit as the reality of the moment hit. "Sorry. I didn't mean to disturb you, but were you just going to sit in Kelly Travis's office naked?"

She laughed, which came out more like a snort. "No, I brought sweats and a blanket. But I do have her permission—not to strip—but to use her office while the festival goes on."

"Right." I cleared my throat. How the fuck was I supposed to transition into my speech about not taking no for an answer?

Rae continued unbuttoning her shirt, while turned away from me. "So, why are you here?"

"Told you, wanted to talk to you."

This wasn't going well.

"You said that." Her shirt came off, and that silky skin was on display. She looked darker, like she'd gotten sun, along with a few more freckles that had recently come in. Her fingers went up to the center of her back, reaching for her bra. Fuck, she was going to strip with me in the room?

My soul may have actually left my body when she reached around and unclasped her bra, letting it slide down her arms. She was still turned away from me, but even seeing her back—knowing what I was missing—was enough to stun me to utter silence.

This was too much to bear.

"Davis?"

I closed my eyes, trying to concentrate, but she was standing there *in a thong*, with no bra. There wasn't any hope for me.

224

Finally, trying to wrangle at least something, I blurted, "I miss you."

She froze, pausing with the shirt sleeve she was slipping back on. I took that as a good sign and moved closer.

"I think it's ridiculous that I miss you. I mean..." I advanced two more steps. "I never even really had you, yet I feel like I lost a piece of myself. It wasn't just sex to me; it was so much more."

I was right behind her, my lips at her neck as she continued to face the wall. From here, I could see her chest rising and falling rapidly. She still only had one sleeve pulled on, the other half of her shirt hanging down her back. Swallowing the lump in my throat, I slowly raised my hand and touched the base of her neck, brushing a few strands of hair to the side.

When she didn't flinch away, I grew bolder and slowly moved the shirt off her shoulder, letting it slip to the ground once more.

"I miss this freckle; do you even know you have it? It's the cutest fucking thing," I whispered, brushing the tip of my thumb over the tan line at the base of her neck. She shuddered, and I drew closer, now pressing a kiss to her shoulder. The shadows in the room covered us, with just a small slice of light coming in from the shades, and the music from her phone—it felt like a secret we were sharing.

Rae turned her face, with her chin nearly resting on the shoulder I'd just kissed. Flicking my gaze up to meet hers, I moved my lips over the space again, bringing my hand up to gently hold her waist.

Her lips parted, those blue eyes staring with a heat that burned as hot as the thing searing my chest.

"What do you want from me, Davis?"

I knew she wasn't asking what I wanted in this moment. It was a question that came from a broken place, and the way her lip wobbled told me she needed to know if I wanted a future with her.

Grabbing her other hip, I pulled her flush against my chest and whispered in her ear.

"I want to take you home and let you steal my flannels. I want you in my kitchen when I make you breakfast. I want you on my

225

chest when I wake up. I know I'm not perfect, Rae…but give me a chance to show you."

She spun in my arms, twisting her fingers into the hair at my neck. Her naked breasts pushed against my shirt, and I suddenly needed there to be less clothing between us, but that would come. Right now I just needed to hold her.

Moving my hand up her back, I crushed her against me, my nose stuck in her hair, inhaling her scent. Fuck, I missed it.

I barely had her for any time at all, but I'd already become an addict.

"You showed me what it would be like—" I wrestled with the words I wanted to say, and pushed out what I could manage, "and then you just walked away." It came out crushed, like broken glass, but I couldn't control it. I was feeling so much as I caged her in with my arms.

She hiccupped, which made me dip my chin and lean back. Gripping her jaw, I lifted her face, and sure enough, there were fat tears trailing down her cheeks. My chest burned again, this time with something other than self-deprecation. This time it was that I'd caused her to feel pain.

"Hey." I swiped at her tears. "Talk to me, baby."

Shaking her head, she hiccupped again, her lips quivering. "I just…I didn't want to leave you, I felt like"—sniffling, she darted her eyes to the side—"I had no other choice."

"But why?"

Shaking her head again, she buried her face in my chest.

"Will you come home with me tonight?" I waited for her refusal, unwilling to hope.

Her voice shuddered as she gave it to me anyway. "Yes."

I wouldn't press about the entire weekend, even though in that moment all I wanted was her to promise not to leave me no matter what happened. Instead, I'd take advantage of what time we had before she had to get back.

"You're supposed to be relaxing and eating before you get back, right?"

She hummed in response.

Trailing the line of her thong down the crack of her ass, I smiled against the side of her head. "Well, what if I help you relax, and then you can eat?"

"In here?"

"Are you morally against having sex in Kelly's office?" My finger moved lower, making Rae moan.

"Not at all," she gasped, pushing her breasts into my chest. "In fact, she was a bitch to me when we were in high school. Fuck her office."

Rae wrapped her legs around my waist when I lifted her, holding tight to the collar of my shirt.

"Then I know exactly what we need to do." I turned and lowered her to the sofa. The thing looked expensive; too bad I was about to eat Rae's pussy on it.

"Take these off." I snapped her thong against her hip, and she gave me a seductive smile in return but complied and leaned back, completely bare, on the couch.

I palmed my erection through my jeans, already hard as stone.

"Spread your legs." I watched as she did as I said, showing me that slick, pink pussy. "Hands on your tits, push them together." Rae did as I said, and while she rocked her hips forward, I peeled my shirt off and kneeled before her. I had to give my cock some relief, so I unbuttoned my jeans and pulled them down just halfway, allowing some breathing room.

Then I leaned forward and shoved my hands under Rae's ass, dragging her closer, until her core met my mouth. There, I plunged my tongue deep inside her then slowly pulled it out and drug it up over her clit.

Rae let out a low whimper while rocking into my touch. I knew we didn't have all the time in the world, and I wanted my dick inside her at some point, so I focused on licking over her mound, moving to her clit and sucking. I'd lean back to see what I'd done, only to lap at it in small circles. I heard cursing—begging—from above me, her hands having slipped from her breasts and now gripped my hair with an iron fist.

I flattened my tongue, swiping up and down, making a mess of her cunt, knowing it would ruin the sofa beneath her. With one last suck of her clit, she came, with a hard cry and fierce tug of my hair.

Moving back, but keeping my hands in place, I spread Rae's legs wide—watching her orgasm drip down the length of her slit and trickle to the sofa.

"This is leather, you know...pretty expensive," I continued, watching her glistening heat. "Guess what you're going to do now?"

Rae's chest was still heaving when she gasped out, "What?"

"Sit up, press that soaked pussy into that leather, and open up that beautiful mouth."

I stood, holding out my hand to help her sit up. She did as I said, sitting on the couch and rocking her hips, still too worked up to stop. Her eyes went to my boxers, her tongue darted out to wet her lips, and I knew she was ready for me.

Her fingers dug into the elastic band at my waist, and once my erection bobbed free, she was after it with a moan.

Her fist went to the base of my cock, her tongue swirling the tip, and then she was going all the way, taking as much of me as she could. Those blue eyes tipped up, meeting mine as she gagged, and hell, it was so fucking hot. I pressed my hips forward, fucking the back of her throat, but it was too much. I was already ready to blow, and it wouldn't be in her mouth, or on her body. I wanted inside that tight heat.

Shoving my hand into her hair, I slowly pushed so she'd let me go.

"I need to be inside you," I whispered, trying to contain how out of breath I was. She didn't normally make me lose my breath like this when sucking me off, but fuck if this time wasn't taking all the air out of my lungs. She didn't even have to suck; just touching me would have done it.

"Come here." I moved her to the desk that was near the window.

Through the shades, we could see the entire festival sprawled out before us. "Look at what you did." I stroked down her back, pushing her forward, so her chest pressed into the desk. "Keep your eyes on the window." I reached for the drawstring to open the shades and pulled them until there was an unobstructed view.

Then I aligned myself with her center and pushed into her from behind.

She was so tight, and so fucking wet.

Pulling out, I hissed as I slammed back in.

"Look at what you did, Rae." I moved my hips, entering her slowly. "I'm so fucking proud of you."

The desk creaked and groaned as I picked up speed, my dick slamming into her heat over and over.

Rae whined, grasping for purchase on the desk as I hovered over her back. Her fingers caught on stray papers, pulling them off, and then she went for a mug of pens. "Fuck, fuck, fuck…" she gasped as I fucked her into the desk.

"I want you to come as you watch what you created, Rae. Keep your eyes on your dream, as I fuck you so good that you feel like you could fly."

I moved my fingers around her hip, rubbing at her clit, and that was it. She arched her back, screaming my name as I pumped furiously in and out of her, until I was coming too.

"Rae, fuck, baby…so fucking good." I said breathlessly, my chest heaving up and down as I bent over her body, peppering kisses on her neck.

"I'm not done," she rasped, pushing back at me to stand on wobbly legs.

The fuck she wasn't.

"What?"

Her blue eyes darted back to a spot behind me.

I watched as she walked to the leather desk chair that had been shoved to the side by me. Then with a coy smile, she sat down, letting our joined releases leak out of her.

"She's going to hate us so much." I laughed, lightly rubbing at the small beard I had growing. Was it too late to be self-conscious about how I looked? Lately, I hadn't been thinking too much about it.

"Serves her right. Now if you don't mind...feed me. I'm starving."

"Say no more." I grabbed the salad, popped it open, and handed her a fork.

30

RAE

THE FLANNEL SHIRT I WORE HUNG LOOSELY ON ME AS I SAT IN THE window seat of Davis's office. We were in his work building, where he was typing a few things into the computer and shuffling papers. Dove and Duke were curled on either side of me as I watched the trees sway and flutter under a rogue wind. Yesterday was a blur, still too insane to even process. I couldn't believe I had actually done it.

I had met with nearly every single business owner in Macon and had presented options to help get their shops updated, with fresh marketing plans and hip ideas that could bring in customers. It took all day, and after my "lunch" break with Davis, we headed back down—hand in hand—where I resumed meeting with people and talking with locals. Music had played in the background, stringed lights popped on once the sky turned dark, and Davis stood nearby the entire night, bringing me treats that he'd bought from all the different shops.

When it was over, he grabbed my hand and walked us to his truck, where he then drove us to his house. I didn't even bother with an overnight bag, since I always wore his clothes or none at all when I was here. Sure enough, the second he got me inside, he stripped me and put me in the bath. Once we were dry, we watched Seinfeld until I fell asleep on his chest, my hair tangled in his fingers. It was the most peaceful night's sleep I had ever had.

I woke to him kissing along my jaw and down my neck, until he slid down my frame, spreading my thighs. He lazily swept his tongue over my clit until I was pulling his hair, at which point his palm planted on the back of my thigh, pushing it against my chest as he buried his face in my pussy until his name spilled from my lips.

Then he showed me the toothbrush and loofah he'd bought me. I had no idea when, but there were several little things popping up around his house that had been purchased for me. Once I was all clean, we headed down to tend to the eggs. This time, we kept our clothes on, but there were so many smiles from Davis that it was still swelling in my chest like a thunderhead. He'd kissed me, too—lingering kisses that burned my lips and singed my heart in the best sort of way.

"Babe," Davis said, sounding like he'd tried calling me a few times. I snapped my gaze over, seeing that he was standing, his laptop shut.

"Ready to go?"

"Yeah, of course. Did you get all your work done?" Secretly, I wanted to hold the blow torch for him or something, maybe wear that cool helmet and see if I had some hidden talent for welding.

He smiled, walking around his desk. "Yeah, your big town festival—it got me thinking about a few things, and different ways I could help too."

He swooped down to grab me, and my arms shot up to go around his neck automatically. "You did? In what way?"

This was another silly thing, but Davis carried me, all the time... and I loved it. A girl could get used to that sort of thing, so I told him that he needed to stop, so I didn't rely on it, but it only made him carry me more.

"I was thinking about donating a few things to some of the businesses, for their outside aesthetic."

"You're talking so dirty right now, I can't even." I fanned my face as he scaled the stairs, carrying me down each step.

He smirked but kept going until we cleared the building and

headed back to his house. The dogs trailed behind us, sniffing things out as we drew near to the porch.

"I just thought it could help, and I figured I'd have to coordinate with you to do it. That way, if you dump me again, I still have an excuse to see you."

He set me down. "I see, so really this is an insurance policy."

"Exactly."

I smiled, walking into the kitchen, where I pulled open the fridge. He'd made breakfast, but I wanted to prepare lunch for us. The nice thing about Davis living so far out meant he always had ingredients. He'd taken me out to the big double garage on the opposite side of his warehouse, and there were *five* freezers out there. One was literally full of junk food and vodka.

I prepped lunch while Dove and Duke watched my every move, and Davis fumbled around with something in the living room. Whenever the television was on, he watched funny sitcoms or survival shows—both of which I appreciated, so it was perfect. I liked the noise of it too, especially when Davis lapsed into his quieter side, which was more often than not. I didn't mind that either. When I needed him to talk to me, he would, and that was all that mattered.

I curled into Davis's side after I consumed my turkey sandwich, watching the survival show in front of us. I was still exhausted from the event, so I closed my eyes and drifted off. When I woke up, Davis was looking down at me while stroking my hair.

I stretched. "How long was I out?"

"Only an hour."

Still longer than any other time I had taken a nap. I was about to move away from him, when he stopped me by gently holding my arm.

"Hey, I actually wanted to talk to you about something."

My belly swooped like we'd just stepped off the tallest building. I was still terrified he'd press for the reason I had left before, and I knew without a doubt that I would eventually need to tell him, but I was still so terrified of his response that I couldn't bring myself to say anything.

"Okay," I replied quietly.

Davis pulled me until I was sitting on his lap and he was caging me in with his arms. I liked this position, it meant he didn't want me to go anywhere. I watched his solemn face as the shadows from the waning daylight flickered across the room, a few slices of light cutting into his hair. On instinct, I ran my fingers through it.

His grip tightened around me as he silently let out a sigh.

"Last time you were here, you asked about my family. I know I didn't open up or elaborate and I know that's probably part of why you left."

"No, it wasn't that," I admitted quietly, gathering the strength to say more, but he shook his head, cutting off my attempt.

"I don't need to know, not as long as you're here. That's all that matters. But I still wanted to open up to you. I want you to know how..." He paused, seeming to build up the nerve to finish his sentence, "serious this is to me, Rae. I haven't ever had a relationship. I've never had a girlfriend of any kind, just random hookups. You're not that to me. You never will be, even after...if this..."

He trailed off again, and I could sense that nerves were eating away at him. To calm him, I pressed a kiss to the space next to his eye, and then on his brow. His hand moved up my thigh, and he continued. "Whatever happens after this, you're important to me. So, I want to tell you about my family, okay?"

My heart raced and my lungs burned to return the sentiment. I wanted to tell him how important he was to me, how he'd always been, but instead I just nodded silently.

"Let's start with the basics. I have two parents. They're still married, and they live in Florida. I don't see them. We...don't speak."

The question of why was on my tongue, but I knew he needed to get through this at whatever pace he needed to.

"I have a brother, but he lives with my parents, and we don't speak either."

My poor pathetic heart, it was going to erupt soon if he didn't start explaining.

To encourage him, I stroked the hair at the back of his neck and the tip of his ear. Slow, steady, peaceful.

"As you know, my real name is Thomas. That was the name I grew up with, and my brother was Timothy. My brother and I, we're just two years apart, so as kids we were always doing the same things at the same time. I think my mom...she had these hopes that she'd have two boys, and they'd become best friends."

The small shake of his head told me that wasn't what had happened at all, and my gut began to sink. Suddenly, I wasn't sure if I was prepared for this story.

"Tim was different from me. He was peculiar...always sad. No matter what we were doing, he would be bummed about it. He hated everything, including me. I wanted to build forts in the forest, go to the pond, catch frogs... Our summers were always spent outside, but the older Tim got, the more depressed he became. It got to the point where I just stopped trying to get him to come with me. My mom resented me for it, but I couldn't force him to be happy, and if he did come with me, he was just a downer."

My strokes along his ear and scalp continued. I wanted to be a silent force of support, to remind him he wasn't alone.

"I knew Mom and Dad had a few fights over getting him on medication or taking him to see someone. Dad was against it, said they'd pump him full of so many meds we wouldn't recognize him anymore. Mom was just desperate, and worried that Tim would start harming himself. It was a fucking mess, and I didn't know how to deal. I was fifteen when the arguments became more and more insistent, and when I tried to check on Tim—see if he was okay, what with hearing all their bullshit about his depression and what to do with him—but he refused to talk to me. Wouldn't even open his door. By then, we were in high school, but Mom decided to home-school us. Not for me, for him. They had slowly taken bits and pieces of my life away and used the scraps to frame a new family, one that was lonely and sad. We stayed away from town, stuck to the mountain, so I lost all my friends, and my brother hated my guts. I was lonely."

I briefly remembered the first time I had ever seen Davis. He was devastating. Dark hair, eyes the color of a storm, a jaw line that was firm and masculine. Unlike any boy at my school, unlike anyone I had ever seen. I knew then I'd love this man for the rest of my life, but I did remember the cloud that seemed to follow him. It was a part of his allure, like a rope thrown out as bait, for anyone stupid enough to get caught in his thralls.

As he talked, I began putting together a timetable in my mind.

"They couldn't agree on what to do for him, except make sure he had a healthy diet and got exercise, which was just walking the dog. But up here, you know, we only really get sun during summer, and even then—it's short lived. It wasn't enough. When Tim was fourteen, he started talking about death a lot, and I knew in my gut we needed to get him help. So I went to my mom and told her."

"That was the right thing to do," I whispered, unable to hold back from adding something to this painful story. How difficult that must have been for him to tell his mother, knowing it could make things worse between him and his brother.

Davis slumped his shoulders and his whole body seemed to curve inward, taking mine with it. It felt like a cocoon. Just the two of us.

"Mom had him in a therapist's office just a week later. Dad was furious and blamed me for it. When Tim got back, he was furious too—but deep down, I knew I had done the right thing. He was diagnosed with severe depression, anxiety, and a few other things, but he needed meds and the doctor suggested a few changes."

"Sunshine," I muttered, thinking that was probably why they had moved.

He nodded, moving his hand up and down my thigh in an anxious fashion.

"After a few months of Tim going to therapy, my parents essentially forgot I existed. I used to blame them for it. My friend's lives looked so fun on social media, compared to mine. They were going to football games, and getting tacos and ice cream with girls. They were going to dances, and again—meeting girls. You can probably tell where my mind was during that time."

He laughed, and I smiled, feeling glad that he could find a way to smile about it, but the truth of his life felt like a broken piece of glass that he was trying to peer through to find what used to be inside.

"So, when I turned sixteen, I was ready to get my license. I'd been driving my dad's truck on all the mountain roads and clocking the time. He'd thankfully started paying attention to my demands to go into town and get a job. I think he was at such a loss with my brother, on how to help him, that helping me at least gave him something to do—or at least alleviated some of the guilt. So, I got my license. My dad let me drive one of his old, beater work trucks into town, and I got my first job doing construction. It was shitty pay, and shitty work, but it got me out of the house, and I needed that more than anything else at that time in my life."

I had a feeling the shoe was about to drop.

"I made a few friends; Gavin was one of them. He introduced me to a few of his buddies from school, and even though I was still homeschooled, they invited me to hang out with them. For the first time ever, I felt like I had a life. Then my brother's therapist wanted a session with me. Apparently I had been brought up a few times in the meetings, and she began to worry about my role in Tim's life."

"Is that normal, or even allowed?" I wasn't familiar with every aspect of therapy, but that seemed odd.

Davis brushed his thumb over the space under my shirt, right along my hip bone. Heat flared where his skin touched, and I tried to relax, realizing that some questions he might not be able to answer, depending on how difficult they were for him.

"The therapist had asked my mother, and she gave her approval, so I went in. The therapist talked about how I needed to take more of a role in supporting him. She wanted me to take Tim with me to hang out with my friends. Wanted me to encourage him to branch out and socialize. I was only sixteen. She knew this, and yet she put all the fucking pressure on me to fix my brother, and I resented the wrong person for it. I still hate myself for feeling the way I did and doing what I did…"

A choked gasp was caught in my throat. "You were a child."

The thumb on my waist moved closer to my rib cage, in a caressing gesture.

"My parents didn't see it that way, and suddenly I was required to take Tim with me everywhere I went. Except he hated my friends, and town. He hated *everything* because of the depression. I resented him, and eventually my friends stopped inviting me places. I was a stupid teenager, but I still wish I could go back and just sit with my brother in a dark room, listening to his music and just tell him he was perfect, just the way he was."

Davis paused, stroking me gently. I kept expecting him to continue, but the silence lapsed. So, I touched his jaw and brought his face up to mine.

"That's enough if you need it to be." I pressed a kiss to his lips.

His throat bobbed, as he shook his head.

"I want to tell you all of it…it just might take me a second." A few more silent moments passed before he continued.

"I had to take my brother with me to work one day, just after I turned eighteen. He was sitting in my truck, just waiting for my shift to get over. But Gavin had invited me to a party. I wanted to go, but I didn't want to drag my brother with me, so once my shift was over, I walked past the truck and headed to Gavin's, to ride with him. Tim jumped out of the truck, asking where I was going. He sounded…so panicked. I'll never forget the sound of his voice when he asked me. I felt like such an asshole, but I laughed and told him he could either come with us, or if he wanted to leave, he could drive my truck home. He was sixteen, he had the keys. It just seemed like it would be fine."

Davis was trembling under my touch, reliving the pain of whatever happened. My throat constricted with tears as I waited for him to finish, although part of me wished he wouldn't.

"I knew he didn't have his permit, and he hadn't had nearly as much practice as I had at his age, but truthfully, I thought he'd wait for me. In my head, I'd go to the party for an hour or so, come back, and it would have taught Tim a lesson not to be so antisocial. So, I left. Got in Gavin's truck and went to the party. My mom called my cell thirty minutes later. I was still at the party as I pulled my cell up, and when I saw her name flash across it, I knew. Deep down, I knew nothing would ever be the same.

Tim had gotten into an accident. When I arrived at the hospital, my mother slapped me. She was shaking so hard she couldn't breathe. My father wouldn't look or speak to me. Tim was in the intensive care unit for two weeks; he almost didn't make it. And during those two weeks, I just wanted to die. I wanted to disappear. I hated myself."

Letting out a heavy sigh, he tipped his head back, staring at the ceiling, as if the rest of the story was up there.

"He was in and out of hospitals for a few years after that. Either his body had some sort of complication, or he needed to be checked in to a mental health facility. The accident made his depression a million times worse, and my parents blamed me entirely. I blamed me. It was my fault. I worked all the time and started going to online community college. Slept on Gavin's couch for six months, because being home was the worst fucking feeling. Then they moved... without me. My dad sent me a text, telling me they were selling the house and to come get my stuff if I wanted to keep it. That was the last time I ever spoke to any of them."

My throat was so tight from choking back a sob that I was nearly about to explode. I had known Davis was tortured back then...I knew he carried a burden, but I had never imagined it being this heavy.

"I slowly just turned into this massive prick that everyone hated, and I decided a while ago that I didn't want to fight it, especially because I didn't think I was worth saving."

"You are," I argued, close to his ear, still stroking his hair. "You're worth saving, talking to, forgiving. Have you..." I wasn't sure how to ask this, or if he'd freak out on me for it. I tried again.

"Have you tried reaching out, and they just didn't respond, or—"

His head shaking from side to side told me enough. He'd let them go, and he never went after them. He'd nearly done the same with me, but here we were because he chased me.

"I think someday, a long time from now, you should try calling.

239

Try telling them you love them, and just see what they say. You never know, it might be all the healing you need."

His arms came around me tight, then he was moving me until I straddled him.

"Maybe."

I knew he didn't want to talk about it anymore, so I leaned forward and kissed his nose, whispering, "Thank you for telling me."

His response was to pull my hips closer while capturing my mouth in a searing kiss. I threw my arms around his neck and kissed him back. I knew he didn't feel worthy of anything, but this—this thing between us—it was still good. *He* was good. He was everything, and I wanted to remind him of that.

So I did.

With my mouth, with my body, I reminded him until the sun slipped behind the trees, and the stars came out with a brilliance that made my breath stall. I let him hold me, let him use me, and more than anything, let him touch a tangible love that he didn't even know he already had. The timetable clicked for me, and I realized that while I was loving Davis, he was dealing with heartache. He'd had my love that whole time. This time, I'd be sure he knew it was me that gave it to him.

31

DAVIS

THERE WERE LITTLE THINGS I LIVED FOR NOW THAT I NEVER realized I would care about before. Like when Rae talked to the hens. I had talked to them plenty before, but hearing her talk to them was becoming an addiction. I watched as she spread feed around the pen, smiling at all the clucking birds.

"Little queens, that's what all of you are. Don't let anyone tell you different, and if Duke or Dove make you scared, I'll personally buy balloons and leave them near their food bowls. They're terrified of them, you know."

I laughed quietly, nailing in a few boards to secure the hen house. I had a few other projects to do now that the weather was turning cold. It was another thing I'd never looked forward to before, but having Rae curled up under a blanket with me next to the fire would live at the top of my list of reasons I loved the colder weather. We'd been dating for over three weeks now, figuring out a new normal where she still went home to her parents and worked during the week, but came home with me every weekend. Sometimes, she'd still show up at my house in the evening mid-week, after helping at the diner, saying she missed me.

I loved those nights—when I wasn't expecting her, but she'd

show up anyway. I was addicted to her, and if I had my way, she'd live with me. Fuck, honestly—if I had my way, she'd be married to me.

Chills spread down my spine like it always did when I thought of how that would go. First, I would have to admit something else to her...something I'd been burning to say for weeks now. Every time I worked up the nerve, I'd just chicken out, but after that day where I spilled my life story to her, and we'd made love the rest of the afternoon, ending up in front of the fire...it just shifted something between us. It was like something clicked into place, and every day after that I had just been falling harder for her.

"You're coming tonight, right?" Rae suddenly asked, walking up behind me to exit the pen.

Her best friend was having a dinner party, and Rae had asked me to go as her date. It wouldn't be the first time we'd gone out, but it would be the first time we were together in a more intimate setting. I had asked if she wanted to go to Gavin's for dinner a few weeks back, but she had some reason she couldn't go. By going to this, I was hoping we could eventually or gradually work our way to both sides of our friendship table. Gavin was my best friend, just like Nora was hers, so I needed Rae to be okay with him.

"Yeah, I'll be there."

She gave me one of those smiles that stirred my cock and warmed my heart.

"Okay, good. You're meeting me there since I'll be leaving early to help her set up."

I silently nodded, going back to my project. By the time I'd made my way upstairs, Rae was in my shower, scrubbing her hair with the shampoo I'd ordered for her. When she realized I had bought it for her, and her own mud boots for the animal pens, she'd cried. It wasn't the reaction I was going for, but thankfully they were just happy tears.

Peeling out of my sweaty clothes, I tugged the glass door open and walked in, standing right behind her. She spun, her eyes squeezed tight as she started rinsing the soap out of her hair.

"Hi, beautiful."

She smiled, giggling under the spray. "Hey, handsome."

I loved showering with Rae; it was another one of those items that I was now addicted to in life: The way her dark hair looked when it was soaked, hanging down the center of her back. The way water dripped down her breasts, traveling in rivulets down her stomach, over her mound, and in between her thighs. She was mouthwatering, and every single time we showered together, I was hard as fucking stone within seconds.

She knew this, and from how many times we'd fucked in the shower, she expected it. She turned back to the wall, now that the soap was gone, and reached for her conditioner. Once she lathered her hair up, I reached around her and turned the faucet off.

"Hey!"

"You need three minutes to keep that in your hair, do you not?"

Tugging her hips back, she let out a small laugh. "Yeah, but I usually shave my legs during that time."

"Then do it, I'm not stopping you."

She gave me a skeptical look, reaching around me for her shaving gel and razor then lifting her leg to the ledge and dragging the razor up her shin. That's when I kneeled behind her and took advantage of her position.

"Fuck!" Rae braced the tiled wall with her free hand as my tongue swept up the crack of her ass, swirling into the tight hole.

"Sure, but first I want to taste you," I said, then sunk three fingers into her while my mouth returned to her slit. I focused on pushing my tongue into her tight heat while rubbing her clit with my fingers.

"Davis," she gasped again, dropping her razor.

I loved when she gave me all of her attention. I was always touching her—when she was reading or watching television, sometimes even when she was cooking, I'd stick my hand down her pants and my fingers into her center. I'd work her while she tried to concentrate, until eventually, she'd give in and surrender to my touch.

"Lift your leg higher, put it on the other ledge."

She did as I said, holding onto the wall for support, so I had complete access to her.

I worshiped her with my mouth and fingers until she was rocking into me, curses falling from her lips.

Right before she climaxed, I pulled away and stood to my feet.

"You son of a bitch!" she gasped, mouth parted, nipples hard.

Smirking, I gripped her by the waist and twisted her until her back was against the wall. I slid the tip of my cock into her but didn't go any further. She moaned in response, wrapping her legs around me tightly.

"You're not going to like this," I rasped, biting her ear lobe.

She rocked in response, letting out a small whine. Using one hand, I reached for the faucet and turned it to the left.

Water hit my back, but it was her eyes that had me focused. "This will give you something to look forward to."

Her eyebrow lifted in doubt. I smirked as I pushed the head of my swollen head in further.

"I'll owe you one." I kissed her and then set her down.

Swatting at my back, she shrieked, "Are you kidding me?"

Laughing, I exited the shower and pressed a kiss to the door. "This way you'll come home to me worked up and ready to take my cock."

I laughed as I entered the bedroom, loving the creative curses that fell from her lips as she washed out her conditioner.

THE DINNER WAS HELD at six, and I arrived a few minutes early to make sure the girls didn't need any help with anything. They waved me off, telling me to go make sure the backyard was all set for the guests. Nora had added patio furniture and a string of lights over her faded pergola, but otherwise the yard itself was still a work in progress.

While outside, I heard someone muttering curses from the other side of Nora's fence.

"Is she really turning those on again?" the stranger grumbled. I walked to the fence and peered over.

"What was that?"

Suddenly Colson Hanes popped into view, an old friend of mine that I hadn't seen in forever.

"Davis?"

"Cole, what the hell are you doing over there?" I held my hand out, and he took it in a friendly shake.

"Shit, man I haven't seen you in forever."

Shaking my head, I eyed his yard, seeing how dark it was. He had a few solar lights around his garden, but nothing as obnoxious as Nora's bright lights. The contrast nearly made me wince.

"So, you live next door, huh?" I gestured toward the back yard.

From what I could remember of Cole, or Colson, was that he played ball but was fascinated with books. He was always reading, doing research and different study projects. I hadn't kept up with him after everything happened with my brother, so I didn't know what he ended up doing.

"Yeah, just moved in about a year ago. She doing some sort of dinner party thing?" His tone was a little terse, which made me curious about his relationship with Nora.

"Yeah, Nora is hosting it, but uh…well, what are you doing tonight? Want to come?"

He laughed, full bellied, tossing his head back. In the shadows it was hard to see him, but he still had blond hair, a hard jaw, and the build of a football player.

"Nah man, she hates me."

I shrugged. "She seems friendly enough to me. Two of her dinner guests canceled, and she's pretty bummed about it. I think if you bring a bottle of wine or something, she'd be grateful to have you."

He seemed to mull it over for a second, then asked, "Her boyfriend going?"

That led to a slew of other assumptions about their relationship, but again, wasn't my place, and I didn't really care that much.

"Doesn't have one that I know of. It's just my girlfriend, and a few other women. I think I'll be a little outnumbered… You'd be doing me a favor if you came."

"Wouldn't want you to be outnumbered…and I do have a brand-new bottle of wine, and a few other things I could bring over."

"Then it's settled. Dinner starts in about fifteen minutes."

"Yeah, see you in a few."

Walking back to the house, I heard Rae laughing with Nora, and the sound of it seemed to warm the whole house. Nora was pretty cool, and only gave me a thumbs up when she saw me for the first time after her little pep talk. We'd never spoken about Rae again after that, but she seemed like a good friend, and for that I was grateful. But now, I was worried that maybe I should have asked her before inviting Colson over. I mean, they were neighbors, they had to be friendly, right?

"Okay, everything is ready!" Nora called out, right as the doorbell rang and two more women came in, bearing some sort of cracker and cheese tray and a bottle of wine. Nora greeted them, Rae went in for hugs next, and then everyone started finding spots around the table.

"I'm so bummed about Chelsea and Brad not coming," Nora complained, while pulling her chair out. "It just feels a little uneven or something."

Right as she said it, the doorbell rang again.

"Who's that?"

"Uh…actually, Nora—" I started, pushing in Rae's chair as she took her seat then trailing behind Nora as she headed to the front door. "There's something I need to tell you. I have this buddy, and—"

She swung the door open, cutting off my explanation. Colson stood there, wearing dark denim, a nice button down, and he had a bundle of flowers in his hand, along with a glass bottle of cold brew coffee.

"Uh…" Colson waited for Nora to say something, but she just stood there frozen.

Clearing my throat, I moved next to her, "Nora, I hope it's okay that I invited Colson, he's an old friend of mine. Turns out he's your neighbor!"

She seemed to snap out of it, moving to the side to let him in, her eyes wild and her jaw tight as she replied, "No, totally fine. Welcome."

Colson clenched his jaw and hesitated before taking a step inside.

The murmurs at the table died down as we returned to the dining room, until Rae saw us and let out a loud gasp, followed by a horrific coughing spell.

"Shit, are you choking?" I moved to her side. Her face was turning purple.

After a few more sputters, she waved me off. "I'm fine."

But alarm was apparent in her gaze as she tracked Nora's stiff movements. Colson had thrust his arm out, holding the flowers, his head dipped, not meeting her eyes. He looked like a third grader handing wildflowers to his crush.

"Thank you." Nora sounded like a robot, with absolutely no feeling in her voice at all.

Next came the coffee. "Here."

"Uh…thanks." Again with the robot voice, except now curiosity had woven a way through.

Colson cleared his throat, explaining. "It's for tomorrow…I'm always exhausted after I entertain. Thought it might help."

Seemingly over the small talk, he took the empty seat next to me and tucked himself into the table.

"Why did you invite Colson?" Rae whispered in my ear while one of the women at the end of the table started talking about some work story, entertaining everyone while the food was being passed around.

I turned to her, whispering back, "He's an old friend. I haven't seen him in years. It felt like the right thing to do."

She let out a sigh, sipped her wine, and drawled a curse word under her breath.

"Is that not okay?"

I didn't get the chance to hear her response because Nora spoke up.

"Colson, you could have brought your girlfriend this evening. She's not at home all alone, is she?"

Rae kicked Nora under the table, making her friend grunt and lean forward with a wince.

Colson blanched as though he'd been the one kicked as he replied. "Nope."

Nora's eyes narrowed into slits, her cheeks warming as she sipped more wine.

Rae tried to carry the conversation, but Colson piped up next, interrupting her.

"How come your boyfriend isn't here, Nora? I was hoping to meet him."

Rae had chosen that moment to sip her wine, which was unfortunate because it came sputtering out from her mouth a second later.

"Are you okay?" Nora leaned in and asked.

Rae wiped at the edges of her mouth and rasped, "Fine, but I need to go to the bedroom and change."

"Oh no, I don't think that you do…" Nora argued, raising her voice as Rae stood.

"I'll be right back. Um babe, can you come help me with the zipper?" she asked, poking me in the back. Her shirt didn't have one.

"Sure."

"I can help you, Rae. I can go," Nora said, half standing from the table.

Rae waved her off. "Don't be silly…it's your dinner party, we'll be right back."

I scooted back and followed Rae to a back bedroom, where she shut us in and started pacing the room.

"What is going on with you and Nora?" I asked, taking a seat on the guest bed. This wasn't Nora's room because I'd seen it when I helped hang all the blinds and shades in the house last week.

"She hates Colson. Well, no, she loves him…but hates him."

"Oh shit, I didn't know…"

"I know, and I'm not mad at you, but we have a real situation on our hands right now."

I watched her ass sway in the tight jeans she wore tonight, completely distracted. Her top was tight, showing off the curves of her breasts too, dipping low enough to see almost to her stomach. All I could think of was how I had stopped us in the shower, and how stupid that was.

"Are you listening to me?" She stopped in front of me.

I laughed, shaking my head as I grabbed her by the hips. "No, you're hot as fuck, and all I want to do is shove my dick so far inside you that you forget what day of the week it is."

"To be fair, I never know what day of the week it is, so that's a pretty low bar."

Lying back on the bed, I brought her over until she was straddling me.

She clicked her tongue. "This is not the time. We have to go back out there, and we need a way to get Colson out of here. Nora is getting drunk, and when she's drunk, she does things like make secret wedding boards for her and Colson."

"No fucking way," I laughed, while moving her over my hard on.

Her sultry moan told me she felt how badly I wanted her.

"Now isn't the time for this." She rocked her hips again, rubbing against the steel rod under my jeans. "Definitely not the time, and I would not want you to unzip your jeans and pull out that gloriously veined masterpiece and fuck me with it."

"No?"

"Definitely not…"

"I thought you spilled wine all over yourself. That means you need to get out of these clothes. Besides, don't I owe you?"

She looked down at her clothing. "You're right."

"I know, so…"

Peeling her top over her head, she tossed it to the ground and then stood above me, unzipping her jeans and slowly peeling them down her thighs.

In just a bra and panties, she settled back over me, and at some point, I had already pulled my dick out.

"Now, let's see…I think I need to inspect you for any wine that might have gotten on you."

She hummed, rotating her hips into my erection. "How will you do that?"

"I'll have to start here." I moved her underwear to the side so I could see her pussy.

"Hmm, nothing seems to be here." I rubbed up and down her center.

"Now where?" Rae gasped, tossing her head back.

"Lift up, and I'll show you."

She did as I said, lifting enough to fit over my shaft, but she didn't sink down.

I took the opportunity to pull her down onto me in one swift move. She cried out while grabbing my shoulders.

"I have to do a thorough examination, just to make sure there's nothing in this sweet cunt of yours."

She began mewling as she rotated her hips, riding me so hard and fast that she couldn't contain the sounds she was making.

"Fuck, fuck, fuck," she cried, pushing her hand into her hair while bouncing on my dick. The sight of her robbed me of breath, her fair skin flushed by desire for me, her plump breasts bouncing as she fucked me.

"Yeah, baby, just like that." I watched as my cock went in and out of her slick heat.

She slammed her hips down, while jutting mine up, splitting her in half with my erection, "You're such a good girl, taking my cock so fast and so hard, knowing that door isn't locked, and anyone could walk through it at any second."

"Shit, I forgot about that," she said huskily, moving her hips faster.

"Then you better milk this cock for all its worth and come, baby."

I slapped her ass then gripped her hip to hold her in place while I lifted my hips to fuck her harder.

Instead of going faster, she slowed down, fucking me slowly while pushing her breasts together.

"Shit, these fucking tits." I sat up, pulled the material of her bra down, and lapped at her nipples, shoving my face in between the two. Her hands moved from my chest to the headboard, where it slammed into the wall from our movements.

"Fuck me, Rae. Fuck me," I rasped as the headboard slapped against the wall with more force, and while I knew Rae was trying to stop it, she finally let go and clenched around me on a gasp.

"Oh my God, I'm there! I'm there! Davisssssssssss."

"Shit, the whole fucking house is going to hear us," I panted, laughing as I came so hard it made my vision blur.

Right as Rae sagged into my chest, she panicked.

"Shit, I can't believe I left her alone so long with Colson. I have no idea if he's still breathing."

Jumping off me, she snatched up a box of tissues and began cleaning herself up, then she tossed the box to me. Once I had situated myself back into my jeans and zipped, I sat up to see Rae with one leg in her jeans, hopping to get the other in.

I decided I didn't want to keep this feeling inside anymore. It felt so good when I had opened up to her about my family and my past. I knew if I just said it, even if she didn't say it back, that I'd feel better, and this burning in my chest every five seconds would ease up. Taking a deep breath, still watching her struggle with her jeans, I confessed.

"I love you."

She stopped moving, completely frozen mid-wiggle, still facing away from me.

"To be completely clear, I'm *in* love with you."

Right as I finished the last word, the door flew open, and Rae screamed and fell over.

"I knew it! You were fucking at my dinner party, and with Colson Hanes here. Our friendship is over, Rae. *Over.* Don't call, don't come by, and do not text me."

"We did not!" Rae lied, and not very well.

"It smells like sneaky sex in here, *and* you're naked."

Rae clicked her tongue. "I had to change from the wine. Davis is dressed, see?"

Nora narrowed her eyes on me.

"We could all hear the headboard, assholes! You better not have gotten a speck of man juice on that comforter!" she yelled, slamming the door shut again.

"Guess that means Colson left if she just yelled that at the top of her lungs?" I asked, moving off the bed and bending down to grab Rae's shirt.

"Guess so," she replied softly, her eyes fixed on the copper button of her jeans. "I have a feeling everyone is gone, and that she's not doing well. Nora never yells like that when people are around. Go ahead and head home. I'll call you when I'm all finished up."

She raised on her tiptoes and kissed me.

Grabbing her by the waist, I pulled her to my chest and slid my hand up her back.

Softly moaning into my mouth, I moved to gain better access to that tongue, and right as I did, the door flew open again.

"I'm not joking, Rae! End of our friendship. Get your ass out here now!"

Rae laughed into my mouth and darted out the door, pulling her shirt on as she went—leaving the void of what I'd confessed behind.

32

RAE

I WAS ELBOW DEEP IN DISHES, COMPLETELY BLOCKING NORA OUT AS she rage-cleaned her table. Normally, I would be a better friend, but Davis had just fried my brain. I wasn't sure how to process what he'd said, and the one person I wanted to talk to about it was currently cussing in Moldavian.

He loved me.

He was *in love* with me.

But that couldn't be right, because he didn't know the real me. He'd spilled his entire life to me, his deepest secrets, and I hadn't told him about mine. I didn't deserve him.

"Rae, did you hear me?" Nora snapped, coming up next to me to load the sink with wine glasses.

I stared at her, dumbfounded. "He loves me."

A singular brow went up, while her face remained twisted with annoyance. It was her way of silently saying she heard me but wasn't quite committed to listening yet.

Shaking my head, I returned to the sink, rinsing glasses.

"I'm sorry, it can wait. Tell me what happened with Colson, and don't yell it at me. Calmly explain it to me while I hand you the dishes I rinse."

Deflating a bit, she conceded and stood shoulder to shoulder with me at the sink.

"He loves you. Like, loves loves...or thinks you're adorable?"

My chest did that thing again where I felt like my lungs had grown a pair of wings.

Tipping a glass around the water, I handed it to her. "He said he loves me, then, to clarify, he said he's *in* love with me."

"He clarified?"

"Oh yeah, nice big fat—you can't miss my meaning—clarification," I deadpanned while scrubbing at a tray.

"What did you say?" She gently set glass after glass in her drying rack.

Turning off the sink, but keeping my hips pinned to the counter, I let out a sigh. "Nothing...you came in, it was madness...but how could I explain that I loved him back, or that I have loved him for most of my life?"

A frown tugged at my best friend's face as she processed what I wasn't saying.

"You still haven't told him?"

"I think you'd know; I mean...I assume he'll have a fairly big reaction."

The silence in the room pressed in on us as we stood at the sink. The shade above was still open, and from the lights strung up in the back, we could make out a silhouette across the fence. The figure faced Nora's yard, sipping on what looked like a bottle of beer.

"Is he just drinking in the dark while watching your yard?" I asked, leaning over the sink to get a better view.

Nora gripped my shoulder, pulling me away from the sink and yanking the string, forcing the shade to slam shut.

"I can't figure him out, and it's driving me crazy!"

"What do you mean? What in the heck happened?"

She shook her head, walking back into the living room. Falling onto the seat next to her, I tipped my head back, thinking about Davis and the dogs, wondering if I should pick up a few of their favorite treats, and some whipped cream for Davis. He loved licking it off me, and I loved when he—

254

"Rae!"

Shit.

"Oh my God, you're useless when you think about him."

"I'm sorry! Go again, I'll do better."

She turned, tucking her knee under her, and I did the same, so we were focused.

"When you guys left, he asked me how long I planned on being in the area. Which was a weird fucking question, if you ask me. It made me irritated, so I asked him why he thought I had a boyfriend."

"Oh, Nora."

Brown curls danced along her shoulders as she pushed her hand through them.

"He gets under my skin. He wouldn't answer me, and instead he asked why I thought he had a girlfriend. So, I told him he said he did when he walked in on me practically naked. He laughed at me, Rae. *Laughed.* Said I was hung up on the past, like a teenager, and told me I needed to grow up."

Oh shit, this was bad. Very bad. "Did you throw something at him?"

"I wanted to, and after he said that he started flirting with Tasha…"

Letting out a sigh, I gripped my best friend's hand and tightened my hold.

"I lost it, Rae. I'm so embarrassed. I just…it was too much, and when it was noticeable that I was upset, everyone stopped talking, and that's when we heard you guys going at it in the room. You were being very loud, by the way. *Super* rude."

Flames engulfed my face as I let her hand go and covered my eyes. "I'm so ashamed. I had zero intentions of having sex. He just sort of pulled me on top of him, and he's kind of irresistible when he wants to be. Did I tell you we had sex in Kelly Travis's office?"

A grin split my friend's face in half as she fought back a laugh. She covered her face to stop it, but it didn't do any good.

"That bitch deserves it."

"Right? That's what I said."

Silence fell back over us after a few seconds, and Nora heaved a sigh.

"So, after that, I yelled at everyone to leave, told them the night was ruined, and that I wasn't feeling well."

"Did Colson just leave, or——"

I wasn't sure what I was hoping for. Maybe some optimism that my friends crush was interested in her. He seemed to be... I mean, unless he was just insanely bored and wanted a free meal, but why get her flowers, and bring her something as thoughtful as cold brew coffee? And the question about her supposed boyfriend still threw me.

"He hesitated...asked if we could talk in the kitchen for a second, but I told him no. I demanded he leave."

See, there *was* hope. Now to just cultivate it carefully.

"Well, what now? I mean, you've made contact..." I asked hesitantly.

Standing up and stretching, she let out another defeated sigh. "Now, I hide. Maybe go on a trip. I've been wanting to go on a trip for a while...maybe head to Portland? Want to come with me?"

Half of me wanted to. It sounded so fun to get away with my best friend, but I needed to confess to Davis, and even then, the idea of leaving him for any amount of time didn't set well with me.

"I'll let you know, okay?"

"Okay, I'm headed to bed. I love you. Thank you for being here."

Standing, I clicked off one of her lamps and headed for my purse. "Sorry about the sex."

Nora laughed, clicking off two more lamps. "At least something exciting happened at my dinner party, and hey——you christened that room. Now when my parents stay over, it won't traumatize me."

"Why would they stay here when they live in the same town?" I said with a laugh, pulling on my jacket. The weather had started to cool drastically, and every morning on the mountain there was frost and a thin layer of snow greeting us.

"Oh, well..." She paused, her face flushing red.

Worry gnawed away at my stomach. Something wasn't right.

"What's going on?"

Nora crossed her arms, looking down. "It's just...they've decided to sell the shop. They're moving. Headed to Arizona to a retirement community. They plan to visit often, though..."

"What?" I had just thrown the little business festival. It was supposed to help.

Nora already knew where my mind was, which was why her face was flushed red.

"I know, Rae. I'm so sorry. You did amazing; it has nothing to do with you. They're tired of the cold. Dad's construction business is in the process of being sold, and Mom can't keep up with the shop anymore. It's just too much for them."

Tears actually burned the back of my eyes, which was mortifying. This wasn't something to cry over. It was just a dumb marketing festival. It wasn't a fix-all idea. Maybe it didn't do anything but leave a sticky memory for parents and lift spirits momentarily.

"Don't do that thing where you trash all your ideas and tell yourself lies. You did amazing, Rae. Amazing. My parents are just done being in Macon, that's all."

I nodded, knowing in my heart she was right and that it made sense, but my head warred with the idea, unwilling to accept that I had failed. I didn't want to lose a single business. I wanted to succeed, and what if a big company bought the shop and put a diner in it, or some other form of competition to my parents?

"Go home, Rae. Go see Davis, tell him you love him too, and let all this go. It was never your mess to begin with."

I couldn't even respond, so I just nodded and left her house.

IT WAS late by the time I parked in front of Davis's house. Stars blanketed a dark October sky as a thin tendril of smoke lifted from the top of the house. A warm sensation of belonging wound its way around my heart, calming me to my core. This place had become home to me, and all I wanted to do was snuggle under the covers with the man I loved.

Taking each step, one at a time, I tugged on the screen door, smiling as I usually did when I remembered that first kiss. Once I pushed open the front door, two short barks greeted me, followed by the sound of nails clicking on the hardwood.

I dropped my purse and took off my shoes, leaving my coat.

"Hello, you two, did you catch any rabbits today? Trap any cougars?" I kneeled, scratching their heads as they affectionately shoved their wet noses into my neck, licking at my jaw.

"They found a snake in the back yard. A big one, so they both enjoyed a fat piece of raw chuck roast for dinner," Davis answered, walking into the living room, bare chested and sipping something hot. My stomach swooped at the sight of him, at the way that longer piece of hair always dipped a little far, cutting into his forehead like a Disney prince.

I loved when he walked around in a pair of denim jeans and no shirt, and the way those eyes seemed to burn when they roamed over different parts of my body. I hadn't even realized I was still kneeling until he walked over and held out his hand.

Taking it, I stood and marveled at the seductive smile curving his sensual lips.

"Hi."

Swallowing the thick, horrific confession I needed to give him, I smiled back.

"Hey."

Without another thought, I pressed my lips to his, and all was right in my world. His firm grip attached to my waist, his mug was set on the table to our right, and then both his hands were moving up my back and he was walking us to the wall.

His tongue delved deeply into my mouth, his head slanting to the side as I watched him move for move, sinking my fingers into his hair.

"It's never enough," he breathed in between kisses. "Having you, loving you...it's never enough."

There it was again...the reminder that I needed to come clean.

I pulled back, pushing that longer piece of hair back away from his brow and took a deep breath. "I love you too. I've been in love with you for a while now, but there's something I need to tell you."

His smile was so big, it nearly broke my soul in half. I had never seen him so happy.

"Whatever it is, it has to wait." He picked me up, grabbing my ass, as my legs went around his waist.

Then he walked us upstairs, kissing my neck, and catching my lips with every step.

Once we'd entered his room, he gently lowered me until my feet were pressed into what should have been a woven rug but instead it was plush and soft.

"What…what is this?" My eyes greedily searched the transformed space.

Davis slowly walked to the new dresser on the left side of the room. Before, a wooden rocking chair had sat there, along with a side table and lamp. Now it was a dresser that matched the one on his side of the room. On top was a nice-looking circular mirror, along with a few other more feminine touches.

"This is yours." He grabbed my hand and walked to the door to the right. It was a closet, packed full of hunting gear last time I checked. Turning the knob, he clicked the light, revealing an empty space, with white shelving inserted, along with three racks for shoes, two big rolling drawers, and enough space for hanging clothes.

"This is your closet," he said, gently tugging my wrist, and pulling me back into the room. "I asked Nora about what sort of bedding you might like, and she told me to watch the episodes of Gilmore Girls after Lorelei renovates her bedroom, and to find something that matches the bedding she had."

A tear escaped as I laughed, because his bed looked just like that. Fluffy pillows, with a massive, snowy white down comforter that looked soft enough to be a cloud. There were white rugs on the floor, brightening up the space, as well as a large new armchair near the window on his side. Black and white photographs added contrast to the room, along with a few framed photos of people I hadn't ever seen before.

"Is this your family?" I nearly sobbed, moving to the small frame.

Cradling it in my hands, I traced the face of the man I had loved while I was in high school, standing next to someone who could be his twin, except he had longer hair and glasses.

"Timothy," I said out loud, and then took in the sight of his mother and father, both dark- haired, good-looking people. They seemed happy in the photo, at least marginally.

"Figured maybe I should start putting out more of these, and, I don't know, maybe try and call sometime."

My throat felt tight as I carefully set the photo down and registered there was a photo of us next to the one I'd just picked up. It was of that day we'd tried to go on a date to a five-star restaurant. So, we were dressed nicely, but the weather turned, delaying us so much that we decided to just stay back, but Davis felt bad, so we hiked to a remote lake. He danced with me along the banks and then held my hand, leading me into the water. Rain splintered the calm surface as he pulled me to him, and still wearing my black lacy dress, and him in his nice green button down, I kissed him, while he thrust his wrist out and took the photo. It was a beautiful photo, stunning with the way the mountain stood in the background and the shading of gray and blue.

"Move in with me." He pressed a kiss to my lips gently. "Go to bed with me every night and wake up with me every morning."

I swiped at my face as more tears came. I had to tell him; I knew this—but how? He'd just told me he loved me, and now this. He had a framed photo of us in his bedroom. No, what he wanted to be *our* bedroom. I was so done for, so insanely overwhelmed, I couldn't breathe.

"When did you even have time to do all this?"

I didn't deserve this. Any of it.

"Bits at a time. You haven't looked in that closet for a while, so that was easy to keep hidden. The rest I just finished today once you left for Nora's, and then finished up before you got home."

Pulling both my hands in his, he started leading us out of the room and down the hall to the very last bedroom on the floor. It faced the backyard, with a gorgeous view of Mount Macon.

"This is your office," he said quietly. "I wanted you to have a space to think up all those amazing ideas to save our little town. You have so much to give, Rae. You just need space to create it all."

Covering my mouth to catch the sob creeping up my throat, I stared at the beautiful white desk, already set up with a printer, monitor, and a bulletin board that had a note tacked to it that read, *I love you.*

He tangled his fingers with mine and asked again.

"Move in with me."

"Yes," I breathed, "of course I will." I finally gave in, because fighting him was futile, and I didn't really want to. I wanted to live with him. Hell, I wanted to marry him.

"I have to tell you something though, and it might take a bit to explain."

"Save it for tomorrow." He kissed my lips. "Please. I just need to be with you, in our bed, on those fancy new sheets, and watch how beautiful you look under the glow from the fire. Give me a night where I get to love you completely, with my body and my soul."

Nodding, I gave in and let him sweep me away.

I let him slowly undress me, and with every piece that left my body, he kissed me reverently. I let him love me the way he wanted to, and selfishly, I let myself love him back, just as eagerly. I was starved for him, so when he laid me down in our bed, naked— pinning my hands together, and sinking deeply into me—I took every piece of it for myself.

33

RAE

I WOKE UP IN THE BED I NOW SHARED WITH THE BOY I ONCE dreamed of marrying. Turning to the left, a bit of daylight broke through the shades, right as a piece of paper crumpled under my face. Tugging it free from the pillow, I blinked to adjust my eyes as I read the note.

Good morning, Beautiful—

I have a delivery to make a few towns over. I usually stay there for the day and visit with my grandfather. He doesn't know who I am due to the dementia, but I still like to see him. I know you have to tell me something, you've been amping up to it, so let's talk after dinner tonight. Your parents begged us to come over, and I have already turned your mom down at least three times, so we need to at least show up for a little bit, but afterward, I'm all yours.

-Love you

Davis

Smiling at the note, I snuggled deeper under the covers and decided I'd take my time in bed this morning.

But then it hit me again, making my stomach dip. Excitement tugged me into action, tossing the covers off, and walking into the bathroom to shower. I couldn't wrap my brain around moving into this beautiful home with him. Getting to wake up and use the shower every day…I felt like a princess.

After dressing, I checked on the dogs, who were resting in the living room.

Right as I started petting them, my phone rang.

"Hey," I replied cheerily to my best friend, heading to the Keurig, prepping coffee.

Nora sounded sleepy. "Hey. I wanted to check in about how things went after you told him."

Ugh, that felt like a pin in my balloon, effectively popping it.

"Um, we didn't talk about that last night. He actually asked me to move in." My smile returned as I realized a silver key was on the counter, right where Davis had first ripped my leggings open. A keychain was attached with a silver star, and my name was etched into a small metal charm.

"He left me a house key!"

Nora made an annoyed sound on the other end, and I felt a little guilty for how loud I had just squealed.

"Rae…" Nora exhaled, sounding like she needed to reprimand me. "You haven't told him yet, and he asked you to move in?"

Why did she make it sound so bad?

"I'm telling him tonight, and it's not like I didn't try…he just kept wanting me to wait until today to tell him."

"Don't hide behind that excuse. You should have told him weeks ago, and you know it."

Hot irritation burned under my skin. I just wanted one day to enjoy this feeling…this beautiful, exhilarating feeling of being wanted and loved. I felt like my teenage self was coming back to ruin my happiness. I didn't understand why she couldn't just disappear once and for all.

My silence spurred her into letting out a sigh.

"I'm sorry, I just want you to have it all, and that includes being honest with the man you love. You can't start this life on a lie, Rae."

I knew she was right, but at the moment, I resented her for it.

"I'm telling him tonight." I left it at that and disconnected the call. I needed a break, and selfishly, I wanted to enjoy this feeling a little longer before I had to risk it all on telling him the truth.

I HADN'T HEARD from Davis for most of the day. I had texted him a photo of the key and then told him I couldn't believe I would be moving in, blabbering on about how happy I was about it. He finally texted back a few hours later with a heartfelt, "I can't wait, baby."

That settled my nerves, helping me smile through my meetings. I realized after last night that I didn't want the news about Nora's parents to stop me from being effective. These three businesses hadn't been able to participate at the vendor fair, so I reached out and asked if we could meet. It was last minute, so it wouldn't be until later that afternoon that I sat down and began talking with them.

But as the day faded, my anxiety peaked.

I couldn't stop thinking over what would happen when Davis heard the truth. I had imagined his face when I explained it. The best case scenario would be telling him similarly to how he told me his big secret about his past. I'd be in his lap, and he'd be stroking my skin until it all slipped free, then we'd fuck all evening.

Simple.

I'd be free to move in and start my life with him.

"Hello, thank you for coming!" I greeted the first business owner to bustle through the coffee shop doors. Rachel, the barista, walked over to us to take our orders. This was something I had suggested implementing, to add more ambiance as well as encourage more tips. Relaxing into the notion that I was already seeing little improvements from my town fair, I decided this meeting would be a success, and regardless of Nora's parents, I would save this town.

If it was the last thing I did, I'd leave my mark on Macon.

"Let's get started, shall we?"

BY THE TIME the meetings were finished, I was starving and so excited to see Davis. We hadn't told my parents that we would be moving in together yet, considering it just happened, but I was excited to see their faces when I took a few boxes with me tonight.

Davis's truck was parked along the curb, already inside, and my mother had likely already made dinner. I couldn't believe how late I ended up being, but one of the owners ran late and then begged me to make an exception and wait for her. I was a sucker, and blamed Nora's parents for it entirely.

Right as I opened the door, I could smell dinner cooking.

"Mom, dinner smells good!" I called out, toeing off my shoes and hanging my purse and coat. "Sorry I'm late."

No one was in the living room, but I heard voices coming from the back of the house—oddly enough, from my bedroom.

Curious, I made my way down the hall. I could hear my mom rambling about a memory, or something she'd done a few years prior.

Leaning my shoulder into the door frame, I smiled at the sight before me. Mom had photos spread out on my bed, while Davis looked down at the glossy images strewn about.

My mom was mid-story, retelling the time I had come home late in high school, and that's when things started to click and panic bubbled up in my chest.

Surging forward, I gawked as the sick realization hit me in the face. My mother had found my photos, or had her own, and my teenage years were on full display—painting my comforter in pathetic hues of acne, short curly hair, and braces. My heart hammering into my throat, I tried to catch Davis's gaze, but he was staring down at a picture that he'd pulled free from the protective plastic, pinching it between his thumb and finger.

It was of me, on my graduation day. I had worn the same outfit into the library that night he saw me.

"I can explain..." I whispered, my voice hitching as he refused to meet my eyes. It made my mother tip her head up, a smile already in place, but my eyes were on the man next to her.

I went to him, kneeling in front of him.

"You have to let me explain. That's why I wanted to show you first." I was mumbling so fast I wasn't sure he was hearing me; tears clouded my vision and fire had engulfed my face.

My mother's face seemed to transform as she looked between Davis and myself. "Rae, what are you talking about?"

"Why did you pull these out?" I snapped at her.

It wasn't her fault, it was mine, but hurt and fear warred in my chest smashing and destroying all that was left of hope.

"Davis spilled the beans about moving in together, and well, you were late, and he wanted to get a head start on packing up a few of your things. We started with the boxes in the closet, when we found your old albums. You two are getting so serious now, I thought it would be okay." Her face contorted into misery, like she'd truly done something wrong.

"I'm so sorry," she whispered, closing the scrapbook.

"It's not your fault, Millie," Davis said evenly, standing from the bed. "Is it, Rae?"

The ice in his tone was like a knife to my chest.

"Please…please just let me explain."

"Explain what?" my mom repeated.

Davis let out a small scoff as he shook his head back and forth, tossing the picture on the bed like it meant nothing to him. The irony that he'd touched me so intimately in this bed made this entire moment hurt so much worse.

"Explain that she's been lying to me since the first day she met me. She's been lying to you, and to Roger—to all of us."

Shaking my head, and pursing my lips, I tried to make him see. "No, that's not it. I—"

"Just stop, Rae…before you embarrass yourself any further."

He was walking away, and my heart felt like it was coming out of my chest.

I followed him out the door as he stormed to his truck.

My feet felt like lead as I trailed after him, as though I was following in the same exact footsteps that led me to heartbreak before. "Please wait, please! Just hear me out, there's a reason I—"

He spun on me; in the waning light of day I could barely make out the tears welling in his eyes.

"Tell me that while I told you my deepest, darkest secret, you couldn't bother to tell me yours? That you once followed me around, had—what? A freakish obsession with me?"

Hurt flayed me open, but I powered through.

"That's why I couldn't do it, because you hated me so much that you actually had Carl hand deliver a note so that I would find you fucking someone else. You knew I was in love with you! You know how much I wanted to be with you."

Shaking his head, he stepped back. "That wasn't me. I never once gave that fucker a note, and I sure as fuck wouldn't have given it to him to meet you. You were nothing to me back then, Rae. You were a fucking kid; you actually think I liked you?"

"No...of course not, I just—"

"So you actually showed up and thought I'd fuck you in the library instead? Freshly graduated from high school, barely eighteen...that I'd choose you over women my own age?"

"Stop..." I pleaded.

This was too much, all my embarrassing fears were being tossed out on the lawn at my feet, and it was too much. I had thought he'd handle this with care. I thought because he loved me...

"So, was this your ultimate long game then, huh? Move back, get me to fall in love with you, pull the rug out from under me months later, once I ask you to move in? 'Surprise, I'm the freak that used to stalk you!'"

"I didn't stalk you! And no, of course not, I didn't even—"

"Stop lying!" he roared.

"You know the pathetic thing about all of this? If you'd just been honest with me, if you'd just told me the truth, I wouldn't have cared!" He roared angrily, veins protruding from his neck and forehead.

I flinched, never hearing him yell so loud, and my heart spasmed uncontrollably.

"You chose for me—you lied. You..." he trailed off, shaking his head. "Maybe you really are as pathetic as you always seemed back then." His scoff was the final nail in my proverbial emotional coffin.

He spun, and this time I didn't try and follow.

I sunk to the ground, tears streamed down my face as I watched as the only man I had ever loved speeding away, taking my dignity and pride with him.

34

RAE

W RAPPING MY FINGERS THROUGH THE HANDLE OF THE WARM MUG did little to help ease the crack in my chest or the anger roaring in my head. He didn't even give me a chance to explain, and for someone who said they loved me and wanted me to move in with them…well, that was just shitty.

If you'd just been honest with me, if you'd just told me the truth, I wouldn't have cared…

"So, you first saw him when you were in high school?" my dad gently asked.

Both he and my mother were sitting across from me at the table. They'd eaten their dinner, but I didn't have an appetite, so I drank more tea. At first, I didn't want to talk about what had just happened, but they had heard everything, and after this, they deserved to know.

Giving him a small nod, I explained when I first saw Davis in the diner, and how my crush had developed.

"Carl knew?" Mom asked, her face dipped in a somber slump.

I gave her a small nod as well. After I explained everything, they seemed shocked, and now they were just clarifying tiny details.

"He tried to talk me out of liking Davis; he was worried about me."

Dad grunted and shook his head. "He should have told us."

"He never tried to dissuade you from being friends with Davis?" That was something that had me curious. It was no secret that Carl didn't like Davis, and after our little showdown, about that day where he'd made it seem like Davis was asking about a different girl and not me—we hadn't really talked again. But if Carl had such a problem with Davis, then why…

Suddenly it hit with sickening clarity, nearly making me double over.

It was *him*.

Carl had given me the note. Only it wasn't from Davis, it was from *him*. But how did he know Davis was going to be there that night, and why would he want to hurt me like that?

So I'd finally get over him, no doubt.

"Carl was never a big fan, mentioned it had to do with the past…but he never interfered or commented after our initial relationship that had started with Thomas."

"Is he the reason you wanted to move so suddenly and go to college clear across the country?" my mother asked, whipping her head up as she finally connected one of the dots I hadn't talked about yet.

"Yes. I was mortified by what—well, what I thought he had done to me. I was heartbroken, and I just wanted to get as far away from him as possible."

That seemed to break my mother, as she finally stood and walked over to me and gently cradled my face in her hands.

"We made you come back, and we forced you around him." Tears welled in her eyes. "I'm so sorry. You tried to fight it…you tried to warn us without telling us."

She gave a little hiccup, and it was an invisible thread to one of the lacerations in my heart. I needed this. To hear that they loved me, that they stood on my side. Part of me worried they'd still side with him.

"Dammit, I'm sorry, honey. We caused all this mess by forcing you two together…" Dad said, shaking his head. "Crazy twist of fate, though, if you ask me."

Crazy indeed.

My mom lowered her face, kissing the top of my head and then released me.

Dad rubbed at his chest, like he'd been doing lately. "Well, you tell us what you need—anything at all—and you have it."

"Look, I understand that what you heard out there in the yard didn't sound the greatest, but what I really want is for you to still be there for him. I want you to be the same support system you've been while I was away, and I want you to continue to allow him to support the diner."

"But, we—"

Shaking my head, I stopped him. "Dad, promise me…please."

They both nodded, quiet and somber.

"Just don't leave again Rae, please. We'll protect you, and if it's between you or him, you know we will always choose you. Over and over again. You're the easiest choice, sweetie. Okay?"

My dam of sobs nearly burst free, but I needed to keep them in for just a little while longer. "Thank you, and I won't leave. This is my home. I'm not going anywhere."

I MANAGED to get in my car, with my packed bags. It wasn't that I didn't want to be around my family, but I knew them too well. The first thing they'd try to do was create a civil meeting for Davis and me, where we talked through our issues in a safe space with moderators.

My parents were peacekeepers, and I loved them for it, but I didn't want to risk being forced into that or getting a surprise visit from him.

He had made himself more than clear about how he felt about me, and seeing me wouldn't be something he'd risk either.

Halfway down the road, I had to pull over because the crack in my chest finally overcame me, with gushing tears and an ugly cry that could rival a dying beast. I wanted to just get it over with, cry and be done with it...put my love for Davis into a small box, and tuck it into my closet, just like all the previous Davis items. But even after half an hour, the tears wouldn't stop. It was as though the rejection from when I was eighteen never healed over, and then I poured acid into the wound.

For a brief second, that moment I had pulled over on the side of the mountain popped into my head. That serpentine river, the tall trees, the feeling of being completely undone.

I needed more of that.

I needed to get away from Macon for a while and clear my head.

Swiping at my face, and taking a few clarifying breaths, I finished the drive to Nora's. A swarm of brown curls bounced as she ran from her door the second I pulled into her driveway. I hadn't texted or called her, so that must have been my mother's doing. I stepped out of the car and crumpled into her arms.

"I'm sorry, honey." She rubbed my back in soothing circles.

I sobbed with the ugly cry again, shoving my face into her shoulder as she held me. She said something soothing, but I couldn't make it out. We stood there for much longer than we should in small-town, nosy Macon. But I didn't care. The gossip would travel about our fight, and then they'd add in this little bit about me falling apart in Nora's driveway, and they'd know I was the one dumped.

"Come on, let's get you inside." Nora put her arm around me and pulled me into her house. Once she closed the door, I sat on her couch, recounting what Davis said through a few gasps and hiccups.

"What an idiot! Why would he think this is your big plan? You resisted and rejected the guy for weeks when you got here. He had to chase you down, not the other way around."

"Thank you!" I held my hand out, a wad of tissues was tucked between my fingers. "And he wouldn't even let me fight with him. I think that was the hardest part; he wouldn't hear me...he just acted like I was still that girl in the library. The annoying child that he would always look past and ignore. He treated me like a disease, or like something he was ashamed of. Not like he'd just asked me to move in."

How could he go from loving me so wholly to hating me so intensely?

"We need to get out of here, Rae. Let's just go on a trip."

She didn't need to convince me; I was completely and entirely on board.

"I'm already packed." Except for the things I had left at Davis's house.

"I'm going to pack. Why don't you go lay down in the guest room for a while, and I'll let you know when I'm ready, okay?" She stood and marched down the hall.

I headed to the guest room, where just the day prior, I'd been with Davis.

I fell apart again.

It was like visiting a tomb, the echo of when he said he loved me was loud in my head and battered at my heart, but tangibly, there was nothing there. It was empty.

I ripped off the comforter we'd laid on and threw it in the corner. Then I wrapped in the sheets and curled into a tiny ball and let more of my heartbreak through.

35

DAVIS

DEALING WITH EMOTIONS THAT SEEMED TOO BIG FOR MY CHEST wasn't a new sensation for me. When Timothy was in his accident, I felt like my heart would combust completely. It rammed against my chest as though it wanted to burst through it. It felt the same now—except different.

The wound in my heart wasn't the same. Because I had given this stupid fucking thing over to Rae, and now I wasn't sure what the fuck to do because it wasn't as though she gave it back. It was as though she had just uncovered that she'd had it the entire time, carefully holding it, waiting for me to realize that it was in her hands.

Protected.

Cared for.

Maybe that was why it was so easy for me to love her...maybe because she'd loved me first for so long.

Fuck.

Didn't matter, she had lied.

There was no hope for a relationship of any kind, not on the level I was hoping for, where she fucking lived with me—not when she couldn't even find it in herself to be honest.

This was shit she should have told me when we first met.

Although…

"Hey, dumbass," Gavin yelled over my head, walking out onto the patio. "You weren't answering your phone, so I just came over, hope that's okay."

Misplaced rage simmered under my skin, making it pop. "No, it's not fucking okay. What if Rae had been here? You can't just walk in. She lives here now." The words felt like dust in my mouth, making something strange happen in my chest. It felt as though something had gotten caught there and wouldn't budge unless I let some of these fucking tears free.

"Sorry, man…you're right, I wasn't thinking," Gavin said remorsefully. "Is she here? I just mean, I didn't see a car out front."

That made the burning in my chest worse. "She usually parks in the garage, unless she gets in late and she doesn't want to walk that far in the dark."

I was rambling, like an idiot. I knew I was, but I couldn't seem to stop.

"She doesn't even know that I bought her a new car. It's a Jeep, with heavy tread—thirty-fives, a roll cage, and enough protection in the snow that even if she fell down a cliff, I'm pretty sure she'd be okay."

Gavin shifted on the lounger, his brows dipping to the center of his forehead, but he didn't say anything.

"I was going to surprise her for Christmas. I had this whole plan," I laughed, rubbing at my chest absently. "We'd drive it to go pick out a Christmas tree, and while we were out, I was going to ask her to marry me…"

"Fuck, man," Gavin finally said, with a slight crack in his voice.

I realized then that the tears I was holding in had been forced out, and my best and *only* friend was sitting here witnessing me fall the fuck apart.

"Shit." I swiped at my face. "Doesn't matter anymore…she's gone."

Gavin seemed to hesitate, adjusting in the lounger again. "What…uh—what happened?"

Groaning, I shoved my hands into my hair and leaned my head back. "Found out she was the girl...the one that used to follow me... the one in the library."

A few seconds passed before he finally exhaled heavily. "Holy fuck."

"Yeah, just found out last night."

"Did she confess to stalking you in the library?"

Shaking my head, I tried to gather the small pieces of that night into order. "She said she was given a handwritten note from this piece of shit that works at her dad's diner. I don't know the whole story because..."

The words died on my tongue because I wasn't sure how to explain that I hadn't given her a chance to talk...to tell me everything. I hadn't given her a chance for anything. I just told her to fuck off and called her pathetic.

More pain pierced my chest, making me nearly double over.

"You okay, man?"

My chest burned, my head pounded, and I felt like I was going to be sick.

"No...I...fuck, she's gone. She's not coming back..."

Because when I hurt people, they never did.

Gavin moved closer, putting a firm hand on my shoulder. "Man, you're falling the fuck apart. I'm confused. If you want her, even after the past, and all the stalker shit, then just tell her that."

"I can't." I barely got the words out.

"Why, what the hell happened?"

I crushed her, again...just like before. I completely crushed her and made her feel stupid for something she couldn't control. I shamed her for liking me. I made it seem like I would have never chosen her compared to the one-night stands I had selected. The women who I never called again...the ones who could never compare to her.

What the fuck had I done?

I KNEW there wasn't much I could do in terms of damage control. I had said what I said, in a moment of rage, and ruined the best thing I ever had. I knew there was no coming back from what I had said, and how I made her feel, but I couldn't just sit at home. I had to do something with this anger simmering under my skin.

I hadn't slept the night prior. Just drank, looking at photos on my phone of Rae. Her smile was so wide in each and every picture. She was happy, and I looked...fuck, I looked healthy. Whole. The most complete I ever felt in my entire life. And in one moment of fury and pride, I just let it all go. So, I was after the one person I could take some of this anger out on.

I waited until I knew for sure that Roger and Millie had gone home and watched as more and more employees left through the back. Once I was sure Carl was alone, I slipped inside, but immediately realized I wasn't the only one who'd had the idea to confront the bastard.

Thankfully I was still in the darkened space of the small hallway when Rae burst through the back door, stomping to the kitchen. Even seeing her like this, anger radiating from her in waves, made me want to reach out and touch her.

"Carl!" she yelled, her boots clicking on the floor as she caught him by surprise. I carefully moved where I could watch and stay hidden.

"String bea—"

Her hand flew up. "Don't!"

Carl's bushy eyebrows caved as his posture deflated. Fucker probably knew what was coming. The whole town was already gossiping about our breakup; wouldn't take much to connect the dots.

"How could you?" she rasped, her fists clenched tight at her sides. "How could you give me that note? How could you crush me that way?"

Carl's head lowered, his hands slowly sinking to the counters.

Rae continued on. "You, of all people, knew how much I loved him. You knew how badly it would hurt me to see him there, especially after thinking he finally saw me!" She was shaking, her voice trembling, and fuck, it felt like her words had grown talons and were suddenly tearing at my chest.

I had an idea of how she had felt for me. Obviously back then I had chalked it up to teenage obsession. I thought she'd outgrow it, but I had no idea why she'd been in that library. Truthfully, she likely *would* have outgrown her crush once she matured, but Carl forced the pain, so it stuck with her forever.

"I just wanted you to be over him. You were finally old enough to actually be interested in him, and it—" Carl hesitated. "It scared me."

"Why?" Rae yelled, slamming her hand down on the counter. "Why did it scare you, and how the fuck did you even know he'd be there with…" She trailed off, her voice shaking.

If I had walked in on Rae fucking someone else, it would kill me. Straight up remove my ability to breathe and exist, and if I had to replay that image for any length of time… Jesus, I had no idea she'd been carrying that for so long, but it finally made sense why she hated me so much when she met me for what I had assumed was the first time.

Carl shook his head. "At the time, I was dating Pam. She was the librarian. A few days leading up to that night, she'd let it slip that she'd be off early because Davis would be there working late. Then she'd dropped that she hoped he didn't meet up with anyone because he'd apparently done it before. The boy had built a bit of a reputation for having company while working late on city projects. Honestly, I just took a shot that he wouldn't be alone."

Rae shifted on her feet, her arms now crossed over her chest.

"So, there was a fifty-fifty chance that I'd go, and he would have been alone?"

What would have happened if I had been?

Nothing. Back then, she was a kid to me, I would have asked her to leave. But Carl didn't even know me. How did he know Rae wouldn't have been hurt, or worse? What a fucking prick.

"Guess I was right about him being a player, since he broke your heart," Carl snidely remarked, tossing his rag.

Rae's jaw set, and her lip wobbled. "You broke my heart, Carl.

Not him. He had no way of knowing, and it was completely unfair that someone intruded on his privacy. All these years, I assumed he'd just sent that note to hurt me—to be cruel. Turns out, you were the only cruel one in the scenario."

Taking a steadying breath, she moved her hands and declared, "I want nothing to do with you."

Carl surged forward, worry etched into his features. "You don't mean that…"

She stepped back, and a fierce protectiveness swept through me. If he tried to touch her at all, even to give her a hug…

"I love him, Carl…with all my heart, and I was going to have a future with him. That's not happening now, but that doesn't change the fact that I can't have people in my life who don't support my choices."

With one last look at the man, Rae turned to leave, while I ducked further into the shadows.

I waited there long enough to let her words sink in. It was slow, like a block of cement. Her saying our future wasn't happening now…it fucked with my head. I still wanted one with her. Still, her lie and the fact that I had nearly gutted myself to be vulnerable with her…it hurt.

I loved Rae. To my very marrow, I did—but I didn't know if I could trust her. Even getting over that she was worried how I'd respond, assuming I had given her that note, how could she still have thought that after being with me? After hearing something so deep and personal to me, how could she assume that I—

Well fuck, I guess in the end, I responded exactly how she feared.

Wasn't that some shit?

Shaking my head, I waited to ensure she was gone before pushing through the back doors and inhaling the cold October air.

36

DAVIS

Three days after Rae had confronted Carl, I started to lose my mind.

I thought it would make me feel better if I confronted the asshole who had put Rae leaving into motion, but then that moment was stolen by my little spitfire, who wasn't exactly mine anymore, and that's what kept swirling around in my head.

Over and fucking over again.

She wasn't mine anymore.

Each day my disgust over how I had treated her that night in her parent's yard would grow. The look on her face kept running on repeat in my head. I'd try to sleep, but then I'd see her face when I called her pathetic and she crumpled to the ground.

Then my brain would remind me that she had lied and chose not to trust me with her truth.

She chose to keep from me this thing that tied us together, this fundamental thing that required her honesty. Her being obsessed with me when she was in high school wasn't something to be ashamed of, but if we wanted a future together, a real one, then it would have to be built on mutual trust and honesty. I was vulnerable with her. That was her moment to tell me who she was…to explain to me that once upon a time she loved me.

The more I thought over the timeline we were together, the more our first breakup made sense. It was the day Gavin came over, and we talked about Rae. She must have overheard us, and right after that she…

Left me.

How could I have actually accused her of trying to set all this up? God, I was an idiot.

All I knew was after three days, I missed Rae. My dogs missed her, the entire house seemed to miss her. It felt empty and cold without her, and I hadn't slept a single night in my bed, because she wasn't in it, and I couldn't stand to look at all the things I put there for her. I had slept on the couch, but then that reminded me of her…and so, I slept on the floor, next to my dogs…where I fucking belonged.

Driving toward Roger and Millie's house felt like swallowing nails. I wasn't anxious; I was ashamed. So, the feeling wasn't even tied to my nerves. It was in my blood, roaring at me to fix the colossal mistake I had made on their lawn just days before.

Parking and starting up the walk, I paused when Roger pushed through the door and met me halfway.

"Roger, I—" I started, but his stern expression stopped me. I had never seen him look so hurt and angry, and he had every right to be.

"Just turn around and go back, Davis."

I paused, trying to wrap my head around him calling me that instead of Thomas. It was a sucker punch.

"I have to be the one to love my daughter, because you broke her heart, and there needs to be some man in her life willing to mend it. So, just go…live your life, be happy, but leave us be."

He gave me one last look and turned around, leaving me there on the sidewalk with my heart lurching uncomfortably and my stomach twisting.

I stood there, staring. My eyes watered, my throat bobbed, and I tried to convince myself to turn around, but they were the only family I had.

They were it, and now they didn't want me.

Maybe if I tried to explain that I loved her, that it was a mistake. Maybe if he…

Blinking, I shook myself out of it, and without another thought, I spun on my boot, heading for my truck.

I knew they wouldn't be happy with me, but deep down, I had assumed our connection would go deeper, and preserve our relationship that had existed outside of Rae. I was an idiot, because Rae had always been a part of us—a part of me—even not knowing she was, there was a tether that had kept us connected.

With shaking hands, I went to the only other place I could think of, now realizing Rae's car wasn't even in front of her parents' house. With every block, I began to think over what I'd say to her… how I would go about patching this up. I couldn't just act like she hadn't lied or omitted her part in my life. I had to face that, but if Rae wasn't ready…or—

The realization that Rae might have given up on me hit hard and fast. Why was I assuming she'd still want to talk to me, after what I said?

Fuck.

Still, I had to try and see her, because I was going insane without at least laying eyes on her.

Pulling in front of Nora's house, I saw Rae's car parked in the driveway. Gripping the steering wheel, I watched the car like it might suddenly combust or disappear then slowly took a calming breath. It was a few seconds later, seeing my breath cloud in front of me, that I walked. The early mornings had turned cold as fall set in, and with it took more time from me being with Rae. She was supposed to be starting each of these freezing cold mornings with me, up there, on the mountain. She was supposed to be there to see how beautiful the leaves looked when they started turning orange and feel how good the hot tub felt on those bitter early mornings.

Curling my knuckles, I pounded on Nora's door, and waited. Nothing happened.

I knocked again and hit the doorbell for good measure, but still nothing.

Maybe she was asleep and couldn't hear me? It was past eight in the morning; she'd be up, they both would. I knew their phone call habits by now, and every morning around seven, they were on the phone with each other.

I was about to walk around back when Colson's voice stopped me. Across the small fence that separated his yard from Nora's, he walked to his truck and clicked over the ignition to get it started. He wore heavier, lined clothing, and thick-soled boots—likely on his way to work.

"She's gone. They both are," he called, walking a few steps closer to the half fence. "Left a few days ago, her and someone that looked like your girlfriend from that dinner party."

Shit. I hadn't anticipated them leaving.

"You know where they went?"

Colson shook his head, flicking his cold gaze behind me once before clenching his jaw.

"But, uh...you okay, with your girl and everything? She seemed pretty upset the other day when she got here. I was fixing my truck and heard her crying pretty hard."

Shame smothered my response, to the point it felt difficult to breathe. I didn't want to stand here and hash out all my problems with someone I hadn't kept in touch with, but it wasn't like the rest of the town didn't already know something. Hell, he probably knew but was trying to be polite.

"Just fucked some things up. I'm trying to fix it."

Colson gave me a pitying look before stepping back toward his truck. "If it helps, I heard Nora yell something about three days of no responsibilities...that should put them back home today or tomorrow."

"Thanks, man." I gave him an appreciative nod and returned to my truck.

I could wait, and during that time, I'd figure out what to say to get Rae back.

THE HOT COFFEE warmed my fingers and burned my tongue. I deserved it, because I was stalking Nora's house like a psychopath. Every day, I had been back, seeing if they'd returned, watching for a pair of headlights to pull in. While they were gone, I called Rae's phone, but she never answered. I hadn't quite braved texting her yet, because I didn't want to say shit through text, even if it was just asking where she was.

I still wasn't sleeping, and my face and body showed it. I hadn't shaved in days, my hair was shoved under a hat, keeping the greasy, matted mess down, and I had to ask Gavin to go to my house and take care of all my animals yesterday. I wanted to be here when she got back.

I had to be.

I just needed a chance to explain myself.

Hearing her voice in my head, begging for the same opportunity, haunted me while I sat across the road, waiting for Nora's car to pop into view.

Hopefully, Rae would be merciful and allow me the chance to say a few things, because after so long without her, I had several words I wanted to share. But with each passing day, those words kept boiling down to just three.

Flicking my gaze down the street, a flash of blue caught my eye, and my heart rate spiked.

Nora.

Slowly, the car made its way down the street and carefully maneuvered the smaller space to the left of Rae's car and parked. I was out of the truck, marching across the street, ready to pull Rae's door open and just hold her in my arms for five minutes before I said a single, fucking word. But Nora's head popped up, and her blue eyes narrowed in a determined way that reminded me way too much of when Rae got pissed.

"She isn't here."

I stopped short, the air leaving my lungs in a rush. "What?"

I edged closer, so I could hear her better.

284

Clicking her tongue with clear annoyance, she exhaled. "She isn't with me. She boarded a plane in Portland, and we parted ways there. I headed home, and she headed…somewhere else."

No, she wouldn't do it again. Not to the town, not to her parents.

Not to me.

I forced myself to form the words burning in my head. "Where did she go?"

"Colorado, I think." Nora leaned in to grab a bag and then slammed her car door shut. "Look, she just wanted a little more time away to clear her head. She wasn't ready to potentially run into you. Which, given you're already standing here, was a good call on her part."

"I just need to talk to her."

I tried defending why I was waiting here, clearly stalking her premises, but I was starting to forget why it mattered. I loved Rae, I wanted her back, and I'd do whatever it took to get her.

"Well, that's dandy, but she broke a bit when you called her pathetic—all of her. Past her, current her…you stomped all over all the pieces she hid from the world, all the things she hated about herself. You lit it all on fire, and now you think there's still something left?" She huffed, shaking her head while walking to her front door. "I wish I had your confidence."

I wasn't confident. I was desperate.

"I know that I messed up. I know I don't deserve another chance, and now I realize why she broke it off the first time with me, but it isn't over. I don't care how long it takes her to realize that, but it's not. If she chooses to leave again this time, I'll chase her."

Nora watched me with an expression like someone who was watching a rabid animal, but I didn't care. I walked back to my truck and decided it was time to get home and start believing I had a chance to win her back.

37

RAE

Hugging my pillow to my chest, I let another tear slip down my cheek. Now that Nora was gone, I was free to cry and break without shame. Not that I was embarrassed to cry in front of her, but I could tell that she wanted to cheer me up and felt defeated every time I slipped back into misery. That was one of the reasons I chose to continue my "vacation." The other was I just simply wasn't ready to see Davis around town again.

Colorado seemed like a good spot. I could see the Rockies, and learn how to hike. It was something I had wanted to do ever since that serene moment on Mount Macon, when I veered off on the side of the road.

While the mountains around me did seem to hold some magical healing properties, nothing I saw compared to *my* mountain.

Two days into my trip, the realization made me cry. I had assumed all mountains would make me feel whole, the way Mount Macon had. I hated how wrong I was, and how desperate I was to go home. Maybe it was time. I had originally planned on a week, but every single day just proved to be more and more painful of an experience than the first time I had left home. Time was supposed to make this pain recede, make it more manageable.

That was how it worked the first time…but now, I had memories to war with.

There were pictures on my phone of Davis smiling, while kissing my stomach, a few of him laughing, while holding me. I had images of him shirtless, while watching me from over the brim of his coffee mug. Pictures of Dove and Duke, of the hens, and the goats. I had an entire life on my phone, and I couldn't seem to just put all of that in a box and watch it leave my life. I wanted to cling to all of it with bloodied fingers.

But that was the old me. The one who thought she could force someone to love her.

Not anymore.

I had to grow up and start accepting that not everything would be that simple. Davis didn't want me, and I had to let him go.

THREE DAYS later I received a text from Nora.

Nora: You coming back soon?

I had left the text all morning while hiking around a small summit with a group of tourists who wanted to safely explore the area. Once I was back in my tent, I tugged it free and bit my nail.

Me: Yeah, not sure when…everything okay?

Part of me being here only worked because I wasn't staying in hotels. I was camping, and I knew it wasn't safe to do it alone, but I had joined this group that had elderly women and a few tourists visiting from Korea and Japan. Everyone was so friendly and helpful that it quickly became like a little family.

Nora: Everything is fine…um…just, well, there's a bit of a situation, but it's fine.

Furrowing my brows, I typed back.

Me: What do you mean? Are my parents okay? Are yours? What's going on?

Nora: Everything is fine, both our parents are fine. I'll tell you when you get back, it's okay. And I know you don't have a lot of battery life.

She wasn't wrong, our little group had a battery pack that we took turns sitting and charging at the truck stops that had showers and charging ports. Then we'd all share the pack when we needed a little juice for our phones.

Me: Are you sure?

Nora: Yeah, you blocked what's his face, right? He hasn't been calling or texting?

What's his face being Davis.

Me: Yeah, I blocked him. I haven't heard anything, are you sure everything is okay?

Nora: Yes, go hike, heal, and then come back when you're ready.

I hesitated a second, but realized she was right. I needed to heal. I owed it to myself to stay.

Me: Okay, love you.

"YOU DID AMAZING!" I congratulated Ellis, my seventy-two-year-old tent mate, tossing a handful of nuts into my mouth.

"I was sure I was about to slip." She smiled, her face bright and flushed with exhilaration.

Speaking while chewing, I shook my head. "I knew you had it."

We were still hiking around smaller summits, ignoring the looks of more experienced backpackers and native mountain climbers who were used to the altitude of Colorado and the cold. It was freezing, and while our tour guide, Jonathan, promised it was still perfectly safe to camp in October, more and more of our group had begun to fizzle out. Ellis and I had decided to share a smaller tent to help with the warmth. Ellis was out here giving herself a second chance at life after she finally left a marriage she never wanted after nearly thirty-five years.

I felt a kinship with her for that. It was obviously different from my situation, but we were both single and finding ourselves now.

It was when I ducked back into the tent that I found a new text from Nora. She'd been texting more and more often, but just little things here and there, nothing earth shattering. I also had been calling my parents twice a week to check in, so I knew nothing too crazy was going on back home. From the sound of it, the grump had gone back to avoiding the town, or at least that's what I assumed since I hadn't heard anything about him.

So, I pulled out a protein bar and read through her messages.

Nora: Okay...so, you've been in Colorado for two weeks. I miss you.

Nora: It's not just that I miss you. There's been some things happening here...I haven't exactly been honest about it, because I wanted you to have your time...

Nora: You need to come home, I think it's pretty serious.

What in the actual hell? I was about to pull up her contact to call her when my mother's name flashed on my screen.

"Hello?"

"Rae, honey..." She sounded so gentle, the exact opposite of the panic in Nora's messages.

"Hi Mom, everything okay?"

I chewed my bar, moving around a few of the items in my backpack, sorting out my dirty and clean clothes.

"Well...honey, things aren't so great here. You need to come back." My stomach clenched tight with nerves. First Nora, now my mom. What on earth was going on?

"Mom, what's wrong? Nora mentioned something and—"

"It's Davis, honey. He's... you just need to come back."

Worry wound around my heart like a rope, pulling tighter and tighter with each second that passed as I tried to find the right words to say, but the only thing coming to mind was panic.

"Is—" I couldn't even ask, because what if he wasn't safe? I closed my eyes, bringing a shaky hand to my head to push back my hair. "Is he okay?"

My mother paused, and the silence seemed to tear a new fissure in my heart. I was too far away. If something had happened to him, I would never forgive myself.

"His brother died, honey. He's not handling it well—"

Oh my God. No. That couldn't be right.

He was going to call; he was going to get closure.

"Rae?"

"I'm sorry, did you say his brother?"

"Yes, honey, his brother Timothy. He passed, and—" I tuned the rest out. I couldn't listen to her tell me that Davis lost the only person who was tied to his redemption. The only person who could have made him whole.

"Sweetie?" I could hear my mom echo from the phone speaker, her voice cracking, and she must have heard me sobbing because I couldn't control it anymore.

"I'm coming. I'll be there as soon as I can."

I didn't need to hear anymore. Hanging up, I started throwing my things inside my backpack, rolling up my sleeping bag and tucking away all my belongings.

Ellis found me trying to tie an extra pair of boots to the side of my bag with shaking fingers. She pulled me into a tight hug, whispering soothing things while rubbing my back. I sobbed, releasing all my fears to her in a muttered rush. I was too far away, and I needed to get back to him.

Assuming he even wanted me. I pushed that thought away because it didn't matter. I loved him, and he needed me. Even if he wasn't going to love me back, I would be there to support him.

That's what love did. It made us loyal idiots, ready to jump off a cliff for the people we cared about. I was about ready to board the most expensive flight I could find, just to get back to him, when Ellis turned to me, pocketing her phone.

"I found you a flight. It leaves tonight from Denver. It will get you to Portland; that's as close as I can get you."

I nodded, tears falling from my lashes as I processed how Davis must be feeling. I hated that I didn't know when his brother had passed, and I hated even more that I had blocked him, and now if I opened the door for communication, he'd reject me.

It had to be in person.

"I'll have someone pick me up and take me the rest of the way.

Thank you so much, for everything." I hugged her close and got inside the Uber I'd called then prayed my flight wouldn't be delayed.

38

RAE

My father greeted me as I exited the airport. I didn't bother checking any bags, just abandoning anything that wouldn't fit on my carry on. I didn't want to waste a single minute getting back home. This time, I had no issues asking for a ride, knowing my parents wanted me back as soon as possible.

"Dad!" I called, running into his arms.

He clutched me to his chest tight before releasing me and helping me with my backpack.

"Mom's at home?" I crawled into the passenger seat and buckled. I knew I looked like I had been camping for the past two weeks, but I didn't care. I hadn't given a single glance to anyone who turned their nose up at me on the flight. Ellis had not only booked my flight, but she had paid for it, and made sure I was in first class, so at least I wasn't shoulder to shoulder with anyone during the flight.

I had to call her and tell her I was safely with my dad. A text would have to do, though, because I was going to grill my dad for details.

As he pulled away from the lane and exited the airport, I tried to breathe through my nose and calm my racing heart.

"What happened? How come no one told me?"

I had begun piecing things together, from what Nora had vaguely texted about something happening but it not being a big deal. She had to be talking about this, which made me furious. She had to know that I would want to know…

Although, I had never shared with her Davis's devastating past. Still, she had to know that this would have been something I needed to be made aware of.

Dad let out a heavy sigh. "His brother passed some time ago, but we just found out." I was trying to sort through what that meant when he spoke up again. "Shortly after your breakup, Davis came to the house."

I hadn't thought he would even try…but I guess he did have his own relationship with them.

"But I—I refused him, and I know what you said, but your mother and I—we were furious with what he'd said to you on the grass that night, so I told him not to come back around."

The crack in his voice told me he was beating himself up pretty horribly for what he said.

I watched the blackness outside the window and tried to keep the tears at bay, needing in this moment to be strong, if not for me then for the people who loved Davis.

"After that, he found out from Nora that you hadn't returned, and I think something in him snapped. He was around town more often than normal, checking in with businesses, following up on things you had set up with them. He started doing projects where he replaced the local shop signs, and adding little rustic fixtures here and there. No one from city hall had signed off on anything; it was all in the works, as far as we knew."

Shaking my head, I confirmed his thoughts. "I hadn't met with them yet; I was waiting until I had a chance to chat with all of the business owners, or at least until I had a proposal to show them."

"Davis must have found it. He was carrying around one of your notebooks and started barking orders at people. He found out Nora's parents were moving, so he bought their shop. They weren't ready to sell, but he didn't want to risk competition moving in. I think he was trying to do anything he could to keep your dream alive, and then…"

My throat was tight, my vision blurred with tears as I continued watching the city lights along the interstate.

Dad's voice shuddered as he continued. "Then he just disappeared…gone. He wasn't coming into town for anything, not parts, not food, not gas…and that worried both your mother and I, so we drove up to his house and found him drunk, staring at a black-and-white photo of his brother."

My heart lurched, remembering that photo of his family that he had finally pulled out.

"Millie started cleaning, and we had brought him a meal, but we realized he wasn't doing well. For a few days, we thought he'd come out of it, but it just seemed to get worse. When we'd ask what we could do, or get for him, he'd just repeat your name."

There were so many feelings happening inside me, it all felt combustible, like any second a fuse would ignite and all of me would explode into a thousand pieces.

What did it mean that he said my name? Had he forgiven me, did he want me?

"What happened after that?"

Dad let out another heavy sigh, bringing his hand to his forehead.

"Then he started trashing his house, saying he didn't deserve any of it. Not after what he said to you, not after what he did to his brother… Honey, your mom and I were taking shifts with him, but he got into his pickup truck and took off while your mother was dozing. We still haven't found him."

Oh my God.

A gasp caught in my throat. "What do you mean, you haven't found him?"

I couldn't lose him.

With shaking fingers, I brought my phone out and stared at our message thread from before I had blocked him. I reactivated him while on the plane, and now that I was off, a part of me hoped it would ping with a notification from him. I hoped that somehow, he would just know that I was here, ready to talk.

Unable to hear anymore, I curled into a ball against the door and shut my eyes, hoping I wasn't too late.

WE ARRIVED in Macon as dawn broke. The town slept, but I could see what my dad had talked about regarding the signs and the shops. Most of them were half finished. I watched as we passed store after store, but Dad kept going up, until we were on Mount Macon and pulling into Davis's driveway.

Our driveway, I had to start saying that in my head because I *was* moving back, and we were going to get through this.

A thin layer of snow covered a few patches on the ground and the pitch of the roofline, but otherwise the forest floor was just cold. I looked up to see the tendril of smoke that was always curling out of the chimney this time of morning, but it wasn't there.

The absence felt as cold as knowing Davis wasn't here.

As soon as we parked, I was out the door and running up the steps.

My mother opened the front door, holding a blanket around her shoulders, her face tight with worry.

"Oh honey." She threw her arms around me, letting the blanket drop, revealing that she'd slept in her clothes. I wondered how many nights she'd done that.

"It's okay, Mom. We'll find him."

I knew we would. I could feel it.

Now that I was home, I felt more at peace. Everything still smelled like him, and that alone was enough to encourage me to prepare, and more than anything, be calm.

I took my things upstairs, and went into our room, where the bed was still mussed from when Davis had slept in it. None of my things were moved from the dresser. I hadn't moved everything in yet, but I had left a few outfits here over time. So, I showered, and then I dressed.

I cooked my parent's breakfast, and then I started to clean.

"Rae, honey, now that you're here, we should come up with a plan. Dad was thinking of calling in the town to help look for him."

With the sleeves on the flannel I had stolen from Davis's closet rolled to my elbows, I gathered the few plates and started rinsing them.

"Rae?"

Smiling up at my parents, I shut off the faucet. "No, we don't need to do that. In fact, I actually need you both to head back home. If you want to come up here, you're more than welcome to, but please be sure to bring all the boxes I had packed up that are in my room."

"Surely, you're not serious about not going out there?" my dad asked with an incredulous tone.

"I know him, and I know he'll come back. What's important is that I'm here when it happens. If a bunch of people go looking for him, he won't come down. Clear out. He'll know I'm home."

My parents gave each other long looks, but it was my mother who folded the blanket she was clutching, laying it over the back of the couch. "Let's go, honey. I could use a good night's sleep."

My dad was reluctant. He rubbed at the back of his neck, scrunching his eyebrows together, but with a soft hand on his arm from my mother, he relented with a sigh.

Once they were gone, I went to start a fire, but realized there was no wood.

That was okay. I had watched Davis do it enough times that I knew what to do. I walked out back and off to the side, where the wood pile sat, and saw that there was still plenty chopped, it just needed to be brought inside. So, I gathered as many logs with my arms as I could and started a fire in the hearth.

Then, I cooked.

I tossed chicken into the crock pot, and started low music on Alexa, turning on small lamps as the day waned. I made our bed, cleaned our bathroom, and took a bath.

I watched the stars come out, while sipping tea on the back porch.

Then I slept alone in our bed, hugging the pillow that smelled like him to my chest.

The next morning, I heard gravel crunching under tires, and threw off the covers, running downstairs.

Flinging the door open, it was my parents' SUV that rolled to a stop, not the big truck I was hoping for. Alongside their Rover was my small Toyota, being driven by my mom.

My father had brought up my belongings, just like I asked. Not a single time did he or my mom question me or what I wanted as they helped carry my extra suitcases upstairs. When they were ready to leave, Dad placed a kiss on my forehead and then left.

I carried on, like I did the day prior, checking to ensure the goats and hens were fed and cared for, and made a fresh fire. I made a new meal in the slow cooker, chuck roast this time. I figured we'd freeze whatever didn't get eaten, which would help keep us stocked through the winter.

Then, I went upstairs and began unpacking my boxes. Clothes went into the closet; shoes were unpacked, and all my little effects were dispersed throughout the room. Next to my bed, I plugged in the chargers for my e-reader and cell, and brought up the book Davis had read to me by the fire.

That night, I took another bath, and this time, a few worried tears slipped free.

I believed with all my heart that Davis would come back for me. I knew he would, deep down, but my bravado began to slip with each day that passed.

IT WAS the fifth day of going through the motions when I realized I might be wrong.

Then, like an avalanche, guilt smothered me as I thought of him out there, likely dead and lost, not rescued, and all because of me. There wasn't heavy snow on the mountain yet; there wouldn't be any real reason to worry. Still, it gnawed at my gut.

Opening the front door, wearing just one of his long shirts, I watched rain pelt my car as hard as bullets.

I considered, not for the first time, hiking around locally, maybe seeing if I could use my recent introductory hiking skills I had learned in Colorado to try and find him, but it would have to be once the rain stopped. I left the door open as I curled up under a blanket on the porch swing and watched the tall trees sway under the heavy downpour and small rivulets fall from the workshop roof. I watched, willing Davis to show up, praying his truck would come into view any second. Hoping the rain would drive him away from the mountain and into my arms. I watched as the rain drowned my world, until my eyelids grew heavy, and I finally let them close.

39

DAVIS

In retrospect, I should have made sure that extra gas can was in the back of the truck before I took off. But I wasn't thinking when I left.

So, three days ago, when I saw the tiny curl of smoke lift from the spot down the mountain, where I knew my house was, something in my gut churned. While I was home and Millie watched over me, not once did she try to start a fire. I didn't think she knew how.

Roger hadn't either, though he might know how—but why would they be in my house if I wasn't there? The hens and goats would be fine for a few days, and I just needed some space to clear my head. Away from the walls that reminded me of her, of her smell, and her things still in my house.

I needed to stop the cracking in my chest, but all around me seemed to be emptiness. But now, there was someone in my house. I knew it wasn't Gavin, and while I hadn't taken my phone with me, I knew if I had my cell and called him up, he'd tell me the same thing he did a week ago, that he was still in Georgia, visiting his family.

No, deep in my bones, I knew it was her.

She'd come back.

Elation quickened my steps, which became increasingly difficult with the rain that had started and made nearly impossible as the downpour continued through the night, and next day.

Now, I was a mere mile from home, and my dogs had given up on waiting for me—they took off running. I wasn't too far behind when I finally crested my drive, and sure enough, her car was parked in front of the house.

She was home.

Home.

Here. Waiting.

I briskly covered the rest of the space between the driveway and the house but stopped dead when I realized who was curled into a ball under the blanket on the porch. Her dark hair curly from the rain, her face was clear of any makeup, and she slept, likely through my dogs trying to wake her, and now the gravel crunched under my boots, and she didn't stir.

Was she alive?

Fuck. That thought punched through me on a new level after hearing about my brother. Shit, if I lost her…I couldn't—

Shaking my head, I pushed the thought away and dropped all my gear on the porch, crouching down and scooping her into my arms.

She still slept as I walked with her into the house and shut the door. Little lamps were on, warming up the space, along with a fire that was getting low, and it smelled like she had been cooking something.

Walking up the stairs with Rae in my arms, I clutched her tightly to my chest and pressed a kiss to the side of her head. She stirred a moment later, right as I walked into our room. Bypassing the bed that looked freshly made, I carried her to the counter in the bathroom.

Tender fingers moved up my chest, over my clothes, until she was cupping my jaw.

Pinning my forehead to hers, I just breathed her in. A burning sensation threatened to rip me open as I realized she was here, in my arms. For just a brief moment, all was right in the world again.

"You came back," I murmured into the minuscule space between our faces.

Her fingers moved up, over my ears and to my neck.

"So did you."

The sound of the pounding rain echoed around us as we stayed connected. Her on the counter, in my arms, my forehead pinned to hers. I knew the words would come, eventually, but she seemed to realize it would take time.

So, I moved. Lifting the shirt I recognized as mine over her head, leaving her naked save for her tall socks and underwear.

She began unbuttoning my flannel, starting at my throat and working her way down, until she was pushing it off my shoulders.

I skimmed the skin along her rib cage, letting my fingers greedily graze. A whooshing seemed to fill my head as I began to trace patterns into her skin, marking it. Memorizing it. It was the dull silence that filled me ever since she left, and then my brother—he'd been gone, out of my life, but there was always this lingering hope that he'd come back. That we'd fix our broken mess and be together again, if I could just fucking speak to him.

Now, he was gone, but Rae—she was here. She was back, and she…a lump caught in my throat as I thought about losing her.

"I'm sorry," I whispered between us as she pulled my shirt up and over my head. "But you're mine." I shivered as her fingers twisted the copper button of my jeans, loosening them and pushing them down my hips. "Always, forever"—I kissed her neck as she pushed my boxers down next—"mine."

Grabbing her left foot, I peeled the sock off, and then the right. My dirty fingers reached for her underwear, tugging it gently down her legs. Then she gathered her hands once again at the base of my neck as I pulled her to my chest.

Walking us into the shower, I turned the hot water on and let it fill with steam before pressing her back into the cold tile wall. Her lips found the space next to my eye first, then my ear, and slowly along my jaw, until she captured my lips in a kiss made up of a wild hope that seemed to tear through her as she moved her body against mine.

Starved and rough, she rocked her hips against mine, tugging my hair back and kissing along my neck.

I allowed her to, because I couldn't fathom that she was here, in my arms again. I didn't deserve her; fuck, she'd probably only came back because her parents guilted her into it. But I was too selfish to care at the moment.

Letting her down, she grabbed a bottle of shampoo and tugged on my hand.

"Sit."

I did as she said, trying to relax into the hot spray.

Her fingers were in my hair as she poured shampoo into it, lathering and scraping my scalp clean. Closing my eyes, I let her work and tried to let the last week slip away.

Most of it went. The stress from losing her, the hole in the center of my chest, the fear that I'd never hold her again or kiss her lips. It all melted away, until only the crack of pain regarding my brother was left.

Rae moved over me and began using a bar of soap, washing over my back and then over my chest, in slow and sensual movements. Then she rubbed the bar of soap in her hands, lathering up, and kneeled in front of me to wash my cock. It felt intimate, far more intimate than anything we'd done. Instead of picking her up again and fucking her against the wall, I rinsed and turned off the spray, helping her out of the shower.

Not grabbing a towel for either of us, I carried her, soaking wet, to the bedroom. Tugging the blanket off, and pulling it around our naked bodies, we curled under the covers. Then I pulled her to my chest, curving my body around hers.

Silence seemed to envelop us, just as tightly as I was holding her to my chest. It threatened to drown out any hope I had of fixing what I broke, so I cleared my throat and confessed.

"I didn't mean any of it…" I let my apology wane in the silence, hoping she'd stop me there, allowing me the coward's way out. *Hadn't I done that one too many times though?*

"I was just hurt that you hadn't told me. But please believe me, I didn't mean it, baby. Forgive me." I kissed her neck, wrapping my hand around her, until my palm was over her stomach. "I know I don't deserve to have you here with me—to have you at all—and I don't want your pity. I just want you, the real you, even if that means it takes a while for you to forgive me."

She turned in my arms until she was facing me, wrapping her hands around my neck again, tangling her fingers in my hair.

"You will never get pity from me. Ever." She pressed a kiss to my jaw then frowned. "I'm so sorry I didn't tell you. I was scared, especially after I heard you and Gavin talking about me. I just freaked out."

I thought back to that day Gavin had shown up and shook my head. "I'm sorry, it's shitty that we talked about you. I hate that you had to hear any of it."

"I know, and I know I should have told you, and I kept meaning to do it, but it just never felt right. I was embarrassed about that part of my life. I was so ashamed."

I pulled her closer by the hip. "It's a part of our past, and it will always be safe here"—I grabbed her hand and placed it over my heart—"always. But I know I don't deserve your forgiveness. I can't imagine how painful it was that night you walked in on me..."

She closed her eyes, breathing through her nose. "I thought it was you just being cruel. For so long I believed that I was just a joke to you."

"Never." I pressed a kiss to her nose, then her lips. "I heard your confrontation with Carl."

"You did?"

I nodded. "Your dad has a theory that he had a vendetta against me after he heard what I had done to my—"

My voice broke off, unable to form the word.

Pain crashed back into me like a freight train. She seemed to understand, as her hand came up, cupping my jaw.

"I'm so sorry," she whispered. "I'm so, so sorry."

Tears burned my throat, and in this moment, with her, the only person on this planet that I trusted with my life, I let the tears for my brother fall, and I let the woman I loved hold me while I fell apart.

I didn't want to cry. I hated that the tears wouldn't seem to stop coming. I hated how weak it made me feel. So, gripping her jaw, I turned until she was under me. Blue eyes stared back, two pieces of ocean tossed into my stone-filled world. How did I ever miss it? They were the same ones that stopped me when she was in that library, the same electric current that tugged at my chest when she found me.

The same chord rippling through me all these years later, meant for me.

Mine.

Pressing my lips to hers, I moved my hand down her body until I held her by the hip. Her tongue slid against mine, deepening our connection, reminding me how starved I've been for her. Pushing her leg wide, I rose above her, settling in between her thighs, bracing my arms on either side of her face.

"You're mine, Rae," I whispered, pressing a fevered kiss to her lips. "For fucking ever, do you understand me?" I slowly slid inside her heat, feeling her warmth wrap around me.

"I can't be without you." I moved, thrusting hard as she jolted forward, letting out a low moan. "Never again," I rasped into her skin as I fucked her slowly. "Never again."

Biting down on her shoulder, I rotated my hips, moving faster as she began meeting every stroke of mine with a hard thrust of her own.

"Never," she whispered, running her fingers up over my chest. She lifted her leg so I had better access. Pushing my hands under her ass, I pulled her to me while thrusting deep inside her.

The connection was so much stronger than any other time we'd fucked, it was messing with me to a degree. It made me feel stripped of any armor I'd put over my heart as protection against her.

I was still moving inside her when she tucked my hair away from my face and smiled.

"I love you, Davis Brenton. I've *always* loved you."

I broke.

Shoving my face into her neck, so she wouldn't see my tears, I increased my speed, pulling her ass against my cock, over and over, until she clenched around me and began crying out my name.

I released inside her, panting with every pump, until I was spent.

We waited there, both of us panting while she drew words into my skin. Then she sealed what we did by saying, "Only yours." She slowed her breathing, while staring at me with those big blue eyes, and smiled. "I've only ever been yours."

RAE WAS STANDING in our kitchen, barefoot, with just one of my shirts on, when I decided I was done waiting. Three days had passed since I came back, and nearly every waking moment had been spent inside each other.

It seemed to be the only way I could effectively communicate my feelings. I wasn't ready to talk, and while Rae hadn't pushed me to, I knew we couldn't just keep having sex every time the pain of losing my brother began to surface. It seemed every time my chest felt like it was about to cave in, I'd just grab Rae, spread her legs, and slip inside. She seemed desperate to help me get past the pain too, so she was more willing than ever to do anything and everything I wanted.

Which included quite a few kinky nights in the truck. We'd go driving, in hopes that it would help me talk, but every single time, I'd just grab Rae by the hair and pull her mouth to mine, and suddenly she was naked again, straddling me until the windows fogged and we had nothing left in us but to drive back and eat dinner, or go to sleep.

I knew we couldn't keep it up, especially because Rae had to get back to work at city hall and meet with the businesses regarding everything from when she was away.

But seeing her now, in our home, the place I wanted to start a life with her, it finally happened. The words came out.

"I was waiting for you...or at least, I was trying to. The town, for once, had embraced my help with fixing up the outside of their shops, and several guys even offered to help whenever I needed it. Colson jumped in too, offering materials and labor..." I trailed off, taking a sip of water while Rae carefully watched me in silence.

Moments passed, then she finished her sandwich and moved to the barstool next to mine.

"I was feeling good, and like I wanted to keep improving, so I decided I'd call my mom and dad for the first time." Shaking my head, I scoffed in disgust. "I actually thought you'd be proud of me for calling them."

"Davis…" Rae whispered, her voice cracking as her hand came out to grip my arm.

"My mom acted like she didn't know what to say. Apparently my brother passed away six weeks ago from medical complications and pneumonia, but they never even—" My throat burned as I tried to push the rest of the words out. "They didn't tell me."

Rae was there, pushing her way into my arms as she cradled my face in her hands, swiping at the goddamn tears that had started.

I rested my head against her shoulder as she held me, and I broke all over again. This time without alcohol to curb the pain, and this time without the fear of never getting her back.

She was here, and while I was still splitting in half, I knew she would make me whole.

40

RAE

TWO MONTHS LATER

THE HENS WERE HAPPY, EVEN IN THE WINTER—THEY SEEMED TO thrive. I knew there was some life lesson in there, something about nature being able to teach us all we needed to know, but I was too exhausted to catch it.

My life, since returning to this place—since returning to Davis —has been a bit of melancholy intermixed with bliss. It was difficult to be truly happy when Davis still carried such sadness, but we worked through it.

Most days, he just needed to sit in the silence and allow it to swallow up his pain. On those days, I tried to hike and give him space. The dogs loved going with me, and I found that I enjoyed Mount Macon more than any other mountain or summit. Even in the winter, as snow covered the ground, it was a form of therapy I knew that I would always need.

A few times, I had tried to get Davis to come with me, but he'd choose to go on a drive all alone. He did that for a few weeks, until I asked where he was going.

That's when he finally took me.

He drove thirteen miles north, and down a long winding road, until we found it.

His old house.

It was empty, and Davis only stared at it. He never once wanted to look inside or break in to visit his old home. I didn't blame him.

But then we'd walk, and he'd take me to the tree fort he and Tim would use, back before his brother became too old for it, or too moody. Davis said that during a short period of their lives, Tim would play in the woods with him, in that tree house, and they'd pretend they were pirates, sailing the vast sea of whatever world they had created at the time.

So, for months, Davis had been driving out here, trying to say goodbye to his brother. He'd yet to find the words, and I wasn't about to pressure him to try. Instead, I would sit with him, hold his hand, and let him process.

Sometimes I would bring flowers, or vodka. Other times, I'd play with his hair as he laid his head in my lap and we just sat in nature, and secretly, I would pray to whoever was listening that it would heal the man I loved.

With each passing day, it seemed it would.

"THE OFFICIAL TERM IS RUSTIC CHARM," Lee Hanes said as his husband came up beside him, pulling him into a tight hug. "Rustic chic," Dane argued, and we all laughed.

"Whatever it is, I love it!" Mayor Gains said, typing away on her cell as she walked down Main Street. Over the past few months, the town upgrades had finished—just in time for Christmas. Our town had a ton of tourists traveling up here around the holidays for the skiing and snowy mountain experience.

I had helped ten different residences transition their guest homes or basements to rentals, so they could have a way to create extra income. We also had drummed up different festival ideas that would be specific to Macon. The people from the mountain that had normally kept to themselves started frequenting the town more often, and even started donating to different charity events.

It was the happiest and most excited I had seen the people of

Macon, and that included my grumpy boyfriend. He had started attending online therapy sessions and meeting with my dad once a week to talk about Timothy, to remember him. While there were some rough days and even harder nights that we had to work through, he was starting to turn a corner with his pain regarding his brother. There was a long way to go, and I knew it would require dedication, patience, and love, all of which I had to give. I helped and supported him as much as I could, and in turn, he'd show me how much he appreciated me with little gifts, like a brand-new Jeep to drive home during the winter. Or a new standing desk to work at, a new laptop, and tablet. I told him he had to stop, but he enjoyed spoiling me, so I just accepted them.

But what I loved more than anything was our home. There were little upgrades we added that made it feel like ours, and with Christmas coming, we were headed up the mountain to track down a tree. I was beyond excited, especially because the tree excursion would include a few people from town. My parents, of course; Nora, Gavin, his girlfriend Tiffany, and as requested by Davis, Colson Hanes.

I hadn't told Nora yet, and I wasn't sure how to even bring it up. For two months the two neighbors seemed to be at war with one another, and it got so bad that one night she even went back to her parents' house, just to avoid going to jail.

I tried to explain this to my boyfriend, but he didn't seem to care. He said that Colson was his friend, and he wanted to start cultivating healthy friendships and start branching away from the mountain, and for that, I couldn't begrudge him. It was something his therapist had encouraged.

Tonight, however, I was excited because Davis wanted to take me on a date to celebrate all the success of our little town renovation. It was just as much his to celebrate as it was mine, considering he'd donated materials and labor in finishing the signs and fixtures for all the store fronts, so there was a matching aesthetic theme of rustic charm throughout Macon.

I hurried to my parents' house, since it wouldn't make sense to go all the way home to change before dinner. There, I showered, did my hair and makeup and waited for Davis to text me where to meet him.

I had been waiting nearly half an hour, toying with one of my mother's puzzles, when there was a knock at the door. Swinging it open, I saw that the stoop was empty. I stared at the doormat, and then the door, spying a folded piece of paper taped to the wood.

Tugging it free, I closed out the cold air and flipped open the note.

Meet me at six thirty, in the library. I have something I need to show you-
Love, Davis

That was odd. He'd already finished up the library as far as I knew, but maybe he found something that would need more attention.

A tiny thrill still ran through me at his delivery method. Why not text me that he needed to meet me, unless he was just trying to be funny? He'd started to do more of that lately with his therapy sessions, too—more jokes, more pranks, more laughter.

I loved it.

Dressed in a short black dress, with a warm overcoat and sexy black heels, I navigated the snow and ice pathetically slowly while entering the library. I had been back dozens of times, but going in the dark definitely sent a zing up my spine as that one terrible memory surfaced.

I pushed it down as best as I could as I walked along the newly exposed wood floors, careful not to trip on my way. The lights were out, save for a few in the back. It felt eerily similar, which I wasn't loving.

My heart rioted in my chest that we were allowing this, and my fight or flight instincts were screaming at me to get out, that this scenario had hurt us before, but I trusted Davis.

Implicitly.

Finally, rounding the last row of books, I found the man in question in the exact same spot I did that night, save for the table. It had been swapped, from the looks of it—thank God. He wore a dark suit, which accented his fresh haircut and clean jawline. The way his eyes heated as he took me in nearly broke me. It felt the same as seeing him that night, but now it was me he was feasting on.

"I felt something that night, you know. It was like a jolt of electricity through my breastbone." He pointed at his chest, and I finally realized there were candles and flowers on the table, along with two empty dinner plates and a brown bag, which probably contained our dinner.

I set my bag down and shrugged out of my coat as my heart twisted in my chest, like a leaf in the wind.

"As soon as you left that night, I stopped with"—he paused, twisting his lips—"that person...and I didn't even know why."

He stepped closer, and the knowledge that he hadn't continued to fuck that girl after he saw me was a tiny balm to a rather large scar.

"I couldn't get that look in your eyes out of my head, or the way you looked at me, like I was yours and I was being unfaithful. I know that sounds crazy, but it's what I felt. It messed with me. Then you up and disappeared. I looked for you, hoping you were okay, worried about you."

He stepped even closer. The storm in his eyes wasn't raging tonight; it was just a nice calm navy blue—the color of the sea at night.

"I think you knew I was always supposed to be yours, Raelyn Jackson. I think you knew all along that we'd be here someday." He was toe to toe with me now. "I think you knew there was no way once I started flirting with you that you'd be able to resist me."

I laughed, shoving at his chest.

He caught my hand in a gentle gesture, and then went to one knee. My breath stalled in my lungs, my heart pumping so hard I worried it would flop out on the ground.

"Rae," he whispered, eyes transfixed on me, "in this place that drove you away from me...this place that caused you so much hurt...let me fix it, let me heal it. In this place, say you'll be my wife. Say you'll be by my side for the rest of time, and wake up to me each morning and sleep with me every night."

Was this really happening? Had he just proposed in the library

—the place where it all fell apart? My dumb, stupid heart was a melted pile of goo. I was crying, nodding and hiccupping as I agreed to marry Davis Brenton.

He stood, hugged me to his chest, and then slipped a diamond ring on my finger.

"I love you, Raelyn, and I know you've loved me longer, but I plan to love you harder." He pressed a kiss to my lips, and I simply nodded.

My heart had been broken in this building years prior, but now it was made whole. And while the way I chased my mountain recluse wasn't admirable, the method in which he won me over was the most beautiful journey. Because anything that has a little bit of sorrow and sunshine is worth saving.

I'm just grateful my rain cloud finally decided he wanted a bit of sun.

EPILOGUE
A YEAR AND HALF LATER

Davis

DOVE AND DUKE RAN AHEAD OF ME AS I SLOWLY MADE MY WAY UP the ladder, scaling the tree house that once belonged to my brother and I.

Rae didn't even know I had bought this property, not for any reason except that I wanted it to be mine and couldn't stomach anyone else ever touching these memories of mine that would now be like relics. Tim had carved his name into the wood of the tree, and there were still secret stashes of treasure we'd buried out in the woods.

This place would stay with me until I was ash and dust, and then if my kids wanted it, they could have it.

The letter had arrived exactly one week after my wedding, and it made me think that maybe he hadn't written it, until I read what was inside and it was confirmed when another letter had arrived after my son was born.

So, when I started to feel his absence in a way that was unbearable, I'd come out here and I'd read the very first one again.

And I'd find a way to feel him while sitting in our tree house.

Hey Idiot,

Mom discouraged me from starting the letter that way, but this isn't for her. I know it's been a while…which isn't entirely your fault, in fact, I know it's largely on me. We were cowards, and not a single person ever once put blame where it belonged for that accident.

I was the one who chose to drive. I was the one who didn't know how to because I was too fucking scared to try.

It was me. Not you.

I allowed them to blame you, I know that was fucked up, but deep down I envied you. I look up to you, bro. Living the life I always thought would fulfill me…you should know I never wanted it though. Not once.

I wasn't meant for this world…I can't explain it, but I know it. Which is why this stupid shit with my lungs doesn't scare me. Death has slowly been coming for me my whole life, it feels like an old friend is waiting to greet me.

I'm not afraid of death, but I am afraid of my loved ones not living simply from a place of misplaced grief.

So, I plan to write you five letters in total, one for each big stage of your life, in hopes that you have them. If you don't then sucks for you, you won't get my letters. I made mom swear to this with a notary and everything. I have backups in place too, so get married, have kids, grow your business into something truly magnificent and live.

Please, I ask…just live. I love you.

I have always loved you…you never did anything wrong, Thomas. Not once. I was just fucked in the head, and it took me a long time to understand that it didn't make you a bad person for not being fucked like me.

So, in death, I hope to bring you life.

Love you big bro,

Tim

I HOPE you enjoyed this book, and are as excited about Nora and Colson's book as I am. It's already up in the Amazon store, so click here to find it.

HAVE you heard of the infamous deleted leather couch scene? This was a scene a bit too hot/different for the book. In fact, as hot as this book ended up being, there were a few scenes too hot for the final version. But, I saved them for you and decided to compile the few into a fun little FREE book, plus a fun bonus scene from a surprise character. So, CLICK here to grab your copy.

A NOTE, WITH LOVE FROM ASHLEY

A little personal note about this book. Often times I'll get asked what inspired a book, so I thought this time, I'd just drop a note about it here.

I wish I had the space to really dive deep into my past, and touch on the purity culture my church exposed me to that framed and shaped so many damaging thoughts I developed about myself—but that would be an entirely different book. Short version: I went to public school, but had on this invisible hat that essentially said, "I'm better than all of you because I'm pure, and waiting for my husband."

It was horrific that my developing hormones were tethered to such a shameful narrative that droned on and on in my head for so long. It wasn't until I was seventeen that the self-inflated balloon popped.

I'd fallen in love.

This guy was five years older, much like Rae and Davis...so I very much understood where Rae was coming from when Carl went to such lengths to stop her infatuation. Similarly, my own family went to great lengths to stop my growing obsession with the older guy who'd captured my attention.

This guy took advantage of my heart, my inexperience, and the fact that he attended youth group (don't even get me started on the blending of ages and lack of accountability to protect minors) and he knew what he was doing. He'd had several girlfriends...and I was just one in a long string of women he'd abused. He led me on, but I was a minor, so of course, after about six months of crossing nearly every single boundary I had promised to never cross until marriage (except for the biggest), he ghosted me.

And I broke.

I completely unraveled and did things that to this day, make me cringe. I stalked him. I waited outside his job. I left him notes, tucked under the windshield wiper blades of his car, I just needed to know what I did wrong.

Now, I often tell my teenage daughters about my past, and of course, they have been raised completely differently than I was. But I am an open book with them, and so this story was discussed last summer, and my fourteen-year-old asked me, "aren't you sort of embarrassed that you did all that?"

Her question, while asked in a total second-born type of tone, got me thinking.

Romance doesn't look the same in every story, and the broken parts are certainly never identical. Heartbreak looks different on everyone, and while I was personally embarrassed by this at the time, it is still part of my story.

I think there are many of us who experience breaking past the point of sanity, which is why I really dislike stereotypes around mental health. We all have moments that break us emotionally and even mentally, and in turn, some of us get to choose how we use those broken pieces.

I chose to take a few jagged pieces from my past and craft a story about a girl who loved someone, who didn't love her back. In this case, she got her happy ending. In mine, I did too. Mine just happened to come when a different hero entered the story, and that's okay too. Romance looks different in every story, which is why each one is so unique.

So, in the end, it was me who inspired this story and in the first draft, there was much more of her heartbreak and embarrassing moments that hit the page. However, in order to streamline an already long book, it was mostly cut out, but it was still so cathartic for me to write. So, if you were one of the thousands or millions of people who endured ghosting, or a break-up that felt one-sided- I see you. You aren't alone.

ALSO BY ASHLEY MUÑOZ

Mount Macon Series

Resisting the Grump

Tempting the Neighbor

Small Town Standalones

Only Once

The Rest of Me

Tennessee Truths

New Adult College

Wild Card

King of Hearts

The Joker

Romantic Suspense

Glimmer

Fade

Anthology & Co Writes

What Are the Chances

The Wrong Boy

Vicious Vet

ACKNOWLEDGMENTS

There are so many people to always thank for these books, and the list only gets longer with each one that I write, so here we go.

Firstly, to my husband and kids for sacrificing so much and always allowing me the space to create and do what I need to do to hit my deadlines. Thank you for the encouragement, support, and jokes. I don't deserve any of you.

Secondly, to my personal, virtual assistant- Tiffany. Thank you so much for standing in my corner for as long as you have, you never give up on me. We've seen the lows and experienced the highs, but through it all, you're always there. I couldn't do this without you.

A huge thanks to my publicist, Sarah Ferguson, and the entire team at Social Butterfly that have made every aspect of this book such a success. And honestly, Sarah…all the text conversations about the cover, I can't even express my gratitude for putting up with all my indecisions.

Thank you to Amanda, my cover designer- you always put up with so much from me. Usually and always we end up going with the first photo you send me, but I make you show me at least fifty mock-ups before I finally go back to the first. This cover is perfect, and I couldn't be more grateful for your brilliance regarding the colors and tweaks.

To Liz, Will and Julie- thank you so much for sharing your special moment with me, and allowing me the opportunity to use your photo for this cover. I am so grateful for you.

Another huge thanks to my agent Savanah who will undoubt-edly push this book to its fullest potential as she does with every other book that's in her care. I am so grateful for you and all your hard work that you put into getting my books into every available platform for people to enjoy.

To my beta readers, Kelly and Amy. My ride or dies, thank you much for always pulling through, and for helping me craft this story into something worthy of celebrating and being proud of.

Brittany Taylor, thank you for being my sounding board when all the madness of this publishing world gets to my head. Thank you for being my friend and for always being there for me whenever I need you. I love you to the moon, and every new galaxy they find and back.

To my Book Beauties, thank you all for your love and support for this book and all my others, I love you all and am so grateful for you.

Lastly, but certainly not least- Thanks to God for creating this gifting within me, and for loving me through all the dreams I constantly grab ahold of.

ABOUT THE AUTHOR

Ashley is an Amazon Top 50 bestselling romance author who is best known for her small-town, second-chance romances. She resides in the Pacific Northwest, where she lives with her four children and her husband. She loves coffee, reading fantasy, and writing about people who kiss and cuss.

Follow her at www.ashleymunozbooks.com

Made in the USA
Coppell, TX
11 October 2022

84453258R00194